MR. SINFUL

by

SERENITY WOODS

Copyright © 2017 Serenity Woods
All rights reserved.
ISBN: 1973757753
ISBN-13: 978-1973757757

DEDICATION

To Tony & Chris, my Kiwi boys.

CONTENTS

Chapter One 1
Chapter Two 9
Chapter Three 16
Chapter Four 18
Chapter Five 23
Chapter Six 25
Chapter Seven 29
Chapter Eight 34
Chapter Nine 42
Chapter Ten 50
Chapter Eleven 53
Chapter Twelve 56
Chapter Thirteen 62
Chapter Fourteen 72
Chapter Fifteen 75
Chapter Sixteen 83
Chapter Seventeen 86
Chapter Eighteen 94
Chapter Nineteen 102
Chapter Twenty 105
Chapter Twenty-One 108
Chapter Twenty-Two 110
Chapter Twenty-Three 115
Chapter Twenty-Four 119
Chapter Twenty-Five 121
Chapter Twenty-Six 125
Chapter Twenty-Seven 129
Chapter Twenty-Eight 131
Chapter Twenty-Nine 138
Chapter Thirty 140
Chapter Thirty-One 144
Chapter Thirty-Two 149
Chapter Thirty-Three 151
Chapter Thirty-Four 158
Chapter Thirty-Five 166
Chapter Thirty-Six 169

SERENITY WOODS

Chapter Thirty-Seven	175
Chapter Thirty-Eight	179
Chapter Thirty-Nine	180
Chapter Forty	188
Chapter Forty-One	191
Chapter Forty-Two	195
Chapter Forty-Three	205
Chapter Forty-Four	208
Chapter Forty-Five	212
Chapter Forty-Six	219
Chapter Forty-Seven	220
Chapter Forty-Eight	225
Chapter Forty-Nine	227
Chapter Fifty	230
Chapter Fifty-One	232
Chapter Fifty-Two	239
Chapter Fifty-Three	247
Chapter Fifty-Four	252
Chapter Fifty-Five	258
Chapter Fifty-Six	262
Chapter Fifty-Seven	264
The Heartfelt Series	266
About The Author	273

Chapter One

"Hey, everyone, Faith's got a sex problem she needs to talk about."

It was very late on a hot February evening, and Faith had almost dozed off, lying on the cool tiles with her feet in the pool and her arm across her face. However, as Eve threw the comment into the conversation like a hand grenade, Faith winced and sat up, sensing an impending explosion. She didn't have long to wait. The three guys sitting around the pool with her and her best friend were quick to voice their opinions on the subject.

Her brother was first. "Jeez, why the hell do I want to know about that?" Dan looked dismayed, as he always did when his little sister's sex life was the topic of conversation.

The other two shouted him down, however. Toby, who'd also been semi-dozing after his half-a-dozen beers, now sat up in his chair and turned it to face her. "Come on, give us the details."

Rusty, laconic as ever, lying stretched out on a sun lounger, just said, "Oh yeah," and winked at her.

Faith refused to be embarrassed. She'd known them all for ten years, since she was twelve and the boys were sixteen. She wasn't about to start being shy now. Still, she looked at the glass in her hand and cursed Eve for mentioning the issue. She'd only found out about it the day before, and she was still mulling over the details.

"Have another glass of wine," Eve said. "Then spill the beans." She'd just got out of the pool, and as she leaned over Faith, drips fell from her wet blonde hair. She offered Faith the bottle of Sauvignon Blanc they were halfway through.

"Thanks." Faith glared at her and took the bottle to top up her glass. She shouldn't really have another. She'd been drinking all evening during the party—she found it difficult not to when the weather was so warm. Summer in the sub-tropical Northland of New Zealand was hot and humid, and they spent most of their evenings in and out of the pool, trying to keep cool. Now most of the Waitangi Day party guests were gone, and only the five good friends were left. Faith was tired and ready for bed, but they were all unwilling to end what had been a beautiful sunny day and a fun evening. Which was why they were still sitting by the poolside in the dark, the only light from the solar lamps around the fence, the girls with their feet in the water, listening to the cicadas and the occasional mournful cry of a kiwi bird in the bush.

She sipped her wine and cleared her throat. "Okay, I'm writing a new series of articles for the magazine, and they'll also appear on my blog."

Her brother shook his head. His hair, light brown like hers, curled around his forehead and neck, and she made a mental note to remind him to get it cut. "I still can't believe there are so many people interested in listening to you witter on about nothing," he said.

"Thank you, Daniel, for that vote of confidence."

Eve waggled her finger at him. "You shouldn't mock her—you know she's the magazine's most popular writer. And her blog's been voted the best on women's matters in the southern hemisphere."

Toby grinned. "A blog about ironing and lace curtains?" As Faith opened her mouth to protest, Rusty reached out a foot and pushed Toby's chair sharply so he nearly fell in the pool, and he squawked. "Hey."

Rusty raised an eyebrow at him. "Don't be so patronizing. She deserves a bit more credit after all her hard work."

Faith nodded. "When you've read it, then you can pass comment on it."

Toby snorted. "Why would I want to read a website about periods and stuff?"

"Don't be such a bloody Neanderthal," Faith said. "I hope it's a bit more interesting than that."

"It is," Rusty said.

"Like you've read it," Toby scoffed.

"As a matter of fact, I do read it. Every week." Rusty shrugged as everyone looked surprised. "Hey, rule number one, know thine enemy."

Faith laughed, pleased he'd made the effort. "Sounds very sensible to me."

He grinned. "So, what are the new articles about?"

"Well, I did one a few weeks ago about women's sex lives. It was really popular, and it raised some very interesting statistics."

"Like…" Dan prompted.

"Like the fact that four out of ten of the women who commented rarely have oral sex performed on them."

"You're kidding." Dan spoke, but they all looked horrified.

"Nope. And for women over thirty, sixty-five percent of them had sex less than once a week."

Eve sighed. "Well that's something to look forward to."

Faith nodded. "It's quite a shocking statistic. Anyway, they've asked me to write a series of further articles about ways to spice up your love life." She sipped her wine. "I've had a think, and I'm going to call it Seven Sexy Sins. I'm going to base it on the seven original sins, with each one relating to a sexy sin. The idea is that your average housewife, who's struggling in the bedroom, could show her partner the list and work through them with him."

They all nodded. "Sounds like a good idea," said Dan. "So, what are the seven sins then? Run them by us, see if we agree."

"Okay." She took another sip. "Number one: envy. I'm thinking of relating this to watching porn, you know, looking at other people's bodies and what they get up to, so housewife and hubby can come up with some ideas for things to do themselves."

They all seemed to agree with that. "Two?" asked Toby.

"Sloth. Oral sex. Letting your partner do all the work."

"Absolutely." Dan frowned. "I still can't believe four out of ten women aren't getting it."

Faith cleared her throat. She had her own views on that statistic but didn't want to share just yet. "Three, gluttony. I'm thinking…sex and food. Whipped cream, chocolate sauce. Spreading it on and licking it off. Like in *Nine and a Half Weeks* with Kim Basinger. Remember the ice, and the strawberries?"

"Oh yeah," Rusty said.

"Sounds calorific," Eve commented.

"Well, there are low-fat options if you're watching your weight. And ice doesn't have any calories in it."

"True. Number four?"

"Pride. Having pride in your own body—doing a striptease for your partner. Dance of the seven veils and all that."

"Another good point," said Toby. "Five?"

She grinned. "They're getting a bit naughty now. Number five's wrath." She saw Rusty's lips begin to curve. "You can see where I'm going with this one. Some light bondage. Nothing scary, fur-lined cuffs or scarves, tying each other up."

"Six?" Rusty asked, looking more interested with each sin.

"Avarice. Greed. For orgasms. Multiple. As many as you can both manage in one night, using as many methods as you can think of, oral, sex toys, you name it."

They all started laughing. "I hate to ask what seven is," said Dan.

"Well, it's lust. But ending on a nice, romantic note. Tantric sex."

"What's that?"

"Thinking about sex all night and then not doing it at the end," Faith said.

"Sounds like your average night to me," Toby said ruefully. He hadn't had a date for several weeks.

They all grinned. "Actually," Faith said, "in this case I plan for it to mean taking time to just be with one another. Not touching, looking into one another's eyes, then when you do get down to it, taking it really, really slow."

Unintentionally, her gaze met Rusty's. He'd been watching her as she spoke, an elbow on the arm of the sun lounger, resting his head on his hand. His reddish-brown hair, which had given him his nickname from a very young age, was curly and ruffled from repeated dips in the pool. His real name was Richard, but she'd never heard him called it. He wore only his swimming shorts, and the hot sun had turned his arms and chest a deep brown. Unlike the rest of them, Rusty hadn't been drinking, and his eyes were half-lidded from tiredness rather than alcohol. But there was still a spark of something deep within them, twinkling like a faraway star, something she couldn't quite place.

As he caught her gaze, he sipped his soda and winked at her, and she stuck her tongue out at him before looking away and saying, "So, what do you think?"

"Sounds interesting," Dan said. "What's the problem?"

"Well, my readers like it when I talk about my own experiences. I think it makes them feel more normal, and it's one of the key successes of my blog."

"And?"

Faith glanced at Eve, who smirked. Faith shrugged and looked down at where her legs were making circles in the water. "Well…the trouble is…I haven't actually done any of the things on the list."

She closed her eyes. The admission was not an easy one. They'd all been friends for so long that she knew about their love lives intimately. Toby was always explicit in describing his sexual encounters and left little to the imagination. Dan was a bit more circumspect with his little sister, but Eve—who'd been dating him for over six months now—gave her more of a rundown than she needed. And Rusty… Well, she'd consoled more of Rusty's ex-girlfriends than she cared to count, who were all more than willing to explain how they thought he loved them because he'd done this, and this, and this… So all in all, she had a good idea that between the three of them, the guys had probably covered every one of the seven sins she'd just detailed, and a few others to boot.

There was a moment of silence. She left it for as long as she could bear before looking up.

Toby's eyebrows had disappeared into his thick black hair. Dan looked uncomfortable. Rusty was studying her, head still tipped to one side, a slight frown on his face.

"You're kidding me," Toby said.

She swooshed her legs around in the water. "No."

"Not even…"

"No." For the first time that evening, she felt her cheeks redden. Damn it. She'd promised herself she wouldn't get embarrassed. Her blog addressed the most intimate questions in women's lives, for God's sake—she discussed everything from sexual issues to personal medical problems. How could she let a tiny thing like this get to her?

"But…" Toby looked aghast. "You've had boyfriends."

"Yes…"

"Selfish bastards, by the sounds of it," said Rusty.

Dan sighed. "Well I for one am glad to hear my little sis isn't that sexually experienced."

"Oh come on." Toby rolled his eyes. "That's hardly fair. How old are you, Faith, twenty, twenty-one?"

"Twenty-two."

"Twenty-two, Dan! I mean, honestly. Do you want her to be one of the four out of ten women who don't get oral sex?"

Faith's cheeks burned even hotter. Toby grinned at her. Dan looked even more uncomfortable. And Rusty… He studied her, his green eyes still lit with that emotion she couldn't quite place. Why was he looking at her like that? She looked back at her feet, studying her painted toenails.

Dan cleared his throat. "Well, you can still write the articles, can't you? Just do some research on the internet."

"I can. It's just… Well, it's sod's law I get this commission after I split up with Jason. Not that he would have been much help," she added.

Toby laughed. "I knew he was a wet blanket. You need someone with a bit more know-how." He waggled his eyebrows.

Dan pointed his beer bottle at him. "Don't even think about it."

Faith sighed. "Dan…" Ever since their parents had died in a car crash three years before, her brother had become increasingly protective of her. Most of the time she welcomed it, but his fatherly attitude toward available men had begun to irritate her recently.

Toby shrugged. "What? I'm just saying, surely you'd rather your little sis be shown the delights of lovemaking from someone you know and trust?"

Faith grinned. "'The delights of lovemaking'? You're kidding me, right? If I need a quick shag around the back of the bike sheds, you'd be first on my list, sweetie."

They all burst out laughing at Toby's indignant face. "I'll have you know I'm a very considerate lover."

Eve patted his knee. "Of course you are, dear."

"I'm just saying, the offer's there."

"Thank you." Faith sighed. "But I guess I'm just going to have to use my imagination."

"Or watch a shed load of porn." Dan got to his feet. "I'm going to bed. Coming, hon?"

Eve took his outstretched hand. "Sure. See you guys."

They all said goodnight, and Dan and Eve disappeared inside. Toby yawned. "I'm off too. Want me to walk you home, Faith?"

"It's okay," said Rusty, "I'll drive her—I'm going past her house."

"Okay. See ya." Toby winked at Faith. "Don't forget—the offer's always there. I hate to think of you suffering."

"Thank you for being so thoughtful," she teased. "Goodnight."

He kissed her on the forehead, nodded at Rusty and walked off.

Faith stretched. "What time is it? I'm shattered."

Rusty looked at his watch. "Nearly one."

"Jeez. I've got a meeting in Whangarei tomorrow at nine. My eyes are going to be bloodshot."

He laughed. "Come on then, let's get you home."

They walked to his car, and she opened the passenger door, sighing as she saw the usual pile of books and papers on the front seat. "Rusty, honestly."

"What? My marking gets lonely if I leave it in the classroom. I like to give it a little ride home and back." Rusty taught history at the local high school.

"You know you're supposed to actually do the marking if you take it home?"

"You are? Damn, now I know where I've been going wrong." He cleared the seat, dumping everything in the back.

"I still can't picture you teaching." She slid into the seat. "Do your students write 'Love You' on their eyelids like they do to Indiana Jones?"

"Not quite." He got into the driver's seat, started the engine, and headed out of the drive toward Kerikeri.

She sighed and closed her eyes. She hadn't told the others that she felt depressed about not having tried anything on the list she'd compiled. True, she was only twenty-two and had plenty of time to meet someone and experiment, but she hadn't even had a sniff of a date since she split up with Jason. She'd slept with two guys in her life, and neither of them had been inspiring in the bedroom. Like most of her readers on the blog, she was desperate to meet someone warm, funny, and sexy, but at the moment the possibility seemed light years away.

"You okay?"

She opened her eyes and smiled at Rusty. He was still bare chested, and she could feel the heat from his sun-brushed skin. If only his students could see him now. "Yeah. Just tired."

"You look down."

"I'm sexually frustrated. I need to be screwed senseless a few times and I'm sure I'd come good. Pardon the pun."

He laughed, his gaze leaving the road to glance at her. "You're not considering Toby's offer, are you?"

She stared at him, startled. "Good Lord, no. Why?"

"I just wondered."

"I mean, can you imagine? I love him dearly but I don't quite think he's the sort of guy I'm looking for."

"No." He smiled. "Have you got anyone else in mind?"

"No. That's part of the problem."

He stopped at a T-junction, but there was nobody else on the road. He glanced across at her again before he pulled away. "What about me?"

Chapter Two

It took a moment for his words to register. Then she burst out laughing. "Good grief, what is it with you guys tonight?"

He didn't laugh. "I'm serious."

She sobered. "What?"

He slowed the car and pulled up outside the house she shared with Eve when Eve wasn't staying with Dan. He put the car into park and turned off the engine. Then he turned in his seat to face her. The moon was nearly full, and there was enough light for her to see the mischievous smile on his face and the glint in his eye.

"I'm serious," he said again. He gestured with his hand, pointing from himself to her. "I'm offering my services."

She stared at him, her mouth falling open. "What are you saying, exactly?"

"You need to do some research for your articles. And I'm happy to help."

"You want to help me research the seven sexy sins? Personally? Like, not in books?"

"Absolutely. Sounds like great fun." They studied each other for a moment. Eventually he gave a short laugh. "You needn't look quite so shocked." His eyes twinkled. "Don't you find me attractive?"

She gave him a wry look. "Of course I do—you know you're sex on legs. That's hardly the point."

"So what is the point?"

"Dan would kill you if he knew you'd even suggested this."

"Toby suggested it—he didn't kill him."

"Toby wasn't serious."

Rusty snorted. "Of course he was. He'd give his right arm to get you into bed."

Shock rippled through her. "What are you talking about? I'm just Dan's little sister. I'm hardly the target of anyone's sexual fantasies."

"Have you looked in the mirror lately?"

"I…" She looked down at herself before looking back up. "What do you mean?"

"I mean you're not twelve anymore. You're not even fifteen. You're a grown woman, with all the relevant…attributes. You must be aware every guy at the party tonight fantasized about seeing you naked at some point."

"Rusty!" Her cheeks grew hot. Inside, however, she glowed at the thought that he saw her as an adult and not only as Dan's younger sibling.

He laughed. "Faith, honestly. Are you that naive?"

She looked down at her hands. Yes, she thought, I *am* that naive. In spite of the fact that she advised women more than twice her age on her blog, and she wasn't a virgin, she knew she was more innocent than most girls in their twenties. She was the youngest of their crowd, and she'd thought they'd always seen her as the baby. She'd never considered they saw her as a sexual possibility, and she wasn't sure how she felt about it.

She shifted in her seat. "I don't understand. Why say this now? That night we kissed at my eighteenth birthday party… The next day you cold-shouldered me. I'd assumed you weren't interested in me."

She hadn't mentioned it since it happened. It had surprised her at the time. It had been six months before the death of her and Dan's parents. Blissfully unaware of what the following year was to bring, she'd been dancing in the garden, and Rusty had caught her hand and dragged her with him into the lemon trees. She'd gone laughingly, the sound of cicadas loud in her ears and the scent of lemons and mandarins in the air, expecting a quick peck or a teasing grope from an old friend to mark her coming of age, which she knew she'd be expected to resist with feigned indignation. Instead, however, he'd cupped her face in his hands, studied her for a moment and then kissed her. He'd brushed his tongue with hers and slipped his hand through her hair, making her heart thunder with unexpected passion. She'd gone to bed excited and dreaming of him, but the next day he'd been his usual self, cool and offhand. She'd felt hurt and a little stupid for being childish enough to think it meant something, but had done her best to forget it ever happened, wanting to keep his friendship, even if she couldn't have anything more.

"Do you remember what I looked like the next morning?" he said.

"I don't…oh wait, you had a black eye, didn't you? You said you walked into a lamppost on the way home."

"It wasn't a lamppost—it was Dan's fist."

Her eyes widened. "You're kidding me."

"No. He saw us. And he knocked me flat into a pile of gorse. Fucking stung, I can tell you."

She laughed, covering her mouth with her hand. "Oh Rusty, I'm sorry."

He grinned. "No worries. I backed off after that. I didn't want to lose his friendship, and I realized he was right. I'm no good for you, Faith. Hell, I'm no good for any woman. I'll never make a great husband. I'm under no illusions about that."

She frowned again. "I hate it when you talk like that."

"Well, it's true."

"No, it's not. Just because your dad's a prick doesn't mean you'll be the same."

He shrugged. "It's in the blood, and I'm not going to give it a chance to rear its ugly head."

"Rusty…"

"Look." He shifted in his seat. "This isn't about me—it's about you. I may be useless long term, but I'm not bad in bed."

"I think you're underestimating yourself, from what I've heard."

"Well, that's very kind." He gave her a sexy smile. "Don't you think it would be fun to practice your seven sins on me?" His green eyes were hot and lusty.

A strange shiver ran through her from her toes to the top of her head. They studied each other for a while. A smile crept onto her lips at the teasing look in his eyes. "Stop looking at me like that."

"Like what?"

"Like you're imagining doing each of the sins to me."

"I am."

"Well stop. This is crazy. I'd be mad to agree."

"Why? I thought we were friends."

"That's what I meant." She frowned. He was so gorgeous. She didn't have any trouble admitting that. And she was happy to admit this wasn't the first time she'd wondered what he was like in bed. His girlfriends had always enthused about his talents, even after he'd dumped them, and she'd been curious from a very young age as to what he got up to under the covers. But she'd always considered

Dan's friends to be off limits because he'd been so adamant that was the case, so she'd never considered any of them seriously. And because of that, they'd all grown to be close friends.

He reached out and took her hand. "Don't look sad."

"I couldn't bear to lose you."

"Lose me? Why would you lose me?"

"Afterward. Wouldn't it be weird?"

He shrugged. "Toby and Eve dated before she went out with Dan."

"True, although that was several years ago."

He studied her for a moment. He brushed her knuckles with his thumb. The gesture wasn't sexual, but it made a frisson of desire run through her. She was attracted to him, very much. He tipped his head, his gaze resting on her lips. "You know it was only a matter of time," he said.

"What?"

"Before we got down and dirty."

Her eyes widened, and her heart thumped. Rusty wasn't helping her out of the kindness of his heart. He really wanted to go to bed with her. Rusty Thorne, who, let's face it, knew his way around the bedroom and could teach her a trick or two. The thought made her dizzy.

Then her brain kicked in. *This is a bad idea.* How many girls' hearts had he broken over the years? She knew what he was like, how he refused to commit.

But he wasn't talking about a long-term relationship, was he? He was talking about a finite agreement, seven sexual encounters. A tutor in the ways of love, to teach her all the things she'd never experienced. As a professional educator, Rusty saw it as his duty to instruct those less knowledgeable than him.

She licked her lips. "I'd want a contract."

His lips curved. "A contract?"

"Specifying it would be for seven times only."

"Of course."

"Don't make fun of me, Rusty."

"I'm not." But his eyes were amused.

"This is all about research. I'd have to take notes."

He gave a short laugh, but nodded. "Okay."

"I mean it. I'd run the show. My work's important to me. I'd want to get it right. If we did this, it would be for exploring these seven sins with the aim of writing the articles. No messing around, no getting sidetracked."

"I understand."

She looked at his mouth. She could still remember how soft his lips had been that night he'd kissed her. "Strictly business."

"Absolutely." He met her gaze. "Can I kiss you now?"

Her heart pounded. "Absolutely not. I haven't finished yet."

"Okay."

"The contract will state that this remains secret. No telling any of our friends and definitely no telling Dan."

"Well, obviously. I'd like to keep my balls intact."

She bit her lip, trying not to smile. She was serious about this. "And if we did go ahead with it, we couldn't go to your place or mine. A motel, out of town."

"Sure. Sounds fun." In the darkness of the car, his green eyes were the color of a forest stream, wild and mysterious.

A thrill of excitement ran through her. Was she really considering this? Having sex with Rusty? Carrying out each of the seven sins with him? Watching porn, letting him lick chocolate sauce off her, letting him…oh dear Lord…perform oral sex on her? She couldn't. Could she? She swallowed. "Why did you say 'it's only a matter of time'?"

He shifted in his seat, moving closer to her. "Because I've been waiting for it to happen. Haven't you?"

"No," she whispered.

"Liar." He was inches away from her now. "I've wanted you since you were eighteen." He leaned forward and brushed her temple with his lips. "Actually, longer than that. Only I don't want to sound like a pervert."

"Rusty…"

"I'm going to kiss you now."

She wanted to refuse but found she couldn't. His arm was along the back of her seat, tanned and muscled, sprinkled with reddish-brown hairs, his bare chest inches from her fingers. Why hadn't she noticed before how tall he was, how broad his shoulders were? "No tongues," she warned him, heart thumping. "Not till the contract's signed."

He chuckled. "Okay."

She let him close the last few inches, wondering if it would feel strange to kiss a guy she'd known almost half her life as a friend.

She closed her eyes. His lips brushed hers. They were warm and dry, and he kissed her languidly. He smelled of chlorine, sunscreen, and hot, scorched skin, and he tasted of Coke and mint. Her heart thundered, and she was hit with the full force of the memory of her eighteenth birthday and how she'd felt when he kissed her in the garden among the lemon trees. But she sat still, reminding herself that this wasn't a big romantic gesture. This was purely business. Like checking the hooves of a horse before you bought it.

She'd thought he was only going to kiss her once, but he continued to plant light, soft kisses on her mouth, very correctly keeping his tongue well out of the way.

What the hell. She opened her mouth and brushed his lips with her tongue.

He lifted his head. "I thought you said—"

"I lied." She slipped a hand into his russet hair, curling her fingers in his ruffled locks.

He laughed, wrapped his arms around her and pulled her close. If the first kiss had been like the gentle sweep of a wave, the next one crashed over her with all the force of a tsunami. He kissed her deeply, his mouth hot, and he cradled the back of her head with his hand. She caught her breath, finding it difficult to exhale as he pressed her to him and brushed her tongue with his, filling her with a hungry need and an ache between her thighs.

Eventually, they both pulled back, breathing heavily, and he ran a hand through his hair. "Wow. I'd heard of spontaneous combustion, but I've never experienced it before."

She wiped her lips with the back of her hand, shaking.

He studied her, smiling. "Too weird? You don't feel like you're kissing your brother or anything?"

"No, certainly not that." It hadn't felt weird at all. It had felt very…right. And very hot. "I'd better go in." She picked up her bag.

"Wait." He caught her hand as she went to get out. "Are you okay?"

"Sure." She met his gaze and smiled. "You kiss nicely, Thorne."

"You too, Hillman." He tucked her hair behind her ear. "So, are we on?"

She pressed her lips together and nodded. "Sure."

"When shall we start?"

"How about Saturday night? I'll book a room somewhere."

"Okay." His smile grew into a mischievous grin. "You want me to sort out the porn?"

"Nope. You can leave that to me. I want to check out some of the websites and educate myself."

He laughed and nodded. "So, until Saturday?"

"Until Saturday. Have a good day at school tomorrow." The students had only recently returned after the Christmas break, and it would be a busy day for him.

"You too. Are you going to start your article?"

"Yes. I can tell the world I've found someone to play with."

"I'll read it. I'm guessing I'll be anonymous, though."

Her gaze fell to his mouth, and she shivered at the memory of his lips on hers, his tongue plunging into her mouth. "I'll call you Mr. Sinful."

"Hah!" He leaned over and kissed her again. "I look forward to reading it."

She let him kiss her before drawing back, and gave him a cautionary look. "I'm not inviting you in."

"I wouldn't dream of it."

Her lips twitched. "See ya later."

"See ya."

Chapter Three

Faith Hillman's blog

Well, any of my readers out there who have been following my progress over the past week, as I try to work out how on earth I'm going to write this series of articles on the Seven Sexy Sins while being a single woman, are going to be pleased to know: I found a volunteer! A very willing volunteer, I have to say. He's agreed to help me out with my research... starting this weekend. So, get yourself prepared for a rollercoaster of a ride...

We're starting with Envy. And the Sexy Sin relating to Envy is going to be porn. I'm going to experiment and find some different types. I'm a bit embarrassed to admit that I'm pretty naive when it comes to this stuff. I mean, I know it exists, and I've come across a few websites (pardon the pun), but I've never sat and watched any videos. Especially with a guy.

So, what research do I need to do? What questions do I need to ask Mr. Sinful? (That's his codename, by the way.) For a start, I'm thinking: what turns guys on more? Girl/boy or girl/girl? (Obviously differs from man to man, but I've got to start somewhere.) I'm presuming with Mr. Sinful that it's not boy/boy. Mr. S., if you're reading this, correct me if I'm wrong. And what will turn me on more? Will it be embarrassing, cringe-worthy, or sexy? Will it teach me anything I don't know? Will I find the men (and women) attractive or sleazy? Am I going to be able to stop giggling for long enough to actually get down to doing anything?

Leave me your comments—please, girls, I need your help on this! I'm out on a limb here. We're all in this together, here to support each other. God knows I need it!

*

An excerpt from the 437 Comments

Patsy: Faith, jeez, you gotta tell us more than that, girl. What's Mr. Sinful like? Where did you find him? How on earth did you even approach the topic? We need to know these things!

Faith: Can't tell you where I found him. It's a secret. And in answer to the last question, he suggested it himself, LOL. Desperate to help me out, he was, *nothing in it for him at all. But I was happy to agree. Mr. S., look away now. *Whispers* He's gorgeous. Don't tell him I said that.*

Chapter Four

The week seemed to pass slowly, and yet suddenly it was Friday night, and the next day Faith was due to meet Rusty and launch the first of the seven sins. Her heart pounded every time she thought about their date. Why? she kept asking herself. It's only Rusty. But then that was the problem, wasn't it?

She was on her way to Dan's house. He'd rung and asked her to pop around, and she'd been happy to jump in the car, desperate to take her mind off the coming mission. She hadn't really thought this through. She'd accepted Rusty's proposal when she was half-drunk, using the organ located below her navel rather than the one in her skull to make the decision. The fact that she hadn't been laid in a few months might have had something to do with it. But she was also aware that the latent attraction she'd tried to ignore for the past few years had leapt to the surface with amazing speed.

It was only a matter of time, he'd told her. Had she thought that too? Certainly, after the kiss in the garden, she'd daydreamed about him, but as time had gone by and he'd shown no sign of wanting to develop a relationship, she'd tried to let go of any feelings she had for him.

But of course, they'd always been there. If she was honest with herself, she knew she'd fancied him from the moment he'd walked in with Dan when she was twelve. She'd been fixing her bike in the garage and had looked up to see this lanky guy dressed in black, whose brown hair glowed red in the sun like copper wire heated in a Bunsen burner. She'd fallen for him right then, but he'd always had a girlfriend on his arm, and after a few years Faith had talked herself out of the belief they would one day get together. The kiss hadn't helped, but she'd managed to move on.

Until now. And now they were going to have sex. And not just any sex—an exploration of the most intimate things a guy and a girl could do together. They'd gone from stationary to light speed in seconds. How had that happened?

She drove down to Dan's house and pulled up outside. Toby's car was there. And so was Rusty's.

"Shit."

Should she just drive off? But that would look too obvious. She'd told Rusty he had to pretend nothing was happening—she could hardly go and do the exact opposite.

Cursing, she got out of the car and let herself in the front door.

They were all in the living room, and she stopped dead. They'd obviously heard her pull up. Dan was standing, arms folded, in front of a chair he'd placed in the center of the floor. Eve sat on the sofa next to Toby, both sipping a beer. They said hello and grinned. Rusty sat in the swivel chair at Dan's computer desk, a Coke in his hand, halfway through a crossword. Dressed in his customary black T-shirt and jeans, he looked no different than usual, and yet her heart gave a very unusual thump as he glanced up. He nodded at her. His look, before he smothered it, was plainly apologetic.

"What's going on?" Faith put her hands on her hips.

"Come and sit down," said Dan, pointing to the chair.

She didn't move. "You've got to be kidding me. Twenty questions?" They always carried out this ritual when one of them was trying to keep a secret.

Her brother glared at her. "Sit."

She was tempted to turn around and walk straight out of the door but knew she had to play it cool. She closed the door behind her, walked past them, and sat on the chair, Eve and Toby in front of her, Rusty to her right, just in her line of vision.

Dan stood in front of her, arms still folded. "Okay, so who is he?"

"Who's who?"

He tipped his head. "You know perfectly well who. Eve read your website, and then I read it. You said you've found someone to help you out with your research."

Faith lifted her chin. "So?"

"So, who the hell is it?"

"I'm not going to tell you, Dan. I'm allowed to have some secrets in my life."

"No, you're not. I want to know who he is, and I want to meet him."

She burst out laughing. "And ask him about his prospects? Jeez, Dan, where are you from, 1852?"

"I'm serious." He looked pained. "You can't ask any guy off the streets to have sex with you."

"Dan! He's not just some guy off the streets. I've known him a while."

"How long?"

She gave him a cool look. "A while."

He glowered at her. "Tell me his name, at least."

"Mr. S."

"His real name."

"Er… No."

"Faith, he could be a freak, or a pervert or something."

She bit her lip. Out of the corner of her eye, she saw Rusty chew his pen and knew he was trying not to laugh. "He could be. I'm hoping."

"Faith!" Her brother looked horrified.

"What?" She felt a rush of exasperation. "I'm not sixteen anymore, Dan. I'm twenty-two, for God's sake. And I'm hardly a virgin."

He looked across at Eve. "Help me, please."

Eve grinned. "Come on, Faith, spill the beans. We won't tell anyone."

Normally, Faith would have told her roommate all the gory details. But this time she was going to have to work through it on her own. "I'm not ready to talk about him, not yet. It's a new relationship. Nothing to do with you. I want to keep him to myself for a while." She could feel Rusty's eyes on her, burning on her skin like lasers, but she didn't look at him.

Dan looked at Toby and then at Rusty. "Come on guys, talk some sense into her."

Rusty shrugged and cleared his throat. "I think we should mind our own business—I'm sure Faith knows what she's doing."

"Well you're a big help." Dan glared at him. "Toby?"

Toby gave her a wistful look. "I'm just sorry it's not me." He held up his hands as Dan shot him a glance. "What? I'm saying it's not!"

Dan was growing increasingly frustrated. "Look, we all watch out for each other. It's what we do." He gave her a pleading glance. "Don't do this, love. Talk to me about it first. You know I worry about you."

"Dan, I was at university for three years, and you didn't seem that bothered about my sex life then."

"Absolutely I was, but anyway, that was different."

"Why?"

"Because this is…" he shivered, "…creepy."

Faith laughed. "It's really not. Sweetie, there's no need to worry. I wouldn't pick any old guy. He's nice. You'd like him."

"I want to rip his head off."

She said nothing, aware of Rusty shifting in his seat to her right.

Dan studied her sulkily. "Are you going to be careful?"

She closed her eyes. "Please don't say what I think you're about to say."

"I feel it's my responsibility to remind you about having safe sex."

Rusty cleared his throat again. "Come on Dan, give her a break. Any guy worth his salt will follow the edict of the President of the USA."

Dan raised an eyebrow. "Which is what?"

"Always come with protection."

Faith giggled. She pressed her lips together as Dan glared at her. "Relax. I'll bring my own, just in case," she said.

"It's not a laughing matter." He was beginning to look angry, and that made her cross.

She stood up. "Dan, stop it. You may act like it, but you're not my father."

"I'm the closest thing you've got, and you *will* listen to me."

Fury flared. "I won't. I don't have to do what you say. I'm desperate for sex, I'm going to meet Mr. S., and I'm going to screw his socks off over the weekend. Deal with it."

Rusty coughed into his Coke. Luckily, everyone else was so shocked at her statement that nobody noticed his reaction. It took every ounce of self-control she possessed not to turn and look at him.

She glared at her brother instead. "I'm a grown woman now, Dan. I appreciate that you want to look out for me. But I don't need babying anymore. So back off." And she walked out of the house, banging the front door behind her.

She stormed to her car and got in, then sat there for a moment, glowering, not wanting to drive off while she was in a rage.

After only a minute or so, Rusty came out. He saw her sitting there and came over. She pressed the button to lower the window.

He ducked down and leaned on the windowsill. "Hey."

"Hey." She met his gaze before she looked away and slid the key into the ignition.

"You okay?" he asked.

"Yeah."

"He means well," he pointed out.

"I know." She blew out a breath. "I wish I hadn't said that about him not being my father. I just wish he saw me as a grown up, not a kid anymore."

"I don't see you as a kid, if that helps."

She glanced up at him. Her lips curved up.

"And I can see right down your front from this angle," he pointed out.

She gave him an exasperated look but laughed nevertheless.

He grinned. "So, what's the plan for tomorrow?"

"I've booked us in to Seaview Lodge in Paihia, you know, the one on the seafront?"

"Yep."

"I'll meet you there? Around seven?"

"Sounds good." He raised his eyebrows. "Are you really going to screw my socks off?"

"You'd better believe it, buster." She met his gaze. Was she really going to do this? Heart pounding, she put the car into drive. "I'm going now."

"I'll see you tomorrow." He stood, then, as she began to pull away, he called, "Hey, Hillman?"

She slowed the car. "Yeah?"

He bent forward again and said softly, "You show me gay porn, I'm walking straight out."

"Sure thing," she said seriously. But she was laughing as she drove away.

Chapter Five

Faith Hillman's blog

A quick update before I head off tonight for the big event.

I spent a few hours today looking at some porn websites (and I can't believe I'm admitting to that on my blog!) I admit that my eyes nearly fell out when I saw some of the stuff that's out there. For those of you who, like me, want to try some erotic videos but are a bit nervous about coming across something alarming, I'll list the best ones I found under this post—these are sensual rather than hard core, and I've written a brief description underneath each so you can see what they contain. I've downloaded these on my iPad, as I don't want the motel to complain about what I'm watching on their Internet!

So, I have a few choices for Mr. S., and it will be interesting to see which one he picks. Or maybe we'll watch all of them. Hell, might as well go for it. Don't know when I'm going to get the chance again!

Wish me luck, ladies. I've shaved my legs, picked out my sexiest underwear (no enormous pants à la Bridget Jones) and I'll give you all the gory details tomorrow. Don't worry Mr. S., not those sorts of details. You can have a little privacy. (But not much.)

*

An excerpt from the 534 Comments

Patsy: Can't believe Mr. S. reads the blog. Does he read all these comments as well? You're a lucky man! Faith is one hell of a girl. You give her the time of her life, you hear me?

MrS69: Yes, I'm here, and yes I read everything you naughty ladies are saying. And I hear ya. Don't worry. I've been waiting for this a long time. I have every intention of playing with her all night long...

Patsy: *fans herself* oh my word.

Faith: Stop getting my readers all hot under the collar. And 'MrS69'? Honestly.

MrS69: Which sin does the 69 come under?

AnnaC: Technically number 2, I suppose. But you might have to invent an 8th, Faith.

MrS69: Now you're talking.

Jules: I thought you'd already done the contract, Faith? Mr. S., can you slip in a clause while she's not looking?

Faith: There'll be no slipping in of anything while I'm not looking.

Jules: ROFL!

Eve: LOL, Faith. Mr. S., I hope you like her choices.

MrS69: I'll let you know tomorrow...

Eve: Can't believe you won't tell me who he is, Faith. Mr. S., do I know you?

*MrS69: *smiles**

*Eve: Be like that. *crosses arms**

JillS: How do you feel about your sex life being public knowledge, Mr. S.? We're all eagerly awaiting details.

MrS69: As long as she doesn't get her ruler out, I'm fine with it. Now I've got to go, got a date tonight. See you there, Faith. Hope you're feeling energetic.

Faith: Oh my.

Chapter Six

At half past six on Saturday, Faith shook as if there were an earthquake in her stomach while she unpacked her bag in the room of the motel. It was ridiculous. At this rate, Rusty wouldn't be able to get near her for the aftershocks. Her heart pounded, and her palms were damp. She wished she'd remembered to bring some wine, but as Rusty didn't drink, she hadn't even thought about it.

At least the room was nice. She'd been worried a standard motel room would feel tacky, so she'd booked a deluxe suite, and to her delight, it had a view across the Bay of Islands, a large room with a king-size bed, and a huge sunken tub in the bathroom that looked very tempting.

She'd arrived early but now wished she hadn't, as the waiting was stretching her nerves to breaking point. She checked her appearance in the mirror a final time. She wore a plum-colored short-sleeved fitted blouse with a long, light, black skirt, and underneath she had a set of expensive, black lacy underwear she'd invested in for this very purpose. She'd clipped her long brown hair up loosely, letting tendrils curl around her neck, and had applied the simplest of make-up, just a little eyeliner and mascara, and a slick of lip gloss. She'd shaved her legs, moisturized, put on perfume, eaten a breath mint—in fact done everything she could think of to make herself irresistible.

Had it worked? She frowned as she looked at her reflection. She would never have described herself as beautiful. She was slightly too tall, her boobs weren't big enough, her mouth was a little wide, and she had far too many freckles to be anything approaching breathtaking. But she looked as good as she could, and that was the best she could hope for.

She paced the floor, hoping he wouldn't be late. At ten minutes to seven, however, there was a knock at the door.

Heart pounding, she went over and opened it.

Rusty stood outside, leaning on the doorjamb, dressed in a black, casual short-sleeved shirt hanging loose over jeans, looking so thoroughly edible it made her mouth water. "Hey." He held up a bottle of wine. "For you."

Her lips twitched as she took it. "Are you trying to get me drunk?" She backed away and let him in.

He followed her into the room. "Do I need to?"

"No." She smiled, a little shyly, and put the bottle on the table.

He glanced around the room. "Wow, nice place. I was thinking it might be…"

"Seedy?"

He grinned. "Maybe a little."

"I didn't want it to be. I wanted it to be…nice."

His warm gaze came back to her and fixed on her face before running briefly up and down her. "You look…nice."

"Thanks. You too." Her mouth had gone dry. Where on earth were they going to start?

He came closer to her and took one of her hands in his. "Are you okay?"

"Nervous, actually."

He squeezed her fingers. "Want to go for a walk along the beach?"

She felt a wave of relief that he understood how she was feeling, but she hesitated. "I don't know, should we? What if someone sees us?"

"We're friends, love. You wouldn't normally think twice about being seen with me."

"Yes, but tonight… Half the women in New Zealand know what I'm getting up to."

"Yes, but they don't all know what you look like, right? Come on. Just a short walk. I'll buy you an ice cream."

"Okay."

They went out, and she locked the door, pocketing the key. The motel was right on the seafront, and he took her hand, led her along the row of shops to the ice cream bar, and bought them both a cone.

They crossed over the road onto the beach, walking slowly down to the water as they ate their ice creams, and both slipped off their shoes, letting the cool water wash over their feet. Faith lifted her skirt to make sure it didn't get wet. She saw him glance at her legs, but he didn't say anything.

Was this just too weird? Usually they talked non-stop about all sorts of things, but now they were hardly speaking. She was conscious that he was one of her best friends. But, although she knew him well, she was also intensely aware of him next to her as she had never been before, his bare arm inches away from hers, as if he were magnetic and she were made of iron, inexorably drawn to him.

They reached a pohutukawa tree that overhung the beach, still heavy with its red Christmassy flowers and, finishing off his ice cream, he ducked under the branches and walked up to the trunk. She followed him, heart pounding as he indicated for her to turn around and face him. Dropping his shoes, he pushed her backward and she moved until her back was against the tree.

"What's up?" He spoke gently, his eyes warm as if they'd captured some of the evening's summer sun.

"Nothing."

"You've hardly spoken."

Some of the rapidly melting ice cream ran onto her fingers and she licked them. His eyes followed her tongue, and she stopped and swallowed. "That's what's up."

"What?"

"You're looking at me like…"

He smiled slowly. "Like what?"

Her eyes met his. He was so gorgeous, he took her breath away. She wanted to smear the ice cream all over him and lick it off. "You know perfectly well what like. And it's weird. This is how Lois Lane must have felt when she found out Clark Kent was Superman. It's like, I know you so well but suddenly I feel I hardly know you at all."

He chuckled. "Well, I'm not wearing my underpants over tights for anyone."

She was too nervous to smile. "Rusty…"

"Are you having second thoughts?" He reached out and tucked a stray strand of hair behind her ear. "You want me to back off?"

Her gaze rested on his lips. She desperately wanted him to kiss her again. "No. God, no. I'm just…nervous."

He stepped closer to her, until he was almost—but not quite—touching her. "About what?"

"You," she whispered, heart thudding. "And me. About what we're going to do."

He bent his head, his russet hair falling across one eye, and his lips brushed hers softly. "We don't have to, if you don't want to."

"Rusty, if I don't have you tonight, I swear I'm going to die."

He laughed, slipped a hand behind her head and kissed her properly. She threw the rest of the ice cream away for the seagulls and brought her arms up around his neck. He pressed her to him, his other hand in the small of her back, and she felt him hard against the flat of her stomach.

Somehow, it helped lessen her nerves. She'd worried he was going to become aware she was still Dan's younger sister and turn awkward, like the day after he'd kissed her on her eighteenth. But the feel of him against her made her realize he wanted her as much as she wanted him. They weren't kids anymore—they were both adults, and he wanted her more than he was worried about Dan finding out. He wasn't going to back off. This was really going to happen.

The kiss was the nicest she'd ever had, with the promise of the evening before them, the feel of the sand between her toes, and the taste of Rusty's chocolate ice cream in her mouth. They drew apart reluctantly, but a deep thrill reverberated through her at the thought that things weren't going to end there. They were going to go back to the motel room, and then…

"Come on." She couldn't wait any longer. She picked up her shoes, grabbed his hand, and led him, laughing, back across the road.

She let them into the motel room, and he closed and locked the door behind them. He surveyed her with a smile. "Should I sign the contract now?"

The contract—she'd nearly forgotten about that. "Yes, please." She retrieved it from her bag and spread it on the small dining table. She gave him a pen, expecting him to give a quick scribble at the bottom, but instead he pulled out a chair and sat.

"I'm not signing till I've read it," he stated at her raised eyebrow. "In case you've slipped in another clause."

"Like what?" she asked.

"You might want to keep me tied up in your room as a sex slave or something."

"You want me to cross that one out?"

"I didn't say that." Smiling, Rusty put his chin on his hand and read.

Chapter Seven

The contract filled one page, and she'd obviously typed it up and printed it herself. Rusty surveyed it with amusement.

I, Richard Henry Thorne (Rusty), agree to help Faith Alison Hillman (Faith) with research for the seven articles on the Seven Sexy Sins.

This research will extend to seven sexual encounters exactly, one sin at a time, no more, no less. After these seven encounters have been completed, the sexual relationship between Rusty and Faith will be terminated.

I promise to answer any questions Faith has relating to the Seven Sexy Sins and my participation in them. I also promise to do whatever she asks during these sexual encounters.

I promise not to disclose this sexual relationship to anyone, and I agree to keep the fact that Mr. Sinful is my secret identity to myself. This sexual relationship exists only in the arena of the seven encounters—I promise not to let it affect any meeting I might have with Faith and my friends (i.e. no touching Faith up when she's bending over, etc, even if I think nobody's looking).

I promise to try my best not to let these seven sexual encounters affect my friendship with Faith when the relationship is over.

Signed:
   Date:

Rusty looked up, his eyes meeting Faith's. She raised an eyebrow. "Well?"

"'No touching Faith up when she's bending over'?"

"I thought it best to be clear."

"Does it sound like something I'd do?"

"Er...yeah."

"Fair enough." He looked down at the document and then back up at her. "'I also promise to do whatever she asks during these sexual encounters'?"

"You have a problem with that?"

"I don't know. Should I?"

Her smile softened. "All I meant was that I'd be grateful if you'd…keep on track. Not get off topic. Because I have a deadline to meet."

He nodded. "Okay." Sighing, wondering what he was letting himself in for, he wrote his name at the bottom and signed it. She took the contract and folded it, slipping it back in her bag.

Their gazes met. He smiled. He could see the pulse pounding in her throat and he knew she was nervous.

It surprised him, because although he knew she wasn't that experienced, she wasn't the kind of girl to tie herself up in knots about things like this. Faith was a Kiwi girl, down-to-earth, up-front, beautiful, kind, and sexy in a girl-next-door kind of way. He'd known her a long time, and it had been obvious to him for years that they'd eventually end up in bed together, as obvious as the sun rising in the east or water flowing downhill. Because of that, he'd assumed that when the time came, they'd both leap into bed and have a fun-filled, short-term relationship that he'd still be thinking fondly of for years to come.

He hadn't expected her to be nervous. And oddly, he hadn't expected his own stomach to be fluttering a little, his breathing to be faster than it usually was.

It was because of the blog, he thought—knowing your every move was about to be broadcast for half the women in New Zealand to see was bound to make a man a bit apprehensive. He was also more conscious than he thought he'd be that she was Dan's little sister. Dan would floor him if he ever found out what Rusty had offered to do.

But if he thought they were the only reasons, he was fooling himself. He liked Faith. He wanted her to have a good time. And he was more excited than he thought about getting her into bed. She looked gorgeous tonight, all curves and flushed cheeks. He had to fight not to pull her into his arms and kiss her senseless straight off the bat.

But what would she think of him once they got into bed? She'd teased him for years about his sexual exploits. Maybe she'd built him up in her mind to be sexually amazing. He thought he was okay, but he didn't know if he was anything special. What would he do if, afterward, she said *Is that it?*

He had to just take his time. Things would happen naturally, and he was sure they'd both enjoy themselves when they got started.

"Come on." He went over to the big TV at the foot of the bed and turned it on with the remote. "Got your iPad? I'll try to hook it up to the TV."

She pulled it out, and he played around with the Bluetooth until he got it working. Then he handed her the iPad back.

"Okay," he said. "What's up first?" He'd seen on her blog that she'd mentioned she'd picked a few videos out.

She tapped on the screen. "It's got to be this one called Ocean's Eleven Inches. That can't be real."

"Wow. Are you trying to make me cry?"

She chuckled and brought up the video, then put down the iPad. She turned to look at him and gave a hesitant smile. "You...want to get undressed now?"

"Nuh-uh."

She looked disappointed and relieved at the same time. "No?"

He went over to the kitchen area, undid the bottle of wine, poured her a glass, and got himself a Coke. Then he brought the drinks over to the bedside table and handed her the glass of wine. "Later on, I'll be more than happy to help you off with your clothes. Now...I think we just need to relax."

She smiled. "Okay."

He climbed on the bed, plumped up the pillows and made himself comfortable. He patted the space on his left. Faith moved next to him—and put a clipboard complete with several sheets of paper and a pen beside her.

"What's that?" he asked.

"Well, I've got to keep a record."

He stared at her, startled. "Of what?"

"Length, firmness. Girth."

"Girth?"

She started laughing. "Rusty, come on. I'm kidding. I'm just going to ask a few questions every now and again."

"Jeez, Faith..."

Her grin faded as the music started, and she reached hastily for the remote control. "Turn it down..."

He held it away from her. "There's nobody in the room next to us."

"You could hear that on the beach a mile away."

"It just sounds like a bad nineteen seventies disco, don't worry about it."

She laughed, turning it down slightly. "It does, a bit."

"Well, these things aren't usually known for their soundtracks."

"Or their production values," she observed, raising an eyebrow at the tacky opening screen. Smirking, he leaned back, his arm along the pillows behind her.

He looked down as she curled up next to him. She sipped her wine, glancing up as she realized he was watching her. "What?"

He smiled. "Nothing." He didn't like to say she'd suddenly looked very young. Guilt stabbed him at the thought of what Dan would say if he knew what was going on. But he wasn't taking advantage of her. She was a grown woman, for Christ's sake, and she was going to go ahead with this research for her articles with or without him. Surely, she would be better carrying it out with him—a good friend who would look after her—than with some idiot she'd only known for five minutes.

Rusty knew he had a reputation in the bedroom, and he liked to think it was well-deserved, but he knew he had to be careful here. This was all about Faith and letting her explore her sexuality in a safe environment. He loved her—she was one of his best friends—and he had to make sure he let her lead the way and have fun with a man who wasn't going to hurt her, or think about anything other than her pleasure.

He made himself think of the contract. She'd drawn it up specifically because she didn't want anything long term—she only wanted seven sexual encounters, and after that, it would all be over. He didn't have to worry about how he was going to end it, or how she would feel afterward. This was purely business, a good deed for a good friend.

He glanced at her, getting a perfect view down the front of her cleavage, and gave a silent groan. *Don't kid yourself, dude.* This wasn't all about helping Faith out. He'd thought about having sex with her for years. If this wasn't a dream come true, he didn't know what was.

He let his arm sink lower until he'd draped it around her shoulder. And smiled when she didn't pull away.

MR. SINFUL

Chapter Eight

Faith's eyes nearly fell out of her head when the actor in Ocean's Eleven Inches first appeared. Even clothed, his equipment was impressive. "Whoa, Jesus. You've got to be kidding me." Rusty started laughing, and she looked up at him in alarm. "That's got to be fake, right?"

"I suspect not, sweetheart, or the film would be probably called Ocean's Four-and-a-Half Inches."

"But… It's not genetically possible, is it?"

"I think it's possible, but not very common. Let's just say I don't think you should judge your future lovers—including me, by the way—by this standard."

She laughed and kissed his cheek before turning back to the DVD. "I can't take my eyes off it."

"Does it turn you on?"

"Ah… Not so much. More 'elephant in the room'."

He chuckled as she lifted up the clipboard and wrote a few notes. Then she leaned back against his arm and nibbled her pen as her eyes went back to the screen. "I'm guessing these sorts of films aren't big on plot."

"Oh no, there's a story. You just have to dig deep." He pointed at the screen and she had a sudden vision of how he must look in the classroom, explaining the Reformation or the Renaissance or something. "You see," he continued, "this one's about a young lady, who's quite clearly got lost in the big city…"

"In a very short skirt…"

"In a very short skirt and with surprisingly little material in her top, and she's wandered into this paper manufacturers, and this very kind man has agreed to help her out…"

"By removing her clothes…"

"Yes, by helping her rearrange her clothing…"

"I'm guessing it's quite cold in the warehouse."

He grinned. "And now she's dropped something down the back of the photocopier…"

"Yes, and she's reaching over to pick it up, and—whoa! Jeez!" They both winced. "That came out of nowhere," said Faith, eyes wide.

They watched for a few minutes in silence. Eventually Rusty looked down at her and started laughing.

"What?"

"You know those glasses you can buy in joke shops, where the eyes are on springs and fall out as you lean forward?"

She glanced at him before looking back at the screen. "Are you surprised? I mean…this is my first porn movie. It's a bit…"

"What?" He ran a light finger along her jaw and she looked up at him. His eyes were tender. "You okay? You want to turn it off?"

"No, no…" He totally had the wrong idea. "It's just… It's more…um…explicit than I thought it would be."

"You thought they'd be having tea and crumpets? You know the definition of porn, right?"

"Don't make fun of me. I saw some pretty eye-boggling stuff while I was surfing around. But I didn't watch much of it because I wanted to wait until I was with you. I thought it would be more…suggestive and arty. Almost, I don't know, kind of pretend. This is very…real."

"I'm not making fun of you, sweetheart." He bent his head and kissed her. "There are some films like that. And I think they probably appeal more to women. Slightly more romantic. But guys prefer this sort of stuff."

She pressed her lips together, still feeling the brush of his mouth. "Do you?"

"We're a pretty basic species."

She scribbled a few notes on her clipboard. Then she leaned back against him and sipped her wine. Ocean's Eleven Inches, huh? Glancing up at Rusty mischievously, she wondered what the movie would be called if he were in the starring role. She was desperate to find out and pondered on whether to start taking off her clothes. But even though he smiled at her, something in his eyes made her hold back.

She continued to watch the video for a while, leaning her head on Rusty's shoulder. He smelled nice, some aftershave with a spicy scent that made her tingle. On the screen, the man and woman continued to have sex in a variety of positions, and she studied them, occasionally jotting down notes. And all the while Rusty drew small, circular patterns on her shoulder with warm, light fingers.

"Well?" he asked after a while, watching her write something down. "What's the verdict?"

Her gaze rested on the screen. "Don't know, really. It's sexy, in a kind of mechanical way. I think the acting puts me off. She's so obviously faking it."

"Yeah, I don't think there's an Oscar on the way anytime soon."

She looked up at him, and their gazes caught, snagged, held. He lowered his head and kissed her again, long and lazily, his hand moving from her shoulder to brush the nape of her neck, tangling in the curls tumbling from her head.

When he eventually pulled back, she surveyed him. "Okay, so give me a score. How turned on are you?"

He raised an eyebrow. "By the kiss?"

"No, silly, by the video."

"Out of what?"

"Ten. One being a striptease by your elderly maiden aunt, ten being a striptease by…er…"

"You?"

She grinned. "If you like."

He glanced at the screen and shrugged. "Seven?"

"Ooh. Fairly high then."

"That surprises you? What's your score?"

She studied the DVD. "Five-and-a-half? Six? He's not all that. I couldn't see myself fantasizing about him."

"Oh, and who do you fantasize about when you're alone in your room, young Faith?" He ran his fingers all the way up her arm, making her shiver.

"Um…" She could feel her cheeks growing hot. "Brad Pitt." She pushed herself off the bed to cover her embarrassment, refraining from reminding him that Pitt's character's name in the proper version of Ocean's Eleven was Rusty. "Let's have a look at Forest Hump. See if that does the trick." She concentrated on finding the movie on her iPad—and on banishing the memory that had jumped into her head. She couldn't possibly look at him. Brad Pitt. Brad Pitt, that's all. With the second movie playing, she snuggled back up to him, and they settled back to watch.

Faith studied the film. It consisted of an orgy in the middle of a forest, featuring half a dozen guys and a few more girls, all butt naked and writhing around in various positions. Only half her attention was on the screen, however. The rest of it centered on the guy currently sipping his Coke and making occasional comments about the movie.

She was becoming increasingly aware that Rusty hadn't done anything more than kiss her. She'd expected him to be undressing her by now, playing with her as they got more turned on, but he hadn't made a move on her at all. Was he waiting for her to do something? And if so, what? And why? He didn't strike her as the sort of guy who needed an invitation to get intimate. Was he having second thoughts?

Now she had that to worry about, as well as her own nerves. Trying not to think about it, she watched ten minutes or so of the movie, attempting to concentrate on her article. Rusty was still talking to her normally, making her laugh with wry remarks about the actors or their actions, but she wasn't stupid. Something was holding him back.

"So what about this one?" she asked eventually.

He sipped his Coke and looked at her. "Probably better than the last."

"Why?"

He glanced back at the screen. "The young ladies seem to be enjoying it more."

"Is that important to you too?"

"Well, I think watching someone enjoying themselves is more of a turn on than seeing someone wincing."

"I guess. For most people." She smiled. "Out of ten?"

"Eight." He sipped his Coke again and grinned. "And a half." He watched her write it down. "You?"

"Mm, probably around an eight." Before she could stop herself, her gaze slid to his jeans. Quite clearly, he was eight-and-a-half out of ten turned on. And yet still he made no move toward her.

"Let's try the last one," she said, pulling her iPad toward her. Maybe a bit of girl-on-girl action would get him going.

She changed the movie to On Golden Blonde and leaned back. His arm fell naturally around her shoulder, but his fingers had stopped lacing patterns on her skin, and this time he didn't kiss her. She said nothing, curling up in the circle of his arm, watching as the movie began to play.

For the first time, she felt a rush of sexual heat right from the start as the two blonde women started making out in the shower. There was no evidence of a plot, and much more subtle music, and the production values were even worse, if that were possible. But for some reason, it seemed much more real because of it, and the two girls actually looked as if they were enjoying themselves.

"Oh yeah," said Rusty, the first vocal indication since they'd started watching that he was enjoying himself.

"You like?"

He glanced at her before looking back at the screen. "Sweetheart, take it from me, girl-on-girl wins every time."

She frowned. "When I asked you what kind of movie you wanted, you said it didn't matter."

"I lied."

"Why?"

He glanced at her again. "I didn't want you to think I was…"

"What?"

"I dunno. Perverted."

She laughed. "That word again. What's perverted about this?"

He shrugged. "Some women think it's weird, a guy liking two girls together."

"Really?"

"Faith, come on. Some women won't watch porn at all, let alone anything not boy/girl in the missionary position."

"I suppose." She watched the girls on the screen playing with the shower spray, knowing her breathing was quickening and her panties were growing damp. "I don't understand people who think like that."

"And that's what makes you you, love." His hand was back to caressing her shoulder, although he still didn't make a move.

Why didn't more women watch porn? Why did the world pretend to frown on it when quite clearly it could be a useful tool for stimulating your love life? She scribbled a few notes on the clipboard. "Out of ten?"

"Eleven and a half."

She laughed, clipped the pen onto the board, and put it down by the side of the bed. "Okay. Enough writing." She finished off her wine, observing the two blondes kissing and touching each other, watching Rusty watching them. For the moment, his attention was fixed on the screen, and she could see the pulse beating steadily in his neck. The room was warm. His russet hair curled around his temples, and moisture glistened in the hollow at his throat. She was tempted to reach up and lick it, but something stopped her. He was so sexy, so hot, she wanted him to rip off her clothes and throw her on the bed and do unspeakable things to her, but he still didn't move.

Moving closer to him, she reached up a hand and brushed his cheek. "Come on, Rusty. Kiss me."

He turned and smiled at her, lowering his lips. He kissed her softly, his hand coming back up to stroke the nape of her neck.

She kissed him for a minute or so, and then, when no further movement was obviously going to occur, drew back to look at him. The room was cast in twilight. Cicadas were beginning to call from the orchards to the west, and the cry of seagulls echoed occasionally through the open window. The whole place smelled of lemon and jasmine, and of salt from the sea. The atmosphere was warm and sultry, and a bead of perspiration ran down between her breasts.

She studied him for a moment. Was he having second thoughts? Did he not find her sexy? Did he not fancy having sex with her?

As she looked deep into his eyes, however, suddenly she realized what was wrong.

Rusty was nervous.

She almost laughed out loud, but stopped herself in time. He knew she was aware of his previous sexual exploits, and after ten years of joking about who he'd done and what he got up to in the bedroom, he was very aware there were going to be no secrets anymore. And she was sure the fact that she was Dan's little sister was also playing heavily on his mind. Rusty wanted her, she knew he did, but his sense of duty, and honor, and possibly a fear of what she would think of him when she saw what he was really like in bed, were overwhelming his desire. He'd promised he'd teach her, and maybe now he was worried she'd find him wanting.

She felt a rush of affection for him, and a hot, sudden sweep of desire. If she didn't do something, this wasn't going to happen, and basically, if it didn't happen, she was going to be disappointed as hell. She was going to have to take charge. As soon as she realized that, all her nerves disappeared.

She got off the bed and walked around to his side. He watched her, his green eyes curious, slightly wary. She stood next to him and put her hands on her hips. "I have something to say."

"Okay…"

"Let's get one thing straight." She reached around her back to slide down the zipper on her skirt. "I'm not your girlfriend." She let the skirt fall to the ground and stepped out of it casually, flicking it to one side with her foot. "I'm not your date." She saw his eyes drop to her black lacy panties, and watched his chest rise with his intake of breath. "And I'm not a girl from a bar you need to impress."

She climbed onto the bed and sat astride him, the movie still playing in the background, the room filled with the low sighs of the two girls pleasuring each other. She flicked a glance at the screen, saw one girl lower her mouth onto the other girl's breast while her fingers moved between her legs. She looked back at Rusty in time to see he'd followed her gaze, although now he looked back at her. His green eyes were dark, some emotion moving mysteriously beneath the surface, an emotion she couldn't quite fathom.

She moved her hips, feeling the swell of him beneath his jeans, hard against her swollen, sensitive sex. He swallowed, and she knew he was aroused but was also forcing himself to hold back. His eyes were almost begging. He wanted her to talk him into it. He needed her to persuade him.

Slowly, she began to unbutton her shirt. His eyes went wide as satellite dishes, but he still didn't touch her. Her heart pounded, but she made herself act coolly, her fingers sliding down the cotton, unbuttoning one by one. "While we're here, I'm not your friend." Nearly all the buttons were undone now. "And I'm nobody's sister." She opened the final button, parting the sides of the blouse slowly to reveal her black bra. His gaze dipped to her breasts, lingered, and came back up to her face. She felt a surge of excitement—his eyes didn't look like her friend's anymore. They were hot and filled with desire. A man's eyes.

She slid the blouse slowly off her arms and dropped it onto the floor. Then she leaned forward, bracing her arms on the bed either side of his chest, and brushed his lips with hers. "I'm just a girl, Rusty, a girl who wants you, very, very much. I don't need to be romanced, and I don't need to be cajoled. And I swear, if you're not inside me in, like, two minutes, I'm going to tie you to the bed and carry all seven sins out on you in one go, whether you like it or not."

Chapter Nine

Their eyes met, locked. There was a brief moment of silence. Rusty blinked, his eyes going slightly out of focus. Then, to her surprise, he grabbed her by the hips and tipped her onto her back, rolling so he was on top of her. His weight pinned her to the mattress, and he looked down at her, his lips curving. "You're a bad, bad girl. You know that?"

"Moi?" She batted her eyelashes.

He gave a little shake of his head, his red-brown hair falling across an eyebrow, lust lighting his eyes like fireworks. "It's a good job my self-control is legendary. You're hot enough to make a man come with a single touch."

She laughed, thrilled, excited she was turning him on. And she was, she could see it written all over his face, feel the evidence of his desire pressing between her legs. "It's a shame you're not wearing any socks," she said.

"Eh?"

"I'm desperate to screw them off."

He gave her an admonishing look. "For God's sake, Faith..."

"Rusty..." She was almost begging. "Please..."

He laughed and kissed her, the playful peck turning immediately into a full-blown passionate embrace as she opened her mouth. Their tongues brushed and her teeth grazed his bottom lip, making him sigh and cup her head so he could deepen the kiss further. She began to feel dizzy with lust, desperate to have him inside her. But he continued to kiss her, his weight pressing her into the mattress, deliciously heavy and solid between her thighs.

Eventually, his mouth left hers and pressed firm kisses down her neck, pausing as his lips met the swell of her breasts. He lifted his head and looked for a moment, bringing up a hand to trace the creamy-white skin above the lacy cup. "God, if I'd known you were this hot, I'd never have waited this long..." He lowered his mouth and traced his tongue along her feverish skin, pressing kisses against the lace, but it wasn't enough, it seemed, because he rolled again so she was on top. He moved a hand behind her back, took her bra clasp between his thumb and forefinger, pinched it, and it popped open, just like that.

"Smooth," she commented, impressed.

"Not my first time."

"Thank God." She meant it. She was relieved he knew what he was doing. She needed him to lead her down this exciting, slightly scary road.

He drew the bra down her arms and threw it onto the floor. She sat up, and her face grew warm as his gaze rested on her breasts. He looked at them as if they were ice cream sundaes and he was desperate for the cherry on the top. "Fuck me, Hillman, where the hell have you been hiding those?"

She burst out laughing, which quickly turned into a half-groan as he caught her hands, linked their fingers, and pulled them above his head, forcing her to lean over him. Raising his head, he closed a hot mouth over her right nipple, and the breath caught in her throat. "Oh God…"

Her head tipped back as he sucked, his tongue circling the sensitive area, and she arched her back, which somehow just made it even more sensitive. Her heart pounded, and she widened her thighs and pushed down against the hard length in his jeans, arousing herself on him. He moved his mouth from her right nipple to fasten on the other, and he released her hands so he could bring his down to cup her breasts. He brushed his thumb across the nipple he'd just left, which, wet from his mouth, was excruciatingly tender and receptive.

She was close to coming, and she didn't want to yet, not until he was inside her. She lifted herself up slightly, but clearly he didn't want that. He caught her hips and rolled one last time—a fateful move, because they were nearer the edge of the bed than they realized. The momentum carried them right off the mattress, and with a startled squeal, she grabbed hold of him, falling right on top of him onto the carpet.

He shifted at the last moment to cushion her fall and then lay there for a moment, winded. "Ouch," he said eventually. She started laughing and he joined in. "Are you hurt?" he asked, running his hands down her sides.

"No." She pushed herself to her feet and held out a hand, hauling him up. "But then I had something soft to land on. You?"

He groaned as he straightened. "Only my pride."

"Is that one of your fancy moves?"

"I'm pleased to say that was the first time I've been so engrossed I've fallen off the bed."

She blushed at the compliment, letting him pull her toward him, and he wrapped his arms around her. She put a hand up to her hair, where a section had loosened. He squeezed open the clip and threw it onto the table. As the locks tumbled down, he spread them around her shoulders, smiling. "You're so beautiful."

"Thank you." Out of the corner of her eye, she saw movement on the TV and looked at the screen. His gaze turned to follow hers, and they watched for a moment as the two blondes made love, still in the shower. One aroused the other with a vibrator, and the water cascaded over them both, turning their skin to satin.

Rusty turned back to her, shaking his head.

"What?"

"This is just, like, every man's dream."

She pretended to look at her watch. "I think your two minutes are up."

"I'm trying, Faith." He pushed her backward to the wall, which she met with a bump. Her hands fumbled at the buttons on his shirt as he began to kiss her again. She pushed it off his shoulders, and he let it fall to the floor.

She ran her hands up his chest, admiring the muscles she'd seen in the pool so many times but never thought she'd get her hands on. She brushed his nipples and threaded her fingers through the reddish-brown hairs as he watched her, enjoying her admiration. Then she began to fumble at his belt.

He stopped her hand. "Let me, it's quite hard."

"Well, praise the Lord."

"I was talking about the belt."

"Hey, I'm not complaining."

Laughing, he undid it, opening the buttons of his jeans. She caught his hands as he went to push them off. "No, don't, leave them on. You look so damn sexy."

He stopped. "Yes ma'am."

"That's my boy."

He pushed her against the wall, moving one hand up her thigh. His eyes met hers, and she felt her cheeks flush as he slipped his fingers inside the black lacy panties for the first time. She opened her legs for him, sighing.

"Am I wet enough?" she asked innocently.

He gave a deep, sexy laugh, sliding his fingers through her warm folds until they were slick and coated, then arousing her gently. "You're kidding me, right?"

She let him stroke her for a while before adding breathlessly, "So we don't need any lubrication then?"

"Ah…not so much."

She moistened her lips with her tongue as he continued his skillful stroking. "So you'll be able to slide in and out easily?"

His eyes were hot and exasperated. "That's it. I can't wait any longer."

"Oh, thank goodness."

He retrieved a condom from his pocket and tore open the packet as she slid her panties off. Releasing himself from his boxers, he began to roll it on.

"Wow." She stared, eyes wide. *Oh my God, I'm looking at Rusty Thorne in all his glory.* "Seriously Rusty, wow. My very own re-enactment of Ocean's Eleven Inches."

"Hardly, but thank you for the lovely compliment." Ready for her, he placed both hands under her backside, and, to her shock, lifted her and wrapped her legs around him.

"Rusty!"

He paused, holding her still, and she felt the tip of his erection press into her. His eyes met hers. "Are you sure about this? Last chance."

She nearly cried. "For fuck's sake…"

He pushed his hips and slid all the way into her, deep as he could go.

Faith gasped as he stretched her, filled her. He stopped moving, his mouth a fraction of an inch from hers, exchanging breaths with her. All amusement fled, and a deep, dark desire clawed its way up her, a hunger she'd never felt before. She'd never, ever wanted a man this much, never craved someone with this intensity.

He breathed out in a long, controlled exhalation. Lowering his lips to hers, he kissed her deeply. Then, very, very slowly, he began to move.

Faith felt dizzy with desire. The hairs on his chest grazed her nipples, making her gasp again, and her swollen sex was excruciatingly sensitive. She wanted it to last forever, but within minutes she was sighing, her lids fluttering. "Oh God…"

He kissed her eyelids. "Come on, Faith, hang in there. I've only just started."

"Ah I can't, it's too…"

He stopped moving. "Multiple orgasms aren't till number six."

"Rusty…"

Holding her tightly, he lifted her off the wall. She threw her arms around him as he carried her over to the bed, where he turned, sat, and lay back, still inside her, pushing her up so she sat astride him. "Count sheep," he demanded. "Distract yourself." He ran his hands up her body and cupped her breasts, brushing her nipples.

Sighing, she arched her spine, enjoying the feel of her hair falling down her back, so close to coming it was like exquisite torture, but wanting to savor the moment. To the side, she caught a brief glimpse of one of the blonde girls reaching an orgasm, face creased with pleasure. Oh God. She tried to picture sheep jumping over a fence, but clearly, that wasn't going to work.

Rusty was obviously having trouble coping as well. The sight of her breasts thrust toward him appeared to have pushed him to the edge. For the last time, he rolled her and moved her legs up. He pushed himself up until he was almost kneeling, looking down at her with an expression of such tenderness, such desire, that she just melted.

"Pretend I've got socks on," she said. She wrapped her legs around him and lifted her arms slowly above her head, stretching underneath him. "Come on, Thorne, show me what you've got."

"Oh, man…" He began to move, more insistently this time, bending to kiss her.

Faith ran one hand down his back, slipping it beneath his jeans. She could feel he was still holding back, worried about hurting her. He was so sweet. But she didn't want sweet Rusty. She wanted the hot, rough man she knew he could be.

She dug her fingers into the tight muscles of his butt. "I'm going to come, honey. Harder." He gave a slight shake of his head and murmured something, but she missed it, too busy gasping as he slid one hand beneath her and lifted her, deepening his thrusts. "Oh, jeez, yes, don't stop…" Her muscles tightened. "Rusty…"

"Let it go, babe."

She screwed her eyes up and squealed as she came, the orgasm so strong it almost hurt. He swore loudly as her muscles contracted around him, and he shuddered as his body pulsed. The feel of him swelling hot and hard inside her was exquisite, and intense waves of pleasure rolled over her for what seemed like an eternity.

For a few moments afterward, there was only the sound of breathing, accompanied by the cicadas out in the orchards. He leaned his forehead on her shoulder, and she pressed her lips into his hair.

Then, quietly, Rusty started to laugh. "Fucking hell."

Faith joined in. "Oh my God."

"Are you going to write about that on your website?"

She collapsed into giggles, and he winced and withdrew from her, rolling onto his back. She pushed herself up and looked down at him, meeting his eyes, which were light with amusement and other emotions too, tenderness, affection, and more than a little admiration. She kissed him. "Thank you."

He raised an eyebrow. "Hey, I had nothing to do with that. That was all you."

"Yeah, yeah." But she was pleased with the performance. Surely, she must have matched at least some of his previous exploits? She kissed his lips again. "No wonder you have a reputation."

"Sweetheart, a man's only as good as his woman makes him." He brushed his fingers against her cheek. "So I must be terrific."

She gave him a longer kiss this time. When she lifted her head, his eyes were hooded, dark with lazy satisfaction. He glanced over at the TV, where the other blonde was now pleasuring her friend. "You want to turn that off?"

She picked up the iPad. "You had enough?"

"Well that's going to make me start all over again, so it's probably best if you stop it."

She laughed and pressed stop.

He sat up, reaching for a tissue on the bedside table to dispose of the condom, and buttoned himself back into his jeans. Then he flopped back onto the bed. He sighed and raised his arm to look at his watch. "You want me to go now?"

Lying on her side, watching him, she raised an eyebrow. "You want to go?"

His eyes met hers, and his lips started to curve. "I didn't say that. I thought this was a one-at-a-time thing."

She studied him for a moment. She honestly hadn't given any thought as to what to do after they'd finished. She'd already paid for the room, so should they just go their separate ways?

She ran her gaze down him and slowly back up. He looked incredibly sexy lying there, bare-chested, hair mussed, sleepily sated. Suddenly she wanted him to stay more than anything in the world.

She shrugged. "We do have the room for the night. And the bath's big enough for two, if you want to join me." She pushed herself up and off the bed and walked over to the bathroom. Then she turned and looked at him, giving him a saucy smile. "And I still have a few videos left on the iPad. I think a little more research might be in order."

He rolled onto his side to face her, propping his head on a hand. A smile spread slowly across his face. They looked at each other for a moment.

"God," she said, "you look good enough to eat."

"Not till sin number two."

"Maybe we could have an advanced showing…"

"Oh no." He got up and came over to her. "Your rules. One sin at a time, no more, no less, remember?"

"Damn it. Stupid contract."

He pulled her to him. "You need to exercise some restraint, Hillman."

"The word's not in my vocabulary."

"So I'm beginning to understand." He brought up a hand and brushed her cheekbone.

She smiled. "That was fun, wasn't it?"

"Hell, yeah."

"Six more sins, Rusty."

"Mm. When are we doing the next one?"

"Same time, same place?"

He raised an eyebrow, looking pained. "A whole week?"

"I only publish one article a week. But I don't expect you to wait."

"What do you mean?"

"We're not exclusive. I don't mind if you want to see someone else in the meantime."

He frowned. "I don't cheat on my girls."

"We're not dating, love. It's just a business partnership, remember?"

"Even so…" He put his hands on her hips and pulled her closer for a kiss. "No one would match up to you, anyway."

She felt a wash of pleasure, which she quickly squashed. They were flattering words, but she was hardly going to be the last conquest on his list. "Yadda, yadda. It's up to you. I'm just saying, I know what your sex drive's like, and if you need someone else to…you know, help you out midweek, I'm not going to complain. Long as you wear a condom."

He looked startled. "Jesus. Miss Romantic." He studied her for a moment. "Are you planning to see anyone else?"

"No."

"Then I won't either."

"Whatever." She smiled mischievously. "Guess you'll just have to put up with adjusting the antenna."

He stared at her. "Doing the what now?"

"You know. Clearing the snorkel. Buffing the banana. Five-knuckle shuffle."

"Faith Hillman, for God's sake, where on earth did you dredge those terms up?"

She laughed. "I did an article on masturbation."

He shook his head, turned her around and slapped her bare backside. "Get in there and put the bath on. I'll get the magazines."

"Yes, sir."

He muttered something under his breath and walked off. Grinning, she put in the plug and turned the taps on in the huge tub. What a great night this was turning out to be.

Chapter Ten

Faith Hillman's blog

Evening all. I'm back! All good. Walking like John Wayne when he's got off his horse, but feeling great. LOL.

But seriously, now. Wow. I mean, WOW! You girls have seriously got to watch some porn. It was sooooo worth it. By far the biggest success was the girl-on-girl movie. Not that Mr. S. would have turned his nose up at any of them, I think, but the girly one definitely got him going, and me too, I have to say. Ocean's Eleven Inches made me wince in places, Forest Hump was better but a bit unbelievable. On Golden Blonde was, like the little bear said, just right: realistic, gentle, erotic, and sexy.

I think the biggest thing I've learned out of all this (apart from how hot Mr. S. looks lying there in just his jeans) is that guys are turned on by us being turned on. And it helps if we don't mind that they're turned on by something other than us. It doesn't mean they'd rather be with the girl on the TV, or even that they're lying there picturing the porn star underneath them. Watching someone else have sex is hot, reading about sex is hot, looking at photos of naked men and women is hot, and there's nothing wrong with admitting that, or getting turned on by it. It's not perverse (you listening, Mr. S.?), and it's not dirty (well, only if it's done right). Nothing that two consenting adults get up to in the privacy of their own homes (or motels) is wrong, providing they're both willing and happy to go along with it. IMHO. And I think—and correct me if I'm wrong, Mr. S.—the thought that a man's partner has made the effort to try something different, especially something he sees as a little bit naughty, is the ultimate turn on. So go for it. Worked for me!

*

An excerpt from the 647 comments

LilyP: I will, Faith, I promise. This weekend. Hubby doesn't know what's going to hit him. Thank you for all your advice. I hope Mr. S. appreciates how lucky he is.

MrS69: He does.

Patsy: *Woo hoo!*
WendyS: *Mr. S.! We wondered where you were! Did you have a good time?*
MrS69: *I did. Can't you tell by the huge smile on my face?*
AnnaF: *Did you enjoy the porn?*
MrS69: *Meh. *grins**
WendyS: *Girl-on-girl, eh?*
MrS69: *What can I say? I'm a man of simple pleasures.*
Eve: *I'm sure I know you...*
Patsy: *He sounds like every other man I know.*
Eve: *True.*
SashaT: *We've been talking about how to approach the topic of watching porn with our fellas, Mr. S.*
MrS69: *Yes, I've been reading your comments. You wicked lot.*
SashaT: *You think we should do it?*
MrS69: *I don't see the harm in trying. I'm no marriage guidance counsellor, but I find it difficult to see how any decent guy would be upset by his partner trying to turn him on.*
LilyP: *Not everyone's as nice as you, though, Mr. S.*
Faith: *Stop massaging his ego, everyone, it's big enough already.*
MrS69: *Hello sweetheart. You can massage whatever you like, love.*
WendyS: *ROFL!*
HelenB: *Come on guys, get a room.*
MrS69: *Yeah, Faith, stop leading me astray.*
Faith: *Hah!*
CissyT: *So come on, dish the dirt. How many times did you do it?*
MrS69: *Oh now, I don't kiss and tell.*
Faith: *Three.*
MrS69: *Huh.*
Patsy: *LOL, Faith tells us everything, Mr. S., you've got to deal with it, I'm afraid.*
Faith: *Strictly business, remember?*
MrS69: *Fair enough. Okay, once on the bed (although we fell off), once in the bath (mutual... ah, you know), then back to the bed (a bit later).*
Patsy: *You fell off?*
Faith: *He's very soft to land on. I didn't hurt a thing.*
MrS69: *I have a bump on the back of my head the size of a walnut. I'm lucky I didn't get concussion.*
Faith: *Eek, you didn't tell me that!*
MrS69: *I didn't want to spoil the moment. I went ouch, remember?*

Faith: Sorry sweetheart.

MrS69: It was worth it.

SashaT: You two! What a pair. And mutual... Can you elaborate?

MrS69: No.

Faith: Masturbation.

MrS69: Faith! Jeez...

Faith: What? We're helping the women of Oceania to develop their sexual relationships. We're proving there's nothing to be ashamed of.

MrS69: I guess, but... I'm blushing.

UnaN: You are so sweet!

Eve: Did you both stay the night?

Patsy: It's all gone quiet...

WendyS: Hellooo?

Yolanda: That means they did!

MrS69: Might have.

Yolanda: I knew it.

MrS69: Well, I was knackered. She wore me out. I slept right through to check-out time and she had to tip a glass of cold water over me to wake me up.

Patsy: I think we've finally embarrassed her. I bet she was good, was she?

MrS69: Sublime.

WendyS: Thank you for coming on here and talking to us. We do appreciate it.

MrS69: No worries, ladies. Remember, you're all beautiful, in your own way.

Faith: Oh, for God's sake... I go for a Coke and you're chatting up half of New Zealand.

MrS69: They thought they'd finally embarrassed you.

Faith: Nah. I'm not easily embarrassed.

MrS69: I'm beginning to understand that. I've gotta go now. Work to do.

WendyS: What job do you do, Mr. S.?

MrS69: Goodnight, everyone.

Chapter Eleven

Wednesday evening was the first time she met Rusty again after their assignation at the motel. They'd all agreed to meet at the local wine bar, as they occasionally did halfway through the week. Faith walked in at about eight fifteen, a little late, and saw them all in their usual corner on the sofas, talking. She paused for a moment. Dan and Eve were on one sofa, Eve stretched out with her feet on the arm, leaning on Dan, his arm around her. Rusty and Toby were on the other. Usually, she would have walked straight up and sat between them, but today...

Dan glanced over and saw her, and she waved as she walked to the bar and ordered herself a glass of wine. She didn't look over while she waited, flicking instead through the bar menu, although she wasn't hungry. She was nervous about striking the right casual note with all of them. They had always been affectionate as friends, exchanging hugs and kisses, and she'd never thought about it before, but suddenly she was very aware of any contact she had with them, and not just with Rusty, either. His comment about Toby being keen to get her into bed had shocked her, as had Rusty's eagerness to volunteer himself. Perhaps she truly had been naive in thinking a man and a woman could be friends. There was a topic for another article there, somewhere.

She paid for the wine and carried it over to them, pausing for a brief moment as she debated whether to pull over a chair, but then Toby patted the sofa between him and Rusty, and she sighed and climbed over Rusty's legs to sit between them.

Toby leaned over and kissed her on the cheek. "Hey, gorgeous."

"Hey, Faith." Rusty's arm lay along the back of the sofa, but he moved it as she sat.

She leaned back and propped her feet on the low table in front of her. "Hey, guys."

"You're late." Dan took a slug of his beer. "Been off with Mr. S., have we?"

Eve laughed. "No, she's not seeing him until Saturday." She waggled her eyebrows at Faith. "Ready for sin two?"

"I've just walked in the door. Can we talk about something else?"

"No," said Toby. "Come on, dish the dirt. What was he like?"

"You'll have to read the website."

"I did." Toby grinned at her shocked face.

Faith looked across at Dan. "Have you read it?"

"No. The last thing I want to know about is what you're getting up to beneath the sheets."

"It's good reading," said Toby. He winked at her. "Three times in one night, eh?"

Dan rolled his eyes. Faith giggled. "Don't torture him."

"I can't believe you fell off the bed," said Eve. "What would you have done if he'd been knocked out?"

"Made myself a cup of tea," said Faith. "I'm sure he would have come around eventually."

They all laughed. Faith risked a quick glance up at Rusty. His eyes were warm with amusement. "So you enjoyed yourself?" he asked.

She shrugged. "It was all right."

Eve laughed. "I think that's an understatement, judging by what you said on the website." She looked mischievously at Toby and Rusty. "He sent her a Valentine's Card."

"Oh?" Toby raised an eyebrow. "What did it say?"

"What was it, Faith? Looking forward to Part Two, or something."

Faith just shrugged again. She'd been surprised when the card arrived. It was the first Valentine's card she'd ever received, apart from a hand-drawn one when she was eight from the kid next door. She'd known Rusty had meant it as a teasing gesture, but still, it had made her glow, and she'd put it next to her bed where she could see it as she dozed off.

Rusty sipped his Coke. She was pretty sure he'd done it to cover up a smile.

Eve caught her eye. "Do you think you'll carry on seeing him after the articles are done?"

"No, we have a contract. Seven times only."

"Well, not quite," said Rusty.

Faith's heart thumped. "What do you mean?"

"You've already done it three times on the first night."

She gave him a sarcastic look. "Seven meetings, then."

"You made him sign a contract?" said Dan.

"Yep."

"And he agreed? What an idiot."

Faith raised an eyebrow, aware of Rusty shifting next to her. "I didn't give him a lot of choice."

"Even so. What if he really likes you?"

"He does really like me. We're having sex, Dan."

"Stop reminding me. I meant what if he wants to carry on afterward?"

She sipped her wine. "He won't. Come on, it's just a bit of fun. These guys do it all the time." She gestured to Toby and Rusty. "They're always off with girls for a couple of weeks. You don't go on at them about it."

"They're not you." He caught her gaze and held it. His eyes were tender, affectionate, and held a hint of worry. "I know what you're like. You're going to fall for this guy, and he's going to break your heart."

Faith felt a rush of heat rise in her neck and up into her face. She made herself stay looking at her brother, however, even though she was acutely conscious that Rusty had stiffened. "No, I'm not. That's what the contract's for. Seven times, Dan, that's all. We're both perfectly aware it ends after that." She sipped her wine again. "You guys aren't the only ones who have needs, you know. It is possible for girls to have sex without the heart being involved."

"Tell me more about these needs," said Toby.

She thumped him. "Shut up."

"No, I'd be interested in hearing more," said Rusty.

"For God's sake, you lot. Can we change the subject, please?"

They all laughed and Dan started talking about work, and Faith allowed herself to breathe out finally. She had seven weeks of this to get through. Talk about self-imposed torture.

Rusty moved in his seat again, widening his legs a little so his knee came to rest against hers. She didn't look at him, but she was aware of the comforting gesture, the small token of support. It would be fine. They were both on the same wavelength, and there was no way Rusty was going to get serious about her, or vice versa. It was just sex. Hot, steamy, passionate sex, true, but just sex.

Chapter Twelve

Thursday and Friday passed with agonizing slowness. By Friday lunchtime, Rusty was beginning to think Saturday would never come.

He sat in the corner of the staffroom, working on some notes on Nazi Germany for the period six lesson as he ate his sandwiches. After a while, however, he sat back with a sigh. It was no good, he couldn't concentrate. Titillating fantasies about what was going to take place on Saturday night kept creeping into his head.

Flicking a gaze around the room, making sure nobody was heading his way, he went onto the internet and brought up Faith's website. He knew she posted the first half of her weekly article on Fridays, and he'd been waiting for it to pop up on the site. Sure enough, as the light orange and pale green leafy border sprang up on his screen, he saw she'd finally posted her entry.

He read it with interest. It was a detailed account of oral sex, which included historical references, amusing quotes, and medical advice. As usual, it was well-written and informative, researched and interesting. And funny. She was very skilled at being able to give her readers details, while making sure she didn't preach. He could see why she'd won awards for the site, and why she was so popular. It was odd to think she was relatively inexperienced in sex matters. She spoke confidently and authoritatively, even while openly admitting she hadn't had much personal experience. He felt a twinge of pride at her obvious talent, and also a sneaky feeling of smugness that he was introducing her to some of the areas she was so obviously innocent about.

He flicked over to her blog. This was a lot more informal, and tended to be where she relayed her true feelings. He read that day's entry with interest.

Okay, Sin Two tomorrow. Sloth. Aka laziness. As you'll see on the website, I've linked this to oral sex, i.e. letting your partner do all the work.

Hmm. So. How do you all feel about oral sex? Do you like having it performed on you? Do you enjoy performing it on your man? I'm embarrassed to say I'm incredibly inexperienced about this. I've never had it performed on me and I've not gone down on a guy. There's no real reason for that... It's a long and rather dull story. Suffice to say I haven't done it, and I'm looking forward to it.

Any techniques you ladies have I should know about? Anything I should or shouldn't do? I've got the general idea. (Especially after watching the porn). But any tips would be welcome.

Rusty's lips curved, and he scrolled down to read the comments. Some of them made his eyebrows shoot up. It always surprised him how willing she was to discuss such intimate details with strangers. But then that was obviously part of her attractiveness for these women who were struggling with their personal lives. They were able to be frank and honest, and Faith was never shocked, and never made them feel embarrassed or ashamed of what they were feeling.

At the bottom, he saw his codename mentioned and stopped scrolling to read.

SashaT: *We just hope you'll pass on anything you learn tomorrow, Faith. We need all the help we can get.*

Faith: *That's what these articles are all about. Sharing. De-mystifying. There's no magic to sex. Well, there is, but you know what I mean.*

SashaT: *Would you say Mr. S. was magic?*

Faith: *Yes :) But don't tell him I said that. I won't hear the end of it.*

A surprising rush of pleasure washed over him at her words. Checking the staffroom once more, making sure nobody was looking over his shoulder, he logged in to his account, typed in a comment and posted.

MrS69: *Hey Faith :)*

He sat back to wait, finishing off his sandwiches. Sure enough, a few minutes later...

Faith: *And... speak of the devil...*

Patsy: *LOL, have you been lurking?*

He grinned and typed again.

MrS69: *A little.*

SueAnn: *What can you tell us about oral sex, Mr.S? *grins mischievously**

MrS69: *Is that where you listen to her talk about it for hours?*

Faith: *Sweetheart, that's aural sex.*

He laughed. She played off him perfectly. He got up to get himself a coffee. When he came back, there was another comment waiting.

Penny: *Mr.S., we've been giving Faith tips on showing you a good time tomorrow.*

MrS69: Oh, like?

Faith: Apparently keeping one's teeth out of the way comes highly recommended.

That made him nearly spill his coffee with laughter. He bit his lip as some of the other teachers glanced over at him, eyebrows raised. Sedately, he typed in his response.

MrS69: *winces* Good advice.

He opened a new tab, surfed for a bit, then went back to see if she'd replied. She had. He stared at the comment, startled.

Faith: The good ladies are roughly divided on spitting or swallowing.

He shook his head. She was doing it on purpose. He typed in his reply.

MrS69: You enjoy embarrassing me, don't you?

Faith: Immensely.

He rolled his eyes. Little minx. She deserved to have her backside slapped for that. He daydreamed about it for a little while before the next comment pinged up.

Lily: (Can't believe I'm asking this question, but Faith keeps telling us to be frank, and, as you're here, Mr.S... *Takes a deep breath*) Do you think it's offensive if a girl spits?

Oh, good lord. He could almost hear Faith laughing at his embarrassment. Still, it was a fair enough question, and wasn't that what this blogsite was all about—being honest and up front? Turning his laptop slightly as someone sat at the table next to him, he typed in:

MrS69: (Can't believe I'm answering this question.) But no, not at all.

Lily: I'm so sorry to be so crude. It's just... I like going down on a guy, but I don't like the taste of... you know... and it puts me off doing it, because I don't want to upset him by spitting it out.

MrS69: No worries. Faith's here to answer the questions that other people won't ask. And so am I now, it seems! But I'm happy to advise... Just keep a tissue handy for surreptitious disposal. It's kind of a turn-off if you go green and have to run to the bathroom.

Lily: ROFL, I see what you mean.

Faith: Oh my God, I swear I've split my sides.

MrS69: Little tip for you there, love.

Faith: Duly noted :)

He grinned. He could just imagine her sitting at her desk, head tipped back, laughing. He could picture her long brown hair curling down her back, her eyes closed like they had been when she was sitting on top of him, trying hard not to come…

He sighed. This wasn't good. He was getting all aroused, which wasn't a good idea when he was about to head off to class.

It was nearly time for period six. Trying to concentrate on work, he walked over to the pigeon holes and retrieved his post, washed up his cup, scrounged a new board marker off a colleague, and then came back for his laptop. Five minutes left. He read the last few comments.

SueAnn: You two are going to have such fun tomorrow.

Faith: *fans herself slightly*

Patsy: Don't worry Faith. We all know you'll enjoy it. You promise you'll tell us all about it?

Faith: As much detail as you can bear.

Lily: Have a good evening tomorrow, guys. Take each other to heaven and back.

Mischievously, he typed in his final comment as the bell rang.

MrS69: I just hope the bed has a strong headboard. She's gonna need it to hang on to. Got to go now, work calls.

Patsy: Oh my God. Faith, you are so lucky.

Faith: Meh. He's all talk. :)

Laughing, he closed the lid of the laptop and went off to class.

*

Rusty was already at the motel when Faith arrived the following Saturday, around six thirty. He watched her get out of the car and smile at him.

"Wow," she said. "You're early."

"Couldn't wait." He came over and took her bag, kissing her cheek. "I've got the key and paid for the room."

"I told you not to do that—my expenses will cover the cost."

"Sweetheart, it's the only thing stopping me from feeling like some sort of gigolo."

She laughed out loud at that. "Fair enough." She smiled up at him, and his heart rate increased. She wore a beautiful light orange halter top he could imagine untying to reveal her delectable breasts, and a floaty chocolate-brown skirt that was very nearly transparent. She'd caught up her lovely hair in a clip again, revealing her long, slender neck. Did she have any idea how crazy that drove him?

She lifted out another bag, which he knew would contain wine, Coke and probably chocolate, which she considered a post-coital necessity. She smiled at him. "You want to go for a walk first or something?"

"Nope. Can't wait." He took her hand and dragged her up the steps to their room.

Her eyes danced as he unlocked the door. "You hot for me, Thorne?"

"Practically volcanic. Get in there." He smacked her butt as she walked past him.

Inside, she barely had time to put her bag on the table before he kicked the door shut and backed her up against the wall.

"Oh my." She gasped as he pressed himself against her and began to kiss her neck. "Someone's horny tonight."

"Oh yeah." He bit her earlobe and then sucked it. "And so am I."

"I meant you." A sigh escaped her lips.

"And you're not turned on at all," he murmured, sliding his hand up her skirt.

She shook her head. "I haven't thought about you at all this week." Her eyes were glazed, though.

He went to say something but the words vanished, as, to his shock, he found she wasn't wearing any underwear. "You naughty girl." Eyes wide, he moved his hand between her legs. He chuckled as he found her already wet and swollen. "Yeah, right. You're not turned on at all."

"Rusty! Whatever happened to foreplay?"

"Foreplay's to get you in the mood. I've been in the mood since about twelve p.m. Sunday."

She laughed and then, as he slid his fingers inside her, sighed and groaned. He began to arouse her, lowering his mouth to hers, and she brought her arms up around his neck. She felt loose and soft in his arms without the constriction of any underwear.

"God, you're so hot," he murmured, grabbing her butt as he pressed himself hard against her.

"What's with you tonight?" She sighed as he stroked her breast. "Not that I'm complaining."

He nuzzled her ear, smelling the fresh minty aroma of her shampoo, the flowery scent of her perfume. "I've been thinking about this all week. I haven't been able to concentrate. Lord knows what I've been coming out with in my lessons."

Chapter Thirteen

Faith smiled. He was adorable like this. She caught his face in her hands, and gave him a happy kiss. "Where do you want me, sweetheart?"

He laced his fingers with hers and walked toward the bathroom, bringing her with him.

"Another bath?"

"Shower this time."

"I had one earlier. I'm clean, honestly."

He chuckled, opened the cubicle door, and turned on the hot water, letting it heat up. While he waited, he put his arms around her and began to undo the neck of her halter. "This is where your first lesson in oral sex begins."

"Oh?"

"Cleanliness is next to godliness, babe."

"I just said, I've had a shower."

He stepped a bit closer as he lowered the top and revealed her breasts to his gaze. Looking down at them, he cupped them in his hands and brushed her nipples with his thumbs. She caught her breath, and he smiled. "I don't mean you, sweetheart. You smell delicious." He kissed her temple, inhaling as he nuzzled her ear. "But we're researching your article here. And the first thing your readers need to understand is that the most important thing about oral sex is…it's nicer after a shower."

"Ah."

He reached in a hand to test the water. "Explain to your ladies, if they want to give it a go, first of all they should introduce the ritual of bathing or showering. Make it part of the act so it becomes ingrained that if he wants it, he has to keep clean."

"That's excellent advice." She began to undo the buttons on his shirt. "Is that why you wash all the time?" She knew he showered at least twice a day, as well as straight after any sport, and was a big fan of nice-smelling, subtle aftershaves. Even now, she could smell something with sandalwood and lemon, light and fresh.

"You've uncovered my secret," he teased as she pushed his shirt off, letting it drop to the floor.

"Like wearing clean underwear in case you get run over by a bus." She began undoing his belt.

He laughed. "My mum used to say that."

"Mine too." She felt the pang of sadness that often swept over her at the thought that her mother was no longer around. Lowering her eyes, she paused for a moment and then continued undoing the belt buckle.

He brushed her cheek, making her glance up. His green eyes searched like a flashlight deep into her, seeing the emotion she'd tried to hide from him. He'd been amazing when her parents died, a rock for Dan, who'd fallen apart, helping to organize the funeral, sorting out financial matters, being there when they were too low to do anything but sit with their heads in their hands. He'd held her while she cried, wiped away her tears. Why the hell hadn't she known it would finally come to this? Hadn't the signs been there all along?

Grasping the bottom of her halter-neck, he lifted it over her head then pulled her skirt down and let her step out of it before placing it to one side. He put his hand in his pocket and pulled something out, keeping it hidden, then he slid off his jeans and boxers and kicked them away too. "In you go."

She stepped in the shower. While she wet her hair, he disappeared into the living room briefly, reappearing carrying a bottle of something. He opened the cubicle door and joined her, filling the tiny space so she had to press herself against the tiles to give him room.

"What's that?" She nodded at the bottle.

"Shower gel. Very silky." He put the item he'd had in his hand on the soap dish—it was a condom.

"What's that for?"

"You want me to draw you a diagram?"

"Do we need a condom for oral sex?"

He didn't reply for a moment. He put the bottle down and rubbed his hands together. Starting with her shoulders, he brushed along her arms and down her body, massaged her breasts gently, and then moved his hand lower, between her legs. She had to catch her breath as he stroked her, and she looked up at him, speechless. His eyes were half-lidded, dark with passion.

She'd always known he was gorgeous, and had never questioned that girls found him attractive, but this was the first time she really understood quite why women loved him so much. He was a sensual, passionate man, a skilled lover, tall, muscular, and lean, handsome and fun. He made her heart pound, even though she knew it was just Rusty, her best friend, the guy she dunked in the pool and bossed around in the kitchen, someone she'd known forever.

He stepped closer and kissed her. "Sweetheart, if I go down on you now, you'll last about ten seconds."

"You're mighty sure of yourself."

He laughed. "I'm sure of you." He kissed her again, deeper this time, one hand sliding easily through her slick, warm folds, one stroking her breast, rolling her nipple. "Think of this like the adverts before the movie comes on."

She struggled to concentrate. "So it's not, like, real sex?"

"Oh no." His fingers were relentless. "This is just a warm up. Not the real thing at all."

"Only it kind of…feels like…the real thing."

"We'll just get rid of some excess energy so we can start again, and take our time."

"Okay." She felt faint with desire. "Stop that. My turn." She pushed his hand away and grabbed the shower gel, squeezing some onto her palm. Then she rubbed it onto his chest. "When did you get all these muscles?" She ran her hands over his ribcage, up to his shoulders, down his arms.

He put his hands on her hips. "You hadn't noticed me before?"

"I…" She thought about it as she rubbed her fingers over his nipples, making him shiver. "I don't think I let myself look too hard. Like staring at a gorgeous pair of shoes that costs five hundred bucks—what's the point in staring when you know you're never going to buy them?"

He smiled, looking down as her hand descended in small, slow circles. Her fingers followed his chest hair where it tapered to a line, and trailed across his flat, hard belly into the thatch of red-brown curls at the bottom. Her soapy hand closed around him, and she proceeded to make sure he was really, really clean.

He closed his eyes, bearing her touch for as long as he could, and when he finally opened them again, they were hot and exasperated. He kissed her, the hot shower soaking his russet hair, turning it the color of mahogany, and the water ran between their bodies, making them shimmer. She tried to say something, anything, to lighten the tension, to make him laugh, but he was too far gone. His kisses were molten hot, insistent. "Okay, that's enough." He tore open the packet and put on the condom.

Gently, he turned her around. He lifted her hands and placed her palms on the tiles. Her heart thumped as he reached around to stroke her breasts. Then he nudged her legs apart and pushed into her, making her sigh.

They stood there for a moment, reveling in the sensation of being so close, so aligned with one another. His hands slid over her soapy body as he began to move leisurely inside her, drawing out their climax with excruciating slowness.

"Jeez, Rusty." Her breath came in gasps, and he gave a sexy laugh. Her eyes narrowed—he wasn't the only one who could play at being naughty. She spread her legs wider, glancing over her shoulder. "Are you going to fuck me properly or not?"

He gave her a warning look, but closed his eyes and thrust into her powerfully, leaning forward on the tiles. She gasped at the sound of wet skin on skin, at the slide of him inside her, and before long, her orgasm exploded. It made her squeal again as her muscles clenched around him, and he exclaimed as he came, pulling her tightly to him.

Afterward, he withdrew and turned her in his arms, and she rested her forehead on his shoulder, only half-conscious of the hot water soaking into her skin. "Oh my God."

He kissed her ear. "You have the most powerful orgasms of any woman I've ever known, do you know that?"

"I have a very strong pelvic floor."

He chuckled. "It feels like you're squeezing me in a vise."

"Oh, I'm so sorry."

"No, no, that wasn't a complaint." He kissed her ear, her cheek and finally her lips. Then he looked at her, his green eyes warm. "So we've finished the starter. Are you ready for the main course?"

"Not yet. I need some real sustenance first."

*

Ten minutes later, they lay on the bed eating chocolate.

"I thought this was for afterward." He broke off a piece and offered it to her.

She took it and put it in her mouth. "It was. But I didn't know we were going to have pre-sex sex. I need to keep my energy up."

He laughed, breaking off another chunk for himself. He lay propped up against the pillows, slightly turned toward her, and she lay on her front, arms resting on a pillow.

She finished the piece of chocolate and took a sip of wine. "This is, like, an absolutely perfect evening."

"Eating chocolate and drinking wine in a dodgy motel?"

"And having hot sex," she said, adding before she could stop herself, "with you."

He sucked on the chocolate as she studied him curiously, his eyes meeting hers, warm with amusement. He raised an eyebrow. "What?"

"I can't reconcile the two versions I have of you in my head."

"What do you mean?"

She pushed herself into a sitting position, her arms around the pillow. "There's the Rusty I've known for ten years, the one who used to like jumping off Charlie's Rock into the river and scaring the shit out of me, who made Dan let me watch horror movies when our parents had gone to bed, who bought me my first glass of wine in a bar." She sipped her wine. "And then there's the other Rusty. Mr. S."

He gave a lazy smile. "And what's he like?"

She watched as he licked chocolate off his fingers. Lord, did he know how much he turned her on? "Sinful. Sexy. Hot. I'd never met him myself—I'd heard about him from other girls, but as soon as I turned up, he disappeared." She ran her gaze down him. He was naked, completely unselfconscious, confident and relaxed in his nudity, and more than aware, she suspected, that his lean, muscled body was starting to heat her up again. "I mean, I've always realized you were popular with the girls. Heaven knows I've heard enough tales about your bedroom exploits from your girlfriends. But it's only now I've really started to see that Rusty myself."

He reached over to get his Coke, displaying his wide chest with its crisp, curling hairs, and his tanned, muscular biceps to her before he turned back. He sipped the soda. "Do you like that Rusty?"

She met his gaze. "I can't see how any woman could fail to." She picked up his left hand, examining his empty fingers. "How come you're still single, after all the girlfriends you've had?"

"I'm only twenty-six. And I haven't had that many. You make me sound like a right tart."

She laughed. "Well, you've had more than me."

"Sweetheart, the Pope's had more than you."

"I've had two boyfriends."

He snorted. "Two eunuchs, by the sound of it."

"Don't change the subject. Come on, tell me, have you ever been in love? I know you were pretty hot on that girl…what was her name? Meredith? Did you love her?"

He shrugged, clearly uncomfortable talking about it. "Not enough."

"Do you ever think you'll relax your guard enough to fall properly in love?"

"Nah." He smiled.

She rested her head on her hand as she studied him. "Do you want kids, Rusty?"

His smile faded and his eyes took on a wary look. "No."

"Why not?"

"You know why not."

"Because your father, and your grandfather, and your great-grandfather were all bastards?"

"Something like that."

"It doesn't run in the blood, love."

He said nothing, and she knew he was thinking about his brother. Cole, three years older than Rusty, had proved himself every inch a Thorne. A troublemaker throughout his school years, he'd got into a bad crowd, been arrested at twenty-one for burglary, spent six months in jail, and since then had been in and out of court on various charges. He got his girlfriend pregnant at twenty-five and had been decent enough to marry her but so far hadn't exactly proved to be the ideal parent or husband. A drunk and a gambler, Cole was unreliable, hot tempered, and basically unpleasant. Faith had often wondered if Rusty had been switched at birth.

"You're so different from them," she said, reaching out to stroke his cheek. "You're educated, you have a profession, you're responsible and reliable… There's not a nasty bone in your body. How on earth can you think you're like them?"

"The same blood runs in my veins." His eyes were shadowed, dark.

"I know. But it's just blood, Rusty. It doesn't mean anything."

The amusement had completely disappeared from his face, though, and she could feel the way he'd withdrawn from her. Suddenly she wished she hadn't said anything. Had she spoiled the evening? Was he going to say he had to go now?

His gaze fell to her lips and then to her breasts. To her relief, by the time he looked back up at her, he was smiling. "Enough about me. I'm much more interested in discovering how you've made it to twenty-two without doing any of your seven sexy sins."

She clutched the pillow to her, letting the intensity of the moment go, glad he'd decided to move on. "I don't know. Just never got around to it. I didn't go out with the two guys I've been with for long."

"You were at university for three years. You must have had other offers. And there was no Dan around to watch over you. I would have thought you'd have gone crazy with all that freedom."

She shrugged. "Mum wasn't quite the 'wait till you're married' sort, but she did impress upon me when I was younger that I shouldn't sleep around. Besides which, I went to uni not long after the accident. I wasn't ready to share myself with lots of different people. I kept myself to myself and concentrated on my studies. I didn't want to open my heart. I was quite keen to protect it."

"Have you ever been in love?"

She thought about it. "No, I don't think so. I've thought I was, several times. But I don't think it was the real thing. Not like you see in movies, or hear about in songs. The kind of love that means you can't concentrate on anything, that makes you ache when you're not with someone. I've never had that." She stopped, thinking about the way she'd felt all week, waiting to see him again. But that wasn't the same. That was just about looking forward to investigating the next sin, to increasing her sexual experience. Not the same thing at all.

He reached out and started to pull the pillow away from her. She clung onto it for a moment before letting him slide it out of her fingers. He threw it on the floor, took her hand and linked their fingers again. "Well, I, for one, have no idea how you've managed to stay relatively innocent for so long." He pulled her toward him, wrapped his arms around her, and rolled so he was leaning over her. He nuzzled her neck, kissing her ear. "You're obviously a sex kitten deep down."

"I've never thought of myself that way."

"It's been obvious to me for a long time." He lifted his head, running his fingers lightly up her thigh. His green eyes were warm, intense. "Are you ready for your second sexy sin, Ms. Hillman?"

A frisson of excitement and nervousness ran between her shoulder blades, and her mouth went dry. "Um…"

He kissed her, nibbled her bottom lip, and ran his tongue across it. "What's the matter, Faith?" He rubbed his nose against hers.

"I'm nervous."

"About what? It's only me."

"Don't you see? That's the problem."

He brushed a strand of hair away from her face. The amusement faded from his eyes, to be replaced by gentleness. "Sweetheart, I'm so pleased I'm going to be the first to do this for you. I love you, I'm incredibly fond of you, and that's what makes this so special."

Faith looked into his eyes. She knew he meant he loved her as a friend. But her heart did a little tap dance all the same.

He trailed his hand down from her face and then drew spirals around her breasts, brushing the nipples occasionally, making her catch her breath, then traced light lines across the flat of her stomach.

She sighed, and he kissed her while he slid his fingers even lower, into the already hot, wet part of her. They slipped deep inside her to collect the slick moisture, and then returned to begin arousing her even more.

She opened her legs wider, welcoming his touch, and his mouth left hers to kiss her cheeks, her eyelids, her neck.

"You're so sexy." He ran his tongue around her ear, making her shiver. "You drive me crazy, do you know that?" His deep voice seemed to ring throughout her, at the right pitch to set her whole body vibrating like a bell. "With your hot little ass and your tight, firm breasts and this incredible mouth…" He kissed it again. "I sat there and watched you talking to Dan and Toby and Eve on Wednesday, and all I could think about was picking you up and carrying you off somewhere so I could do bad things to you."

"Oh," she said faintly.

His lips hovered a fraction above hers, teasing, just out of reach. His fingers were firm, stroking her insistently. "I want to bury my mouth in you. I want to taste you, Faith. Are you going to let me taste you?"

"Yes." Her nervousness had vanished, to be replaced by a hungry desire for this sexy, provocative man.

He reached behind him and threw all but one pillow onto the floor, lay on his back, and placed the last pillow under his head lengthways. The room was subsiding into twilight, and somebody had lit a barbecue on the beach somewhere—the subtle smoky smell complementing the sweet scent of the jasmine that was rising again. Music also filtered through with the aromas, either from one of the other motel rooms or from the beach, slow ballads and lazy acoustic guitar, Jack Johnson, maybe, or John Mayer, the notes spiraling with her thoughts.

His eyes were dark, intense. He was no longer the friend she'd known for millennia, replaced instead by the lover she was beginning to adore. She moved up the bed, maneuvering herself astride him, and his hands guided her down onto his mouth.

Faith leaned her arms on the headboard of the bed, her heart thumping. She closed her eyes as he kissed the soft, sensitive skin of her inner thigh. He brushed his lips there, sending a tingle through her. Then he swept his tongue right through the hot center of her.

"Fuck!" She inhaled sharply, tensing at the unfamiliar feeling. He gave a short, brief laugh, and his hand stroked the outside of her thigh in response, but he didn't stop. Forcing herself to relax, she gave herself over to him as he began to arouse her slowly with his lips, teeth, and tongue.

She rested her forehead on her arms. The sensations he was creating were incredible. He caressed her thighs and hips and brought a hand underneath to stroke her, parting her lips with his fingers to access her clit. He slipped his fingers inside her, deep inside, his thumb joining his lips and tongue in teasing so that she groaned and widened her thighs, begging him to take her further.

So he did, slowly, making it last as long as he could. He drew out her pleasure until in the end he was barely touching her, each little brush of his tongue, graze of his teeth, or sucking of his lips making her teeter on the edge of the chasm, until eventually she pleaded for him to let her fall. And so he covered her sweet spot with his warm tongue, slid his fingers back inside her, and held her tightly across the thighs with his other arm as her orgasm exploded within her like fireworks.

Chapter Fourteen

Rusty let her lift herself off him and collapse onto the bed. He looked across at the sliding doors to see the twilight settling, and watched a moth hover around the lamp outside, although it didn't come in. There were no lights on, but the full moon that hung low in the sky like a Christmas bauble lit the room, and as he turned his head to look at Faith, he saw her skin glowing, luminescent like an oyster shell. She looked as if she were made of marble, each muscle delineated by light and shadow, like a Greek statue of a gracefully reclining woman, sculpted with a careful hand.

She took his breath away, and for the first time since they'd slept together, Rusty forgot she was his friend, forgot she was Dan's sister. She was beautiful and exotic, and he felt an unfamiliar rush of his blood, a thump of his heart. Not just desire, although there was that as well. But a kind of awe, of wonderment and admiration.

"Don't move," he said as she stirred, lifting her arm from her face. She stopped, arms above her head, and he lifted onto his elbow to look down at her, shivering at the way her pupils were so large her eyes seemed entirely black. He let his gaze skim over her, noting her sudden intake of breath, her unnatural stillness. He followed with his hand, tracing light fingers along the swells and valleys of her womanly figure, across the hills of her breasts, into the dip of her navel, the small hollows beneath her hipbones.

He moved his fingers where his mouth had been, just a light brush, reveling in the way she was so wet and swollen, rich and velvet, before continuing up her body once again. Her eyes glittered in the darkness, reflecting the moonlight, and he shuddered.

What was wrong with him? Had she cast a spell on him? His lips hovered above hers, caught in a brief second of time. Her arms were above her head, her hair wild and mussed, and she was breathing heavily, even though her body should be calming by now. He brushed her lips with his own and watched her breathe in, knowing she would be able to smell her own arousal on him, feeling himself harden at the thought. She opened her mouth, and he dipped his tongue in and kissed her deeply. His hand cradled her head, his other arm tucking underneath her to bring her closer to him. For maybe the first time, he let the full force of his passion, his desire for her, show in the kiss, and when he finally released her, she was gasping, her chest heaving, her mouth bruised and red.

He felt a fleeting surge of guilt. He had to remember this was Faith in his bed, Dan's sister, the young girl he'd fancied for so long but, in spite of her two partners, was still innocent, still fresh. He had to remember to treat her tenderly, to respect her. To let her lead the way.

She didn't say anything. She pushed herself up and climbed off the bed, then reached out a hand to bring him to sit facing her. Keeping her dark eyes fixed on his, she sank between his legs onto her knees. He was so turned on he couldn't have been any harder. Breathing heavily, leaning back on his hands, he watched as she studied his erection with interest. He swallowed as she closed a hand around him and stroked for a while, casting him one final, hot glance before lowering her mouth.

He tipped back his head and held his breath as she began to move her head up and down. Her mouth was warm and wet, her tongue tantalizingly rough on his sensitive skin. He looked down, watching her release her hair from its clip so it fell around her face, then sweep it to one side so it brushed against his thigh, silky soft.

He groaned aloud, gasping as she began to take him deeper and deeper inside her mouth. He moved his hand to rest against her head and slid his fingers through her hair, unable to stop moving his hips forward with each dip of her mouth. But she didn't seem to mind and gave a deep sigh low in her throat, lifting up slightly so she almost swallowed him whole.

It didn't take long, only minutes, before he'd reached the end of his self-control. "Faith…" His hand tightened in her hair, and heat flooded through him, focusing in his groin. She hadn't lifted her head, and he hoped she was ready, because he couldn't hold back. He came in her hot mouth, totally unprepared for the way she took everything he had to give. As he cried out, she stroked his thigh as he had hers, and only lifted her head when he finally collapsed back on the bed, eyes closed, completely spent.

He felt her lift up onto the bed to sit astride him. He opened one eye and saw her studying him with a flicker of a smile.

He opened the other eye and blinked, staring as she lowered her head a little more so he could see her expression in the moonlight. "Now," she told him huskily, "whenever we're in public, sitting with Dan and Eve and Toby, and I do this—" she licked her lips, "—you won't see me as Dan's little sister, or the skinny girl with braces you used to torture with crickets and cockroaches. You'll think of my lips around you, and me taking you deep inside my mouth, swallowing as you come. Okay?"

He nodded, wide eyed, not trusting himself to speak.

She looked into space, considering. "Tastes salty," she said. "Nice." She licked her lips again. "Want a bit of chocolate?"

Chapter Fifteen

On Tuesday, Faith turned up at Rusty's high school, carrying two trim lattes in takeaway cardboard cups. She knew he had a free period before lunch, and she hoped to catch him in his classroom.

She hadn't spoken to him since Sunday morning. After their intense exploration of oral sex on the Saturday evening, they'd watched the moths play outside around the lamp and the moon rise slowly in the night sky, yellow and heavy, like a bowl of cream. He hadn't said much. She'd tried to lighten his mood, but he'd been unresponsive and monosyllabic, and eventually she'd let him pull her tightly to him, content to drift off to sleep in his arms.

The following morning, he'd been pleasant and affectionate, kissing her deeply before he left, but still quiet, and she'd puzzled about his frame of mind for the next couple of days. He'd never been a particularly moody man, and she was unsure what had made him so reserved. She was worried she'd shocked him. He found it difficult to think of her as anything other than Dan's little sister, whatever he said to the contrary. Was it possible he really had been helping her out of a kind of twisted, familial desire to look after her? Perhaps her dirty talk had made him realize she thought about sex with him in a different way from, for example, him giving her driving lessons or teaching her how to play the guitar. If he thought of himself as an alternative big brother, she could only imagine how much she'd freaked him out. Surely, that couldn't be the case, though? It would be pretty warped if it were.

After two days of worrying about it, she'd decided to confront him, and that was why she was bringing coffee to his classroom. She'd been to the school before, and she'd popped into the reception to pick up her visitor's sticker before circling the edge of the main buildings. His room was right at the end of a new block, the classrooms still smelling of fresh paint and carpet glue, which Rusty worried would make the kids high as kites if they spent too long with the windows shut. The new rooms had air conditioning and data projectors fixed into the ceilings, and she knew he loved the muted blue carpets and light blue walls, and the way he could see through the glass partition to make faces at his colleague in the next classroom when the students had their backs turned.

She ran lightly up the steps and along the pathway, opened the door to his room, and walked in. She stopped abruptly. Crap. He was in there, but so were half a dozen students. "Oh I'm sorry," she said, "I thought you were on a free."

"I am." He was sitting back in his swivel chair, his feet on his desk, amused at her horrified face. "These nuisances won't leave me alone."

The six girls looked over at her, interested in seeing Mr. Thorne's guest. They weren't wearing uniform, which made them seniors. "Hello," said one cheekily, and the others giggled.

"Hi." Faith backed toward the door. "I'll come back later."

"No, come in." He beckoned her forward and sat up. "Actually, you're the perfect person. Andrea here was just talking about taking journalism at uni." He indicated the girl nearest to him, a pretty, earnest-looking blonde, and then pointed at Faith. "Miss Hillman's a journalist."

"Oh?" Andrea's eyes widened.

Faith hesitated before walking into the room. She twisted one of the cups out of the cardboard carry tray and handed it to him. He met her eyes briefly, smiling. "Thanks."

"You're welcome." She took out her own cup and perched on the edge of his desk, facing the girls. "So you fancy it as a profession?"

Andrea shrugged, tucking her hair behind her ears. "Maybe. I write for the school magazine, and Miss Chapman lets me help out with the press releases. And I've had a couple of pieces in the local paper."

Faith nodded, impressed. "That's a great start, at your age. Are you good at English?"

"It's my best subject."

"And history?"

Andrea grinned at Rusty. "Well, obviously."

Faith smiled. "History is a great subject to study if you want to be a journalist. The essay skills, the analysis of social events and primary sources, the politics, the general background... They're all invaluable for anyone who wants to work in the field."

"I keep telling them," said Rusty. "I don't think they take me seriously."

"'You have to know the past to understand the present,'" she quoted.

"Dr. Carl Sagan had a point. Listen to Miss Hillman, girls. She knows what she's talking about."

One of the girls was frowning at her. She turned and whispered to her friend, who looked over at her, wide-eyed. Faith felt a sudden surge of concern.

"Oh my God," said the first girl. "You're Faith Hillman. The one with the website."

"Ah…" Faith stared at her, panic rising. "What are you doing reading that? It's R16."

"I'm seventeen," said the girl. Her friend elbowed her and whispered something else. They both looked across at Rusty, and giggled.

"No, no, no," said Faith hurriedly.

"Are you Mr. S.?" one of them asked him, looking thrilled, ignoring her.

"No," Faith said, more sharply, her cheeks flushing at the thought that these teenagers knew she'd had oral sex over the weekend, and had a pretty good idea with whom. "He's not. Rusty and I are just friends."

They all stared at her and then started giggling again. She glanced at Rusty. "Oh. I guess they don't know your nickname."

"Well, they *didn't*." He stood and started shooing them out like chickens as the bell for lunch went. "Go and get some sunshine you lot, you're all white as vampires."

"You want to be alone…Rusty?"

"That's Mr. Thorne to you. Stop being cheeky. Go on." He opened the door for them and ushered them out before coming back in, locking it behind him.

"I'm sorry." She felt awful. "Have I put my foot in it?"

He laughed. "Nah. You know what kids are like. Fascinated with anything that involves teachers' home lives. They think we live at school. They spent ages trying to find out my first name. That little nugget of information will keep them quiet for a while." He perched on one of the desks and smiled at her. "Thanks again for the coffee."

"You're welcome, again. Rusty…I'm sorry I came by… I just wanted to check we're all right."

He tipped his head at her. "Why wouldn't we be?"

"I…I wanted to say…" Spit it out, Faith. "Did you want to, um, end our contract?"

He studied her for a moment. Then a smile lit up his face. "Hell, no."

A wash of relief made her inhale, and she couldn't stop a big smile spreading across her own face. "Oh. Thank God."

He laughed, but a frown marred his forehead. "Why would you think that?"

"It's just… I thought maybe you were having second thoughts."

He cleared his throat, looked at his coffee cup and took a long swig. Afterward he wiped his mouth with the back of his hand before smiling at her again. "No."

"Oh. Okay. Not feeling particularly effusive today, either?"

"What do you want me to say, Faith?" He sobered, his eyes taking on an intense look. "Do you want me to say I wasn't shocked by what happened Saturday night? Because I was." His gaze rested on her mouth, and she had a sudden, vivid recollection of him kissing her, his hand arousing her with gentle strokes. "I knew you'd be dynamite in bed. But I didn't expect you to be quite so…" His eyes went slightly glazed, as if he was remembering something too. They lifted to meet hers, and for a moment, they just stared at each other.

Her heart thumped. He thought she was dynamite. "So…"

He smiled. "So…what sin's next?"

She studied him. The mischievous look was back in his eyes. His mood seemed to have lifted. She still wasn't sure what had gotten into him, but she was glad he was over it. "Gluttony. Food."

"I'm guessing we're not talking a four-course meal here."

"Nuh-uh."

"What are we talking?"

"That's going to be a surprise. But I do have a task for you."

"Oh?"

"The next location. How would you like to organize it?"

"You don't want to go to the motel?"

"It's fully booked, some sailing regatta or something. I thought you might like to choose somewhere."

"Sure."

His eyes were full of amusement, but she had no idea about what. Did he have a clue how sexy he looked at that moment? He sat back in his chair, hands linked in his lap, and like a typical bloke, his legs were wide apart, but even though he usually sat that way, she couldn't stop herself thinking of the way she'd knelt between his legs and taken him in her mouth.

She looked back up at his face. There was obvious humor there now, and she realized he knew what she was thinking, and he was amused because he'd been thinking exactly the same thing.

She frowned. "Am I ever going to be able to look at you again without thinking of going down on you?"

He gave a short laugh. "I hope not."

He turned his chair towards his desk and held out his hand. "Come here. When was the last time you checked your blog?"

"Earlier this morning." She'd written her follow-up article on the second sin on Sunday, and the last two days her blog had been pretty busy with comments. "Why?"

He grinned. "They're speculating on who I am."

She walked behind him and bent to look at the screen of his laptop. He had her blog up, and he now scrolled to the comments he'd referred to.

Jill: I get the feeling that maybe they work together.
AnnaB: I think she works from home, doesn't she?
Jules: She goes into an office several times a week, I think.
Jill: Maybe he works there.
SashaT: Nah. I think he's a firefighter.
WendyS: In your dreams, Sasha!
Patsy: He's educated.
Jill: What makes you say that?
Patsy: a) you can tell from what he types and b) she wouldn't pick anyone who wasn't.
SashaT: I still think he's a firefighter.

Rusty grinned at Faith. "Shall I join in?"

"Yeh, go on."

He logged in, then added a comment.

MrS69: I'm not a firefighter.

Smiling, Faith left him to it, and spent a while walking around his classroom, looking at the students' work on the walls, seeing how he'd created displays on the Waitangi Treaty and Gallipoli. He didn't tend to talk much about his work, and although she knew he must have a wealth of historical knowledge shored up in his brain, as she looked at the posters, and his distinctive slanted handwriting on the bottom of essays, it reminded her just how clever he was. When he was with the others he rarely mentioned the fact that he'd been to university, probably because Toby was a laborer, albeit skilled, and Dan had taken over as assistant manager in the computer store he'd worked in on Saturdays and had never got to uni. She felt a newfound respect for him, at the way he didn't lord it over his mates because he was a professional and they weren't.

After a few minutes he started laughing, and she walked back to his desk to check the screen.

Jill: Mr.S! Wheee!
SashaT: Aw. There goes my fantasy.
MrS69: Sorry to spoil your day.
Rula: So come on, give us a clue, what do you do? Are you a professional?
MrS69: Are you asking politely if I'm a gigolo?
Rula: Eek, no! Although...

Faith grinned. "Tell them you are. That'll set the cat amongst the pigeons."

He started typing.

MrS69: Faith says to tell you I am.

She stared as he pressed 'Send'. "No! You can't say you're with me at the moment."

"Why not?"

"Because if the girls that were standing here just now read this later, they'll know you're definitely Mr. S."

"Ah. I didn't think of that."

They both looked at the screen as several comments pinged up.

Rula: Faith's there with you now?!
SashaT: I thought you two were only supposed to meet on action days?

He thought about it, then typed:

MrS69: I'm on the phone to her.

"Clever," Faith said.

Patsy: Ask her if she thinks you're educated.

"No," said Faith.

He grinned and typed.

MrS69: She says I'm the cleverest man she knows.

She rolled her eyes. "In your dreams." Although it was probably true.

He laughed.

Patsy: Lol, that doesn't sound like Faith speaking.

MrS69: That might have been artistic license.

SashaT: Come on Mr.S., give us a hint!

Faith watched him frown. He was clearly puzzled. He typed:

MrS69: *perplexed scratching of head* Why is it so important to you to know what I do?

"Because it's a natural instinct to want your man to be intelligent, competent, and able. So he can provide for your children," Faith said.

SashaT: We want to know if you do something hot.

"And that," said Faith. Rusty laughed.

MrS69: I can tell you for certain that what I do is NOT hot. Gotta go now.

He signed off and lowered the laptop lid.

Faith tipped her head at him. "Oh, you're so wrong."

"What the hell's hot about boring a class of thirty children to death?"

She smiled. "I know for a fact you're not boring in class."

"How? You've never seen me teach."

"Well, firstly you told me the number of students taking history over the last couple of years has more than doubled. But secondly, even if I hadn't known that, I do know you're smart, funny, and confident. I know if I sat in on one of your lessons I'd want to jump you by the end."

His lips curved slowly. She looked down at him. She leant on his desk. A bit closer and she'd be able to press her own lips against his smile. "I think I might kiss you now," she warned him.

"As much as I'd like that, I'm not sure we should do it with an audience."

Faith looked up, suddenly realizing the two year thirteen girls who'd guessed his true identity had their noses pressed up against the windows of the classrooms. She stood up hurriedly. "How did you know they were there when you had your back to the windows?"

"Teachers' sixth sense." He gave her a sexy smile. "I swear, if they weren't there I would have had you on the table by now."

His remark took her completely by surprise and she stared at him, blushing. He laughed, pushing himself to his feet. "I have to go and do duty now."

"Sure. Look, what day do you want to meet?"

"Shall we do Friday night this week? Just to stop Dan and Eve getting too suspicious as to why we're both busy on a Saturday night."

"Yes, okay. I can leave the location to you?"

"Yep. Already got an idea."

"Cool."

They stared at each other for a moment. Rusty glanced over his shoulder. The two girls had gone. He bent forward, slipping his hand behind her head, and gave her a brief, hot, hard kiss on the mouth. His thumb brushed her neck before he withdrew his hand. "See you soon."

She nodded, pressing her lips together, following him out of the classroom.

"Thanks for the coffee. And for checking up on me." He closed the door behind him and locked it.

"I wanted to make sure you hadn't gone off me."

He turned to stare at her. "Yeah, like that's going to happen." He gave her an exasperated glare. "See you later."

"See you." She watched him walk off, stopping to talk to a group of students. He seemed so young to be a teacher, but he was clearly confident in the role. It turned her on, seeing him so self-assured. Mind you, everything he did turned her on at the moment.

Mulling on that fact, she walked off in the opposite direction.

Chapter Sixteen

Rusty sat in his car and tapped his fingers on the steering wheel. It was Friday afternoon, shortly after the end of school, and he was waiting in the car park for Faith to show up, ready to spirit her off for the third sin.

She was late. He frowned, watching the last few teachers driving off. Where had she got to? She had a thing about tardiness, and Dan and Toby were always getting into trouble with her for turning up late. He didn't have a problem usually—when you worked to the school bells, you got to be a bit like Pavlov's dog and functioned automatically on hourly intervals. Once he'd even stood up in the bar when a bell rang, making everyone laugh.

Had she changed her mind? He turned the car ignition on, lowered the window, and turned it off again. After her visit to his classroom on Wednesday, he doubted it. But maybe she'd finally talked herself out of seeing him again.

It wouldn't surprise him. Because he'd been having doubts himself. He knew she'd picked up on them. That's why she'd come to his classroom. He'd denied there was a problem. Well, there wasn't, not really. He didn't want to stop seeing her. He didn't regret what they'd done. Quite the opposite, in fact. And maybe that was the problem. He was enjoying himself so much he didn't want to stop. And he knew he had to, after their contract finished. For several reasons. Dan, for one. Faith herself, for another—she'd made him promise it would end after the seventh sin, so clearly she wanted a finite end to their sexual relationship. And he had to end it because of himself. She deserved better than him. If they carried on after the seventh sin, she'd end up regretting it down the line. And then he'd lose her completely, and the thought of never having her as a friend again was too painful to bear.

He'd gotten too intense during the second sin, he knew it. He had no idea why, something to do with the magic of the moment, which made him want to slap himself, because he'd never considered himself particularly romantic. But there had been something magical about that evening and how he'd felt about the woman who'd loved him in the moonlight, the woman whom he hadn't recognized, because she hadn't been his friend Faith, Dan's little sister, skinny and with braces. She'd been exotic and tantalizing, and she'd taken his breath away with her passion.

When he'd first offered his services, he'd wondered whether her naivety and innocence would make sex with her clinical and mechanic—look Faith, this goes here, that goes there, try doing it this way, love. He'd thought she might be nervous and fumbling, and he'd seen his role as educational—no real surprises there considering what he did for eight hours a day, five days a week. Although he fancied her like mad, and he'd always been able to see past her role as Dan's sister, he'd still thought she'd defer to him, and he had to admit part of him thought he'd be the one taking charge.

Her enthusiasm, her passion, had completely taken him by surprise. Although she wasn't very experienced in bed, her eagerness to try everything, and her complete abandonment in their lovemaking, had shocked him. And he wasn't easily shocked. He'd been with wilder, more experienced women who'd known every trick in the book and had been prepared to try them all out on him, but none of them had made him feel like he had the other night with Faith. He'd never lain in the moonlight and worshipped a woman as if she were a Greek goddess. He felt embarrassed now, thinking about it, but at the time it was as if he'd been under a spell, or drunk maybe, although he'd never been drunk, so he had no idea what it felt like.

And now he had five other sins to try, and excitement and impatience blended inside him, along with a hint of wariness. He felt as if he were standing at the edge of a huge puddle, about to step in, and he had no idea how deep it might be. It could come right over his head, for all he knew. He had to be careful. Okay, he was only four years older than, but he was the guy—he had to take charge of their relationship. He had to keep things light and fun. The seven sins were the key—they'd agreed to take part in this scientific experiment, and he had to concentrate on the physical side of things and keep their emotions well out of the way.

At that moment, Faith came around the corner, saw his car, and gave a big smile as she crossed the car park toward him. He got out and leaned on the door, smiling as she walked up to him. She wore a long green skirt and a black camisole top, and he could tell by the soft shape of her breasts and the lack of straps that she wasn't wearing a bra. She possibly had no panties on either. Damn it, three seconds into the date and he had a hard-on. There was no hope for him.

"You're late," he said, softening it with a smile.

"I couldn't get rid of Eve. I think she may have cottoned on to the fact I'm meeting Mr. S. tonight."

"I find it very odd when you refer to me in the third person."

She winked at him, glancing quickly around the car park before coming around the car to the passenger side. She carried a big cooler along with her night case and dumped them on the back seat before climbing in the front.

"I feel like we should have a secret password or something," he said, getting in beside her.

"I did think about wearing my dark glasses and false nose." They both laughed, clipping in their seatbelts.

"If we see anyone we know, you'll have to duck down." He started the car and headed for the exit.

She chuckled, reached across, and squeezed his hand. "I've been looking forward to this all week."

"Me too." He lifted her hand and kissed her fingertips. Glancing over, he saw her brown eyes were warm with affection.

He cleared his throat. "So what's in the bag?"

"Ah, it's a secret. Where are we going?"

"Er…not saying."

"What are you, twelve years old?"

"Takes one to know one." Laughing, they began talking about their day, while Rusty headed up State Highway Ten, out of town.

Chapter Seventeen

He drove for about half an hour, and Faith watched with interest as he headed north toward Doubtless Bay, but turned off at Pungaere Road for the Puketi Forest. Were they going camping? Halfway up the forest road, however, he took another turnoff across the beautiful rolling hills and fields full of cows and horses toward Lake Manuwai.

He smiled at her inquisitive glances. "Okay, stop giving me the third degree." He put his hand in his pocket, extracted a key, and passed it to her. "A colleague at work has a place on the lake."

"Oh. How nice. Have you been there before?"

"Yes, he had a party there one Christmas. It's basic, but it's got a lovely view."

She felt a wave of excitement. "This is such fun. Sex should always be like this."

"It is always like this if you're doing it right."

She knew he'd meant it to be funny, but her heart gave a little jump at the thought that he'd felt this way when he'd had sex with other women. She'd told him she had no problem with him having other lovers. But still…

She'd been unable to stop a smile breaking out on her face when she'd walked up to him in the car park. He'd come straight from school so he was still wearing his school clothes—while not exactly a suit and tie, his black shirt with the sleeves rolled up and smart dark grey pants made the blood rush in her veins. His hair was getting a little long on top, falling forward over one eyebrow. He was gorgeous. He would never be short of female company.

She looked out of the window, trying to act casual. "You always have this much fun?"

He was quiet for a moment. Then she felt him take her hand. When she glanced across at him, his eyes were full of amusement. "Are you fishing for compliments, Hillman?"

"I am female. We kind of like them."

He laughed. "Fair enough. Okay, how about if I say you're the best I've ever been with? Will that do?"

"Compliments, Rusty, not fantastical statements. We can tell the difference."

"Clearly not."

She snorted. "I'm not stupid—you don't have to protect my fragile ego. I'm well aware you've been with some pretty hot girls." She grinned at him. "How are you coping with only having sex once a week?"

"I might last about six seconds tonight, if you're lucky."

She giggled. "How often do you normally have sex?"

"Really, Faith."

"What?"

"I don't kiss and tell."

"It's not like we're dating. It's called historical investigation. You should appreciate that."

"I don't, because it's not, it's called being nosy, and you're not dragging me down that road. How would you like it if I told other women what it had been like with you?"

She shrugged and suppressed a twinge of unease at the thought of him sleeping with someone else when they finally finished their contract. That was none of her business. "I was just…inquisitive. Interested."

"A.K.A. nosy."

"If you say so. Anyway, you never answered my question. I need to know these things for my research. How often do you have sex?"

"As often as I can get it. Now be quiet, we're nearly there." He turned to the right down another road, and then left down a long drive. He threaded the car through the trees, eventually emerging in front of a long, low house perched on the edge of the lake.

"Oh, wow." She was out even before he'd switched off the engine. The house was beautifully private, surrounded by bush and overlooking the vast lake, which glittered bright blue in the late afternoon sun.

"Nice, huh?" He led her over to the house. It had double sliding doors leading onto the large decking, which faced north to catch the sun all day.

He let them in and she wandered around, seeing the open-plan kitchen off the living room and the two bedrooms, small, but neat and clean. She came back into the living room to see him placing the cooler on the work surface, her night case in his other hand. He handed it to her, smiling. "Does the house meet with your approval?"

"Very much so."

"Good. Now, I want you to go and unpack. And don't come out until I call you."

She raised an eyebrow. "Why?"

"Because I said so." When she didn't move, he ushered her into the bedroom.

"I'm not one of your schoolgirls," she protested.

"Faith, for God's sake, I don't need any more provocation. I told you, I'm turned on enough without imagining you in pigtails and white socks." He gave her a hot kiss before going out.

Wondering what he was getting up to, she began to unpack her bag. She placed her toothbrush in the bathroom and hung up her clothes for the next day. Then she took out her notes and began to jot down a few titles and headings, thinking about her next article. As she did so, she had to quell the ripple of excitement and nervousness that shimmered through her. Eventually she put down the pad and lay back on the bed, looking up at the ceiling fan that turned slowly, circulating the air.

Rusty had said sex was always fun like this, if you were doing it right. Was that really the case? She'd never felt this excitement, this anticipation, with either of her other lovers. But then this was different, because of the articles, and their exploration of the seven sins. Ordinary sex, with a partner you'd been going out with for ages, wouldn't be the same, would it? If she'd been dating Rusty for months, or years, her heart wouldn't be racing at the thought of kissing him and feeling his hands on her eager body. Would it?

She closed her eyes. What was he doing out there? She wanted him, badly, had been planning what she was going to do with him all week, since they last parted. It felt as if she'd been in a permanent state of arousal for days. She moved her hands down her body, inhaling as her fingers brushed her nipples. If he didn't take her soon…

The door opened and she sat up, flushing at the direction of her thoughts. Hands on hips, he observed her, raising an eyebrow.

"What?" she demanded.

"You look guilty." His lips curved. "Have you been getting started while I've been busy?"

"No! Goodness." Could the man read her thoughts? Or was her desire really written all over her face? She'd never been a good poker player.

"I don't mind." He came over and pulled her to her feet, nuzzled her ear, and kissed her hot cheek. "I'd prefer it if I could watch, though."

She tried to push him away. "Stop embarrassing me."

He held her tighter. "I like embarrassing you. You go all pink. Like you do before you're about to come."

"Rusty! What's got into you?"

"I don't know." He kissed her ear again, making her shiver all over. "You smell all…womanly. Mint and lavender and…something with vanilla…"

"That's probably the custard I had for lunch."

He chuckled, but didn't stop touching his lips to her neck as his hands began to wander across her body. "Joke all you like, you're not putting me off."

"We should wait. I've got everything prepared…"

"And you've made so much effort, I want to make it worthwhile. I have a plan…"

"Another warm-up session?"

"Yep. Pre-sex sex, as you lovingly called it."

She sighed as he ran a hand up her skirt and reached around to cup her butt.

"You're so wicked," he whispered as his hand found bare skin.

"I'm wicked? You're the one who keeps embarrassing me." She gasped as he pushed her and she fell backward, bouncing on the mattress. He fell on top of her, making her squeal. "Oh God. No. Air. In. Lungs."

"Tough." He kissed her, hard.

Desire shot through her, as if Cupid had injected her with a vial of lust. She opened her legs and wrapped them around him. "Okay, I give in." She wriggled beneath him, pushing herself against his erection. "Come on, Thorne. Squish me flat."

Hot and aroused, not even bothering to undress, they made love in about five minutes, which was slightly better than the six seconds he'd promised her. Faith would have been embarrassed at how little time it took her to achieve an orgasm, if he hadn't nearly beaten her to it.

Afterward, they lay back on the bed, letting the fan waft cool air over them. He looked over at her. "Sorry."

"For what?"

"Being so quick. I did warn you."

She pushed herself up onto an elbow. "You did. I was hardly hanging around, in case you didn't notice."

He rolled to face her and propped his head on a hand. "I did notice, as a matter of fact. You're very easy to please."

"Well, when your guy has all the moves, what can you do?"

He gave a short laugh.

She studied him for a moment. "How many girls have you had, do you think?"

His smile turned into a frown. "Faith…"

"I'm interested."

"I've already told you…"

"You don't kiss and tell, I know." She met his gaze openly. "Seriously, Rusty, I've never spoken to a guy like this. You all joke about sex and who and what you've done, but I never know if you're being serious. You know what my job involves, that I write about this kind of stuff for a living. You're great at helping out on the website, and with this." She indicated the bedroom. "I could do with an honest answer or two."

He continued to frown. "I don't know that I'm comfortable with talking to you about stuff like that."

"Why not? As I told you last time, we're not dating. It's not as if I'm a girlfriend or anything. We're business partners. And friends."

The frown turned back into a reluctant smile. "I guess."

"Consider it part of my education. I know you can't resist educating me."

He sighed. "You know me too well. Okay, what do you want to know?"

She sat up and crossed her legs. "How many girls have you been with?"

"I honestly couldn't tell you. It's not like I've got notches on the bedpost or anything."

"Over a hundred?"

His eyes widened. "Fuck me, Hillman, I've already told you, I feel enough of a gigolo without your help. No, nowhere near a hundred."

"Ball park, then."

"I honestly don't know. Thirty-something?"

"Could you name them all in order if you had to?"

His gaze drifted to over her right shoulder, as if he was trying to list them in his head. It came back to her and he smiled. "More or less."

Her heart pounded. She didn't know why this was so important to her. But she needed to know about him, about whom he'd loved, and why. "How many were one-night stands?"

"Ah...a few."

"Ten? Twenty?"

"Er..." He looked embarrassed. "Probably nearer the latter. University."

"Hmm. Any you didn't know the last name of?"

His lips twitched. "Possibly."

"Any you didn't know the first name of?"

"No... I'm not that bad. Jeez."

"How many times have you been in love?"

The frown reappeared. "Never."

"Never?"

He shrugged. "Don't think so."

"Not even with Meredith? I thought she was special."

He looked out of the window. "She was a nice girl. She wanted things to get more serious. But I..." He let the sentence drift off.

"You didn't feel you wanted to spend the rest of your life with her?"

"No."

"So a more apt description might be you didn't want to fall in love."

His green eyes came back to her. "Maybe."

"Are you ever going to get over this thing you've got about being like your father?"

"I doubt it."

"So you don't think you'll ever fall in love?"

"Not if I can help it."

They studied each other for a while. His gaze was open, honest. She didn't want to spoil the day, and decided not to pursue him down that road.

He seemed willing to wait patiently for her to come up with the next question.

"Who's the best you've had?" she asked.

"I've already told you."

She sighed. "Seriously."

"I'm perfectly serious. Look." He gestured at his face, indicating the absence of a smile. "Why do you think I'm not telling the truth?"

"I think you're being polite. Love the one you're with. I don't see what would be so wrong about you giving me an honest answer. I know it's not me, Rusty, I won't be wounded. You're only my third lover. I'm well aware some of your girls have…" She thought how to phrase it.

"Been around the block?" he suggested.

She giggled. "No, that's not what I was going to say. Had more experience is how I would phrase it."

He smiled. "Yes, most, if not all, were more experienced than you."

"So who was the best?"

He sat up, leaned forward, and kissed her. "One day, I'll say 'you', and you'll believe me. Now, come on. I've got something to show you."

Not believing him in spite of what he said, she followed him out into the living room. There she stopped, staring in surprise at the scene outside. He'd spread a large blanket on the decking, maybe six or seven feet square, and scattered it with cushions. Around the edges, he'd placed a ring of candles, some of which she could smell were citronella, to ward off insects, the rest a variety of colors. He'd lit them all, bathing the area in a warm glow. He'd carried out her cooler and placed it to one side with a couple of plates. And next to it were two glasses, one with wine, one with Coke.

She grinned happily at him. "You old romantic."

He winked back. "Are you ready to reveal to me the secrets of your cooler? Only I'm starving. I haven't eaten since lunch."

"Good. I have a variety of things to whet your appetite."

"I know, but do you have any food?"

Laughing, she led him over to the blanket, and they sat cross-legged on cushions, facing each other. She pulled the cooler over to her and unzipped it.

"So tell me about this sin." He sipped his Coke. "What's the big deal?"

"This sin is about your senses." She rummaged in the cooler. "Specifically, taste and touch. I want to experiment with different foods, and see if some are sexier than others. Many foods are supposed to be aphrodisiacs. I want to see if they work."

"Sounds good. Where do we start?"

"There are a couple of rules—you can only eat with your fingers. And as far as possible, we have to share."

"Feed each other, you mean?"

"Yeah. Or off each other."

He smiled lazily. "Sounds good to me."

She suppressed a shiver. "Okay, sexy food can basically be split into two types: foods that contain chemicals that are conducive to feeling sexy, and foods that look…suggestive."

"Hmm, sounds intriguing. What's first?"

Chapter Eighteen

She pulled out a small box of crackers and a jar. "Caviar."

"Ooh." He watched her spoon a small amount onto a cracker. "So what's sexy about caviar? I'm guessing it's not one of those foods that looks suggestive."

"Not so much. It's supposed to stimulate the formation of testosterone."

"Well, I guess I could always do with more of that. Don't know about you."

She held the cracker up to his mouth. He ate it in one bite while she prepared another, which he then took and fed to her. She closed her mouth over it, feeling his thumb brush her lip as he pushed it into her mouth. Great. The first bite and she was already turned on.

He raised an eyebrow. "What do you think?"

She ran her tongue around her lips thoughtfully. "Slightly salty. Reminds me of something else…" They both laughed.

He scooped some more onto another cracker and helped himself as she rummaged in the bag again. He flexed an arm muscle. "I feel manlier already."

"Well, there you go." She retrieved the next box from the bag, opened the lid, and took out half a dozen jalapeno poppers.

"Chilies?" He looked wary.

"Apparently they help release endorphins, which give you a natural high."

"Where did you get these from?"

"I made them."

"You went to a lot of effort."

She shrugged. "I needed to for my research." She concentrated on his mouth as she held out the grilled chili stuffed with cream cheese and spices. She didn't want him to look into her eyes and see the truth—that she'd prepared every dish with him in mind, unable to stop thinking as she made them about whether they'd turn him on or not.

He bit into the pepper, chewed, and winced. "Fuck, they're hot!"

"What did you expect?"

"One of the milder ones. God, my lips are burning."

"I forgot what a wuss you are with spicy food. Here." She took a small mouthful of his Coke, leaned forward, and kissed him, letting the liquid flood his mouth, the bubbles dancing on their tongues.

She pulled back. "Better?"

"No. But it was still nice."

"Want another one?"

"Ah…no thanks. Do you have any food that doesn't take the inner lining off my mouth?"

She retrieved some more containers from the cooler. "These will be more to your liking, I promise." She popped open the lids. "Homemade guacamole, not too spicy, I promise."

"So what's the background behind this?"

"Avocados contain vitamin B6, which increases male hormone production."

"Are you going to have a moustache by the end of this exercise?"

"I sincerely hope not. They also contain potassium, which helps regulate the female thyroid gland. And…the Aztecs called the avocado tree a 'testicle tree' because when the fruit hangs in pairs it looks like testicles."

"And I'm supposed to find that sexy?"

She laughed. "Here, dip one of these in it for me." She handed him a stick of asparagus, wrapped in bacon.

"Amusingly phallic," he said, scooping up some of the guacamole and offering it to her.

Fixing her gaze on his, she closed her lips over the end and took a delicate bite.

He studied her, his gaze starting to grow hot. "I don't know how you made that look sexy, but you managed it."

"This will kill you, then." She took out a hot dog and made a great display of licking the end before sliding her mouth over it. Giggles overtook her, however, which rather killed the effect.

After this, she continued to unpack the tiny containers she'd carefully fitted into the cooler. Thoroughly enjoying themselves, feeding each other, they made their way through the other dishes she'd prepared, including small, tender pieces of steak cooked in a mustard sauce, salmon pieces that she adored but he wasn't so keen on, and oysters, which he loved but made her shudder.

"Did you know," she told him as she fed him yet another, "oysters change sex from female to male and back, which means they help us to experience the masculine and feminine sides of love?"

He looked slightly alarmed. "Meaning what?"

"That you'll be wearing my underwear before the night's out."

"Ah, but you're not wearing any."

"True." She licked her fingers, not missing the way his gaze followed her tongue. She could see why eating like this was supposed to be sexy. It didn't really matter what food they ate—the act of feeding each other, and observing the other eat, was the reason for the arousal. Watching his mouth close around her fingers, feeling his tongue sweep across her skin, that was the sexy part of this. She thought of what else she had planned, and desire rippled through her. She knew he saw it, maybe in a tightening of her nipples, or the dilating of her pupils, because his lips curved, and he leaned forward once again to kiss her.

When he finally drew back, she glanced out across the lake. The sun was low in the sky and the water sparkled with highlights. The late February mornings had turned cool and autumnal, but the evenings were still warm, and the cicadas were already out in force, chirruping in the bush. She cleared her throat. "How about some sweet food now?"

"Mm." He tipped his head to one side, studying her.

"What?" She flicked him a glance as she brought out the last few pots.

"Nothing." His eyes were full of smiles.

"I know you have a sweet tooth. So I took extra care with choosing these." She opened the first one. "Strawberries and raspberries. Red fruit—the color of love."

"Oh yeah."

She picked up a strawberry by the green stem and held it up. Keeping his eyes on hers, he closed his lips around it, reminding her of the way his mouth closed over her nipple. She swallowed as he bit gently, then brushed his lips with his tongue.

"I love strawberries," he said.

"I know." She took the bitten end of the fruit, wiped the red juice on her lips like gloss, and pouted at him. "That's why I got them."

He reached across and slipped a hand behind her neck, pulling her toward him. He licked her lips slowly, sending little shivers of delight skittering through her.

They fed each other the rest of the fruit, and then she popped open the next container.

"Figs?" he said in surprise.

"Yep. Figs were used by the ancient Greeks in copulation rituals."

"Now that sounds like something I might be interested in." His eyes glimmered with amusement. "Actually, figs were one of the first plants cultivated by humans. Fossilized figs dating to around 9500BC were found in an early Neolithic village near Jericho."

"Useless facts," she said happily as she cut the figs in half. "That's why I love you so much."

The words left her mouth before she could stop them and she bit her lip, keeping her eyes fixed firmly on the knife. Carefully she slit another fig open. She'd told him she loved him hundreds of times before. But not since they'd started sleeping together.

She decided to pretend she hadn't said it and cleared her throat. "Apparently open figs simulate female reproductive organs. Watching a man eat one is supposed to be incredibly erotic." She looked up finally.

"Huh," he said.

She held one up and turned the red flesh around to face him. "Well?"

"Are you going to take your clothes off so I can compare?"

"I don't think so."

Grinning, he took the fig from her. Keeping his eyes fixed on her, he ran his tongue lightly up the middle and then took a gentle bite, his tongue brushing his lips, and again she felt a shudder of desire, giving her goose bumps.

"Two can play at that game." She took out a banana, peeled it, and closed her mouth over the end. Widening her eyes at him, she moved it in and out between her lips.

They both laughed, and he pulled her close to him for the first time, wrapping his arms around her and kissing her properly. "Are you nearly done?" he asked eventually. "I'm too horny to wait much longer."

"Sweetheart, I think you were horny before I even unzipped the cooler." Packing up the plates, she moved everything off the blanket to one side. "There's one thing left."

"What's that?"

She took out a jar of chocolate body paint and showed him the label.

Both his eyebrows shot up. "Now you're talking."

She got to her knees, took a final look around to make sure they couldn't be seen, and then removed her top. Standing, she slipped off her skirt and threw both items into the house before sitting before him naked, cross-legged. Following her lead, he did the same with his shirt, pants, and boxers, and sat facing her. "I'm glad there's chocolate," he said.

"You can't have food sex and not have chocolate. It's another food containing a stimulant similar to endorphins. Apparently, some monasteries in Vienna banned it in the seventeenth century because it inflamed passion."

"The Aztecs discovered it. The Aztec emperor Montezuma drank fifty golden goblets of chocolate a day to enhance his sexual prowess."

"I didn't know that," she said. "Jeez, he must have been fat." She unscrewed the lid of the jar. Inside was a small brush, fitted into the lid.

"Where did you get this?"

"One of my readers gave me a website address." She took out the brush and straightened the handle, clipping it in place. "The idea is that we paint this onto areas we'd like to be licked. Starting with the not so obvious."

"Otherwise it would be a very short exercise."

"My thoughts exactly."

"Go on then, you first."

She dipped the brush in the soft chocolate and touched it to the tips of each finger on her left hand, then held it up to show him.

Rusty closed his hand around her wrist, his thumb resting in the center of her palm, and brought it up to his mouth. Keeping his eyes on hers, he closed his mouth over each finger in turn, sucking the chocolate off. She couldn't decide whether to watch him, finding his hot gaze and the sight of his lips sucking her so arousing, or close her eyes, which heightened the sensation of his tongue brushing her skin.

In the end, she did both in turn, sighing happily as he turned her hand over and placed a kiss in the center of her palm.

"My turn now." She did the same to him, painting his fingers before licking the chocolate off. He gave a low groan as her mouth covered his thumb. She looked up to see his eyes closed, and she kept her mouth there for a while, smoothing her tongue over his skin, closing her own eyes. When she finally looked up again, he was watching her, his eyes hot.

"Do you know what you do to me?" he whispered.

She glanced down at his lap and then back up at him. "Yuh-huh." Smiling, she dipped the brush back in the chocolate, drawing it across her wrist.

"Oh." He brought it up to his mouth and licked it off gently. "This is a very useful lesson in erogenous zones."

"I was just thinking the same." She copied the movement on him. "I can't believe how erotic it is, and it's such a simple thing."

"I know." He watched her run her tongue down his arm, and he shivered. His eyes were growing more intense with desire by the minute. "Show me more."

"I think the whole of my body's one big erogenous zone at the moment." She brushed the chocolate in the crook of her arm, shuddering as he removed it slowly with his mouth.

"I know what you mean." He took the brush from her and painted a stripe from her shoulder up her neck, and then ran his tongue all the way up, making her tip her head to the side with a sigh.

"Show me what you like," she said huskily as she got to her knees.

He dipped the brush in the chocolate and daubed his earlobe, and touched the brush to the spot behind his ear. She leaned forward, her breasts brushing his arm, and licked slowly up to his hairline, taking the lobe in her mouth and sucking the chocolate off. She repeated it the other side, enjoying his sighs of pleasure.

"You now," he said, handing her the brush.

She took it and stroked it firmly across her lips.

He took her in his arms and kissed her, which smeared the chocolate across their faces and made her squeal as he lowered her to the ground. He planted chocolate kisses across her cheeks and chin, and placed dots with the brush on her nose and temples, kissing them off with his chocolatey lips.

After that, things started to heat up. They drew patterns with the body paint across their bodies and down their legs, getting stickier by the minute, trying the backs of their knees and the insides of their ankles, their toes, nipples, and even dobs in each other's navels, which made him sigh but her squeal and giggle.

"Wait a minute," he said eventually, holding up a hand. He looked very mischievous and she felt instantly wary. "I've got something I want to try." He pulled the cooler over and rummaged inside. "I'm sure I saw…ah yes." He brought out a Mars Bar.

"That was supposed to be for afterward."

He shook his head. He put a hand on her shoulder and pressed her onto her back. Slowly, he unwrapped the long, slender chocolate bar, his eyes gleaming.

"Rusty…"

"Open your legs."

She shook her head, eyes wide. "No."

He leaned over her and kissed her. "Think about what you'll be able to tell your readers."

"I couldn't."

He glanced over his shoulder. "There's nobody here."

"That's hardly the point."

He nudged at her legs. "Come on. Isn't this what your articles are about? Pushing boundaries?"

"Even so." She felt deliciously shocked. "You are so wicked, Rusty Thorne."

"And you love me for it." His eyes were hot, almost feverish, and she knew then that he'd heard her saying she loved him. He kissed her and nudged her legs again. "Go on."

She closed her eyes and screwed up her nose, reluctantly opening her legs. "I'm going to regret this…"

"No you won't. I promise." He kissed her again.

She jumped as he brushed the cold bar up her thigh. "Eeek!"

"Just relax." He stroked it up the central core of her, continuing to kiss her. She let him, struggling not to giggle, not believing what she was letting him do. She felt him push it inside her gently, and gasped. He took the opportunity to plunge his tongue into her mouth, kissing her deeply as he slid the chocolate bar up into her. The coldness was tantalizingly shocking, a stark contrast to the heat of her body. As he withdrew it slowly, it made her catch her breath.

He lifted his head. She opened her eyes, her cheeks hot. Then she stared at him as his green eyes gleamed.

"You wouldn't," she warned.

He grinned. Before she could stop him, he took a bite of the bar.

"Rusty!" She squealed, trying to snatch it out of his hand, and he laughed, rolling away from her. They fought for a moment, but he caught her hands and drew her to him, turning it into an embrace, and eventually she gave in and put her arms around him, melting against him like the bits of chocolate still sticking to their bodies.

Before long, he retrieved a condom, put it on, and slid inside her, still laughing at the embarrassed expression on her face.

"You're so sexy." He licked up stray bits of chocolate around her neck and shoulder. "I've never done that before."

"I should think not, you wicked man."

He chuckled, making hot, sweet, sticky love to her until they both came, filling the warm evening air with soft sighs and gasps, as the kingfishers dived into the darkening lake, and the kiwi birds began to cry in the bush.

Chapter Nineteen

Later, after a shower had washed away the stickiness, they walked around part of the lake and watched the reflection of the setting sun across the water.

Rusty took Faith's hand, and she didn't protest. After all, they'd walked hand-in-hand before, just as she'd walked with Toby, Dan, and even Eve, so it was hardly out of the ordinary. And yet it felt strange. Intimate. She looked down as he linked her fingers with his, watching as he stroked her knuckles with his thumb while he talked. Then she glanced back up at him. He wasn't looking at her—he was waxing lyrical about the first European colonists to New Zealand and what it must have been like to land in such a beautiful country after a long journey across the wild seas. His gaze had wandered across the lake, and he was lost in a world of his own, his voice deep and melodious as he related some tale he'd once read about the first missionaries to Kerikeri. He often zoned out like this when in teacher mode, and she knew his students commented on it. Mr. Thorne's gone A.W.O.L. again.

The sun was setting behind him, and the sky burned a deep orange in between the blue. It lit his hair, turning the ruffled, russet-brown strands to scarlet at the ends, silhouetting his attractive, boy-next-door features and wide, sexy smile. She couldn't help it. She brought him to a stop, turned him around, and kissed him, their fingers still linked down by their sides.

"Hmm," he said when she finally drew back. "Were you trying to shut me up?"

"That's absolutely the reason."

His lips curved, and, releasing her hand, he brushed a strand of hair back from her cheek and tucked it behind her ear. The light touch made her shiver, and she saw he'd noticed, a slight frown appearing on his forehead, an intense look in his eyes. For a moment, she thought he was going to startle like a deer, run a mile at the thought that he could make her shiver with a mere brush.

But he didn't. His eyes gleamed, almost triumphantly, and she could see he liked that he'd hooked her, made her see what his other girls saw—the Rusty that made their hearts miss a beat, the Rusty that captivated them. His pleasure irritated her, but still, as he stepped closer to her, bringing both of his hands up to cup her face, she couldn't move, fixed there by his green-eyed gaze.

He kissed her, long and languidly, and brushed her tongue with his, eventually enveloping her in his arms, a heartfelt, deep, passionate embrace that made her heart thump and a sigh escape her lips when he finally raised his head.

"What was that for?" She cleared her throat as she realized he'd stolen her voice somewhere along the way.

He looked deep into her eyes, and for a brief moment, she thought he was going to say something profound. She should have known better. He blinked, grinned and said, "I need a favor."

"Oh?"

He released her, taking her hand again, and continued walking along the lake as if nothing had happened. "What are you doing Thursday?"

"Um…I'm in Whangarei in the morning. Nothing in the afternoon."

"Evening?"

"Nothing. How can I help?"

He looked back across the lake. "There's an event at The Harrington in Waitangi. I'm up for an award for running the Medieval Fair last year."

Faith nodded. The Fair had been a huge success, and she wasn't surprised he'd been nominated. She and Eve had dressed up as nuns for the day and run a medieval hospital, explaining to the kids how medieval doctors used to diagnose patients by drinking their urine. They'd offered them free samples, which were actually watered-down fruit juice, but looked sufficiently urine colored to encourage squeals of disgust from the students. "How can I help?"

"I kind of need a date."

She raised an eyebrow. "And you can't get anyone else?"

He smiled. "I haven't asked anyone else."

"Oh."

"I thought we decided to be exclusive, until the contract ended," he pointed out.

She glanced at him. "I don't mind if there's someone you'd rather take."

"There isn't. You're my flavor of the month."

She smiled, because he'd meant it to be funny, but the phrase stung a little. She had his attention, for the moment. Soon his eye would be wandering, however, and he'd be off chasing another skirt. She wasn't anything special to him—she had to remember that before she got all starry eyed every time he kissed her.

And anyway, what was her problem? He'd never promised her anything other than sex, and that was all she'd wanted from him. Seven encounters and they'd be done. She'd even made him sign a contract stating she didn't want anything else from him. And she'd done that because even though she was curious about what he was like as a lover, she also knew what Rusty did—kissed girls and made them cry. He was a classic nursery rhyme. She had to keep her wits about her and make sure that didn't happen to her.

"Yeah, I'll go with you," Faith said. She slipped her hand out of Rusty's and put both hers in her pockets, hunching her shoulders forward.

Chapter Twenty

Relief swept over Rusty. He hadn't been looking forward to going to the event alone, but he also hadn't felt right asking someone else to go with him while they were having sex, in spite of her insistence that he could date other girls. And he also wanted her there. He wasn't sure why. "Great. It's quite a classy do. Black tie. You got anything to wear?"

She shrugged. "I'm sure I've got an old sack I can stitch some sequins onto."

"I didn't mean—"

"I know."

He stopped walking. She wasn't looking at him, and he could feel the way she'd withdrawn. "What's up?"

"Nothing." She shivered. "I'm cold."

He glanced up at the sky. It had grown cooler, and he could smell autumn in the air. When he looked back at her, he noticed that her nipples stood out like buttons on her shirt. "Come on," he said. "Let's go back to the house."

As they walked, Faith talked a little about her week ahead, impersonal stuff, keeping her eyes on the ground. He listened but searched his brain furiously to try and work out what he'd said wrong. However, apart from the query about whether she had anything to wear—which should have made her laugh—he couldn't think why she'd gone quiet. He'd kissed her, and she'd obviously enjoyed it—he'd seen that in her eyes, and had been pleased because of it. How had he upset her?

She ran lightly up the steps of the decking into the house. He followed her in, trailing her into the kitchen. He leaned against the worktop as she poured herself a drink from the fridge. She was saying something about Dan and Eve, talking too quickly, as if she was nervous. As she closed the fridge door, he caught her hand and turned her. "What's up, sweetheart?"

"Nothing."

He caught her chin in his hand and lifted it, forcing her to meet his eyes. Large and dark brown, they were suspiciously shiny, like highly polished mahogany. "Faith," he said gently. "I know you well enough."

She gave him a smile, but it was forced. "It's nothing. I'm feeling a bit emotional. My period's due tomorrow. Hormones, you know."

"You should have said."

She flushed. "You don't need to know everything about me. We're not dating." She turned and walked over to the decking, looking out across the lake as she sipped her drink.

He hesitated, frowning. Faith was never sharp with him. She was hardly ever in a bad mood, and he'd never known her to be hormonal, in the way that men always joked that women were at "that time of the month". The excuse was convenient, and she would be aware he couldn't argue with it. She didn't want to talk about the real reason she was upset.

He studied her slim form, her narrow waist, and curvy hips. Her long brown hair hung down her back in gentle waves. She looked elegant and graceful, even just standing there, motionless. Should he leave her alone for a while? Suggest they go home? Trouble was, he didn't want to. He was enjoying himself, and had looked forward to spending the night with her. He wanted to take her in his arms and kiss her tears away. But she wasn't his girlfriend. She'd made that quite clear.

She was his friend, however. As he saw her sigh, he felt a surge of affection for her and regretted he'd done something to upset her. He wasn't going to leave his friend unhappy like this.

He went over to his bag, retrieved his iPod and speakers, and plugged them in. He selected a song and pressed Play. Then he stood by the workbench, arms folded, waiting.

The Beatles' song *Here, There and Everywhere* began playing. He knew the song was one of her favorites.

At first, she didn't move. Then, as the music swelled, she turned her head and looked at the floor behind her. Her gaze moved up to his. He met her eyes and smiled. And to his relief, she gave a small, resigned shake of her head and smiled back.

He walked over to her, took her glass, placed it on the table, and pulled her into his arms. They began to dance, and he sang to her as they moved, kissing her temple gently. And when she finally slipped her arms around him and rested her head on his shoulder, he knew she'd forgiven whatever he'd done that had made her frown, for now.

Chapter Twenty-One

Faith Hillman's Blog

So… food sex! It's not everyone's cup of tea, I know. But my oh my… what a sensual experience. What's come out of this sin, for me, is how important it is to communicate to your partner what turns you on. The chocolate paint was perfect for this. You paint it onto your body on the places you'd like to be kissed and touched, and it's a great way to give them ideas, because we all know that men need a little help with foreplay every now and then, and a reminder that's it not all about nipples and the bit 'down there'.

We tried all sorts of food, and again, the key is about taking time to eat, to be with one another, and to think about sex while you're eating. The food itself is pretty much irrelevant—it's the being together and concentrating on the other person that's important.

Mr. Sinful lived up to his name last night. I'm not going to say what he did with the Mars Bar—I will leave it to your imagination. Let's just say that I'm hoping I don't get a yeast infection.

*

Excerpt from the 732 comments
SashaT: OMG! Faith!
Faith: Yeah, I know. He's such a naughty boy.
Ophelia: I've always thought I wasn't easily shocked, but you made my eyes nearly pop out of my head.
Patsy: LOL. Did you have a good time?
Faith: We did, we had great fun.
Patsy: Getting into the swing of it now.
Faith: Yeah, I guess.
Imogen: Am I sensing some hesitation?
SueAnn: Hey, Faith. Are you developing feelings for Mr. S.?
Faith: I always had feelings for him :) He's a nice guy.
SueAnn: You know what I mean.
Faith: I do. And it's all good. I still have the contract. And we're sticking to the terms.

Patsy: We're always here if you want to chat—you know that!
Faith: I do, and thank you so much, that means a lot.
Patsy: We're rooting for you, girl. Whatever happens, we're on your side.

Chapter Twenty-Two

Two days later, Rusty sat on Dan's sofa, Coke in hand, and stared as Dan offered him an evening snack. "Er…"

Toby looked over and burst out laughing. Dan looked across at him and then back at Rusty. "What's the joke?"

Rusty's eyes met Toby's, and he grinned ruefully. Dan frowned and looked at the Mars Bar. "I don't see what's so funny."

"Clearly you haven't read Faith's website," said Toby.

"No…" Dan drew the word out, his eyes wary. "Why, what's she said?"

"You don't want to know." Rusty took the chocolate bar from Dan's hand and opened it.

"You really don't," Toby affirmed.

Dan looked at them both. "A Mars Bar? What did she do with it?" His eyes widened as the penny dropped. "Oh my God, you're kidding me?" He sat with a sigh, massaging his forehead as if it pained him.

Rusty exchanged a glance with Toby and saw that his friend echoed his reluctance to reveal exactly what Faith had gotten up to that weekend. Rusty had guessed she wouldn't be able to keep his little experiment quiet, and he'd been right. Her fans had been exultant that Mr. S. had been so naughty. He was getting quite a reputation. The thought amused him, even though it felt odd that she was sharing their most intimate moments with half the population of Oceania.

Dan leaned his head on the back of the chair and groaned. "I hate this. I hate what she's doing."

Rusty took a bite of the bar and studied his best mate. "She's not a kid anymore."

"I know. But she's still my little sister. I feel responsible for her."

Toby stretched out his legs and put his feet on the table, safe from reprimand, as Eve was working that evening. "You gotta let go, Dan. She is allowed to have sex."

"She's not just having sex, she's having kinky sex. There should be a law against it."

Toby laughed. "There's nothing kinky about chocolate." He thought about it. "Okay, maybe there is, considering what she let him do with it."

Rusty closed his eyes momentarily. He'd never blushed in his life, but he was remarkably close to doing it now.

Dan frowned. "Not only does she let him do this stuff, she tells everyone about it. I can't believe what she's turned into."

"She's not turned into anything," Rusty said with amusement. "It's her job. She writes about sex. She helps women understand there's nothing wrong with experimenting and trying different things."

"I know. And Mum would be horrified." Dan swigged his beer.

Rusty felt a twinge of guilt. He squashed it firmly. He wasn't doing anything wrong. He and Faith were having healthy, happy sex. That was nothing to be ashamed of. Dan was being positively Victorian. "Your mother was hardly a prude," he pointed out.

Dan glared at him. "That's not the point."

"So what is the point?"

"I don't like everyone knowing what she does with this guy." Dan heaved a sigh. "I wish she'd been a nun."

Rusty looked down at the chocolate bar. He could still remember the way Faith's large brown eyes had widened with desire when she'd realized what he was suggesting. He liked shocking her, and he knew she liked to be shocked. Anyone less like a nun, he couldn't imagine. The thought of her in a wimple, dark eyes watching him over a hymnbook, made him smile.

He looked back up, straight into Dan's eyes, so like his sister's. Rusty felt his heart jolt at Dan's direct gaze. "What?"

Dan blinked, and Rusty realized he hadn't been looking at him after all. Talk about a guilty complex. Dan cleared his throat. "I was thinking about this guy, the one she's seeing."

Toby shrugged. "He genuinely seems to like her."

Dan frowned. "But don't you think it's odd?"

"Don't you think what's odd?"

"That he's agreed to do this with her, spend seven nights with her, just like that? Don't you think it's a bit…cold? Calculating?"

Rusty shifted uncomfortably. "It's what she wanted."

"It's what she said she wanted."

Toby sighed. "Girls do like sex too."

"I'm not saying—"

"Yes, you are. You're saying because she's a girl she can't possibly want sex for sex's sake. But she's young, she's only had two lovers, and they hardly sound like they've been the life and soul of the bedroom." Toby got up to get another beer from the fridge. "She wants to experiment a bit. She wants to discover what all the fuss is about."

Dan looked sullen. "So she just picks any old guy? He's obviously been around the block. God knows what diseases he's got."

Toby rolled his eyes as he came back. "Dan, you could be talking about any one of us. We've all had our fair share of partners. That doesn't make us easy, and it doesn't make us Petri dishes for sexual diseases, either. We all use condoms, and I'm sure Faith's making sure he is too."

Dan didn't say anything. He drank his beer and studied Toby, unsmiling.

Rusty frowned. "Faith's not stupid. She wouldn't take risks or expose herself to any danger."

"I'm not saying he's a psycho killer or anything," Dan said. "Although now I'm considering that, thank you very much. I'm just saying…us guys, we're all the same. We play around—we use girls sometimes. We all pretend we're on the same wavelength, but deep down, we know it's different for them, don't we? We're always looking for sex. They're always looking for love. We know we're breaking their hearts when we sleep with them. We just don't care."

Toby laughed. "Jeez, Dan, tune in to the twenty-first century, for fuck's sake. Girls like sex, believe me. They have the pill, they have condoms, and they know how to use them, the same as we do. They're not sitting around waiting for us to ride up like knights in shining armor—they're not offering us sex to get to our hearts. They're offering us sex to get to our dicks. And you're being chauvinistic if you think anything else."

Dan drank his beer, glowering. Rusty got up and walked over to the window, looking out across the bush.

Which of his friends' opinions was right? The truth probably lay somewhere in between. Toby was certainly correct in that there were plenty of women out there who liked sex and went looking for it aggressively. However, Rusty was also aware that nearly every time he'd slept with a girl, they'd wanted him to call the next day. Sometimes he did, sometimes he didn't. But he was aware that when he hadn't, they'd been sitting by the phone, waiting.

He watched a couple of rabbits hop across the lawn, silflaying in the early twilight. Nothing like that was going to happen between him and Faith, though. They were in perfect accord. She'd drawn up the contract, putting her requests into writing, and he'd been perfectly happy with her demands. They'd been up front from the very beginning. Neither of them would get hurt that way.

"Who are you seeing at the moment?" Dan asked unexpectedly.

"What?" Rusty turned, startled.

"You haven't mentioned anyone lately. I can't believe you're celibate."

Rusty walked back to the sofa and sat, also putting his feet on the table. "I met another teacher from Kaitaia at the last History convention. I've been over to see her a few times."

"What's her name?" asked Toby.

Rusty took a swig from his Coke, saying the first name that came into his head. "Laura."

"She hot?"

Rusty just looked at him. Toby tipped his head. "Do we get to meet her?"

"Maybe later."

Dan finished off his beer and put the bottle on the table. "Faith mentioned you've asked her to go to The Harrington on Thursday with you."

"Yeah."

"Laura not available?"

"Nah. She's got a parent evening."

To Rusty's relief, Dan nodded. "See if you can get any more details out of Faith while you're there."

"About what?"

"About this guy. Mr. S., or whatever his real name is." He looked thoughtful. "I want to meet him."

Rusty finished off his Coke. "I'll see what I can do. I'm off now. Essays to mark."

"Okay. See ya Friday?"

"Yeah." Rusty nodded at them and then left. He got in the car, sighing with relief as he reversed and headed up the drive. Keeping

Dan off their backs wouldn't be easy. He was a smart guy, and he was determined. Rusty was going to have his work cut out. He didn't like tiptoeing around his best mate, lying brazenly, sleeping with Dan's sister when he was so obviously upset about it. Were the seven sins worth all this deception?

Rusty thought of the Mars Bar incident and started laughing. Yeah. Absolutely.

Chapter Twenty-Three

"You know Rusty's been given instructions to wheedle Mr. S.'s true identity out of you," said Eve.

Faith paused in the act of slotting in an earring and met Eve's gaze in the mirror. "Oh?" She looked back at her reflection and moved to the other earring.

"Dan's desperate to find out who he is." Eve lay on her front on Faith's bed, providing necessary fashion advice as Faith got ready for the ball. "He wants to meet him."

"Well, Rusty can do his best, but my lips are sealed." She stepped back from the mirror. "Do I need a necklace?"

"Nah. That glittery spray looks so cool."

Faith studied her reflection. She wore a strapless top made of a shiny, chocolate-brown material and a floor-length black taffeta skirt that rustled when she walked. She'd given her shoulders and breastbone a light spray of glitter, making her shimmer in the light. Finally, she'd fixed her hair on top of her head with a sparkly clip, leaving curls to frame her face.

"Will I do?"

"Well enough for Rusty," said Eve. "Put the shoes on."

Faith slipped her feet into her new black high heels. She very rarely wore heels, but the skirt was long and she needed the height to lift it off the floor. "I know I'm going to go arse over tit in these."

"No you won't. You look elegant, sweetie. You just have to act it now." Eve grinned. "He's going to be shocked when he sees you. They all still think of us as fifteen-year-olds."

Privately, Faith doubted that was the case with Rusty, but she didn't say anything.

Eve sat up and put Faith's make-up back in her bag. "You're lucky you're going to this thing. Apparently his new girlfriend's busy, otherwise he'd have taken her."

Faith felt like Eve had slapped her with a wet fish. "New girlfriend?"

Looking down, trying out an eyeshadow on the back of her hand, Eve didn't notice her shock. "Yeah. Called Laura. Another teacher, from Kaitaia apparently. He told Dan about her on Monday."

"Oh." Faith picked up her handbag, checking she had her purse and phone. She was shocked to see her hand was shaking. When she breathed, she felt as if someone were sitting on her chest. What was wrong with her? What did it matter if Rusty was seeing someone else?

At that moment, there was a knock at the door. Eve rolled over and got to her feet. "That'll be him. Wait here. I want to watch his face when you walk out."

Faith felt incredibly nervous. Her body had turned into a cliché, her mouth dry, her palms sweating, and her heart thumping so hard she thought she might pass out.

She had to get a grip. She'd given herself a stern talking to on Saturday after Rusty had dropped her off. She had a contract—seven sins, seven sexual encounters, no more, no less. Anything else was out of the question. Even if she were in the zone for a long-term relationship—which she wasn't—she wouldn't touch Rusty with someone else's barge pole. He was exactly what she needed at this precise moment—a lover who was gentle, imaginative, funny, and skilled, who could show her what she'd been missing, initiate her, if you liked, into the delights of lovemaking. But he had no more to offer than that. He'd admitted it himself.

She took a deep breath and let it out slowly. She was going to think of him as a gigolo, whether he liked the term or not. That way it didn't matter that he was seeing other women. She was just hiring him for the seven sins. Yes, that made sense. Okay, she wasn't paying him, but in her head, the label helped. "It's all about the sex." She made herself say it aloud. Then hoped Eve hadn't heard her.

Their voices echoed from the living room, and she sighed and left the bedroom to walk down the hall. Might as well get this over with. Why had she said she would go? She should have sent him by himself. Serve him right.

She entered the living room and stopped. In spite of all her words, her breath caught in her throat.

Rusty stood by the front windows, looking out across the lawn. He wore a black suit and a crisp white shirt with a black bow tie. He'd combed his normally ruffled locks into place, and his hair looked darker than usual, and sleek. He stood with his hands behind his back. Faith had never seen him dressed so smart. The closest she could remember was at her parents' funeral, where he'd also worn black, but there it had just been jacket, shirt, and tie. He looked absolutely, completely gorgeous.

And at that moment, she knew she was lost.

Eve cleared her throat, and he turned, glanced at Eve, and followed her gaze to the doorway. He stared and his eyes widened. "Fucking hell."

Eve burst out laughing. "Nicely put."

Faith walked up to him. They surveyed each other slowly, conscious of Eve watching them, amused. Faith looked him up and down. Her heart thumped, but she made herself say something in jest. "You look like a waiter."

His lips curved. "Thank you. You look lovely too." He bent forward and kissed her cheek, his hand warm on her arm.

Eve sighed. "I wish I was going. Have a great time, you two."

"I'm sure it will be very dull," said Rusty, indicating for Faith to precede him out of the door.

Eve grinned. "Just make sure if she falls asleep, her head doesn't land in the soup bowl."

They both laughed. Faith opened the front door and walked out to his car. There she paused for a moment in the cool evening air and closed her eyes, trying to still her pounding heart.

She couldn't have done it. Surely. They'd only had sex three times. Well, maybe more than three times, but only three separate occasions. Surely she hadn't fallen in love with him already? It couldn't be. She'd just had this internal conversation, for God's sake. But she knew she was kidding herself. What she felt for him went deeper than sex. Didn't it? How did you know if you were in love with someone, or just in lust?

Whatever she was feeling, it hadn't happened over the past three weeks. The emotion she was feeling wasn't something that had shot up overnight, like bamboo. It had grown like a kauri tree, nurtured over years and years. She'd been falling for him since she was twelve, and she was powerless to do anything about it.

"Are you okay?" His hand rested on her waist, and his voice was full of concern. "You look very pale."

"I'm all right." She risked a glance up at him. Her heart continued to thud. She didn't recognize this Rusty, dark and suave, serious and grown-up. Maybe she and Eve had gotten it wrong—they'd been thinking all along that the guys had them fixed in their heads at the age of fifteen or so, but maybe it was the other way around. Maybe she and Eve had been thinking of the guys as forever boyish, playing computer games, falling off skateboards, and bombing each other in the pool. The trouble was, they still did all those things, and she found it difficult to come to terms with the fact that they'd grown up.

She swallowed. "I haven't had much to eat, that's all. Remind me not to have a glass of wine until I've had a bread roll, at least."

He laughed. "Okay." He opened the car door for her. "Mind your head."

"Thanks." She slid into the seat, tucking her skirt in so he could shut the door.

As she clipped in the seatbelt and he circled the car to get in the driver's side, Faith mused on Eve and her relationship with Dan. Eve had been her best friend at high school. They were the same age and had all grown up together, but at some point, Eve and Dan had obviously seen each other in a different light, and friendship had turned to romance. It was ironic really, considering how strict Dan had been with his friends to ensure they kept away from his baby sister. But then she supposed that was natural—he was older, and he was a guy, and he felt responsible for her because of what had happened to their parents. But he'd been dating Eve for six months now, and Eve already stayed at his house four nights out of seven. It wouldn't be long before they moved in together.

Faith wasn't destined to have the same happy ending, however. Sure, Dan had his hang-ups, but he was merely two-plus-two compared to Rusty's algebraic equation of a psyche. Rusty was so complicated and convoluted she wasn't sure if he'd ever be able to untangle himself enough to have a real relationship. And there was nothing she could do about that.

Was there?

Chapter Twenty-Four

Rusty slid in beside Faith, clipped himself in, and started the car. Only then did he glance across at her. "Just so you know," he said, "I'm desperate to snog you, but I'm worried Eve's watching us out of the window."

She fanned herself. "Oh Rusty, you're so romantic."

He put the car into drive. "Let me just get around the corner and I'll prove to you how romantic I can be."

"Absolutely not, Rusty Thorne. I spent ages applying this make-up, and there's no way I'm going to let you kiss it off until everyone at The Harrington has realized how much effort I've put into it."

"So maybe later then?"

She gave him a wry glance before looking out of the window. He took the opportunity to study her, in between glances at the road. He'd never seen her dressed like this. In the strapless top she looked slender, her shoulders narrow, her generous breasts tightly contained in the boned bodice, but with enough of a swell at the top to encourage his interest. Her make-up was immaculate, and she'd applied false eyelashes onto the top lids, making her look like a film star. The chocolate-brown top brought out her coloring to perfection. She was stunning.

"Stop looking at me like that," she said.

"Like what?"

"Like I've still got bits of chocolate stuck to me."

He met her gaze briefly before returning to the road. "Don't tempt me." She said nothing, and he sighed. "This was a stupid idea."

"Why so?"

"There's no way I'm going to be able to keep my hands off you all evening. You little temptress." To his surprise, she didn't smile. Her eyes were cool, appraising. He studied the road for a bit, then glanced back at her. "What's up?"

"I was just wondering…" She smiled. "It's nothing."

"Faith…"

"Do you wish you were going with someone else tonight?"

He gave her an amused look. "I'd much rather go with you than Toby, if that's what you're asking."

"That's not what I'm asking. I meant Laura."

"Who?"

"Your girlfriend? The teacher from Kaitaia?"

He burst out laughing. "Faith, I made her up. Dan was asking me who I'm seeing at the moment. He didn't believe there wasn't anyone. So I…invented someone."

"Oh." She studied him for a moment, digesting the information. Eventually she asked, "Is she prettier than me?"

He went to react to the crazy question and then realized she was joking, and they both laughed. He picked up her hand and kissed her fingertips. "No, sweetheart. She most definitely is not prettier than you. You are the most beautiful woman I've ever seen. And you take my breath away." The amazing thing was, he meant it.

He could tell she didn't believe him by the glare she sent him. But her cheeks pinkened just the same, and he smiled, squeezing her fingers before leaving her hand to hold the steering wheel.

After that, she seemed to relax a little, and they talked about other things as he drove the twenty minutes or so to the hotel at Waitangi. He thought about what she'd said as he drove, however. She'd been jealous. Hmm. What did that mean? He wasn't sure, but he filed it away in his brain to think about later.

Chapter Twenty-Five

At the hotel, they made their way through the lobby and into the main hall. Faith hadn't been there before, and she felt like a country girl in the big city, wide-eyed and smiling nervously. She accepted a glass of champagne from a waiter, but caught Rusty's warning glance and remembered her promise to eat something before she drank any alcohol. He stole a plate of canapés from another waiter and watched her until she'd eaten half a dozen before he let her have a sip of the champagne.

He then began to introduce her to people, and she soon stopped trying to remember everyone's name, recognizing that she wasn't supposed to and that he was just being polite. She didn't go to many functions and had been nervous about the evening, but in the end, it wasn't too bad. They sat at a table with some of his colleagues from the Social Studies Department, and she ate her meal, which was exquisite, and sipped the champagne as she listened to him entertaining his friends with everything from historical anecdotes to rather lewd gags about the Aussies. She worried that he was going to upset someone until she realized half of the department was Australian and it was obviously a standing joke.

He'd been very careful to introduce her as his "friend" to everyone and not anything more serious. She didn't really expect him to even remember she was there—after all, when she'd gone to a firm barbecue with Toby, he'd deserted her five minutes into the evening and she'd barely seen him for the rest of the night. However, all the while, apart from when they ate, Rusty held her hand under the table, doing nothing more sinister than giving her fingers the occasional squeeze.

She only realized it had been noticed when the awards were finally presented. Although he didn't win, Rusty got second prize for Most Enterprising Teacher, and when he went up to collect his award, the head of Social Studies—a mature, bubbly woman called Ellie—

leaned across the table and winked at her as everyone clapped. "Wow," Ellie said. "Looks good in his tux, doesn't he?"

Faith shrugged, feeling a surge of pride as he took the award from the presenter and shook his hand. "He's acceptable, but don't tell him I said so."

Ellie laughed and gave her an appraising look. "He speaks very fondly of you. You're a lucky girl."

Faith widened her eyes, startled. "Oh we're not… I mean, he's not my… We're just friends," she finished lamely. Her cheeks grew warm as he began to make his way back to the table.

Ellie grinned and winked again. "Yeah, right. I saw you holding hands. And I saw the way he looked at you. Like he had x-ray vision. He's crazy about you, girl. Hang on to him tightly."

Faith couldn't protest because he took his seat at that moment. She gave him a hasty smile, hoping to cover her disconcertion. "Well done." She leaned over to kiss him on the cheek.

He turned his head at the last moment and caught her lips with his own. "Oops," he said, when she pulled back, flustered.

She glanced at Ellie, saw by her smile that she'd seen the kiss, and lowered her eyes, her cheeks glowing. Rusty laughed. "You're so sexy when you blush," he murmured in her ear.

"Stop it." Oh why did she get so embarrassed all the time? It was his fault.

To his credit, he let the blush die down for a while and chatted instead to his colleagues as the evening wore on, although he did continue to hold her hand under the table. Only later, when the band began to play and people started dancing, did he take her to one side and move closer to her.

"Someone will see us," she protested as he rested his hands on her waist and nuzzled her neck.

"I don't care. You smell divine."

"Rusty…good Lord." She'd drunk too much champagne and felt dizzy as he grazed his lips up to her ear. "Stop it—I'll pass out."

He chuckled, looking over his shoulder as the music changed to a slower number. He grabbed her hand. "Come on. We're dancing."

"You're supposed to ask," she protested as he marched off toward the dance floor, unable to free herself from his tight grip.

He reached the area they'd sectioned off for dancing and pulled her into his arms. "I want to hold you, and it's a good excuse to touch your butt." He put his right hand on the area as he held her other hand.

She slid it up to her waist and smiled sweetly. "Not in public. The contract, remember."

"Hmm." He pressed her hip gently with his fingers.

"What are you doing?"

"Trying to see if you're going commando."

She sighed. "I'm not."

"Oh." He looked disappointed.

She met his gaze. The room had grown warm, and his hair had rebelled against whatever product he'd used to hold it in place. It had begun to spring back into its normal style, curling around his temples and neck, shining a deep red-brown in the lights from the stage. His green eyes were affectionate, intense. Suddenly she wanted him so much it hurt.

"Wait a minute." She moved very slightly closer, so she could whisper in his ear. "You don't know what underwear I'm wearing."

"Oh?" He raised an eyebrow.

"Mm." She slipped her hand from his shoulder to his neck and ran her fingers through the hair at the nape, not missing his answering shiver. "I'm wearing an incredibly small pair of black panties. They're hardly panties at all, actually—more just a scrap of lace that hardly covers my... well, you know."

He gave a short laugh and shook his head, rolling his eyes. But she hadn't finished with him yet. She brushed his jaw with her lips, right at the point where his sideburns ended, the spot she knew made him tingle. "I'm wearing a strapless black bra that only just covers my nipples. And black stockings that come up my thighs, ending right at the point that my tan starts to fade. You know the point I mean?"

She saw his Adam's apple dip as he swallowed. His tone, when he spoke, was wry. "Yes, Faith, I know exactly the spot you mean."

She sighed. "It's a shame you won't get to see me. They're very naughty panties."

He pulled back to look at her. They studied each other for a moment.

"That would be in breach of my contract," he pointed out.

She shrugged. "Not if we addressed sin four at the same time."

"Stripping?"

"I can't think of a better outfit to watch you take off."

He grinned. Leading her off the dance floor, he pushed another glass of champagne into her hand. "Wait here."

Chapter Twenty-Six

"Where…" But he'd gone. She sat on a chair, wondering where he'd disappeared to.

She only had to wait two minutes and he was back. His eyes were mischievous, and he winked as he grabbed her hand and headed for the exit. She put her glass down hastily on a table as she tottered after him on her high heels.

"Bye, Ellie," he said to the older woman, who stood talking to some colleagues.

"See you tomorrow, Rusty," she called. "Don't do anything I wouldn't do."

He just laughed, his hand tight on Faith's. She could feel the energy pouring from him. He was happy, excited.

"Where are we going?"

He led her across the foyer, stopped by the elevator, and pressed the button. "Room fifteen," he said, taking a keycard out of his pocket.

"You booked a room here?"

"Yep." He pulled her close and nuzzled her ear again. "Because if I'm not inside you in, like, double quick time, I'm going to explode."

She inhaled sharply, lust sweeping through her, sharp and clean. "Oh my."

"Yes, indeed." He pressed light kisses to her neck. "I'm so hot for you, Faith Hillman. I'm wild about you, do you know that?"

She closed her eyes blissfully. "You're certifiable, that I do know."

The lift pinged open, and he pulled her in after him. The doors slid shut, and immediately he backed her against the wall and began kissing off her lipstick as he'd promised to do earlier that evening, making her gasp with his insistent mouth and hands.

"Pre-sex sex?" he questioned, pressing his hips against her so she was in no doubt as to how turned on he was.

Trying to gather the scrambled egg of her thoughts together into one pot, she pushed him away. "No, not this time."

He pouted. "Why?"

She met his gaze, letting the heat of her desire warm her eyes. "Because I want you hot for me."

His lips curved, and he pulled her to him again. "I'm always hot for you."

"I mean really hot. Combustible hot. Explosive hot." She slid a hand into his hair and tightened her fingers in the red locks, letting her lips hover a millimeter above his. "I want you crazy for me. I want to drive you right to the edge, so you're thinking about me, nothing else but me. I want you to beg me for release."

She pulled back so she could look into his eyes. They were half-lidded with desire, the eyes of a grown man, a man desperate to have her. She felt a swirl of exultancy, thrilled to be in charge of their sexual relationship for the first time since they'd started sleeping together. She knew that when they'd had sex before, he'd somehow held back. She didn't know why, or quite what would happen if he didn't hold back, but she was desperate to find out. She was shocking herself, but she didn't care. Maybe the champagne was making her crazy, maybe she was drunk on love. She didn't know what the future held, but she had him to herself, for now. And she intended to make the most of him.

The lift pinged again, the doors opened, and they drew apart. In silence, they walked down the corridor to the room, and he swiped the card and opened the door. She went into the room, exclaiming as she saw what a beautiful view they had of the bay, which lay spread out before them, the lights of Russell twinkling in the distance, the sea dark under the thin sliver of crescent moon.

She turned to face him. He was watching her, smiling, and he threw the keycard on the table. The room was lit only by a lamp outside somewhere in the distance. In the semi-darkness, he looked predatory, dangerous even, and she shivered at the thought of him touching her.

But it wasn't time for that yet.

She walked over to the TV and picked up the remote. "Music," she said at his questioning eyebrow.

"And there's me thinking you wanted to watch Coronation Street."

She laughed, turned on the screen, and flicked through the channels until she found a music channel. Adverts were showing, so she left it on, turning down the sound slightly, and walked over to him.

She stood before him, looking up into his dark eyes, and licked her lips. "You first."

He raised an eyebrow. "You really want me to do this?"

"Absolutely." She stepped closer and brushed his lips with her own, linking their fingers down by their sides. "I know you've got rhythm."

He chuckled. "I've never denied that."

She kissed him properly, delving her tongue into his warm mouth as she pressed her breasts against his chest. When he started to get more passionate, she pulled back and walked over to the bed, kicked off her shoes, and climbed on. Then she sat, cross-legged, facing him. The adverts had finished, so she turned up the sound. "Off you go."

He turned to look at the screen as the first song came on. It was Michael Jackson's *Thriller*.

He looked back at her. "You've got to be kidding me."

"Nuh-uh."

He folded his arms. "Faith, I am not stripping to *Thriller*. I have some pride."

"It's a very sexy song. Listen to that beat." She started to move to the music on the bed, rolling her shoulders. "Come on, Rusty. Strut your stuff."

He put his hands on his hips and glared at her. "I'm not doing the zombie dance, before you ask."

She laughed. "Come on, sexy. Get your kit off."

Slowly, sighing, he began to pull his bow tie undone.

"Oh yeah." She felt incredibly happy.

He finished undoing the tie and removed it with a flick, in time to the music. She cheered, and he threw it at her, and gradually began to tease his jacket off his shoulders. She turned up the music, her blood surging through her body as he fixed her with a hot gaze. He turned his back to her before letting the jacket drop and caught it before it fell to the floor. He tossed it onto the nearby chair, turning back to face her. The waistcoat he was wearing made him look so hot, she knew she was growing wetter by the minute.

He was getting in the swing of it now and had lost his self-consciousness. He undid the waistcoat and slipped it off. Tipping back his head, he exposed his throat to her, wincing as he struggled to get the tight top button of his shirt undone, and she inhaled at the sight of his strong jawline with its five o'clock shadow. When had he turned into such a man?

Gradually, he began to undo the rest of his buttons in time to the music, keeping his eyes fixed on her. When he got to the bottom one, he parted one side of his shirt, then the other, teasing her with a view of his broad chest, tanned and with a scattering of light brown, reddish hairs, raising his eyebrows suggestively as she clapped with approval.

Leaving the shirt on, undoing his cuffs, he levered off first one shoe, then the other, moving his hips to the music as he did so. She sighed. He was so sexy, she was tempted to forget about the sin, push him onto the bed, and have her wicked way with him, but she made herself sit still.

He bent and flicked off his socks, giving her a nice view of his ass as he did so, before he turned back and began undoing his pants, just as Vincent Price started talking. Rusty rolled his eyes but didn't stop, continuing to pull down the zipper. She sighed helplessly. She would have given anything to have that view of him—white shirt just parted to show his chest, pants open to reveal his black boxers—on a poster in her room.

Finally, he let the pants fall and kicked them off, posing in his white shirt, making her laugh. Then he walked up to her and slipped his shirt off, throwing that on top of the chair. Clad just in his black, silky boxers, he stood at the side of the bed, fixed her with a hot gaze, and slid his thumbs into the elastic. He lowered them, very slowly. She watched, looking back up at his face and then down again as he edged the silky material toward the ground. She could already see his erection straining against the fabric, and she held her breath as the material dipped lower, giving her a glimpse of a line of red-brown hair. He paused, waiting for her to look up, smiling again as he lowered the boxers millimeter by millimeter. Eventually, however, he must have taken pity on her, because he lifted the elastic over his erection, let the boxers drop to the floor and kicked them off.

He stood before her, butt-naked, hands on hips, and raised an eyebrow. "Happy now?"

Chapter Twenty-Seven

Rusty held his breath as Faith moved forward to the edge of the bed. She paused, her mouth inches from him. He ached for her and was desperate to bury himself inside her. But he wanted to see her strip too.

She licked her lips, making sure he could see. But she didn't kiss him. Slowly, she pushed herself to her feet, brushing her breasts against his erection, stroking him all the way until she faced him.

"Sit," she said. "My turn now."

He threw himself on the bed with a sigh. She was obviously determined to torture him. He propped the pillows against the headboard and lay with his hands behind his head, not attempting to hide the fact that he was still hard and ready for her.

She looked across at the TV screen, waiting for the next song to come on. He wondered what she'd do if it was *The Birdie Song*. When it started, however, he just sighed. "Oh yeah, that's fair. I get *Thriller*, you get *Heard it Through the Grapevine*."

"Luck of the draw. Deal with it."

He gave her a determined stare. "Get your clothes off, Faith. Five minutes. I'm warning you."

"Ooh." She gave a pretend shiver, which he wasn't sure she'd faked completely, and began to move to the music.

One thing she could do was dance. He'd watched her many times over the years, at parties and weddings, and sometimes at home in the evenings. She never realized how sexy she looked, never knew that he and Toby often exchanged the occasional amused glance at her innocence.

She'd clearly realized she wasn't wearing many layers and knew the removal of her clothes would only take a few seconds, so for a while she just danced. She threw herself into the music, moving her hips, rolling her shoulders, and leaned over occasionally to give him a view down her cleavage. He enjoyed the performance, feeling himself grow harder by the second. Gradually, she began to undress.

First, she slid the zipper of her skirt down and let the fabric rustle to the floor, inch by inch, to reveal sheer black thigh highs, which looked incredibly sexy. His gaze followed her hands as she pushed the skirt to the floor, stepped out of it and draped it over the chair. She stroked from her knees up her thighs, drawing attention to the tiny black panties she wore. She was right—they barely deserved the name, being only a tiny strip of lace, just covering her mound. His mouth went dry at the sight of her smooth skin, and it took all his self-control not to throw her onto the bed and plunge straight into her.

She reached around, lowered the zipper of her top, and lifted it over her head. Her breasts threatened to pop out of her strapless bra as she raised her arms, and he swallowed, nearly whimpering with desire. Laughing at the look on his face, she danced for a bit longer, taunting him with her revealing underwear before reaching around to flick open the back of her bra. She held the cups to her for a moment, giving him a sexy smile before turning her back to him and letting the bra drop. She turned back, covering her breasts with her hands, continuing to roll her shoulders with the music, before finally, slowly, she slid her hands down her body and exposed her full breasts to his heated gaze.

Just as he had, she tucked her fingers in the elastic of her panties and taunted him for a moment before eventually sliding them down her thighs. She flicked them to one side as the song ended, and came forward to stand before him, leaving the stockings on. "Well?" She climbed onto the bed. "What do you think of sin number four?"

Chapter Twenty-Eight

Faith's heart pounded at the desire in Rusty's eyes as she sat astride his legs.

He surveyed her, his lips curving. "Very nice," he said. He was breathing heavily, and as she looked down at his crotch, his erection swelled under her hungry gaze.

She crawled up him, letting the hard length of him brush against her sex, but didn't allow him to enter her. She paused when her lips were millimeters from his, her breasts touching his chest.

"Tell me what you want, Rusty." She placed light kisses on his lips then to the right along his jaw to his hairline, stopping to whisper in his ear. "How do you want me? Nice and slow?" She ran her tongue around the edge of his ear. "Do you want to kiss every inch of me, taste me, suck me and tease me until I beg you to take me?" She placed her tongue in the shell of his ear, leaving behind wetness, and blew on it gently, making him shiver. "Do you want to enter me, just the tip at first, pushing in slowly until you're completely sheathed? Do you want to thrust incredibly slowly, until we're so sensitive we can hardly bear to move, drawing out our orgasms, making me wait to come?"

She moved back and kissed across his cheek, brushed his lips—which were starting to curve—and then kissed up the left side of his jaw to his other ear. "Or do you want me hard and fast? Do you want to throw me on the bed, or up against the wall, part my legs and ram yourself into me?" She laughed at his soft groan, pressing her breasts against his chest. "Do you want to pin my hands and hold me there as you thrust into me so hard it feels like you're coming out the top of my head?" She bit his earlobe, hard enough to make him gasp. "Do you want to make me scream, Rusty? What do you want?"

She caught her breath, watching desire spark in his eyes. Finally, he wrapped his arms around her and pushed her onto her back.

"What I want," he said with much amusement, running his hand up her stockinged thigh to her bare ass, "is for you to repeat after me: 'My name is Faith Hillman, and I'm a wicked, wicked girl'."

"I'm not wicked." She resisted as he tried to roll her over.

"I'm afraid I have to contest that." He motioned for her to move onto her front, giving her an insistent stare. Catching her breath, she did so, letting him tug her tight against him. He reached over, pulled a pillow from the pile above them and tucked it under her to raise her hips. "You see, you are a very, very wicked woman."

"No, I'm not. I'm an angel."

He pulled down another pillow. "For you to bite on."

"Rusty!"

He laughed, moving up the bed so he could lean over her and whisper in her ear. "I don't think angels strip in quite such a naughty fashion." He brushed her cheek with his hand and ran his thumb over her bottom lip. She opened her mouth, caught the digit between her teeth and sucked. He groaned as she ran her tongue over the pad, and she glanced over her shoulder at him, a thrill running through her at the heat in his eyes. Oh yeah. The real Rusty was coming out to play.

He moved his hand to her breast and cupped it, rubbing his wet thumb over her nipple. She closed her eyes, sighing.

He murmured close to her ear, his deep voice making her shiver. "I don't think angels sigh like that, either."

"You don't think angels have sex? Then I'm not going to Heaven."

He gave a throaty laugh. "Oh, you're definitely not going to Heaven, Faith." He moved his hand to her butt, stroking his fingers between her legs. "There's definitely a little devil in you." He slid his fingers downwards, into the white-hot heat of her, making her gasp. "More than a little."

She opened her legs slightly, letting him slip his fingers inside her. He kept his hand there for a moment, and she tightened her internal muscles experimentally, pleased when he sighed. "You're the devil inside me," she whispered.

He removed his fingers and slid them forward, stroking her gently. "I'd like to be inside you." He nudged her legs even wider. "Wicked girl."

"I wasn't wicked until I met you."

"Oh, so I've corrupted you?"
"Definitely."
He laughed. "Ruined you?"
"Absolutely."
"Spoiled you for other men?"
"Oh." She caught her breath at his expert touch. "Completely."
"Good." He sounded vehement and she blinked.
"You don't want me to have fun with other men?"
"No." His fingers were insistent. "I want you to think of me every time you make love with someone else."
"That's unfair."
"No, it's not." He hooked a leg over her, and leaned heavily, squashing her. "You see, only I can see inside you, Faith. Only I can see the wickedness you carry deep within you. I like shocking you. You know why?"
"No." She tipped her head back, letting him bite her earlobe and graze his stubble against the delicate skin of her neck.
"Because you like to be shocked. It turns me on to watch your eyes widen and your breath catch in your throat."
"I don't do that."
He laughed. "No? Want me to prove it?"
She knew she was taunting him. Her eyes fluttered shut, and her heart thumped in anticipation. "Yes. Show me."
"Okay." He moved his hand to the back of her knee and pushed her leg up gently. Murmuring in her ear, continuing to berate her for her wickedness, he slid his fingers back between her legs. He dipped them inside her, coating them with her slippery moisture. Moving his hand back up, he rested it on her butt cheek and rubbed gently where the skin puckered, lubricating the area. Then, slowly, he slid a finger inside her.
"Oh my God." Her cheeks flamed as she gasped.
"Still think you're an angel, Faith?" He kissed her ear.
"Rusty…"
"Tell me to stop, and I will."
"Ah…" She rested her forehead on the pillow as he slowly moved his finger in and out of her. "Please…"
"Please, what?"
She couldn't answer. He bit her ear, kissed down her neck and, fastening his mouth on her skin, sucked hard.

"Ow!" She shivered with delight.

He pressed his erection against her, continuing to tease her with his finger. "Still think you're an angel?"

"You've contaminated me. You're immoral. Sinful."

"Yadda, yadda. That's why you love me." He finally removed his finger, making her sigh, and murmured in her ear, "I'm going to fuck you now, Hillman, nice and slow." He slapped her butt. "That all right with you?"

She felt faint with desire. "You can't spank me till sin number five."

"Oh… You like to tempt me, don't you?"

He went to reach over for his wallet, but she grabbed his hand. She'd been planning this. She wanted to feel him inside her, skin on skin. She knew he'd never had sex without a condom—he'd confessed that once when they were all talking one evening, and something within her was desperate to be his first. "You don't have to, if you don't want to. I'm on the pill."

He hesitated. "We should be careful."

"I'm clean, Rusty. And I trust you." She glanced over her shoulder. She could see the thought of being inside her without barriers was turning him on.

He stroked her thigh, however, and leaned forward to kiss her. "Dan would kill me if I didn't."

"I would think it's the fall that's gonna kill you, Sundance. Is that really what you're worried about?"

"I guess not." He kissed her. "Are you sure?" When she nodded, he maneuvered himself on top of her and then, in one smooth move, slid inside her. They both gasped at the exquisiteness of the sensation.

He bit her ear. "Wow. You are so wet."

"That's not a polite thing to say."

"You're exceedingly lubricated, Miss Hillman."

She bit her lip. "Don't make me laugh."

"I like making you laugh. Sex should be fun." He placed his hands either side of her and propped himself up, his muscled arms taut and strong, and she realized she couldn't do much except lie there and let herself be soundly screwed, at the mercy of his relentless thrusts.

But she wasn't ready to roll over, metaphorically speaking. "Is that all you've got, Rusty?" She pushed her hips up. "Come on, you can do better than that."

He moved a hand beneath her, lifting her farther, and plunged deeper, making her gasp. "That better?"

"Oh yes."

"And this?"

"Oh my God."

"How about this?"

"Ah…"

He kissed her shoulder. "I never thought I'd meet a woman who'd be as enthusiastic about sex as me, but you've more than matched me, Faith." He thrust again, leaning over her, his breath hot on her ear. "You drive me insane, you realize that?"

"Oh…"

He thrust harder, faster. "Completely crazy…"

"Oh—"

"Completely—"

"Rusty!"

She squealed as they came together. The orgasm was one of the strongest she'd had, and she pushed hard with her hips, screwing up her nose at the intensity of the pleasure.

"Fuck…" He dug his fingers into her waist and pulled her tightly toward him, thrusting so deep she really thought he'd speared her to the bed.

And the pillow did come in quite handy to bite on, as he'd promised.

*

Afterward, she couldn't even be bothered to move, and lay on her front, sighing, as her eyelids drifted shut.

He moved across her to the other side of the bed, and after a while she levered open her lids to see him lying on his side, head propped on a hand, watching her.

He tucked a strand of hair behind her ear. "You okay?"

"Mm." She felt sleepy and sated. She blinked slowly, studying him. "Your chest hairs are curly."

"They are indeed."

"And red. Well, reddy-brown."

"Hence the nickname."

She smiled and brushed the hairs lightly with her fingers. "You don't look like a Richard."

"I don't feel like one, either."

"You'll always be Rusty."

"Yeah. I reckon." For a moment, he didn't say anything else. Her eyelids drooped again. Then he said simply, "I'm sorry."

"For what?"

"For saying those things I said."

She frowned. "What things?"

"That you were wicked and stuff. I didn't mean them. And I'm sorry if I've corrupted you."

She gave a little chuckle. "You haven't corrupted me, Rusty."

"I have. I know I have. I mean, I know you weren't a virgin, but there was something virginal, something pure and unsullied about you. You were angelic before you slept with me."

"And now?"

His lips curved, somewhat ruefully. He touched the love-bite on her neck. "I've left a mark here…and here." He brushed her forehead. "Your eyes are tarnished. They hold a hunger that wasn't there before. They're a woman's eyes now. I've taken away your innocence, and it's not something you can ever get back."

"Maybe." She rubbed her nose lazily. "But I don't see it like that. You've liberated me. It's like I thought there was only one kind of flower, the rose, and it was the only flower any man had ever bought me, and it was nice enough, I mean I'm not going to complain when a guy buys me roses. I suspected there were other flowers out there, but the rose was pretty, and I was satisfied with it…for a while.

"But then…you came along, and opened the door to a wild garden, and you showed me all the different varieties of flowers…bluebells and daffodils and daisies and chrysanthemums… And they're all beautiful, every one, and I love them all." She yawned. "And there are still loads of flowers I haven't seen, and I need you to guide me through the garden, to hold my hand and point them all out to me, or I'll never find my way out. I trust you, Rusty. Don't you get that?"

She stopped, wondering if she'd said too much, waiting for him to make fun of her, to talk about fertilizer or hoeing or something. But he didn't.

A light frown on his face, he studied her thoughtfully. "That was probably the nicest thing anyone's ever said to me."

She shrugged. "You're easily pleased." Her eyelids drooped. She'd had a busy day, three glasses of champagne, and a mind-blowing orgasm, and sleep was overtaking her. "You know, I steal one of each flower as we walk through the garden, and I press it, and keep it here." She tapped her temple. "So I can look at them later, when it's all over."

"Don't let's talk about it. Not yet." He looked sad.

She reached out for his hand and linked their fingers. "You'll still be friends with me, won't you? I couldn't bear to lose you."

"You'll never lose me, Faith. I promise."

Satisfied, for now, she let sleep take her, conscious as she did so of the soft stroking of his thumb on her hand.

Chapter Twenty-Nine

"I wonder what she's doing now?" Toby opened his chips and shoved a good half the packet in his mouth at once.

"I have no idea," said Rusty truthfully, pretending to concentrate on his crossword. He'd suggested to Faith she keep up the pretense that she was meeting Mr. S. that Saturday night to make sure the others weren't getting suspicious. It had worked, thank God.

"They're stripping this week, aren't they?"

"Apparently." Seven down. Marvin makes Beaujolais from the fruit of this plant. Rusty smiled and wrote in Grapevine.

Toby chewed thoughtfully. "I bet she's good at it."

"Hmm." Nine across. American horror actor with a thrilling voice. He sighed and wrote Vincent Price, trying not to think of how she'd laughed when the song had come on.

"Lucky bastard," said Toby. Rusty looked up, raising an eyebrow. Toby shrugged. "Mr. S., I mean. Well, you can't tell me you haven't thought about doing it. With her."

"Might have," said Rusty, lowering his eyes.

"I mean, she's pretty hot."

"Yeah."

"She's got a great ass."

"She's also Dan's sister."

"Doesn't change the fact that she's got great tits."

Rusty gave him an exasperated look.

Toby winked at him. "You don't agree?"

"Faith has very nice breasts. Now shut up."

"What?" Toby grinned. "I bet she goes like a train."

"Dude, honestly…" Rusty glared at him.

Toby held his hands up innocently as Dan and Eve joined them at the bar. Eve glanced across, seeing Rusty's grimace. "What's going on?"

Rusty pointed at Toby with his pen. "He's being lewd."

"Huh. No change there then. What about this time?"

Toby shook his head slightly, alarmed. Rusty shrugged. Serve him right. "He's speculating what Faith's up to at this moment." As Dan glared at Toby, Rusty smirked.

"Nice," said Dan. "Not a conversation I'm interested in." He heaved a sigh, his curiosity obviously getting the better of him, in spite of his words. "What's she doing tonight, anyway?"

"Stripping," said the rest of them, all together. They all laughed.

Dan sighed. "Well, at least that's not too kinky."

Rusty received a vivid image in his head of Faith's eyes closing in bliss as he did something sinful, and he winced, trying to concentrate on the crossword. Thirteen across. A feat that demonstrates or tests the strength of a person's convictions, as an important personal sacrifice. Act of…

"What the fuck?" The other three looked over at him and he rolled up the paper and threw it into the bin. Was the universe trying to torture him?

He looked across the bar to the palms waving gently in the breeze outside. What was Faith up to? He should have talked her into seeing him again tonight. He wanted to hold her close, touch her, kiss her and make her sigh in that way he was sure only he had ever done. But he also wanted to talk to her, make her laugh. He missed her.

The others had started to talk about some TV show that he didn't watch. Surreptitiously, he slid his phone out of his pocket, flipped it open and started a new text.

Chapter Thirty

Faith scrolled through the comments on the latest post of her blog. They were getting more and more numerous with each post. The seven sins idea had clearly claimed the nation's attention. Actually, she thought Mr. S.'s secret identity was probably proving the ultimate draw to the site. Her followers liked discussing what job he did, how old he was, and their favorite topic of all was what was going to happen when sin number seven was over.

Unfortunately, she was supposed to be out with Mr. Sinful, so she couldn't post herself at that time. Instead, she read the comments, feeling slightly depressed.

Jill: Do you think they'll see each other after they finish the Seventh Sin?

Patsy: I don't think so. Wasn't that the purpose of the contract?

Jill: Yeah, I know. They just seem to get on so well.

Faith sighed. Of course they got on. They'd been friends for a hundred years. But she couldn't tell them that.

Jules: I don't know that either of them is looking for a long-term thing.

Lily: Yeah, but, if it happens, you shouldn't really ignore it, should you? That type of thing doesn't come around very often.

Ophelia: Do you think they're in love then?

Faith's heart seemed to stop for a moment. She didn't want them discussing this on her blog. And she certainly didn't want Rusty reading it, but she couldn't say that. She got up, went into the kitchen, and poured herself a drink. This whole thing was starting to get hugely tangled, like a dog on a lead running round and round a table. She sat back down, her hand shaking slightly. A few more comments had popped up while she was away.

WendyS: Oh yeah, they're definitely in love.

Karen: Nah, they're just good friends. You don't have to be in love to have really good sex.

Faith sipped her drink. Huh. It seemed like everybody had a view. But then if she and Rusty didn't know themselves, what chance did her followers have of getting it right?

SashaT: I don't know that we should be discussing this. They're going to read this later, and it could make things awkward for them.

Patsy: I agree. It's none of our business—we're here to discuss sex, not love.

Lily: Trouble is, one can easily lead to the other. The question is whether they both feel the same way.

Faith closed her laptop lid. She didn't want to read any more. She bit her lip as tears stung her eyes. The evening at The Harrington had been bittersweet. Although she'd had her little revelation about the fact that she was falling for Rusty, Faith had known she was still going to have to go through with the sins, because if she backed out, he'd know what was going on in her head. And besides, she didn't want to back out. What she had said was true—he was showing her things about herself she'd never known, and taking her on an exciting journey. She didn't regret starting the affair—or whatever she should call it. But she was very much going to regret ending it.

Unless… She pulled up her legs, wrapped her arms around them, and rested her chin on her knees. Did it have to end? She knew Rusty's views on long-term relationships, and knew he didn't intend to settle down, ever. He was scared that if he allowed himself to love someone, he would hurt them terribly, like every other man in his family seemed to do. Of course, it was rubbish. Wasn't it? He didn't have a cruel bone in his body. He would make an excellent husband and a wonderful father.

But surely his sister-in-law, his mother, and his grandmother had all thought the same thing before they married the other men in his family? They'd all fallen in love, had all thought marriage would be blissful, forever. And they'd all been horribly disappointed. Faith had heard Rusty's mum, Anna, talk about his dad, Luke, and had been shocked at how vitriolic she'd been. Anna tended to keep her feelings to herself when Rusty was around, but when Faith had asked something about Luke, Anna had not bothered to hide her feelings for the man she'd once loved but now hated with a passion.

Of course, part of the problem in his family was the alcoholism that passed from father to son. All the Thorne men suffered and, when drunk, all of them turned nasty. Faith hadn't seen it first-hand. But Rusty had told her about how his father reacted when under the influence—how he'd once wrecked the house, slammed Cole into the wall, yelled at Rusty until he was in tears, and beaten Anna almost senseless, driven mad by some unprovoked fit of jealousy that he couldn't even remember in the morning.

Rusty saw alcohol as an evil demon, a kind of malevolent spirit that possessed the Thorne men when they drank. He never talked about it in front of his friends, and never seemed to mind if they drank, because he obviously only saw it as a family problem. Faith could understand that, because when Dan got drunk he became incredibly funny, Toby just tended to go to sleep, Eve got giggly, and Faith herself, well, it just made her want to dance.

But Rusty had never let himself have a drink, so none of them—including him—had any idea what he was like when he was drunk. He was terrified it would transform him into a monster, like Dr. Jekyll drinking the potion. He was so scared of turning into Hyde that he wouldn't go near alcohol, and she couldn't blame him for that, even though she couldn't imagine him turning nasty.

But it didn't make sense that he'd decided he was too dangerous to let himself ever get close to a woman. Even if alcohol did change him, he never drank, so where was the danger? She knew it went deeper than that, though. He'd seen all the men in his family hurt their women—had seen his grandmother, mother, aunt, and sister-in-law cry because of what the Thorne men had done to them. And sweet, gorgeous, honest, loyal Rusty couldn't bear to let himself ever get in a position where he might do something so terrible to someone he loved.

Of course, he didn't realize he was doing that to every girl he went out with who wanted to continue to see him. Or maybe he did, but thought it couldn't possibly hurt them as much after half a dozen dates as it would if he was horrible to them after a long-term relationship. During one of their late-night sessions around the pool, he'd once announced he wished he could be a monk. They'd all burst out laughing at the thought of Rusty being celibate, but Faith could still remember the serious look that had appeared on his face before he, too, had started to smile. He'd meant it—he didn't want to want women. He wished he didn't have physical urges. It was just unfortunate he had a sex drive that could power a rocket to the moon and back.

One day, someone would convince him to have a real relationship. A woman would come along who he felt strongly enough about, a woman who would be able to persuade him that she was worth the risk.

But was that woman her?

At that moment, her phone sang in her handbag, letting her know a text had arrived. She flipped it open. Rusty's number was at the top. How ironic. She felt herself blush, as if he'd picked up she'd been thinking of him. What was wrong with her? How could she be blushing when he was a mile away?

She read the text, her heart thumping. *What are you up to? Has Mr. S. left yet?*

Smiling, she sent back: *Yeah, he's gone. Miss him :(*

A minute later, another text came through. *He misses you too. Want to meet up?*

She returned: *That's not in his contract.*

After a couple of minutes, as if he was thinking what to say, he replied: *It's Rusty asking, not Mr. S.*

She gave a short laugh. She shouldn't see him. She was only making it harder on herself. But that thought kept ringing through her head, as if it were one of those bells above a shop door. Was that woman her? And his words, *He misses you too*, gave her hope.

She texted back. *Lol. That's ok then. Stone Store, 10 mins?* She started getting ready—took off her trackpants, slipped on her jeans, brushed her hair, and put on a slick of lipgloss, in anticipation of his reply.

Mr. S. is jealous. But Rusty will be there. See you then.

Laughing, she clicked the phone shut and headed for the door.

Chapter Thirty-One

When she got there, his car was already in the car park of the lovely bar and restaurant that overlooked the Kerikeri inlet. She parked next to him and walked past the small wishing well to the Stone Store, the oldest stone building in New Zealand. He sat on the steps to the Store and watched her as she walked up to him, a small smile on his face.

"Hey," she said, perching beside him.

He shifted aside a little to make room. "Hey." He wore his usual tight black jeans and black shirt, sleeves rolled up. His hair was getting long and needed cutting, and it curled around his ears and neck. He ran his hand through it. "I look scruffy, I know."

"Yeah." She met his gaze, seeing something lurking in his green eyes. "What's up?"

He shrugged and picked at some mud on the knee of his jeans. "Nothing. Just wanted to see you, that's all."

She didn't say anything. But she nudged him with her elbow. He nudged her back, and they laughed.

"Wanna Coke?" she asked, nodding toward the bar.

"Sure."

They stood and walked across the road. It was about seven o'clock, and daylight was starting to fade. The weather was warm and humid, the cicadas calling in the bush surrounding the inlet, and a trickle of sweat ran between her breasts. They didn't hold hands—she was with Rusty, after all, not Mr. S.—but still she felt a little zing of electricity as he brushed his arm against hers, enough of a zing to send yet another flush to her cheeks.

The bar was stuffy, so they bought a drink and made their way out the back to the grassy bank overlooking the inlet. There were no free tables, so they sat on the grass under an oak tree, Faith cross-legged, Rusty with his long legs stretched out, leaning back against the trunk. He looked melancholic, although he smiled when she winked at him.

"I've been reading a great book on women in Anglo-Saxon England," she said.

"Oh?" His eyes lit up.

She proceeded to tell him what she'd learned. She knew he'd interject with his own facts and wanted to see him glow, as he always did when he was talking about history. He didn't disappoint her, and was soon telling her about Sutton Hoo and West Stow and pottery techniques. She listened, glad to be able to study him as she did so, pleased to make him happy.

"You haven't got a clue what I'm talking about, have you?" he said eventually.

"I do so! Sutton Hoo. King Raedwald. No skeletal remains present, probably because of the acidic soil."

He laughed. "I stand corrected."

"I like history. And I like listening to you talk about it. You don't bore me."

"I'm glad to hear it."

She smiled. She liked being back with her old friend Rusty again. For the moment, there was no sign of the man who'd driven her wild in bed, no heat in his eyes. He looked across at her, met her gaze, and held it for a while.

"We'll still be able to do this afterward, won't we?" he asked eventually.

"Do what?"

"Talk like this. It's not going to be odd?"

She broke her gaze away and looked across the inlet. Some teenagers were making their way across the rocks, the girls giggling, the guys showing off. Ten-to-one several of them would be in the water before they reached the other side.

His talk about the ending of their affair depressed her. She was stupid to think she'd be the one to change his mind on long-term relationships. How should she answer him? She knew what the truth would be. That of course it would be odd, because she'd have to watch him bring other girls into the bar, his arm draped casually around their shoulders, as she'd seen him do before so many times. He might even kiss them in front of her, the thought of which made her heart stutter and her throat tighten painfully. How would she feel on seeing he'd given a new girlfriend a hickey, thinking of him thrusting into her from behind, murmuring she was the best he'd ever had as he fastened his warm mouth on her neck? It made her feel sick.

Her fingers tightened in the grass, but she made them relax. She sipped her wine and gave him a smile. "Of course we'll still be able to talk."

He nodded, but she wasn't sure she'd convinced him. She didn't want to talk about it anymore—she'd start crying, she was sure. Instead, she changed the subject again and asked him about the upcoming ERO inspection at the school, getting him to tell her about what schemes of work he needed to prepare, and he didn't mention the matter again. They talked for an hour as the sun gradually set, and eventually the grass grew cool on her legs. Regretfully, she said she ought to think about going home.

They walked through the bar to their cars. She leaned against hers, and he leaned against his, just a foot away.

"So, until next Saturday?" he asked.

"Yep."

"Where are we off to?"

"Actually, Eve and Dan are going away for the weekend, so I thought we could stay at my place, if you like."

He smiled. "Sure. And what sin's this one?"

For the first time that evening, she felt her heart rate increase a little. "Wrath."

"Hmm." He studied her, his eyes fixed on hers, and his smile grew as a blush filled her cheeks. "That's my girl."

She touched the back of her hand to her face. "I don't know how you do it. You could make me blush from a hundred yards."

He stepped closer, still smiling, but didn't say anything. He laced the fingers of his right hand through the fingers of her left down by their sides. Then he bent his head and kissed her.

We're in public, she thought, panicking a little, her heart racing, but his lips were so soft, the kiss so gentle, she couldn't bring herself to pull away. He placed his left arm around her, still holding his keys, and tightened his grip so she had to press herself against him. She put her hand on his chest and opened her mouth automatically under his, even though she was trying to keep the kiss light and friendly. He answered with a sweep of his tongue, and that was it, she threaded her fingers up through his hair, and he released her hand so he could pull her against him. White-hot heat flared between them, making her gasp, and she could feel her nipples tightening, an ache beginning between her thighs. Her body desired him, even though she was trying to keep herself distant.

In reply, he pushed her against her car, his body even more traitorous than hers, displaying his passion quite obviously in the hardness of his erection when he pressed his hips against her.

Somewhere at the back of the car park, a car horn tooted, and Rusty lifted his head sharply, even though the driver wasn't targeting them. He didn't pull back, though, and Faith could feel the pounding of his pulse in his neck beneath her fingers. His eyes were dark as they searched hers, his fingers digging into her waist. "How am I going to do it?" he asked hoarsely. "How am I going to be able to let you go?"

Her heart swelled. More than anything, she wanted to ask him to go back to the bar with her and tell Dan and the others they were seeing each other. Then she wanted to take him home to her bed, where they could wake up with each other next morning and for all the mornings after that.

But his eyes, although passionate, were frustrated, bordering on angry. He didn't want to feel this way about her. She had to play this carefully. Women had done it since before the dawn of time—Cleopatra, Eleanor Woodville, Anne Boleyn, Wallis Simpson… They and many more both before and after had had to be clever, conniving, to get the man they wanted. And she was going to have to do the same.

"Don't think about that now," she said softly. She brushed her lips against his. "Think about next Saturday." She let her lips curve and gave him a saucy look. "I have fur-lined handcuffs."

As she'd hoped, the frustration faded from his eyes, desire taking its place. "Fur-lined?"

"Well, play ones obviously. They're symbolic. That's the point, isn't it? It's about trust. You don't have to really tie someone up."

He seemed amused. "Huh."

"You don't agree?"

He nuzzled her ear. "Where's the fun when you know you can escape at any moment?"

A frisson of excitement rippled through her. "Rusty!"

"What?" He pressed his lips to her neck. "Don't tell me the thought of me chaining you to the bed and keeping you as my sex slave doesn't turn you on."

"I…" Oh dear. "Um…"

He lifted his head. He was smiling, and he kissed her nose. "That's what I'm here for. To show you the flower garden." He sounded like he was trying to convince himself.

"Absolutely."

"That's my role," he said.

"Yes, of course. And you're so good at it. How did you become such a gardener?"

He gave a short laugh. "Have a good week, Faith. Thanks for meeting me tonight."

"I enjoyed it." She reached up to kiss him one more time.

"Me too." He touched her cheek with the back of his hand. "I always do, with you."

Chapter Thirty-Two

Faith Hillman's Blog

So... we're onto Wrath. This is one of the (many) areas in which I lack experience. I've read a lot about BDSM, both fictional and real accounts. I have to say... I don't quite get it. I'm not into pain. I don't see how anyone can find it sexy. I don't particularly understand the sub/dom thing, although I suppose I get that more. I like a man to take charge in the bedroom, although I don't think I could play the submissive role without getting indignant or laughing! I don't like the idea of whips and chains or leather stuff. Role play... yeah, maybe, if it's fun. And bondage... hmm, perhaps I can see how that would be sexy... *drifts off into daydream about Mr. S. tying me up...* So we'll see. I think I might struggle with this one. I'll let you know how it goes.

*

Excerpt from the 832 comments
SueAnn: I totally agree. Don't get the pain thing at all.
Georgia: Well, the line between pleasure and pain is very thin, I think, that's the point.
MrS69: Oh, it's wide enough that I'll never cross it, believe me.
Patsy: Mr. S.!
MrS69: Hello :)
SashaT: Ooh, talk to us, Mr. S. Tell us what you're going to do to Faith.
MrS69: LOL, no!
HelenB: So you're not into BDSM of any kind?
MrS69: I'm not into pain, but luckily I don't think Faith is either. I don't think there's anything wrong with this kind of thing as long as everyone's consenting—it's just not my thing. I enjoy sex enough without all the bells and whistles!
Georgia: So you're not going to tie her up?
MrS69: I didn't say that...
Faith: Oh dear.
MrS69: Hello, sweetheart.

SueAnn: Faith!

HelenB: Hey, Faith! Sounds like you're in for some fun!

Faith: Is that what you call it? *trembles*

MrS69: Heh. No need to worry, honey. I promise you'll enjoy it.

Faith: *faints*

Yolanda: I am absolutely green, Faith. I so envy you.

Trinny: Me too!

Patsy: I hope you'll give us a full rundown afterward.

Faith: Of course! There are no secrets between friends :)

MrS69: I must admit, I never thought I'd share my bedroom exploits with the whole of Oceania. Have you seen how many comments you're getting now, Faith?

SueAnn: You realize you can have the pick of any woman you meet after this, though?

MrS69: Hmm…

Faith: Oh, stop it. His ego's going to be the size of Australia at this rate.

HelenB: LOL.

SashaT: So come on, tell us what you're planning. How are you going to experiment with Wrath?

Faith: I'm thinking about dressing up as a schoolgirl, and then he can chastise me.

SueAnn: Ooh…

MrS69: Give you a hundred lines, you mean?

Yolanda: Snort!

MrS69: Oh, you mean put you across my knee? Sure…

Patsy: Jeez, you two.

Georgia: So you're going to try a bit of hanky-spanky?

MrS69: Depends if she's been a bad girl.

Faith: Okay, I'm signing off before I pass out from lack of oxygen.

MrS69: Hehe. See you later, sexy.

Patsy: You two are just the sweetest. Have fun.

Chapter Thirty-Three

It had been a busy week. Rusty had been preparing for the ERO inspection, plus he'd had a parent evening and an after-school staff meeting. They'd texted and emailed each other regularly, but he hadn't had a chance to see Faith all week.

Consequently, he was desperate to see her, firstly because he'd missed her and he was starting to dislike being apart from her, and secondly because he was as horny as a stallion in a field of brood mares. Sitting in the car in front of the rugby ground, he tapped his fingers on the steering wheel and tried to think about inspectors and schemes of work and Henry the Eighth wall displays in an effort to distract himself. He'd been daydreaming all week about handcuffing Faith to the bed and torturing her with various pleasure-inducing methods. Consequently, sporting a hard-on the size of the Sky Tower, he was beginning to worry about embarrassing himself by arriving before the train entered the station, so to speak.

The passenger door opened, making him jump, and Faith slid in beside him. She smelled of autumn, and she looked happy and bubbly as she turned in her seat to look at him. "Hey, you."

"Hey," he said, smiling.

She didn't say anything else but sat with her back against the car door, her eyes dancing.

"What?" She looked gorgeous with her long brown hair tumbling around her shoulders, her beautiful chocolate-brown eyes wide and teasing.

"I thought this time would never come. I've been thinking about it all week."

"Me too." He let his gaze drift to where she'd unbuttoned her white shirt low enough to expose a hint of cleavage and a swell of pale breast. He closed his eyes for a moment, tapping his fingers on the steering wheel again. Down, boy.

She laughed and moved toward him, leaning across so she could brush her lips against his. "Do you need some pre-sex sex, sweetheart?" She moved her mouth to his ear and murmured, "Poor Rusty. All wound up and no one to take it out on." She kissed back to his lips and he sighed, recognizing she was teasing him.

"Unfair," he mumbled.

"Is it?" She moved her hands to his pants, and to his surprise, she undid the zipper.

"Hey."

"Just relax. I've been planning this all week."

He tried to push her away. "I can't, not now—I'm supposed to meet someone in a minute."

"Who?"

"Just a friend. He's got something I need to borrow."

"Oh. Let me know if he turns up." Before he could stop her, she had her hands on his pants again.

"Faith!" He was genuinely shocked and tried once again to push her hands away, but she resisted firmly, and within seconds she'd pulled down his boxers, releasing his very eager erection.

"Oh yeah." She closed a hand around him in delight.

"Whatever happened to foreplay?" He tried to tuck himself back in, scanning the domain hurriedly for the person he was supposed to meet.

"Foreplay's to get you in the mood. I've been in the mood since about twelve p.m. Sunday."

His laughter at her echo of his own words came to an abrupt halt as she shifted in the seat and lowered her head. "Really, Faith, what's got into you? I—oh!" He caught his breath when she closed her mouth around him, and his hands curled into fists as he braced himself against the dashboard. "That's really not a good idea."

She ignored him and continued to caress him with her lips and tongue. She stroked him with her hand and took him deeper and deeper inside until she was nearly swallowing him whole, and it was too much for him to bear. Keyed up, extremely turned on by her forcefulness, he gave in, and in less than a minute, came in her mouth. He tipped his head back on his seat, and his left hand slipped into her hair and cupped her head as she murmured her pleasure.

When he'd finished, she licked him slowly from base to tip as if he were a melting ice lolly and kindly tucked him back in his boxers before she pushed herself up to look at him. He'd been staring at the roof of the car, but now lowered his head to look at her.

She burst out laughing and kissed his cheek. "You should see the look on your face."

"Well, it's hardly surprising. You're turning into a regular little harlot."

"Hmm, and whose fault's that?" Lifting herself up, before he could stop her, she moved across him and straddled him in the driver's seat, squishing herself between him and the steering wheel.

"Faith…"

"What?" She rubbed her breasts against him and nibbled his ear. "It's all down to you, Rusty. You drive me crazy, you know that?"

He rested his hands on her waist, sighing. Her body was soft and pliant, and she smelled wonderful. He didn't know what had gotten into her, but he wished they could bottle it—he'd make a fortune.

A sharp knock on the window made them both jump violently.

Rusty saw the police officer's uniform and sighed. He should have known that was going to happen.

"Fuck!" Faith lifted herself up onto the steering wheel and promptly sat on the horn, making all three of them jump. She panicked and fell into the passenger seat in a most ungainly fashion.

Laughing as he zipped up his pants, Rusty pressed the button to lower the window. "Evening, officer."

The police officer leaned on the windowsill and surveyed the inhabitants of the car with a raised eyebrow. "Good evening, sir. Evening, miss."

"Er, hi." Faith had turned completely scarlet.

Rusty looked back at the police officer, who was trying very hard not to laugh. Rusty winked, encouraging the deception a bit longer.

"I was expecting a couple of seventeen-year-olds, judging by the steamed-up windows," said the officer.

"It's her fault," said Rusty. "Couldn't keep her hands off me." He heard Faith's gasp and bit his lip.

"There are more appropriate places to carry out an assignation," the officer said to Faith.

"I know, I'm so sorry, officer. It won't happen again." She was absolutely mortified.

Rusty couldn't torture her any longer and laughed, patting her on the knee. "It's all right, love, Andy's a friend. He's just teasing." Andy winked in reply.

Her eyes widened, and she glared at them both, making them laugh. Andy passed Rusty the brown envelope he'd been holding. "I can see you'll put them to good use," he said, glancing back at Faith with amusement.

Grinning, Rusty put the envelope in the space between him and Faith. He nodded at Andy. "Cheers, mate."

"Take it easy. Nice to have met you." He nodded at Faith.

"I can't say the feeling's mutual," she said, but smiled anyway as he winked and walked off.

Rusty turned the key in the ignition and started the car. "Don't glare at me like that."

"That was very mean." She looked at the brown envelope. "What did he bring you?"

"Have a look." He reversed the car out, put it into drive, and headed for her house, glancing across as she lifted up the flap of the envelope. Her eyes widened again and she looked up at him as she removed the contents. It was a pair of handcuffs. He winked. "Real ones."

"Oh my God." She stared at him. "And the officer…he's going to know…"

"Yes, Faith. Now I'm not the only one who knows what a hussy you are." He lifted her hand and kissed her fingers.

She went quiet for a while, and he wondered if he'd overstepped the mark. As he pulled up outside her house and turned off the engine, he took her hand again. "You okay? I'm sorry I teased you. I shouldn't have done that."

She gave him a happy grin. "Sweetheart, I'd just gone down on you in a public place. I deserved everything I got." She gave him a warning glance. "You're not to blame for everything I do, you know. I do have a mind of my own."

"You still want to go ahead with tonight?"

"Absolutely. Why on earth wouldn't I?" When he didn't say anything, she leaned over and kissed him. "You are so sweet sometimes. Come on." She picked up the brown envelope and got out of the car.

He followed her inside the house, where she took his hand and led him into her bedroom. He'd seen inside once before, when he'd carried a suitcase through for her, but this was the first time he'd had a good look around. The room was bright, full of color, with spiral mobiles turning in the breeze as she opened the sliding door to the garden, and a double bed covered in a deep purple duvet. He noticed the headboard was made of slats of wood and smiled. Perfect for handcuffs.

"Do you want a drink?" She put her handbag on the table, emptied the handcuffs onto the bed, and tucked the key into the pocket of her jeans.

"No, I'm good."

She came up to him and put her arms around him. "You sure?"

"Mm." Once again he could smell her perfume, something light and flowery, mixed with the scent of the autumn evening coming through the doors. He wrapped her in his arms and held her for a while, enjoying the softness of her body against him. "You smell good."

"You too." She sniffed his shirt. "I like that aftershave, whatever it is."

He made a mental note to wear it again next time they were due to meet. "Thank you."

"You're very welcome, Mr. Thorne." She placed a light kiss on his neck above the collar of his shirt, making him shiver. "Ooh. Do that again." She kissed up to his ear, and he couldn't help but shudder. "Wow. You are so sexy."

"And you're driving me insane today." He dropped his hands to her hips, pulled her toward him and kissed her properly. "What has gotten into you?"

"You," she said, her fingers going to the buttons of her white shirt. She began to undo them from the bottom up, still kissing him, and slipped the top off, exposing her bra.

He pulled back a little to look at her, his heart rate speeding up as he saw the white lacy cups only just managing to hold in her breasts. She was already fumbling at the zipper of her jeans, and he watched as she pushed them down and kicked them off. She wore white lace panties and sheer thigh highs, and a surge of desire, hot and erotic, fizzed through his veins.

"You like?" she asked as he began to push her backward, over to the window.

"Oh yeah." He kissed her until they bumped against the glass and then released her to turn her around.

She placed her palms against the window, leaving hot prints on the glass, and pushed herself back, rubbing her butt into his groin. "Do I turn you on?"

He laughed and stroked her thigh, enjoying the feel of the strip of soft skin between the top of the thigh highs and her panties. "What do you think?"

"Tell me."

"You turn me on. God, Faith, you're driving me mad tonight."

"That's the plan." She sighed as he stroked his other hand up her body and brushed her nipple beneath the lace cup. "You like me being naughty?"

"I think you need to be severely reprimanded." He slapped her butt.

She pushed her hips back again. "You think so? Perhaps you should put me across your knee, like you said."

He was so hard now he could have been made of concrete. He wanted to make her sigh and see her eyes widen the way they did when he shocked her. "Don't tempt me." Another slap followed—this one even harder.

This time she gasped, tipping back her head, her eyes glazing as she inhaled and said, "Ow!"

Instantly he felt a surge of guilt. "Jeez, I'm sorry."

She shook her head, dazed. "What?"

He turned her, closed his eyes, and wrapped his arms around her. What was he doing? He was like a bad uncle who taught a four-year-old to burp the national anthem and say swear words. He should serenade her, take her out to dinner and buy her flowers and chocolates, not slap her on the butt so hard his fingers left a red mark. She was his friend, the sister of his best mate, not some girl he'd picked up in a bar. Dan would kill him if he knew what he was up to.

She put her hands on his chest and pushed him away. "What's the matter?"

"I'm sorry. I shouldn't have done that."

"What are you talking about?"

He couldn't put his remorse into words. "I'm sorry," was all he could say again.

"Rusty…"

He ran a hand through his hair. "I should go."

She put her hands on her hips. "Don't freak out on me again."

"I can't do this, Faith. You're my friend, and Dan—"

"Don't you dare mention my brother!" She pushed him hard and he stumbled back, hit the bed, and fell onto the mattress. She stood over him, eyes blazing. "Move up."

"What?"

"Move up the bed."

He did so, eyeing her warily. He'd never seen her so cross.

"Lie down," she snapped.

"Faith…"

"Lie down!"

Chapter Thirty-Four

He lay back, and she climbed onto the bed and sat astride him. She looked like an Amazon, absolutely furious, and his heart thudded as she leaned over and glared at him with her beautiful brown eyes. "Now you listen to me," she said firmly. "Contrary to popular opinion, Rusty Thorne, you are not the center of the whole fucking universe. I have a mind of my own, and I am not some little fifteen-year-old you're deigning to deflower. I'm only four years younger than you, for Christ's sake."

"Okay."

"You may have been the first person to show me a thing or two, but that does not mean I wouldn't have done these things if it wasn't for you. You've not infected me, and you're not the bloody Marquis de Sade, corrupting your way through the female population of Kerikeri. You hear me?"

"Yes, ma'am."

She met his gaze, and for the first time he saw a hint of humor flicker in her eyes. She sat up and studied him coolly. "Boy," she said. "Do you need to be taught a lesson."

"Um…"

She reached behind her and picked up the handcuffs. Then she beckoned him with the other hand. "Give me your wrist."

Alarm rose within him, and he pushed himself up onto his elbows. "Oh no."

"What?" She tipped her head at him, mocking him. "You can deal it, but you can't take it?" She leaned forward until her lips were inches from his. "You signed a contract, Rusty. You promised to do whatever I asked, remember?"

Shit. "Yes, but—"

"No buts. You trust me, don't you?"

He sighed. How could he get out of that? "Yes, I guess." Closing his eyes, he offered her his wrist. The metal closed around it, and she pushed him back. She leaned over him as she lifted his arms above his head, slid the handcuffs around one of the slats of the bed, and closed the remaining cuff around his other wrist.

He opened his eyes and looked straight into her amused brown gaze. "Hah," she said. "Sucker. Now I'm going to take all the money out of your wallet, strip you, and leave you for Eve to find."

"Faith…"

"I'm kidding! Jeez." She sat back and studied him thoughtfully.

Rusty lifted his arms, hearing a clunk as metal met wood. He felt disturbingly vulnerable. Why had he suggested this? Served him right for thinking he was in charge.

"I'll be back in a sec." She lifted herself off him and walked out the room.

Crap. He stretched his arms to test his reach and found he could just put his hands behind his head, which almost made it feel as if he was lying there out of choice. This wasn't going to end well. He'd annoyed her, and she was going to make him suffer for it. He glared at his groin, which was clearly excited at the thought, and sighed, looking up at the ceiling. What was she doing? He hoped it didn't involve candle wax. Or anything sharp. He wasn't into pain.

After a few seconds, she reappeared, and he was relieved to see only a bottle in her hands. She placed it on the bedside table, and he glanced over, seeing some kind of massage oil.

She raised an eyebrow. "What? You thought I was going to bring water and jumper cables?"

"Don't even joke about it." He watched as she climbed back on the bed and started to undo the belt of his jeans. "Faith…"

"Ssh." She laid a finger briefly against his lips.

"Yes, but—"

She stopped, got off the bed, and walked over to her chest of drawers. She rifled about in one of the drawers, extracted something, and came back to him. She held a silky scarf up. "You keep talking," she told him calmly, "and I'm going to gag you."

"Fucking hell." His heart thumped as she started undoing his jeans again.

Her eyes were dark, intense. "I'm not your trainee, Rusty. And I'm not your protégée. I may be a step or two behind you, but that doesn't make me your subordinate. Understand?"

"Yes, ma'am."

She nodded, amused. "Good." Finally undoing the tight button on his jeans, she pulled down the zipper and slid them off, dropping them on the floor. Leaving his boxers on, she came back to sit astride him and looked down at his shirt.

"You'll have to let me go to get that off," he said, then clamped his mouth shut as she pretended to reach for the scarf.

She fixed him with a determined stare, took hold of both sides of his shirt and, with a big yank, ripped it open, scattering buttons in all directions.

"Whoa!" He lifted his arms automatically, coming to an abrupt halt as the metal clanked on the wood. She pushed him back and spread the sides of the shirt to reveal his bare chest. Then she reached over and got the oil.

"Did I ever tell you I took a course in massage?" She poured a small amount onto her hands, returned the bottle to the table, and began to rub her hands together, warming the oil.

"No."

"See. There's a lot about me you don't know." She placed her hands together on his chest and then parted them, smearing the oil across his ribs. She bent forward to kiss him. "Relax, sweetheart. I'm not going to hurt you."

He said nothing, watching her as she ran her hands up to his neck, across his shoulders beneath his shirt and then down his body again, stopping briefly to circle her fingers on his nipples. He gave her a warning look, and she giggled, continuing to massage him. Gradually, he started to relax as she took time to work her fingers into his muscles, moving to his legs, seeming to enjoy the way her fingers slipped over his skin.

He closed his eyes, sighing, as she stroked down his thighs, her hands strong but gentle. She worked down to his feet, massaging them softly, and then moved back up and started on his arms, caressing his biceps and triceps beneath the short sleeves of his shirt.

He studied her, feeling a wave of affection, strangely touched by her tender exploration of his body. She glanced at him occasionally, and each time he felt his heart thump in response, like a teenager caught peeking at a neighbor sunbathing in the back yard.

Eventually, to his disappointment, she finished and lifted herself off him, wiping her hands on a towel. Then she leaned over him.

Dropping her head, she kissed him, brushing his tongue with her own, and he returned it, relaxed after her gentle ministrations.

She lifted her head. "I'll be back in a minute," she said, and disappeared again.

He watched her go, sighing, and heard her moving about in the kitchen. It took her a few minutes before she came back this time, and when she did, she was carrying two things: a glass of iced water, and a mug of what smelled like tea.

She placed them both on the bedside table. Then she glanced at him. She smiled impishly, and he felt the first twinge of alarm.

"Faith…"

She raised an eyebrow, and he closed his mouth. Standing beside him, first she reached behind her back, unclipped her bra, and let it fall to the ground. She slid her panties down, leaving her stockings on. Leaning over him, she lifted the waistband of his boxers, slid them down his legs, and threw them on top of her own clothes. She raised her eyebrows admiringly at his erection, and he rolled his eyes.

She sat beside him, leaned over, and picked up the glass of water. She took a sip, sucking up one of the ice cubes, and circled it around her mouth. He watched her, his heart beginning to pound again.

She met his gaze, her eyes challenging, daring. Leaning forward, the ice cube between her teeth, she lowered her mouth to his right nipple and rubbed the ice over it.

An electric shock shot through him. "Jeez, Faith."

She circled the ice cube in her mouth and pressed it to the other nipple, letting the cube melt on his hot skin and the icy water flow over his ribs. He sucked in his breath, looking up at the ceiling, cursing quietly. She lifted her head, her eyes dancing, and moved over him, bending to rub the ice over his lips. He took the cube from her and crunched it between his teeth, glaring at her.

She studied him, lips pursed. Then she took another cube from the glass. She circled it once again in her mouth and lifted herself off the bed. Before he realized what she was going to do, she sat astride his legs, arms braced on either side of his hips.

"Faith…"

She crunched the cube, her eyes intense. Then, ignoring his look of alarm, she lowered her mouth right over the tip of his erection.

"Fuck!" The icy cold sensation shot through him, pleasure and pain rolled into one.

She gave a short laugh as his muscles tightened, and she sucked gently until her mouth began to warm. Lifting her head, she reached over for the tea. She took a large mouthful and swallowed before lowering her head once again. He steeled himself, but still gave a jolt as her hot mouth closed over him.

"Oh…" He looked up at the ceiling, his breath coming in sharp gasps, thinking he couldn't possibly get harder than he already was. He glared at her, wanting her to end it, to finish him. Undaunted, however, she did it twice more, alternating hot and cold, and he screwed up his eyes each time, trying not to yell out at the shocking pleasure of it, more than aware of the silky tie still lying by her side.

Eventually she must have taken pity on him, because she lifted her head, breathing heavily, he noticed, and her nipples were tight. Slowly, she moved up the bed, brushing his erection as she did so. She paused when she was leaning over him, straddling his hips.

She studied him, and all he could do was look helplessly into her eyes.

"I'm going to fuck you now, Thorne. Nice and slow." She tipped her head to the side. "That all right with you?"

He closed his eyes and flexed his hands, but didn't say anything. Talk about being given a taste of your own medicine.

She moved atop him and pushed down her hips, and he slid very slowly into her. She was incredibly wet and very swollen, and he exclaimed as she took him inside, closing hot and velvety around him.

She pushed herself upright and widened her thighs, so he slid even farther inside her. She tipped her head back and arched her spine, and he opened his eyes and watched her speechlessly, thinking he'd never seen anything as beautiful as this mad, incredibly passionate woman, who'd decided to teach him a lesson and prove he wasn't the only one who could educate where sex was concerned.

Looking down at him, she let out a long sigh and licked her lips. "I can feel you all the way up, right to the top. Can you feel that?"

He nodded wordlessly. She leaned forward, nibbled his bottom lip, and kissed around his jaw. Then she ran her hands up his chest and across his arms, admiring his biceps. "You're so gorgeous. You drive me crazy, you know that?"

"I'm beginning to understand."

"I've been thinking." She lifted her hips, letting him slide in and out of her.

"Oh no." He shivered.

She kissed his ear. "About what other sins I could invent."

"Oh?"

"Mm." She moved slowly. "Ever had a threesome, Rusty?"

He closed his eyes.

"Well?"

"No…"

She gave a sexy laugh. "I'll find us a nice horny girl, someone with a big chest, and we can play with her all night."

He opened his eyes and glared at her. "There's absolutely no way you're going to Heaven now, Faith Hillman."

She chuckled. "I have other suggestions. You wanna hear them?"

"No."

"How about we make a video of ourselves doing the rudest thing we can think of, and post it on YouTube?"

"Oh for the love of…"

She moved up and down gently, each time pushing back so he slid deeply into her. "Or how would you like to watch me dance in a strip club, pole dance in front of an audience of men, and you can watch me do lap dances for them, and know you're the only one who can take me home?"

He said nothing, struggling to retain his self-control, breathing heavily.

"Are you all right, Rusty?" She kissed him. "Don't you want to hear the rest of my ideas?"

"Faith…"

She whispered in his ear, giving him more glimpses into her imagination, each more innovative and dirtier than the last. Eventually, he went to lift his hands toward her to stop her, forgetting he was chained, and he made a loud clunk as the metal hit the wooden slat.

She stopped and met his gaze, her eyes slightly glazed, and he realized she was having as much difficulty as he was holding on.

"Repeat after me," she said softly, ceasing to move. "Faith Hillman, you are a sexy individual in your own right."

He repeated the words, wishing she'd kiss him, every inch of him throbbing for her.

"I haven't corrupted you," she said.

"I haven't corrupted you."

She let her lips hover above his as she started to move again. "And it's not my fault you're a very, very naughty girl."

He closed his eyes. "Faith, please…"

Her lips touched his gently. "Come for me, sweetie."

He shook his head. "You first."

"Oh no."

He opened his eyes and looked at her, confused.

"Tonight is for you, honey." She kissed him again. "I want to watch you."

He blinked, overwhelmed by her words. He'd never been with any woman who'd been so concerned with his pleasure. Some girls had satisfied themselves as if he were a vibrator that happened to be attached to a body, some had gone down on him as if they felt guilty letting him do all the work. But most had been content to lie there and let him pleasure them, and he'd done so, not realizing it could be any other way. And suddenly he understood he wasn't the only one doing the corrupting. Faith had spoiled him, too, for other women. How could he ever sleep with anyone else again without thinking of her whispering his most secret, erotic fantasies into his ear?

"Come on, Rusty." She brushed her breasts against his chest, ground her hips against his, arousing herself as she moved on him. "Come for me. I know you want to."

And there was really nothing he could do but give in to her demands. She'd owned him tonight, beaten him at his own game, made him realize he'd been kidding himself when he thought he had something to teach her. She'd been right—all he'd done was show her the way. She'd found the path quite easily on her own.

Her hips were relentless, insistent. He looked deep into her eyes, knowing she was going to watch him. She must have seen something in them, something in his expression, because she smiled. Then he felt the hot heat of concentration in his groin, and he swelled inside her, saying her name as he came, conscious all the while of her dark eyes on his face.

And just as the wave receded, she tightened around him as her climax swept over her, and he just lay breathing heavily as she took her own pleasure, powerless to do anything but watch her and think how beautiful she was.

She stayed atop him for a moment. Gradually their breathing slowed, and she leaned forward and rested her forehead on his shoulder. Her hair covered his face, but he didn't mind, because it smelled of mint conditioner, and her skin was warm on his.

Eventually, she lifted her head and met his gaze. He opened his mouth, seconds from telling her he loved her.

At that moment, they heard the front door open and Eve call out. "Faith? You home?"

Chapter Thirty-Five

Faith shot upright, panic threading through her at the sound of Eve's voice. "Shit!" She lifted off Rusty, searched hurriedly for her panties, and pulled them on, followed by her jeans. "I'm coming," she yelled to Eve, finally locating her white shirt and donning it, buttoning it up hurriedly.

She turned to face Rusty, remembering she'd handcuffed him when she saw him still stretched out on the bed, completely naked, eyebrow raised as he waited patiently for her to notice him. "Help?" he said, amused.

"Shit." She froze for a second, hearing Eve mumbling something down the corridor. Where the hell had she put the key?

"Pocket," he reminded her, nodding at her jeans.

Of course. She retrieved the key, freezing as she saw the handle of her bedroom door twitch. Stuffing the key in his hand, she ran across the room, opened the door, and slipped outside before Eve could come in.

"Hey." She ran a hand through her hair self-consciously. Then she froze. Eve's face was white, and as she saw Faith, her features crumpled and she burst into tears.

"Oh my God, what's happened?" Faith steered her toward the living room, over to the settee. Eve sank onto it, her face in her hands as she sobbed. "Why are you back so early?"

"Dan and I had a row." Tears leaked through Eve's fingers. "It was awful. It's all over, Faith. We broke up."

"No..." Faith put an arm around her, shushing her friend as sobs wracked Eve's body. Her mind whirled furiously, half of it wondering what on earth Dan had done to screw up the best relationship he'd ever had, the other half trying to puzzle out how she could excuse herself to go back in and rescue Rusty. She reached across to the table, extracted a tissue from the box, and handed it to Eve. "Shh, now. Come on, tell me what happened."

Eve took the tissue, wiped her face, and blew her nose. She looked up at Faith, her eyes swollen. "Is Rusty here? I saw his car outside."

Fuck. "Yeah, ah, he popped in to help me when my computer crashed." It wasn't the worst lie in the world, he was good with computers, but that didn't explain why he was there at eight thirty at night, and in her bedroom at that. Especially as her laptop was currently on the floor by the coffee table.

Eve leaned across to put her tissue in the bin, and Faith quickly shoved the laptop under the sofa. As she looked up, her heart gave a leap at the sight of Rusty standing there, hands tucked in the pockets of his jeans. He was wearing his shirt, but the buttons were only done up in two places, and she remembered the way they'd popped off across the room when she tore it open.

"Hey." She stifled the urge to giggle. "Did you sort out the computer?"

He blinked, looked down at Eve as she sat up, and said, "Yeah. All sorted." He frowned as he saw her wet face. "Eve?"

"Oh, Rusty." Eve stood, walked up to him, and threw her arms around him. She started to cry again.

"Hey, shh." He looked over at Faith. "What happened?"

"She broke up with Dan, apparently." She studied him calmly, although inside her heart was thudding. He'd rested one of his hands on Eve's waist, while the other stroked her back comfortingly. Eve had buried her wet face in his neck, and was pressing herself against him.

Against her will, Faith felt an uncharacteristic stab of jealousy. Eve had dated Toby, then Dan—was she now making a move on Rusty? Faith shook her head, knowing that was unfair. Eve was upset—she wasn't conscious of her actions. She wasn't even suspicious of his presence at the house, whereas usually she'd have cottoned on in no time. Eve had known Rusty as long as Faith had—they were old friends. Of course she would turn to him for comfort, and of course he would comfort her. She wouldn't expect any less.

It wasn't the fact that he was holding Eve that was bothering her, Faith knew. But it reminded her of what was going to happen once their last two sins were completed. He would be standing there, like this, another woman in his arms, his attention focused on her, while Faith had to watch as someone else laid claim to his heart.

She turned away, her throat going so tight it felt for a moment as if someone were choking her. "Brandy," she said, and walked to the kitchen. She took out two glasses, filled them with ice, and poured a generous amount of the spirit over the top. Her hands were shaking, and she made herself drink a mouthful of it, feeling it sear its way down her throat before she returned to the living room.

She paused in the doorway. Eve had slipped her arms around Rusty's waist, and he'd pulled her close and was murmuring something in her ear as he stroked her back. Faith leaned against the doorjamb, feeling a wave of misery. He chose that moment to look up, and their eyes met. She realized her expression must have been completely transparent, because he frowned slightly, and then his eyes widened. He looked down at Eve and gently moved her arms away before leading her back to the settee.

"Here." He took one of the glasses from Faith and handed it to Eve. Then he lowered to his haunches before her, so he could look up at her face. "I'll talk to him, okay? Don't worry. It's not the end. We'll sort something out."

She nodded and sipped the brandy. Faith heard the rattle of the ice in the glass as Eve's hand shook. She bit her lip, feeling terrible. Her best friend was broken-hearted, and all Faith could think of was herself.

Rusty stood, kissed the top of Eve's head, and walked over to Faith. He took her free hand and led her into the hall. Then, when they were out of sight, he turned her and put his arms around her.

Faith leaned her forehead on his shoulder. Somehow he knew what she was feeling.

They stayed like that for a few seconds before she pulled back. He cupped her face in his hand, stroked her cheek with his thumb. His green gaze was intense, and she had a flash of him as he lay on his back and looked up at her helplessly, completely at her mercy, the memory making her shiver. He searched her eyes for a moment. She bit her lip and closed her eyes. She didn't want him to see what she was trying to hide from him. That she was crazy about him. And that she loved him, with all her heart.

He hesitated for a second. He kissed her, just a soft touch of his lips on hers. Then he drew back, and when she opened her eyes, the door was closing behind him.

Chapter Thirty-Six

Faith talked with Eve for a couple of hours and soon worked out that she was part of the problem. Eve wanted to move in with Dan, but he'd told her that although he wanted to live with her, he was worried about leaving Faith on her own. Eve had blown up, saying he treated Faith like a child, and he'd responded that he still felt responsible for her, and things had deteriorated from there.

Faith listened to Eve talk, feeling a peculiar mix of emotions. Annoyance that Dan was refusing to accept she'd grown up. Guilt that she was somehow responsible for Eve and Dan's argument, even though the rational side of her knew it wasn't really her fault. Irrationally, there was some relief mixed in with it that Dan was still looking out for her, accompanied by a twinge of fear for what would happen when Eve inevitably moved out. Which she should do, obviously—her place was with her boyfriend, Faith was under no illusions about that.

But Faith had never lived alone. She knew many women her age did, and she wasn't afraid of the practical side of things—she knew how to work out the bills, who to call if they had a water leak, and where the baseball bat was if she suspected someone was sneaking about. But she knew she'd miss the company.

When a knock came on the door around ten o'clock, she went and answered it, not surprised to see her brother there. She stepped outside, studying him. "You okay?"

"Yeah." He looked sheepish and tired.

She rested her hand on his arm. "Ask her to move in with you, honey. She loves you, you know."

"I know."

"It doesn't come around very often, Dan. You've got to hang onto it when you find it."

He frowned. "But—"

"Don't you dare say you don't want me to live on my own." She made her voice fierce. "I'm perfectly capable." She couldn't keep it up though, and kissed his cheek. "You've looked after me long enough. It's time to let go."

She was feeling tearful as she turned and slipped on the sandals she'd left outside the door. "I'm popping up to the supermarket. I expect you to be gone when I come back."

He hesitated. "Will you be…" He bit his lip. Then he smiled. "Okay."

She nodded and walked off.

The supermarket was only ten minutes away, and she walked swiftly. She remembered she was wearing a white shirt with no bra underneath. No doubt her nipples were showing through. Great way to attract attention as a single woman, Faith. Luckily, the neighborhood was nice, the pavement well-kept, the gardens fronting the bungalows lined with neat hedges. Still, she crossed her arms over her chest until she reached the shop.

Inside, the lights were bright, and she winced, knowing she must look a sight, her hair tangled, her make-up kissed off. Trying not to think of Rusty chained to her bed, she picked up a basket and wandered around, choosing herself a bottle of wine and a couple of bars of chocolate, feeling miserable. Time to get drunk and fat.

Her phone beeped, and she took it out and flipped it open. It was from Rusty.

Where are you? You ok?

She sighed and sent back: *Supermarket. D&E making up. All good. Thanks for a nice evening. Night.* She pocketed the phone and set her jaw determinedly. She was not going to cry.

Five minutes later, as she added some chocolate fudge brownie ice cream to her basket for good measure, the phone beeped again.

You're not wearing a bra, are u?

She frowned and texted back: *What? How do you know?*

Frozen aisle. Either that or you're very pleased to see me.

She glanced at her chest to see her nipples showing clearly against her shirt and looked up. He was leaning against the cabinet at the end of the aisle, and he laughed as she tipped her head and glared at him.

Pocketing his phone, he walked up to her. "Hey."

"Hey." She balanced the basket on the edge of the freezer, breathless.

He touched her cheek. "You okay?"

"Yeah." She lowered her lashes, overcome by a wave of memory of the things she'd said and done that night, and of how gorgeous he was. He'd changed his top, she noticed, donning an All Blacks T-shirt that stretched nicely across his chest. She'd have to hunt down the buttons of his shirt for him. He was still studying her, smiling, and she shifted awkwardly. "You spoke to Dan, then?"

"Yeah. He'd thrown his rattle out of the pram. He didn't need much convincing to make things up."

"Neither did Eve. What a pair." She sighed. "They were arguing about her moving in with him."

"I know. I told him he should." He shrugged at her surprised look. "I told him he needed to stop worrying about you."

She nodded, pleased at his confidence, but also feeling a strange twinge. He was happy for her to live alone. Did he not worry about her at all?

"Yes, I do," he said, and she stared at him, startled. Had he read her mind? He smiled. "Of course I worry about you, Faith. But one thing I learned from tonight is that you're a big girl now. You don't need Dan, or Eve, or me, to look after you." He brushed the back of his hand up her arm. "But you're always in my mind. You know that."

Her heart rate increased, but she made her pose casual, her voice playful. "Rusty Thorne, getting all tender. That's a first."

"You don't think I can be tender?"

"It's not exactly the first thing that springs to mind when I think of you." She had a vivid image of him pushing her up against the window, slapping her butt, and her cheeks grew hot.

He smiled. He stepped closer to her and slipped a hand around the back of her neck. And then, right in the middle of the supermarket, with half a dozen late-night shoppers looking on, he kissed her.

Faith's heart hammered, but she kept still, accepting the kiss. His lips were soft and cool, and he kissed her for a while, only deepening it when she sighed and opened her mouth to accept his tongue as he brushed it along her bottom lip. He pulled her to him, ignoring her basket as it slid into the freezer, and wrapped his arms around her. He cradled her head in his hand as he continued to kiss her passionately, but so gently it made her tearful.

"Evening, Mr. Thorne," came a pair of voices from behind them.

Rusty lifted his head and glanced across at the two girls who were watching them, giggling. Faith recognized them as students from his classroom, the ones who'd known she was the Faith from the website. Oh dear God.

He nodded at them and cleared his throat. "Evening, ladies."

"Are you giving Faith some extra tuition?" said one girl, and the other nudged her and giggled.

Rusty cast the girls a reproachful glance, but laughed nevertheless. He lifted her basket out of the freezer, took her hand, and led her toward the counter.

"Great," she said. "We are so bad at undercover."

He unpacked her basket onto the belt and took out his wallet. "I'm past caring, to be honest." He waited till the assistant had finished scanning the items, pushed Faith's purse away, and paid for them. "Come on."

He led her outside and started walking back with her toward her house, carrying her bag.

"You don't need to come with me," she protested. "I'm fine on my own."

"I know. You're perfectly capable. You're also perfectly female and it's perfectly dark, and there's no way I'm letting you walk home alone." He took her hand.

She said nothing, enjoying the feel of his warm touch, and his concern, and they walked quietly for a while. Eventually, she felt like she should say something, however. "I think those girls have guessed your secret identity."

"Hmm."

"Will you get into trouble?"

"Well, it's not like we got down to anything in the classroom."

"True."

He scratched the back of his neck. "If any of them start making comments about Mars Bars, though, I'll know the word's spreading."

"I'm so sorry."

"I'll just deny all knowledge. Don't worry about it." He flexed his hand in hers. "What are you up to next weekend?"

"Nothing. Seeing you. Why?"

"It's avarice time, isn't it?"

"Yep. Multiple orgasms all around." She giggled.

He smiled. "Well, I was thinking, we need a good run at it, give ourselves a few hours, eh?"

"Oh, totally."

"So how do you feel about going away on Saturday for the night?"

She blinked at him. A smile spread slowly across her face. "Sounds lovely. You have anywhere in mind?"

"Not really. Maybe over to the Hokianga. A mate has a holiday home there, right on the beach."

They reached her house. Dan's car had gone. Rusty held open the gate, let her walk through, and followed her to the front door. She took the bag from his hand. "I'd like that. Very much."

"Okay. I'll sort it."

She met his gaze. Two sins, she thought, and then she wouldn't be able to look into his eyes like this ever again.

"You look sad," he said.

She forced a smile onto her lips. "Just thinking that Eve's gone. I'm pleased for her, but sad too."

"Hmm." He slipped his hands into the pockets of his jeans. "Are you going to eat that whole tub of ice cream by yourself?"

"Absolutely. Why?"

"I wondered if you wanted to share. Chocolate fudge brownie's my favorite."

"You don't have to feel sorry for me, honey. Or worry about me. I've stayed on my own loads of times when Eve's been at Dan's."

"Who's feeling sorry? I'm seeing it as a golden opportunity to get you alone for the night." He grinned. "It is still Mr. Sinful's evening technically, after all."

He wanted to stay the night. The thought made emotion come rushing up through her. "Are you sure?"

He reached out and brushed her cheek. "I'm sorry, Faith. You were right—I did see you as kind of an apprentice, someone I was training up, so to speak. But you put me right tonight. I've been so arrogant. Will you forgive me?"

His tenderness was too much, and she couldn't stop a tear breaking out and falling onto her cheek.

"Oh don't cry. Now I feel like a complete heel." He kissed her forehead.

She wiped it away. "It's not you, it's me. Don't worry." She looked up at him, seeing his gaze so gentle it made her ache. "Have I frightened Sexy Rusty off forever?"

He laughed out loud at that. "No, he's still here." He took his hands out of his pockets and braced himself on the wall, his hands either side of her. "Want me to prove it to you?" His eyes were suddenly hot again.

For a moment, she was speechless. "Um…"

"I forgot to take the handcuffs with me." He kissed her cheek and around to her ear. "They're still in your bedroom. It's only fair I get a turn."

"Multiple orgasms aren't till next weekend," she murmured, shivering as his lips brushed against her neck.

"I think we need some practice before the big night."

She heaved a sigh, took his hand, and led him inside. Well, she shouldn't really eat a whole tub of chocolate fudge brownie ice cream on her own. She'd only get fat.

Chapter Thirty-Seven

The next morning, Faith had just come out of the shower when Rusty called her into the lounge. He'd set up her laptop and was checking his emails, and had obviously decided to look at her blog.

As she walked in and saw the distinctive colors of the site on the screen, she also saw the frown on his face. "What's up?" She perched on the arm of the sofa, rubbing her hair with a towel.

"I thought they had better sense," he said. "But clearly I overestimated them." He turned the laptop towards her.

Faith studied the comment at the top of the screen.

SJPwannaB: I know who Mr. S. is.

Her heart seemed to come to a stop. She looked at Rusty, who raised an eyebrow and said, "I know."

"One of the girls?"

"Yes. And I know which one. She's always going on about *Sex and the City*. Read on. There's a war taking place."

She looked back at the screen and read the rest of the comments.

WendyS: Ooh! Tell us more!

Karen: Wait, wait. I don't think we should go down that road.

SashaT: Are you crazy? I definitely want to know! Is he a fireman?

SJPwannaB: No, lol.

WendyS: How did you find out?

SJPwannaB: Saw them kissing. But I knew before then.

Karen: You absolutely should not do this, SJPwannaB. This is wrong.

Patsy: I agree. Faith is our friend and she wants Mr. S.'s identity kept secret. She must have a good reason for that.

WendyS: *Blows raspberry* Screw that. They must have known everyone would find out in the end.

SashaT: Where were they kissing?

SJPwannaB: On the mouth.

SashaT: ROFL. I meant where did you see them?

SJPwannaB: Oh... lol. In the supermarket last night.

Patsy: Did they see you as well?

SJPwannaB: Yeah. Faith blushed :)
Patsy: You realize they're both going to read this and know who you are?
Karen: Lol, that shut her up.

Faith read the rest quickly. 'SJPwannaB' had gone offline, but the conversation had continued, with her fans split down the middle between those who wanted to know who Mr. S. was, and those who thought it should be kept a secret.

"Crap," she said.

"I don't think she'll say anything now. She'll know I'm going to see her Monday."

She studied him. "Do you think you should? It's not a school matter."

He looked impatient. "Well, I won't give her detention or anything. But I'll make it clear I'll be very unhappy if I find out she's published my name."

In spite of her worry, Faith couldn't help the frisson of delight that ran through her. "Ooh. You sound all... teacherly."

He looked up at her, eyebrow raised. He lifted the laptop and placed it on the coffee table. Then, before she realized what he was going to do, he leaned back and caught her around the waist, pulling her onto his lap.

She squealed, but he was too quick for her, and he moved onto his back on the sofa, lifting her on top of him, before sliding his hands beneath her bathrobe.

"Your hands are cold!" she protested.

"I'll warm them up then," he said, turning so he could pin her against the back of the sofa, and sliding one hand between her thighs.

"Yow!"

"Serves you right for making fun of me." He nuzzled her ear.

"I wasn't making fun of you," she said. She sighed as he brushed his lips against her neck. "I like your teacher voice."

"A hundred lines, Miss Hillman." He kissed down to her breasts. "'I must not expect Mr. Thorne to keep his hands off me when I've just had a shower and my skin's all soft and damp.'"

"That's a very long line," she said, letting her eyes droop shut as he closed his mouth over a nipple.

He sucked gently, then lifted his head to give her a warning look. "If you're defiant, I get to discipline you."

"Oh, now you're talking."

Laughing, he proceeded to chastise her in his favorite way.

*

After he left, Faith spent several hours trying to convince herself that him sleeping in her bed didn't mean anything. It would have been easier to do so if he hadn't called her, emailed her, and texted her twenty times a day the following week.

She began to grow used to her phone beeping almost continuously, usually with something completely pointless, with him telling her he was having a nice muffin with his morning coffee, or had just sat through a really dull staff meeting where he'd been asked a question and had got caught daydreaming, thinking about the weekend.

At one point, he sent her a text that said: *Can we still do this after sin 7? I'll miss you.*

She'd been in a meeting in Whangarei with a couple of commissioning editors, but they'd broken for a coffee break, so she took the opportunity to text back: *I think your other women would have something to say about that.*

He came back with: *Other women? Makes me sound like a right tart.*

Laughing, she replied: *If the cap fits.*

You'll pay for that later, he said.

She smiled and returned: *Promises, promises. Am I lying, then? Are you taking monastic vows in two weeks' time?*

As the editors came back out, he sent: *I'm seriously thinking about it. No one could match up to you, sweetheart.*

She caught her breath, staring at the screen. He was joking, obviously. He wasn't really thinking about taking vows. But even so, for the second time now, he'd admitted he was going to have trouble when their contract finished.

Her heart seemed to stop. He spoke to her—in one way or another—practically every five minutes of the day, even emailing her from the classroom when the students were working quietly. He couldn't keep his hands off her when they were together. He cared deeply for her—she knew that without having to ask him. And now he was telling her he was having difficulty thinking about sleeping with other women, because "No one could match up to you".

He loved her. She already knew that. But, being an idiot, or being a guy—which kind of amounted to the same thing where love was concerned—he didn't realize he was in love with her. Either that or he did realize it, but he was still determined not to have a relationship and settle down.

"Faith, you coming?" called one of the editors.

"Sure." She would have to think about this later. Clipping the phone shut, she shoved it in the pocket of her jeans.

It would vibrate three times with insignificant text messages before her hour meeting was over.

Chapter Thirty-Eight

Faith Hillman's Blog

So it's greed tomorrow. We're going to try to cram in as many orgasms as we can. The laboratory record is apparently 134 in an hour. An hour!!! That must be fake. Although many women say they can achieve 30 or 40. Well, I've not experienced multiple orgasms before so anything more than one will be an improvement!

*

Excerpt from the 965 comments

Georgia: How many can a guy have in one session?
Faith: It's difficult to say. It depends on the age and health of the guy, and everyone's different. There's no right answer. Mr. S. is young and virile :-) So we'll see.
MrS69: He'd also like to be able to walk the next morning.
Faith: Is that a complaint? Want me to find another lab rat?
MrS69: No… I'm happy to help you out. Just make sure you keep me hydrated.
Faith: Ha! Will do.
SashaT: How many are you aiming to give Faith, Mr. S.?
MrS69: If she hits double figures, I'll be happy.
Patsy: If she hits double figures, we're all going to want your phone number.
MrS69: Heh. I'm a one-woman man.
Faith: For now.
MrS69: Yes, Faith. *waves the contract at her*
Patsy: Aw, don't let's talk about the end yet. You'll make me cry.

Chapter Thirty-Nine

On Saturday, Faith told Dan and Eve that Mr. S. was taking her to Auckland for the weekend. Rusty told them he was staying with the invisible Laura in Kaitaia. Nobody seemed to suspect anything, which was kind of a relief, considering that the previous weekend Eve had nearly walked in on Rusty chained to the bed.

It was ten in the morning, and they were heading west across the North Island to the Hokianga Harbour, a stunning area with kauri forest and waterfall walks inland, and, on the coast, magnificent sand dunes that fronted the sparkling blue Tasman Sea.

Rusty looked gorgeous, wearing navy surf shorts and a light blue top that she would never have thought went with his coloring, but somehow complemented it perfectly. The bright sunshine had lightened his hair, making it even redder. He looked relaxed and happy at the thought of spending twenty-four hours with her.

Faith looked out of the window, seeing the flat-topped volcanoes in the distance with their forested skirts. She'd given a lot of thought to their situation over the week, and had finally come to one conclusion.

She was going to have to talk to him about it.

Well, she couldn't go on like this. One of them had to raise the subject of how they were feeling, and what was going to happen when the contract was over. What had started as a bit of fun and a light-hearted adventure had turned into something much more serious, and it wasn't fair to the relationship to treat it as if it were insignificant and irrelevant. Millions of people never found their soul mate, never had someone feel for them the way she felt for Rusty, or the way she was sure he felt for her. It was stupid to pass it over. They needed to address it.

But not yet. It wouldn't be an easy conversation, and she didn't want to spoil the day. They had a lot of fun to get through first, and she was very much looking forward to it. Twenty-four hours of sex with Rusty Thorne. Yum. What could possibly top that?

They arrived around eleven and found the house easily. It sat just off the beach on a bank of grass, with a large living room that overlooked the sea. The water was a sparkling turquoise, topped with white surf, the sand a shimmering gold.

"Oh." She sighed as Rusty opened the sliding doors and let the warm March air into the house. "It's beautiful."

He came up behind her and wrapped her in his arms. "It's nearly a full moon tonight," he murmured in her ear. "I want to make love to you out here, and watch the moon turn your skin silver."

She turned around to face him. "'Make love'?" she said playfully. "When did we start 'making love'?"

"It's just a phrase."

"Sure it is." She reached up to kiss him, whispering, "And how many times do you think you can 'make love' in one day, hmm?"

"I don't know." He picked her up, making her squeal, and wrapped her legs around him. "But I think we should get started. I don't want to run out of time."

"God forbid." She kissed him, and he carried her back into the house, up to the kitchen, and lifted her onto the worktop.

"Pre-sex sex?" She tightened her legs around him, pressing his now-very-obvious erection to her.

"Just a warm-up." He slid his hands under her top, up her ribcage and cupped her breasts.

"So this doesn't count then." She arched her back as he slipped his hand inside her bra and rolled her nipple.

"Well, I didn't say that. I still think it should count toward our golden total." He stroked her and kissed her until she began to squirm against his fingers. He put his hand up her skirt and pushed aside her panties, and within seconds he was inside her.

She tipped her head back as he pulled her to the edge of the worktop and slid right into her. "Oh…" She looked back at him, her gaze unfocussed. "So what's your guesstimate, then?"

"For what?" He seemed to be having trouble concentrating.

"How many orgasms can a man have in one day?"

"I'm aiming for half a dozen," he said as he began to move inside her, "but I expect you to top that."

"Ooh." She shivered at the sensual slide of his skin on hers. "Six-plus orgasms? Oh God, is this just the perfect day or what?"

"You have no idea," he mumbled, increasing his pace. "I can't believe you made me wait all week."

"All part of the contract." Her breath came in gasps. "Jesus, Rusty. You've been inside me, like, ten seconds…"

"That's… what comes… of making… us wait. Fuck."

They came together, sighing and groaning in turn, and afterward he pulled her to him and wrapped his arms around her.

"One-all," he said.

She started laughing. "You're going to keep score?"

"Well, isn't that the point?"

"I guess."

And so they were off.

*

By lunchtime, it was three-two to her and they needed a bit of R&R, so they made sandwiches, grabbed a bottle of Coke, and had a walk along the beach, shoeless, toes sinking in the soft sand. She took a blanket and spread it by some rocks, and they ate as they talked about nothing and let the cool sea breeze wash over them.

Glancing over his shoulder, Rusty checked the beach. He turned back to her with a twinkle in his eye.

"Here?" she said, slightly shocked.

"This from the woman who went down on me in the car, with a police officer standing outside." He kissed her nose.

"I didn't know he was there at the time."

He wriggled closer and began tracing a hand up her thigh. They'd long since abandoned underwear, and she sighed as he pushed her legs apart and began to stroke her with his warm fingers.

"Even so. It still makes you a hussy."

"Fair enough." She closed her eyes and let the sun warm her face, while Rusty placed kisses on her cheeks and lips, and continued to slide his fingers inside her.

And shortly after that, it was four-two.

*

They walked back to the house, lay on the bed for a while, and talked about the wickedest fantasies they could think of, trying to shock each other, making each other wait as long as they could. Before long, however, her sinful whispers drove him over the edge, and this time he had her on her hands and knees and took her from behind. He stroked her back and ass, and leaned forward to cup her breasts, while outside seagulls cried overhead and the sound of the waves mingled with her soft sighs.

"Five-three," she said, as they both fell onto the bed, gasping. "Oh my."

He looked across at her, and his eyes crinkled with amusement. "You had enough?"

"Well, I might need a few minutes." She giggled. He pulled her into his arms, picked up the duvet, threw it over them, and lay back with a sigh. "Are you going to sleep?" she asked suspiciously.

"I'm getting old now, Hillman, and you're wearing me out. I need to recharge."

"Fine." She snuggled up next to him. "But only half an hour. I'm keeping you to a strict regime."

He fell asleep quickly, and she watched his chest rise and fall evenly and studied his face, thinking how he looked younger when relaxed. The sun slanted across the room and fell across the upper half of the bed, warming them through even as the cool March breeze fluttered the curtains by the open window. The golden rays heated the coppery filaments of his hair and turned the ends to scarlet, the rest of it glowing a deep red-brown. It fell across his forehead, still needing a cut, and she knew if she reached out and ran her fingers through it, it would be tangled but soft, like the coat of the red setter she and Dan had owned as children. Rusty sometimes reminded her of the dog, so good-natured, fun, trustworthy, and loyal. Frequently randy. The thought made her smile.

I love you. She didn't say it aloud. But she thought it with all her heart. She didn't ever want to let him go. She wanted to wake up with him like this every morning, to accompany him on the sometimes happy, sometimes difficult journey of life, to live with him until they grew old together and his red hair turned white. She wanted to do all the things she saw old married couples do—scold him for not eating healthily, nag him to pick up his socks, squabble over the remote control. She wanted to be there when he was having trouble at school. To help him get organized for the inspection, and listen when he needed to talk about his students. She wanted to make love to him every single day of her life, to capture his heart, and make sure he never looked at another woman again.

Surely, he didn't really mean to stay single forever? He'd make a great husband, and such a wonderful father. Briefly, she let herself think about what it would be like to get married, to get pregnant, and to have a baby with him. She'd never really thought about it before—she'd always thought she'd do it one day, like learning to knit and cook quiche. But the thought of a baby—Rusty's baby, with a thatch of red hair and his wonderful green eyes—made her catch her breath.

She bit her lip and forced herself to slow down. Just because they'd had a fantastic few weeks, it didn't mean he would be interested in continuing to see her. She knew he loved her, if only as a friend. But she also knew his thoughts on long-term relationships, even if she didn't completely understand.

For some reason her mother came into her head, and she found herself wondering what her mum would have said if she'd known Faith had fallen in love with Rusty. Her mum had adored both him and Toby, although she'd despaired over them both, especially Rusty, with his roving eye and refusal to stay with anyone longer than about two weeks.

"He's a heartbreaker, if ever I saw one," she'd said one day to Faith, when he'd left the house with yet another girl. "It'll take a fine woman to get that one to commit."

Faith now remembered the way her mother had looked at her, with a twinkle in her eye and a raised eyebrow. She hadn't said anything at the time, not even thinking her mother could be referring to her, but now she wondered if her mum had seen something she'd missed.

"I don't know if I can do it, Mum," she whispered, reaching up to brush a stray hair from off his face. "I might need some help." Her throat tightened, so she curled up beside him and closed her eyes. She had time left yet. She wouldn't get maudlin, not until all hope was gone.

*

He woke her about an hour later with light kisses on her face and shoulders. "Come on, sleepy," he said, lifting the duvet. "We've got a deadline to meet."

"Oh." Still dozy, she started to laugh as he disappeared beneath the quilt and brought it over his head. He kissed down her body, lingered on her breasts for a while, and covered her nipples with his warm mouth. He teased them with his tongue and sucked until she began to sigh. Then he kissed downwards and traced his lips over the skin of her stomach and hips, before he moved down and pushed up her legs so he could bury his tongue in the warm center of her. Still clinging to the last strands of sleep, Faith felt as if she were floating in a vat of melted chocolate, luxurious and sensual, and she gave herself over to his loving mouth and hands. She trusted him implicitly, and reveled in the fact that he wasn't going to stop until he'd taken her to the dizzy heights of pleasure.

Seven minutes later, it was six-three.

"I need to even the score," she said lazily as he emerged from the bedclothes, hair ruffled and cheeks flushed.

"Nah. I've got other plans." And he flipped her over, kissed her from head to toe until her laughter turned to sighs, slid inside her, and promptly made it seven-four.

*

By this time, the clock read nearly half-past three, and she needed chocolate. She brought the bar she'd put in the fridge back into the bedroom.

"Keep your energy levels up," she said, and climbed onto the bed to feed a cube of Dairy Milk into his mouth.

"Yes, ma'am." He sucked on the chocolate, lying on his side, his head propped on a hand. "I'm enjoying this."

"Me too. What a good excuse for having sex all day."

He laughed. "Yeah."

"Have we beaten your previous record yet?"

"Yes, and you're very happy about that, aren't you?"

"What's wrong with wanting to be the best you've had?"

He leaned across to give her a chocolatey kiss. "You were the best I'd had at sin number one, Faith Hillman. When will you start to believe me?"

She met his gaze and couldn't stop herself blushing at the thought of her plans for their future. She rolled over so he couldn't read the emotion in her eyes, stood, and stretched. "You realize I'm not going to be able to walk tomorrow?"

"Ah. I've got a solution for that." He got off the bed and went into the bathroom. The next thing she heard was the water running and the gurgle of a bottle emptying into it. He came back in, smiling. "The bath's huge. Plenty of room for two."

"I thought the point was to relax me."

"Orgasms aren't relaxing?"

She ate another square of chocolate and shrugged mischievously. "Meh."

Laughing, he fed her squares until she pleaded she was full. Then he led her into the bathroom and made her get into the bubble-filled bath before joining her at the other end.

They soaked until the water grew lukewarm, and listened to the radio while they talked about this and that as the bubbles popped and the water warmed her joints. Then he pretended to lose the soap, and she pretended to be affronted, and before she could count to ten, he'd pulled her onto his lap and was kissing her breathless. Soon the water was slopping over the side, and, in a surprisingly short amount of time, it was eight-five.

*

They walked up to the local café to get fish and chips for dinner and ate them on the beach, trying not to drop the hot flakes of hoki on the sand. He talked for a while about his job, and he told her he didn't really have any plans to try to get a promotion. He'd considered becoming head of department, but the current head had been there for a gazillion years and wasn't set to retire for another gazillion, so he knew he was unlikely to get the post any time soon.

"But that's okay," he said, taking the rest of her fish from her when she said she'd had enough. "I have no great aspirations for my teaching career."

"So what are you going to do with the rest of your life?" she asked, not quite as innocent as she sounded.

"Dunno. I'd quite like to write history resources for schools. Some of the ones out there are just terrible, and I usually end up writing my own anyway, so I might as well make some money out of it."

"And you see yourself doing that until you're old and gray?"

"I guess. Toby and I are going to grow old and grouchy together like the old guys in the Muppets."

She laughed and finished off the Coke in the bottle. Down the beach, a young mother walked slowly along the sand, accompanied by a dog and a toddler, two or three years old. The dog bounded off into the surf to retrieve a stick, while the toddler ran ahead toward them, all fat legs and waving arms, still finding his balance. As they watched, he tripped on a piece of seaweed and fell flat on his face.

The mother had turned for a second, throwing the stick for the dog, and the toddler's face screwed up as he bawled out a cry.

Before Faith could even move, Rusty was running the few yards to the child, and he picked him up and set him on his feet, brushing the sand from his face as his mother came up. She swung the baby into her arms and thanked Rusty. Faith heard him say something to them both as he cleaned the toddler's hands of sand, making him giggle and bury his head in his mother's neck.

Rusty came back and sat beside Faith. He wrapped the newspaper into a ball and raised an eyebrow as he saw her studying him. "What?"

"Do you want kids, Rusty?" She couldn't help herself.

His green eyes were light, reflecting her gaze rather than letting it in. Then he looked out at the sea. "No. Family life's not for me."

She screwed the top slowly back onto the plastic bottle. "It seems kind of a shame that you've discounted a whole section of the future because you're afraid of something that might never happen."

He leaned forward, picked up a shell and examined it. Only after a few minutes had passed did she realize he wasn't going to say anything. "Rusty?" she prompted.

"What?" He looked up, and his eyes were cool.

They studied each other for a moment. Suddenly she felt as if she were standing on a seesaw, waiting to see which way it would tip. It was incredibly important that she talk to him about this. She felt breathless with the significance of what she had to say. And she was terrified of saying it, in case it brought all her hopes and dreams crashing down.

"You shouldn't punish yourself for what the men in your family have done," she said. "You shouldn't deny yourself a family life because they've been idiots. You're a good man, honey. Don't let their mistakes form your future. You'd be a wonderful husband, and a fantastic father. You're destined to make some woman very happy. It would be such a waste to refuse to accept that fate." She phrased it as carefully as she could and waited for his reaction.

Chapter Forty

Rusty stood, took a few steps forward, drew back his arm, and threw the shell out to sea. Then he tucked his hands in his pockets and studied the waves.

His stomach felt as knotted as a tangled ball of wool. He hated discussing this with anybody. His friends had brought up the subject several times in the past, trying to convince him he was being stupid, and each time he'd refused to argue with them, listening to them until he couldn't bear it anymore and eventually had to walk out, leaving them open-mouthed and frustrated.

He didn't want to talk about it, because he harbored a terrible secret. He hated his family. He hated his grandfather, his father, his uncle, and his brother, for having this terrible addiction they couldn't control, for being so cruel and pitiless when under the influence of alcohol.

He also hated his grandmother, mother, aunt, and sister-in-law for being weak and letting themselves be treated in such a way. He knew that was unfair, because it wasn't their fault their spouses had mistreated them, and he knew how charming the Thorne men could be, on the surface. But still he resented the women for coming back for more, for letting the men think treating women in such a way was forgivable.

And he hated them all for making him feel the way he did, that he had no choice but to end the spread of the malevolence he felt was in his blood by staying alone for the rest of his life.

Part of him knew how ridiculous he was being. He loved women, and he'd never even spoken harshly to one, let alone mistreated any of his girlfriends. He wasn't stupid—he knew there was no guarantee he'd react like his father or brother, even if he drank. He hoped he was a fair man, a kind one, a person who hated injustice and unfairness, who worked hard at his job, and who loved his friends. But the thought that Mr. Hyde might be lurking deep within him scared him enough to make him stay alone.

And there was also the issue of what might happen if he had kids. Faith had told him it was only blood and it didn't mean anything, but Rusty didn't believe that. Even if the family demon had skipped a generation, there was every possibility it might pass to the next. And he didn't think he could bear to bring up a child, especially a boy, only to see him inherit the terrible Thorne curse.

The truth was, up until now, he'd had it easy. He hadn't lied when he'd said to Faith he'd never really been in love. He'd been fond of some of the women he'd slept with, and he'd dated Meredith probably a little longer than he should have, because it had been a wrench when they'd finally broken up. But generally, he'd found it easy to be fickle in his relationships, to discard women easily before they had a chance to think he was serious.

But then he'd never felt about any woman the way he felt about Faith.

Standing there, staring at the waves crashing onto the sand, Rusty finally realized he'd made a terrible mistake in suggesting he help her out with her articles. He knew she was falling for him and, deep down, he knew he'd fallen heavily for her too. He'd thought they'd be able to keep it simple, that the sex would be fun and frivolous, and it had been, for a while, but he hadn't considered the fact that his heart might get involved.

He closed his eyes. Letting her go would be unbearable. To see her and know he couldn't just walk up to her and kiss her, because she wouldn't be his to kiss. To watch her with other men. To see her get married, and have babies. It made his heart twist, and he bit his lip as emotion welled inside him. But in spite of all that, he couldn't continue to date her. She deserved to find someone who didn't have the sword of Damocles hanging over him, who could give her marriage and children without the threat of danger hovering.

He dropped his head, stared at the sand. He couldn't think what to say.

Suddenly she was in front of him, cupping his face in her hands, kissing him. "I'm sorry," she said, over and over again. "I'm so sorry, Rusty. I shouldn't have said anything."

"I can't," he said hoarsely. "I just can't."

"I know." She put her arms around his neck. He hugged her to him, and she pressed kisses around his ear. "It's all right, sweetheart. You don't have to explain."

"I love you," he said, tightening his arms. He wasn't going to cry, he wasn't that much of a girl. He really wasn't.

"I know." She buried her face in his neck. "I love you too."

They stood there like that for a while. The surf was strangely soothing, cleansing their emotion as it washed away the footprints of the dog in the sand. He felt himself grow calm now that he'd made his decision, although sadness overwhelmed him. He didn't know what it meant for the rest of the night, for the final sin, or for their friendship. If she wanted him, he'd be there. If she wanted to end it now, he'd understand that too.

Eventually, she pulled back. He'd thought her face might be wet, but her eyes were clear, the color of the wet sand, and she smiled as she looked up at him.

"What number are we up to?" she asked.

He stared at her. She could have reacted in a hundred different ways, yelled, cried, walked off, accused him. Her actual words shocked him, and to his alarm, a tear rolled down his face.

She brushed it away, tipping her head. "It was eight-five, if I remember correctly," she said, as if nothing had happened. Her eyes lit mischievously. "I have something in my bag for us to play with, if you're interested."

He rubbed his nose. "I'm assuming it's not Monopoly."

She laughed, picked up the bag with the rubbish from their dinner and took his hand. "Slightly more vibrate-y than that. Come on."

Chapter Forty-One

She led him up the beach and into the house, closing the doors. Daylight was fading and the sandflies would be snapping, and besides, the day had grown cool. She took him into the bedroom and began unbuttoning his shirt while he stood there, studying her, a gentle smile on his face.

She felt calm after the emotion that had washed over them on the beach. It wasn't over, not by a long shot. He thought it was. She'd seen his face when he'd looked at the toddler on the beach. And as he'd stood there looking out to sea, she'd realized the full extent of his angst, and why he felt he couldn't ever get married and have kids. Not only was he still worried the family curse hunkered within him, he also thought of himself like the carrier of a disease, and was terrified at the notion of passing that disease on to his children.

It could happen, Faith knew. But surely it became watered down through the generations? Any children they might have would be half him, but also half her. And the fact was that even if it was like a disease that transferred to the next generation, they'd deal. They'd work together to cope with whatever life threw at them.

Faith wasn't the sort of person not to do something because she was afraid of what might happen. In her mind, you had to weigh the pros and cons, and the thought of having Rusty as a life partner vastly outweighed any potential possible threat of the Thorne demon rearing its ugly head. With her whole heart, she knew Rusty didn't have it in him to be the sort of man that his father and Cole were. He didn't have a violent bone in his body.

Part of her knew that one thing he was worried about was sex. A passionate man with a high sex drive, she was sure he worried sometimes that he was going to hurt her in bed, that he'd overstep the mark and find the demon lurking, ready to play. But Faith was certain there was a difference between the dark desire she often felt inside herself during sex, and an actual desire to hurt the person you loved. Rusty feared the latter, and she knew he couldn't bear the thought of ever hurting her. But she was certain that if he looked deeply, he'd find nothing but love and passion inside himself, and she was going to prove it to him.

Several hours remained before midnight. And she had a few ideas up her sleeve.

She finished the buttons and pushed open his shirt, sliding her hands over his ribs. Putting her arms around him, she reached up and kissed him, a soft, tender kiss, which he returned happily enough, to her relief.

"Are you okay?" she asked, looking up into his eyes.

"Yeah." He brushed her cheek.

"You still wanna play? I don't mind if you say no. Eight-five's a pretty good total for one day."

He laughed and kissed her. "Oh I'm happy to play along, if you want me to."

"You got anything left for me?" She rubbed her hips against his. "Or has the well run dry?"

He grasped the bottom of her T-shirt and lifted it off in one swift move. "I seem to have a refillable tank where you're involved."

She giggled and led him toward the bed, drew back the cover, and pushed him onto the mattress. He slid off his shorts and moved back onto the pillows, and she quickly took off her skirt and climbed on, pulling the duvet over them.

She cuddled up to him and kissed him for a while. Eventually, he pulled back and raised an eyebrow. "You mentioned you had something to play with."

"Later," she said. "I've got something else in mind first." And, winking at him, she began to kiss down his chest. She disappeared under the covers, feeling him sigh as she worked her way down, and his hand slipped into her hair as she finally covered him with her mouth.

She aroused him slowly, tenderly, trying to show him without saying anything that she loved him, understood him, had forgiven him, and wanted to make him feel better.

And when she made it eight-six, she knew it had worked.

*

Afterward, he made her find her play toy, and she retrieved it from her bag and brought it over to the bed, where he was lying facing her, head propped on a hand.

"Oh yeah." He eyed the long vibrator approvingly.

She slid into the bed beside him, flushing as he picked it up and studied it with interest.

"When did you get it?" He tested the button on the top, raising an eyebrow as it started buzzing.

"Er… About two years ago."

His eyes widened and he started laughing. "You monkey! You never told me you used a vibrator."

"Well, it's not the type of thing that comes up in a normal conversation."

"I meant, since we've been seeing each other."

"You never asked."

His eyes met hers, and he held her gaze, his smile growing. "You really are naturally naughty, aren't you?"

"Yep." She lay back on the pillows and wriggled closer to him. "Now are you going to sort me out, or what?"

He kissed her cheek. "Absolutely. But you need to tell me what you like." He kissed her lips.

"And how it feels?"

His eyes met hers. "If you want."

"I'll give you a running commentary. Tell you exactly what you're doing to me."

He blinked slowly. His smile had faded. Without another word, he pushed down the duvet, exposing her to her waist, bent his head, and touched his tongue first to one nipple, then the other. He switched on the vibrator and pressed the tip against her sensitive, wet skin.

Faith inhaled sharply. He leaned over and kissed her, and she opened her mouth to accept the sweep of his tongue, tingling all over as the vibrator continued to buzz against her nipples.

He raised his head to watch her, and she began talking to him, telling him exactly what he was doing to her. Gradually, he moved the vibrator lower, letting it hum over her belly and tickle the sensitive skin of her lower stomach, before he slid it down between her legs, into the slippery folds of her skin.

She sighed and told him how to pleasure her, and he followed her directions. He moved the vibrator inside her for a while before he brought it back up to focus on her clit, and pushed her legs open wide, kissing her in between her whispered instructions.

He aroused her carefully, watching her all the while, and by the time she made it nine-six, she knew they'd moved past the moment that had upset him so much, and that he was ready for the final phase of her carefully targeted plan.

Chapter Forty-Two

Rusty sensed there was something on her mind, but she talked for a while about insignificant matters, and he was happy to lie with her and listen to her voice as the sun set and the moon rose in the darkening sky. A night from full, it hovered above the sea like a flashlight, shining its beam across their bed.

They went into the kitchen and had a final piece of chocolate, and Faith poured herself a glass of wine and drank it sitting naked at the kitchen table, while he leaned on the worktop and listened to her talk about her writing and her plans for future articles. He sensed she was trying to relax him, perhaps to make him forget the tension they'd experienced earlier. Which was fine, but she kept giving him dark glances, and he could almost see her thoughts passing across her eyes, like clouds over the moon. And every time she looked at him, he felt his heart rate increase a little, knowing she was planning something, the thought making him hard in spite of the fact that he'd thought six orgasms was probably his limit for the day.

Eventually, she finished her wine, and his heart began to pound as she placed the glass in the sink, took his hand, and led him back into the bedroom. She stood with him in front of the window, turned him to face her, and backed him up against the glass.

"Are you done?" she asked kindly, stroking his face. "Or do you have enough energy for one more adventure?"

He put his arms around her. Her hair, in the moonlight, was dark, her face a black-and-white photograph of light and shadows. It made her look intense, the color bleached out of her eyes, her pupils so large they seemed almost black. "Adventure?" he queried.

She rested her hands on his chest and licked her lips. Was she nervous or excited? She stroked his curling chest hairs. "Rusty?" Her voice was husky, teasing.

Uh-oh. "Hmm?"

She brushed his nipples. "Next week, when we finish the seventh sin, we're done, right?"

He wasn't going to think about it. "Yes."

She stroked his chest. "Next week, it'll be the last time. It'll be difficult, and there's a lot of thinking involved. Next week, we make love with our minds."

"Okay."

"But tonight… we should concentrate on our bodies."

He said nothing, caught in the mesmerizing darkness of her eyes, afraid to break the spell.

"After we're done, you want me to meet a nice man, someone kind and gentle, who treats me like a lady, don't you?"

His throat tightened, but he managed to say, "Yes."

She moistened her lips again. "So this is my last chance, then, to be a wicked girl?"

He swallowed. What was she trying to say?

She brushed her lips against his. "You've done very well, educating me in the seven sins."

"I don't think I had a lot to do with it," he said, thinking about the way she'd handcuffed him to the bed.

She laughed and traced her fingers up his body, across his shoulders. "There's one more sin I'd like to try, though."

"Oh?"

"Yeah. I wouldn't ask if it were anyone else, but as it's you, Rusty, and I know you want to make sure I go off into the world fully educated, I'm hoping you'll agree." She ran light fingers down his chest, slid a hand lower, across his belly and into his hair, and finally grasped his erection.

He met her gaze, breathless with desire but also wary, wondering what was going through her head.

Her tongue grazed his mouth, and she bit his lower lip, hard enough to make him gasp. "Any ideas what I'm thinking about?"

"No." He could think of a couple of things he'd like to do to her, but he wasn't going to put them into words in case he shocked her. This was Faith, he reminded himself firmly. His friend. Sister of his best mate. He used to put crickets in her pockets. He was there the first time she got drunk and threw up on her mum's sofa. But it wasn't working. He couldn't see any remnants of the girl in the sexy, passionate woman before him.

She leaned over to her bag, reached in, and closed her hand on an item, took it out, and threw it on the bed. He looked down. It was a tube of lubrication.

"Oh, crap." He closed his eyes helplessly.

She pressed her breasts against his chest, drew his head down, and kissed him deeply. When she finally pulled back, her lips were swollen, her eyes dark and taunting. "Come on. Don't you want to?"

He frowned. "That's hardly the point."

"What is the point?"

"You're... Faith," he said simply, trying not to notice the way her taut nipples were tangling in his chest hair.

"You've only just noticed?"

"I meant, you're my friend Faith. Dan's little sister." He sighed as she looked frustrated. "It's one thing to help out a friend, it's another to... to take advantage..." His voice trailed off as amusement grew in her eyes.

"You really think that's all this is—you helping me out?"

"Um..."

"And you still think you're taking advantage of me?" Her mocking gaze suggested the reality was quite the opposite.

He met her eyes. "Ah..." His brain was turning to mush because all his concentration was focusing in the place where she was stroking him. "Stop that."

"No." She pushed his hand away.

He was starting to get exasperated. How could he continue to act gentlemanly, with her best interests at heart, when she was being so damned provocative?

"What's up?" She kissed his neck, letting her tongue trace over the point where his pulse was beating hard beneath the skin. "You think I can't cope with feral Rusty?"

"Faith..." He put his hands on her hips to push her away, but she fastened her lips on his neck and sucked, and instead he instinctively pulled her closer.

"Stop trying to teach me," she said, kissing up to his ear. "Forget about the contract, forget about the sins and Dan and our past and everything except the fact that here, in this room, it's just you and me."

He wanted her so badly. He was so hard it almost hurt, in spite of the fact that earlier he'd thought he wouldn't be able to get another hard-on if she'd paid him.

"I don't want to be your best mate's sister, or your friend." She ran her thumb over the tip of his erection to collect the drop of moisture that had formed there, and he groaned as she licked it. "I want to have all of you. The Rusty that all your other girls have seen. You owe me that."

He hesitated. She didn't realize he'd already given her more emotionally than he'd ever given to any other woman he'd been with. But he knew what she meant. She was aware he held back physically with her. He knew why he did. He was afraid if he gave her everything, they wouldn't be able to go back. He'd already given her a hundred percent of his emotion—if he also gave her a hundred percent of his physical desire, he was afraid he'd scare her or hurt her, and then he'd ruin any chance they had of staying friends after this was finished.

He'd tried so hard to keep this whole thing light and friendly, to think of himself as educating her before sending her off into the world fully primed for whatever guy she ended up with. He'd thought of himself as a friendly uncle—okay, a friendly perverted uncle—helping her out, rather than as an equal. Quite clearly, though, as they'd worked their way through the sins, she'd shown him she was very much more than his subordinate. He'd been arrogant and exceedingly idiotic to think the education had only ever been one way. And now she was tempting him to take that final step that, in his head, he considered a bridge too far for his role as Rusty the Teacher. It would confirm that he was crazy about her, and wanted her more than any other woman he'd ever known. And that wasn't going to end well.

She took his hand that still rested on her hip and moved it to her butt, slid his fingers down between the cheeks of her ass. "I want you here. Will you do that for me, sweetheart?"

"Faith…" He was losing it, and desire surged in him, stirring his blood.

She took his other hand and moved it down over her stomach, between her legs. "You see how much the thought turns me on?" She pushed his fingers into her incredibly wet, hot center. "I've been thinking about this for weeks. I didn't want to ask, but now I know you're a bad boy…" She moved his hand up and down. "It's time to let feral Rusty out, honey. I'm a big girl. I can take it."

The dark craving nearly overwhelmed him, but he reined it in, pushing her away from him hard enough so she fell onto the bed. "A man can only take so much," he snapped, his last stand at trying to keep the boundaries fixed.

He looked for the slightest hint of fear in her eyes, knowing if he saw any, it was all over, not knowing whether he was praying for it to be there or not.

But she didn't look scared, and she didn't cry out.

Instead, she laughed. "Is that supposed to scare me, you big pussycat?"

Completely nonplussed, he studied her, hands on hips, trying to ignore his erection as it strained toward her.

Rolling onto her front, she reached up and pulled down a pillow. "To bite on," she said impishly. Hooking up one leg, she wiggled her butt enticingly at him. "C'mon Rusty. Make my day."

He stared at her for a second. She was so gorgeous, with her skin turning silver in the moonlight, and her long hair lying across her shoulders like dark ribbons. He was fooling himself. Whatever he did with her this evening, they were never going to be able to go back to how they were. They'd overstepped the boundary on the first sin, or maybe it had been when he'd kissed her in the car. Or perhaps it had even been long before, that day she'd stood there in her bikini when she was fifteen, and for the first time he'd seen her not as the sister of his best mate, but as a young woman he'd wanted to kiss. It was always going to end this way. How stupid he'd been to think it could ever be anything else.

And now her ass was pale and round in the moonlight, and she was moving it so enticingly, he couldn't resist her. But if he was lost anyway, what did it matter? At least she was lost with him. Damn the future. All he had was here and now, and here and now, he wanted her.

He gave a short laugh and shook his head. "You are evil incarnate." He climbed onto the bed and leant over her.

She sighed with relief. "Yep." She raised her hips, brushing her butt against his erection. "Oh God, I so want that in me."

"And you'll get it." He cupped her breast and began to kiss her ear. "You're a tart, you know that?"

"Yes."

He tucked a hand under her belly, sliding it down. "Floozy."

"Oh yes." Her eyelids fluttered as he stroked her.

He rolled her onto her back, took her wrists, and pinned them above her head. "Hussy."

"Only for you," she sighed, tipping her head to the side so he could kiss her neck.

He planted slow kisses down her body, taking nibbles out of her as he went, and grazed her with his teeth until she wriggled beneath him. She wrestled her hands free and buried them in his hair as he sucked her nipples hard, and she groaned and raked her nails down his back in response. He kissed her, plunging his tongue into her mouth, and she arched up beneath him, dug her fingers into his hips, and rubbed her sex against his thigh, arousing herself. He slid his fingers into her, and she was hot, wet, and swollen. He played with her until she couldn't bear it any longer, and she caught his hand, her chest rising and falling rapidly. He raised his head and looked into her large brown eyes, the pupils so big they almost encompassed her irises.

Wordlessly, she rolled onto her front and looked over her shoulder at him, moistening her lips with her tongue.

His heart thundered, and he pulled down another pillow and placed it beneath her hips. Leaning over her, he tucked his arm beneath her breasts and kissed her neck. "Are you sure about this?"

She met his gaze. Something within her eyes made his heart miss a beat. They weren't the eyes of the girl he'd known since she was twelve, the eyes of his best mate's sister. They were a woman's eyes. Hot, knowing, and raunchy as hell. The last of his reservations fell away as he looked into them and saw the depth of her desire, rising to match his, eclipsing any familial feelings he'd ever had about her.

She didn't say anything. She kissed his lips, his shoulder, and down his upper arm.

Then, taking him by surprise, she bit him.

"Ow. Shit!" Pain shot through him, and then desire, like thunder following lightning. "You little…" With his other hand, he smacked her on the butt, hard.

She gasped, dipping her head toward the pillow, and before he could move his arm, did it again.

"Fuck." He pulled his arm back and threaded his hand through her hair, tightening his fingers and pulling her head up. He turned her face so he could capture her lips and kiss her, but she bit his bottom lip, making him growl. He pulled back and looked into her eyes. "Right. You asked for it."

"Oh yeah."

Her complete abandonment was making his blood surge around his body. He took the tube of lubrication and squeezed some onto his fingertips. It was cold, and as he stroked her where she desperately wanted to be touched, she jumped and gasped. "Ooh! You could have warmed it up."

"Serves you right for being shameless."

She pushed back against his hand, staring at him over her shoulder with her dark eyes again. "For fuck's sake, Rusty, get a move on. I'm desperate."

Shaking his head, he spread the lube between her legs. Then he leaned over her and pushed a finger gently into her, making her gasp. "I'd even go so far as to call you depraved," he whispered in her ear.

"You can talk." She slipped her hands into his hair and yanked his head down. He kissed her deeply, his finger slipping and sliding in and out of her tight opening. Small moans escaped her lips as his tongue slid in and out of her mouth, matching the pace of his finger.

He inserted another finger and paused, letting her adjust. She gasped, then groaned when he gently stroked them inside her.

"Okay?" he murmured.

She nodded, breathing hard, and so he slid his fingers in farther, up to the second knuckle, stretching her wider.

"Ah…" She bit her bottom lip.

"Just relax." He removed his fingers, gathered more lube, and did it again, and again. Slowly and gently, until she began to push back against his fingers, asking for more. He was happy to comply, and it wasn't long before her breathing was coming in ragged gasps.

Finally, she moved her legs farther apart and opened her eyes, looking up at him with her beseeching dark gaze. "Now, love. Please."

His heart thumped. Outside the window, a kiwi bird cried, and he could hear the crash of the waves on the beach. He moved on top of her, bathed in moonlight. She pushed her butt against his erection.

He closed his eyes briefly, but already knew there was no going back. He rubbed the tip of himself slowly up and down her wet, soft lips, lubricating himself all the way. Then he pressed himself against her.

Her body resisted, and he braced his hands either side of her. She moved her hips, nudging the tip of him. He pushed forward against her tight entrance, and then, in one smooth movement, he slid inside her.

They both gasped. He stopped moving and waited. He let her adjust, resting his head on her shoulder. She was so incredibly tight, it took all his self-control not to come immediately. His hands curled in the bedclothes, and he had to breathe slowly, exhaling to calm himself down.

He opened his eyes and studied her. Her forehead rested on the pillow, and she'd closed her eyes. Was she okay? He went to withdraw, but stopped as he felt her hand on his thigh. She opened her eyes and met his gaze, and a beautiful flush spread across her cheeks.

"Slowly," he warned. As gently as he could, he pushed forward.

She groaned aloud. He made sure he was well lubricated, and continued to move. Gradually, it became easier, and he felt her body relax beneath him as she began to enjoy it.

"Wow," she said. She closed her eyes again, and moved her hips backward and forward, driving him in and out. "Just, oh wow."

"Oh, Jesus." He let her drive the pace, his head spinning from the incredible sensations she was arousing in him. She sighed so erotically, however, that he couldn't stop his hips thrusting forward.

"Oh yes." She buried her face in the pillow as he kissed her neck and bit her ear. "Oh Rusty, that feels so…fantastic."

He shook his head, linked the fingers of their left hands, and held her hips with his right. "You like that?" he asked huskily as he pushed forward. His hand tightened on hers. "You like me screwing you up the ass?"

He was testing her—he thought she might gasp, blush, or just say nothing, too shocked to speak. In reply, however, she lifted her head, glancing up at him, eyes dark, and spread her legs wider. "Oh yeah. Come on, Rusty. Fuck me senseless."

"Whatever the lady wants." So he did, finally giving in to his desperate urge to thrust harder. As he did so, she met each thrust with a push of her hips, matching his speed, crying out for more. And because he couldn't shock her any more than she was shocking herself, he felt no guilt, no fear, nothing but affection and love for this immoral, sinful, beautiful woman who had seen his sexual darkness and was matching it with her own.

Her language became filthier, and when he slapped her ass in punishment, it only made it worse. She brought his hand under her to squeeze her breast, and he tugged on her nipples until she quivered with need, until they were both hanging onto reality by their fingernails, overtaken by their dark desire.

He slipped a hand underneath her and slid his fingers inside her, which was so incredibly erotic he thought he was going to explode. Clearly, she thought so, too, because she screwed her eyes and nose up, which indicated her orgasm was on its way, and then every single muscle in her body seemed to tighten around him.

"Oh fuck, Rusty!" She squealed. "Fuck, fuck, fuck…"

And there was no way he was going to survive that. Hot, black desire swept over him. He tangled his hand in her hair, pressing her into the pillows. Crying out, he came inside her, thrusting hard, giving her a hundred percent of everything he had, and all he could think about was that he loved her, and if anyone else ever did this to her, he'd beat them to a pulp with a baseball bat.

When he'd done, he withdrew from her carefully, and collapsed beside her. Immediately, he drew her up against him, nuzzling her ear. Her face was still buried in the pillow, and his heart thumped, as, when she finally lifted it, tears shone on her cheeks.

"Babe?" He felt a stab of fear. "Did I hurt you?"

She shook her head, rubbing her nose, and gave a short laugh. "You just blew me away, that's all."

"Come here." He wrapped his arms around her. She curled up against him, wiping her tears away.

"Ten-seven," she whispered.

"Yes. And you're right. You are naturally naughty. I consider myself corrected." He tightened his arms around her. She'd met him and matched him, taken everything he had to give, and seemingly enjoyed every minute of it. He felt overwhelmed with emotion, tired, sated, his eyes pricking with tears. He kissed her hair.

She cleared her throat. "Good."

After a while, he said, "Ten-seven's not bad for one day, is it?"

"I'd say that's pretty spectacular."

"Good enough for your website?"

"Yeah, I reckon."

He kissed her hair again. "Night, Faith."

"Night, sweetie." She kissed his chest. Her breathing grew even, and within minutes, she was asleep.

But Rusty stayed awake for over an hour, Faith's ribcage rising and falling under his warm hand, watching the pale moon ascend slowly in the midnight sky.

Chapter Forty-Three

Faith Hillman's blog

Ten-seven! That's ten orgasms to me, seven to Mr. S. I consider that a great conclusion to the sixth sin!

It was a fantastic evening, and I had such a good time. Variety is the spice of life, they say, and if you want to have a go at sin six, the key is definitely to change things up a bit—try different positions, oral sex, mutual masturbation, in the bath, in the shower, whatever you can think of. And the biggest thing is not to worry when you reach your limit. It was a fun task to aim high, but the numbers are irrelevant, really. It's all about focus, I'm discovering. For that afternoon and evening, we thought about nothing else except each other, and that's what made it special.

And... I hope you ladies realize how brave I'm being now, because I'm going to admit something. We had anal sex. Now, I don't know why I feel so shy admitting this. Allegedly eighteen percent of women have it, and I suspect those numbers are low because women don't like admitting to it. Well, I'm here to tell you that I believe nothing you do in the privacy of your own home (or a motel etc) with a consenting adult is wrong. Nobody should feel pressured into doing anything they're uncomfortable with. But there's nothing wrong in exploration. In trying something to see if you like it. The key is lubrication—lots and lots of it—and preferably patience on the part of your man. Take it slow. Believe me, you'll find it worthwhile :)

*

An excerpt from the 1342 comments
SueAnn: Do you think they'll be on today? I can't wait to hear how it went!
MrS69: Evening all.
SueAnn: Mr. S.! Squeeee! We were wondering when you'd turn up. Are you exhausted?
MrS69: Shagged, yes. LOL. Just a little.
SashaT: You are so amazing. Do you have any brothers I can date?
MrS69: Ha! I'm unique, you know that.

SashaT: Aww…

WendyS: How's it going, Mr. S.? Did you have a good time?

MrS69: As Faith said in her article, it was a fantastic evening. She'll be on later to chat. Thought I'd just call in. I realize I'm taking my life in my hands coming on here tonight, though, judging by your comments…

HelenB: Hehe. Ten-seven?

MrS69: Yeah. I think my crown jewels are radioactive.

Patsy: Hahahaha!

WendyS: ROFL!

SashaT: Oh God, you made coffee come out of my nose!

Loxie: And… anal sex?

MrS69: I knew someone was going to bring that up.

HelenB: Can you blame us?!!!

Patsy: I'm shocked, Mr. S. Are you corrupting our Faith?

MrS69: We had that conversation. She insists not. I'm not so sure.

Karen: Can I ask you something?

MrS69: That's what I'm here for (he says, heart sinking)

Karen: No, it's just that I've never tried it, you know, anal, and my boyfriend's hinted a few times, but he wouldn't make me or anything. I'm a bit nervous, but I feel I should try if he wants to. Do you think I should give it a go?

MrS69: Obviously, it's up to you. Don't feel pressured to do anything you don't want to. It's your body, and a partner shouldn't make you feel bad because you are uncomfortable doing something. After saying that, if you want to try anything, discuss it with your partner, whether it's anal, being tied up, whatever. Tell him (or her) why you're wary and that you want to go slow. I suspect they'll be thrilled that you want to experiment. With being tied up, start with scarves, and make it just for show (I suggest not starting with police handcuffs—that backfired on me big time). With anal, as Faith says, use plenty of lube, and start with fingers or a vibrator. Have fun and enjoy yourself! That's the biggest turn on, believe me.

Patsy: Wow, that's quite a speech!

MrS69: Sorry.

Patsy: No, it's brilliant, Faith will be thrilled!

Ophelia: I know it must be embarrassing for you coming on here, but it's really helpful. I'm sure I'm not the only one who's felt encouraged to try stuff.

WendyS: You're not.

HelenB: You're not.

Yolanda: You're not!

Ophelia: LOL.

MrS69: I'm glad. It always surprises me how little some men discuss these things. None of us is born knowing. It always helps to talk.
SueAnn: Speaking of which… How's it going with Faith?
Patsy: You've scared him off now!
WendyS: Aw, Summer!
Jenny: Oh, I was enjoying that!
MrS69: I'm still here. Just thinking.
SueAnn: I'm sorry! We're all rooting for you, that's all. Are you sad that there's only one more sin?
MrS69: Yes.
Ophelia: Awwwww…
WendyS: Oh God I swear I'm going to cry.
SueAnn: Will you see Faith again after sin seven?
Patsy: *holds breath*
MrS69: I signed a contract. Seven times only, remember?
SueAnn: Yes, but it's only a pretend contract, right?
MrS69: I still signed it.
HelenB: Mr. S.! We can all see how much you like her.
MrS69: Of course I like her.
Karen: Nobody else wants to ask, so I'm going to. Faith said "we thought about nothing else except each other." That sounds like more than friendship to me. Are you both falling in love?
SashaT: OMG.
Patsy: Jeez! The million-dollar question!
MrS69: I'm very fond of her. But rules are rules. We both know sin seven is the end, and we're fine with that. Have to go now. Nice chatting to you all.
Patsy: Aw. You're breaking our hearts too, you know that?

Chapter Forty-Four

Faith paused outside the door to the bar, heart racing and her mouth going dry.

They'd returned earlier that day, but she'd made Rusty promise he would go into the bar to meet the others at seven, and she would arrive after eight, pretending she'd just got back.

After their exploits of the night before, Rusty had been quiet, but very affectionate, very tender with her. Early in the morning, dark clouds had filled the sky, and, with the sound of rain on the window, they'd made love with no sign of the overwhelming, dark passion that had enveloped them the night before. Afterward, they'd packed up and left the house, driving back in the rain, not saying much, although he'd held her hand all the way.

Faith had been conscious of needing to give him time to think about what they'd done and how he'd felt the previous night. She knew her plan had worked. She'd matched his desire, and for a while, he'd forgotten she was Dan's kid sister and had treated her like an equal. But she didn't know if she had eradicated his fears completely and made him think a relationship with her was a possibility.

She hadn't really wanted to go to the bar that night, but she'd promised Dan she'd see him when she got back from her weekend with Mr. S., as if he wanted to check she hadn't been chopped up with a hacksaw and dumped in a black garbage bag by some raving lunatic. She sighed, knowing they were going to give her a hard time, especially after what she'd written in her article. But she couldn't stand outside all day.

She pushed the doors open and went into the bar.

As usual, they were sitting over by the window on the sofas. Dan sat on one with Eve, and Faith was pleased to see his arm around her. Eve looked happy and relaxed in his embrace.

Rusty sat next to Toby on the other sofa, and looked over as he saw her enter. Putting his Coke bottle on the table, he stood as she approached. "Hey."

"Hey." She smiled as everyone looked around and Eve and Toby cheered, and she held up her hand. "Thank you, thank you."

"I'll get you a drink," Rusty said, amused. "Take my seat, I'll get a chair."

"Okay." She slid onto the sofa next to Toby, who leaned over and kissed her temple. Dan and Eve studied her, Dan glowering, Eve's eyes dancing.

"So…" Eve said finally. "Ten-seven?"

Faith put her feet up on the table, crossed at the ankles. "Not bad, eh?"

"Seven?" said Toby. "Jeez."

"Well, eleven-eight if you count this morning." Faith started laughing at Dan. "You should see the look on your face."

"What do you want?" he said flatly. "A medal?"

She shrugged. "If a medal's in the offing, I think I deserve a gold."

Dan sipped his beer and said nothing. She met his eyes for a moment, then lowered hers. No doubt Eve had told him about the blog post she'd written. She'd known it would upset him, but she was a grown woman now. She didn't have to answer to him anymore.

Rusty came back with a glass of wine, and Faith took it from him. "Thanks." She watched as he pulled across a chair and sat between her and Eve, an ankle resting on his knee. She didn't dare meet his eyes—she knew she'd start giggling.

"Did Mr. Sinful have a good time?" Eve asked, amused.

"Poor bastard's been sucked dry," Rusty said. "Probably looks like Ramses the Second now." He winked at Faith. "I threw a history joke in there, did you notice?"

She grinned at him. "Did you have a nice time?"

"Eh?" His eyes widened.

"With Laura?"

He blinked, and then his lips twitched. "Oh." He looked down at the Coke bottle. "Yeah. She's…lovely, actually."

Dan looked at Eve, who looked at Toby, who looked at Faith. "Ooh," said Eve, and sang, "Rusty's in lurv."

"Wow," said Toby, "never thought I'd see the day."

Faith said nothing, tongue-tied, taking the opportunity to sip her wine. Rusty cleared his throat. "I didn't say that."

Seeing he was uncomfortable, wanting to distract attention from him, Faith looked at Toby. "Who are you seeing at the moment? You've been pretty quiet."

"No one," he said, disgruntled. "Haven't had any for weeks."

Rusty smiled. "When you eventually get some, it'll be like the explosion of Krakatoa in 1883."

They all started laughing. Faith leaned forward to put her wine on the table and shifted uncomfortably as she sat back. The exploits of the night before were beginning to make their mark.

"What's up?" asked Eve.

Faith shifted again. "I'm radioactive. I could do with a freezer pack to sit on."

Dan shook his head and started talking to Toby, while Eve laughed and got out her phone and began texting someone.

Faith glanced at Rusty, who was watching her. "You all right?" he mouthed, concern furrowing his brow. She nodded and winked. He met her gaze, and they studied each other for a moment. Gradually his lips curved into a smile. His eyes were very warm and affectionate. She'd read his comments on the blog and knew it had been hard for him, but she appreciated the way he'd opened up to her readers.

A sudden gasp made Faith look across at Eve. Faith's eyes widened in alarm, her humor disappearing rapidly. Eve's gaze was flicking from Faith to Rusty, and, clearly, she'd seen the looks that had passed between them.

The penny had finally dropped.

"Oh my God." Eve stood up, an automatic reaction, staring at Faith in shock.

Dan looked up at her, startled. "What?"

Faith gave a small shake of her head and an imploring look.

Eve stared at her, mouth open, and then glanced across at Rusty. Faith followed her gaze. He studied Eve, seemingly calm, but his eyes were cautionary.

Eve looked back at Faith, shut her mouth, and looked down at Dan. "I... I've just remembered... I think I left my hair straighteners on."

Dan let out a breath. "You frightened the crap out of me."

"Sorry."

He sighed. "I suppose we've got to go back now. I was just getting relaxed."

"I'll run you back if you like," said Rusty, getting to his feet. "I need to get some petrol anyway."

"Thanks, mate." Dan stretched out his legs.

"No worries." Rusty got his car keys out of his pocket, glanced at Faith, and motioned with his head for Eve to follow him. Eve glared at Faith, who looked at her hands in her lap, her heart pounding. After grabbing her handbag, Eve walked out after Rusty.

OhGodohGodohGod. Faith picked up her glass of wine and knocked it back in one go. Would Rusty be able to stop Eve from telling Dan? She glanced across at her brother, who was talking rugby to Toby. He'd had his hair cut recently and it stuck up on top. She adored him, and she knew he adored her, and if he found out that the guy who'd been doing all the terrible things to her was actually his best mate, he was going to go ballistic.

Chapter Forty-Five

Rusty and Eve walked in silence to his car and got in. He drove around the corner, parked on the side of the road, and turned off the engine. Then he turned in his seat to face her.

"You've got to be fucking kidding me," she said. "You and Faith? Dan is going to cut your balls off and stuff them down your throat."

"He won't," said Rusty calmly, although his heart thudded and his head pounded with a sudden headache. "Because he's not going to find out."

"He will," said Eve. "Because I'm going to tell him."

"No you're not."

"He's my boyfriend. I can't keep a secret like this from him. That's unfair—you can't ask me to do that."

"Eve... Faith and me... It'll all be over by the end of the week. There's no point in telling him."

She frowned. "What do you mean?"

"Sin number seven. After that, we're done."

Eve studied him. "You're kidding, right?"

"No."

"Rusty, you seriously think the two of you can sleep together and then pretend like it never happened? I've been reading the blog! I know how you feel about each other."

"That's exactly what we're going to do." He glared at her. "You slept with Toby."

"That was different."

"Oh, how?"

"Well, it happened a gazillion years ago, for one thing. And we only did it twice. It was consolation sex—I'd just broken up with Sam. Whereas you guys..." She tipped her head. "I can't believe you're Mr.S." Her eyes widened. "Oh, fucking hell, the Mars Bar! Jeez, Rusty!"

He looked out of the window, unexpectedly embarrassed, speechless. Eve shook her head and laughed. "You poor bastard."

"What's that supposed to mean?"

She studied him again, long enough to make him uncomfortable. "How do you feel about her?" she said eventually.

He dropped his gaze, picking at a bit of mud on the car seat. "I'm very fond of her."

"Huh. Do you love her?"

He sighed and leaned back against the car door. "You know I do. Just like I love all of you."

"That's not what I'm asking, and you know it."

"It's just sex," he said softly.

"There's no such thing," she said, just as quietly.

He huffed at that. "We both went into this with open eyes. She made me sign a contract, stipulating it would all be over after the seventh sin. She made me promise to stay friends with her afterward. Neither of us expected any more from it."

Eve's cool blue eyes grew soft. "This is me you're talking to, sweetie. I'm your friend. Stop treating me like a stranger and talk to me properly. The two of you have gotten yourselves into a right mess, and you're not going to be able to get out of it without some help."

He looked away, out of the window, all his resentment and irritation fading. He leaned an elbow on the steering wheel and massaged his throbbing forehead with a hand. "I don't know what to say."

"Is she in love with you?"

"I think so."

"And are you in love with her?"

His eyes met hers. He didn't say anything.

Her lips curved in a smile. "Well, that changes things a bit."

"No, it doesn't." He ran a hand through his hair. "I don't want a relationship. It ends, next weekend. We've just got to find a way to continue to see each other without it getting in the way."

She studied his face. "Is this all to do with your family again?"

"Don't even go there, Eve."

Her forehead creased. "So you're going to throw away what could potentially be the love of your life, because your dad and your brother are idiots?" He turned in his seat and put his hand on the key in the ignition, but she put a hand on his arm. "Wait a minute."

He sat back, tense and stiff, his jaw set, his arms straight on the steering wheel. "I don't want to talk about it."

"Are you going to be okay with seeing her with other men, Rusty? Because if you don't hold on to her, she will eventually hook up with someone else. However much she loves you, she's only twenty-two. She wants kids, a family, all the trimmings. How are you going to feel when she has a ring on her finger? Or stands in front of you, six months pregnant?"

"Stop it." His hands tightened on the wheel, and he closed his eyes. His headache was making him feel sick. And so was the thought of Faith with a swollen belly, looking up lovingly at her husband. How was he going to cope?

"Oh." Eve put a hand on his shoulder. "I'm sorry, Rusty. I didn't realize."

He went to say, "realize what?" but at that moment his phone rang. He pulled it out of his pocket and flipped it open. It was Sarah, his sister-in-law.

He answered the call. "Hello?"

"Rusty?"

"Yeah. Sarah? What's up?"

"Rusty, can you come around?" She sounded panicky. "It's Cole." There was a crashing sound, and she squealed.

Rusty straightened in the seat, alarmed. "What's going on?"

"He's drunk and he's angry and he's smashing up the living room. I've locked myself in the bathroom with Finn, but Cole keeps throwing things at the door." There was a sniffing sound—she was crying. "Please, Rusty, I'm scared."

"I'll be right there." He clipped the phone shut and started the engine. "I'll have to drop you back at the bar," he said to Eve, reversing, and turning around in the road.

"What's going on?"

"Cole's determined to destroy his family. The fucking idiot. I've a good mind to call the police and get him put away again." He drove too quickly back to the bar and skidded to a halt in front of the doors.

Eve put her hand on the door handle, looking back at him.

"I don't care what you say to Dan," he told her. "If you feel you have to tell him, then tell him. I'll handle it. Don't lie for me."

She said nothing, but squeezed his arm. "You're a good man, Rusty."

"I'm not. But thanks anyway." He watched her get out and then drove away.

At Cole's house, he parked in the road and walked across the lawn. His brother was a slob—a motorbike lay in bits in front of the garage, and there was rubbish across the grass, including a broken bottle, which made Rusty grit his teeth at the thought of his four-year-old nephew stumbling across it.

He went around the back of the house to the decking. As he'd thought, the sliding doors were open, and he stepped into the living room, his heart sinking as he saw several pictures and ornaments lying broken on the floor.

Stepping inside, he avoided the broken glass and paused. He could hear Cole shouting and banging, presumably on the bathroom door, answered by a high-pitched yell from Sarah. He walked across the living room and down the hall, turned the corner, and paused as he saw his brother.

Cole was two inches taller than Rusty and about thirty pounds heavier, with the family's distinctive red hair, though his was a lot longer than Rusty's, and curled in straggly strands around his neck. He was a good-looking man, but his deep-set eyes and a scar on his cheek he'd received during a fight a few years back made him look suspicious and mean. He turned now as Rusty paused, and they studied each other.

"Well, well," said Cole. "Halle-fucking-lujah, the cavalry's arrived." He turned and banged on the bathroom door. "Did you ring him? You fucking bitch."

"Hey." Rusty walked forward until he was three feet away. "Don't speak to her like that. Come into the kitchen, for Christ's sake. I'll make you a cup of coffee."

Cole turned back to face him. His eyes followed a second later—clearly, he was well plastered. "Fuck off, *Dick*. This is none of your business."

Rusty bristled at Cole's childhood nickname for him. "I'm not going until you sober up, you drunk bastard. Sarah's terrified, and so's Finn. Is that really what you want—your family to be scared shitless of you?"

"I saw her with… the guy from the garage. She's having an affair." Cole swayed slightly.

"I'm not!" Sarah yelled from the bathroom. "I went in to book the car in for a service. You asked me to, you crazy son of a bitch!"

Cole's hands tightened into fists. "I saw her put her hand on his arm… And she laughed up at him. Little flirt. I don't know who she's doing behind my back." He leaned his forehead against his arm on the doorjamb.

Rusty frowned, feeling an uncharacteristic sweep of pity for his brother. This was what love did to the Thorne men. Turned them into crazed lunatics, twisted with suspicion and jealousy. He'd felt the exact same thing sitting in the car with Eve, thinking about Faith standing before him, happy and pregnant with another man's child.

And that was when it dawned on him. He wasn't going to be able to be around her anymore. He didn't want to feel those emotions when he looked at her. He was going to have to move away and not see her again. And maybe, as the years went by, it wouldn't hurt so much when Dan rang him and said how she was doing.

He reached out and touched his brother's arm. "Come on, mate. Sit down and talk to me about it."

Cole twitched and threw off Rusty's hand. He ignored him and banged on the door again. "Let me in. It's my house—let me into my own fucking bathroom!"

"Cole!" Rusty grabbed his shirt and pulled him away from the door. "For God's sake, leave her alone."

Cole turned and pushed him, and Rusty stumbled back down the hall. Cole came after him, and Rusty walked backward into the living room, drawing him away from the bathroom. He put his hands up. "Don't do this, come on, calm down."

Cole ignored him, obviously desperate to take out his roiling emotions on someone, and he came forward and aimed a swing at Rusty's head. Rusty ducked, lighter on his feet, alcohol-free, and stepped backward again. "Cole! Jesus, man, calm down."

"Stop telling me to calm down," yelled Cole. "You fucking do-gooder. Can't sort your own life out, so you have to come around here and interfere with mine."

"Yeah, 'cause I'm the one with the problem." Rusty made his tone wry, although the comment stung. Cole was probably closer to the truth than he realized.

He watched his brother carefully. They'd both had boxing lessons as kids, and Cole could throw a mean right hook. At least his brother was focusing on him and not on Sarah and Finn anymore. But that would be scant consolation if he found his teeth shoved halfway down his throat. "Sit down," he said again.

Cole lunged at him. Rusty dodged the punch once more, his feet scrunching on broken glass, and he felt Cole's meaty hands grab his shirt. The next thing he knew, Cole had slammed him against the wall and knocked his breath out of him.

He flung both arms up, knocked away Cole's grip and shoved him hard in the chest. "Okay, now I'm annoyed."

"Ooh," taunted Cole. "Gonna get your feather duster out now and tickle me to death, Dick-head?"

Rusty saw red. He drew back his arm and threw a punch at Cole's face, putting all his frustration and unhappiness behind it. His brother moved, but not quickly enough. Rusty's fist connected with Cole's jaw, and the larger man crumpled and fell backward into the living room. His head met the dining table with a resounding crack, and he went still.

Behind Rusty, Sarah screamed. Rusty hadn't realized she'd come out of the bathroom. She pushed past him and dropped to her knees beside Cole. "You bloody killed him!"

"He's not dead," said Rusty, relieved as he saw Cole's eyes flutter and heard a low moan escape his mouth. He pulled out his phone. "I'll ring for an ambulance, though. It'll get him out of your hair until he sobers up."

As he dialed, he held out an arm to stop Finn from going to his father, conscious of all the broken glass around. But Finn pushed him away, his eyes wet, and ran to Cole's side, saying, "Daddy, Daddy, are you okay?"

Rusty put the phone to his ear, feeling cold inside as he watched Sarah and Finn cover Cole's face in kisses, distraught that he was obviously injured. Even now, they couldn't hate him, despite all the hurt he'd caused them.

"Ambulance, please," he said as the operator answered, and gave the details before he hung up.

Cole was already stirring, and Rusty knelt to help him up, but Sarah pushed him away. Her eyes were wet. "Just go," she said tiredly. "I'll deal with it from here."

"But…"

"It's all right, he won't hurt me now. Thanks for coming around. I appreciate it."

Rusty stood, his head beginning to thud again as he looked at the mess in the room. "Why don't you let me stay and help you clean up?"

"No, go please. He won't want to see you when he sobers up. Just go."

Rusty nodded. His knuckles hurt where they'd connected with Cole's jaw. But what hurt most of all was Finn's little face as he looked up at the man who'd hit his daddy. He didn't understand what had happened, of course. But in his eyes, Rusty was the bad man here. The thought made Rusty sick to his stomach.

He turned and walked out of the house. Sarah shut the door behind him, and the sound was like the closing of the lid on the coffin of his future. Faith deserved better than him and his bad blood. He didn't regret sleeping with her—could never do that—but he did regret that she would find it difficult to accept it when he left.

Chapter Forty-Six

Faith Hillman's Blog

This is just a quick post to answer the emails I've been getting. I'm not sure yet what's happening this weekend. Yes, I know we still have Sin Seven (Lust) to carry out, but there have been some complications, and I'm not sure yet whether we'll go ahead. I'll keep you posted.

*

Excerpt from the 1692 comments
Karen: OMG Faith! You can't leave us hanging like that!
SashaT: Do you think he's told her he wants to stop?
Georgia: Oh no! I don't believe that. He's crazy about her.
HelenB: One of them must have wanted more.
Ophelia: But which?
Karen: I reckon it was him.
WendyS: I don't think so. He kept reminding us about the contract.
Patsy: I don't think it's that. I think someone's found out who he is.
SueAnn: Argh! You think it was SJPWannaB?
Patsy: Possibly. And maybe it's someone that Faith works with or something, and it's caused her problems.
Karen: Oh God, we can't have them breaking up now! What can we do?
Patsy: There's nothing we can do. Faith knows we're here if she needs us.

Chapter Forty-Seven

Faith didn't see Rusty again for three days. He texted her on Sunday to tell her briefly what had happened, and she knew instantly it would cause trouble between them. Sure enough, he only sent five texts on Monday, two on Tuesday, and by Wednesday he wasn't communicating with her at all.

She felt overwhelmed by sadness. She'd booked a motel at the weekend in anticipation of the seventh sin, but she wasn't sure whether he was going to want to go ahead with it. She couldn't bring herself to write on her blog, although she read all the comments, just in case he happened to post. He didn't. She wasn't surprised.

At eight thirty on Wednesday evening, there was a knock at the door.

Thinking it was Eve, or maybe Dan, she walked up the hall slowly. She wore an old, tight T-shirt and a pair of baggy trackpants, with her hair pulled back off her face in a scrunchie. A bar of half-eaten Dairy Milk lay on the coffee table.

She opened the door, and her heart gave a somersault when she saw Rusty leaning against the doorjamb, hands in his pockets. Temporarily speechless, she stared at him for a moment. He wore a black T-shirt and black jeans, and he'd had his hair cut at last—it was still fairly long on the top, flopping over his forehead, but short around the back of his neck, and her fingers twitched at the thought of running her hands up it.

He looked at her, and the smile that had hovered on her lips as she saw him faded away. His green eyes were angry, resentful. She stepped back and to the side to let him in, but he didn't move. He continued to stare at her, his gaze dipping almost insolently over her tight T-shirt. Then he looked away across the garden, although he still didn't move.

She studied him for a moment. She could read his thoughts as clearly as if his head were made of glass. He didn't want to be there.

But he couldn't keep away. He wanted to see her. But he didn't *want* to want to see her.

She hesitated, her heart going out to him. Seeing his brother had ripped him up inside, and he needed consolation, but he didn't know how to ask, because they weren't supposed to be having a relationship. They were supposed to be over at the weekend, it was all terribly messy and convoluted, and neither of them knew what to do.

So she did the only the thing she could have done. She grasped the bottom of her T-shirt, peeled it off, and threw it to the floor, glad she had a decent bra underneath. Pulling out her scrunchie, she shook her head and ran a hand through her hair, challenging him with her gaze.

He stared at her for a moment, a furrow in his brow, all the pain he was feeling etched in those lines. And then he came inside the house, kicked the door shut, and gathered her up in his arms. Lifting her off the ground, he wrapped her legs around him. She pressed her lips to his, and he kissed her hungrily as he walked down the hall. He turned to press her up against the wall, backing her up with a bump that knocked the breath out of her. She gasped, sank her hands into his hair, and ran her fingers up the short, bristly strands at the back, pulling his head to hers. She opened her mouth to welcome his tongue in a fierce, passionate kiss that lit the whole of her body. Little electric shocks shot through her, making her nipples stand on end and a dull throbbing begin between her legs.

He pushed his hips forward and pressed his hard erection against her, almost bruising her, but she welcomed the sweet pain, moaning softly, and tightened her legs around him so it brought him even closer. He muttered something against her mouth, but she didn't catch it, and she thought she probably wouldn't want to hear it anyway. He let her legs go so she slid down him, and his hands went around her back to unclip her bra. Drawing it down her arms, he threw it to the floor, and then he pushed her back up against the wall. He covered her breasts with his hands and squeezed her nipples, making her gasp again. He dropped his head and covered one of them with his mouth, and she inhaled, and inhaled, and inhaled, unable to catch her breath as he sucked hard, so hard it almost hurt. But she knew what he wanted, and she clenched her fingers in his hair, pulling his head. He stepped back, breathing heavily, his eyes so hot it sent a thrill right through her.

Taking his hand, she led him into the living room, over to the sofa. He grabbed the neck of his T-shirt and pulled it over his head, dropping it to the floor, and she slid off her trackpants, pushed her panties down her legs, and kicked them off too. He began to undo his jeans, but she shoved him hard on the chest, taking him by surprise, and he stumbled and fell onto the sofa.

She climbed on top of him and pushed him onto his back. Sitting on his legs, she unbuttoned his jeans quickly. He watched her, his chest rising and falling rapidly, and grabbed her before she could lower his boxers and release him. He pulled her up toward him, so she straddled his legs, and slipped his hand behind her neck, bringing her lips down to his.

She kissed him hungrily, aware of a rising passion deep within her that she couldn't control. She wanted him so badly, loved him so deeply, she was desperate to try and ease his pain, as well as assuage the dark craving that spread through her as he held her hips down and pressed the hard part of him against the soft, swollen part of her. She moved her hips and ground their sexes together, moving herself up and down the length of him, soaking his boxers with her moisture. He responded with a heartfelt groan and cupped her breasts with his warm hands, lifting her slightly so he could fasten his mouth on them, his tongue rough against her sensitive, tender skin, the soft, pliant nipples hardening as he sucked.

She couldn't wait any longer. She pushed down his boxers and directed him into her, pausing as the hot tip of him slid inside. She braced herself on his shoulders, meeting his gaze as she lifted her hips just enough to let him push into her and then slide out again.

He tried to hold her hips, but she caught his hands and pinned them above his head, remembering vividly the day she'd handcuffed him to the bed. He looked absolutely gorgeous lying there, eyes half-lidded, bare from the waist up, his muscular arms tense as he flexed his hands in hers. But still she didn't give him what he wanted—she eased up, pushed down, short, shallow strokes, teasing them both, making him close his eyes briefly before opening them to fix on her with a direct, demanding gaze.

Suddenly, before she could resist, he wrenched his hands free, wrapped his arms around her, and flipped her over and underneath him, a move so slick and professional it made her gasp with approval. He laughed, the first sign that he wasn't really angry with her, and she raised her arms over her head and stretched out. She reveled in the feel of being completely naked beneath him, the coarse material of his jeans rough against her thighs. Still inside her, he braced himself in turn, and she wrapped her legs around him as he began to move with deep, slow, driving thrusts that soon had her sighing in ecstasy.

It didn't take long for either of them to reach their climax, and as he shuddered and plunged deeply into her, his body going rigid, she cried out as a wave of pleasure swept over her, her muscles tightening around him.

He rested his head on her shoulder for a moment, and she put her arms around him and ran her fingers up his spine, stroking his ribs. She placed a gentle kiss on his ear, and he lifted his head and looked at her.

"Hey," he said, and she realized it was the first thing either of them had said since he'd turned up.

"Hey." She touched his face and then ran her hand up into the short hair on the back of his head. "I like this."

He shrugged. "About time I tidied myself up." Faith knew the real reason he'd had it cut, though. Seeing Cole with his straggly locks had reminded Rusty of the fact that they were brothers. He wanted to sever the link, but, unable to do that, he'd at least made sure they looked as unalike as possible.

Gently, he withdrew from her, and she shifted on the sofa, turning onto her side so he could lie next to her, facing her. He met her gaze and gave a heavy sigh. "I'm sorry."

"For what? It was a pretty good shag."

He laughed and cupped her face with his hand, stroking her cheekbone with his fingers. Then he slid his hand into her hair, brought her head forward, and kissed her. The kiss was tender, and it made her sigh softly when he eventually pulled back.

He looked into her eyes again. She could see regret and pain in his gaze. She went to say something, but he pushed himself up and off the sofa, doing up his jeans.

She sat up and drew up her knees, putting her arms around them. "Are you going?" She made her voice casual.

He looked startled. "Come in, screw you blind, and then go home? Jeez, Faith, I'm not that heartless." He paused. "Unless you want me to go?"

She smiled, relieved. "No." She got up and picked up his T-shirt, pulling it over her head. It came past her bottom, the sleeves almost to her elbows. "Come on, I'll make you a cup of tea."

Chapter Forty-Eight

They went into the kitchen, and she switched on the kettle and busied herself putting the bags in the mugs. Rusty sat at the table and watched her, thinking how graceful she was, how beautiful, with her hair sex-mussed and her ass just showing beneath his T-shirt. Why was it so sexy when a woman wore a man's clothes? He leaned an elbow on the table, put his head on his hand, and sighed as she ferreted around for some biscuits, finally finding a box at the back of the cupboard. She placed them on the table, smiling as she saw him watching her.

Finishing the tea, she brought the mugs over to the table and sat opposite. He sipped his tea and watched as she dipped a biscuit into hers and sucked it. "Are you going to talk to me?" she asked.

He looked into his mug. "I don't know what to say."

"Why did you come around tonight? Just for sex?" She shrugged as he looked up. "I don't mind."

"No." He dropped his gaze again.

"To say goodbye?"

His hand tightened on the mug and he made himself relax his grip before he broke it. "I…"

"Rusty?" Her voice was gentle. "It's okay." She reached out and held his hand.

He brushed her knuckles with his thumb. "I just can't, you know? Seeing Cole, I couldn't… I just can't."

"It's okay." She squeezed his hand. Then she sipped her tea. She seemed calm, composed. How on earth was she so calm?

He cleared his throat. "Can we do it now?"

"Huh?"

"The seventh sin. I don't know that I can wait for the weekend. I need to…"

"Finish it?"

He met her gaze, choking up. "Faith…"

"You don't have to. I can make it up. It doesn't matter."

"No. I signed the damn contract. I promised. I'll do it."

She sat back, withdrew her hand, and took another biscuit. "If we do, you do as I say. Follow my rules."

"Sure."

She gestured at the packet on the table. "You look spaced out. Eat a biscuit—it'll ground you."

Smiling, he took one and dunked it. "I'm not surprised I'm spaced out, after what you just did to me."

"Er, excuse me, I kind of think you did the doing."

"You took your top off." She had no answer to that, and he smirked before taking her hand again. "I'm glad you did. I couldn't think what to say."

"I guess we didn't need words."

"No."

They sat and drank their tea. She hadn't turned on any lights, so the room was cast in twilight. She finished her tea, got up, and put the mug in the sink. Rusty finished his and handed his mug to her. She put his cup next to hers and looked at them for a moment. Then she came over to him.

"Come on." She took his hand and led him back into the living room.

Chapter Forty-Nine

Faith turned to him, wondering if he could hear the pounding of her heart. "Take off your pants and sit down."

"Yes, ma'am."

She went over to the cupboard in the corner, extracted some candles, and started placing them around the room and lighting them. Soon a warm glow bathed the room, and the air filled with the scent of lavender, rose, and sandalwood.

She went over to the iPod on the table and chose a slow playlist she'd been concocting for this very purpose. As the music started playing, she smiled at Rusty where he sat on the sofa, arms along the back, watching her. She kept the volume low but danced for a while, and he rewarded her with a smile, albeit a sad one.

She felt strangely euphoric, in spite of the fact that she knew this was the last time they'd ever make love. It was as if the future had vanished and there was only the here and now, and the here and now was wonderful. Rusty Thorne sat on her sofa in only his boxers, red hair falling across his forehead, looking at her the way he looked at Roman architecture, with a sense of wonder, as if there was nothing more beautiful in the whole world.

Elton John's *Sweet Painted Lady* came on the iPod, and Rusty raised an eyebrow. "Seems appropriate."

She came closer to him, still dancing in his T-shirt. "Are you calling me a tart?" He continued to stare at her, eyebrow raised, and she started laughing, grasped the bottom of the T-shirt, and pulled it off. She continued to dance, naked, and linked her hands on the top of her head, singing to the music as she swayed around the room.

Rusty said nothing, still watching her, sighing occasionally, and eventually she took pity and went over to him. She sat astride him, on his thighs, and took his hands in hers.

"Are you sure about this?" She kissed his fingertips. "It won't be easy."

"I'm sure." His eyes were a rich green in the candlelight, like emeralds, glittering in the flickering flames. He linked his fingers with hers. Again, she felt a swell of euphoria, of pleasure that he was there, all hers for the next hour or so, completely under her control.

She slid a little more down his thighs, widening her own, but not quite touching his body. "Tantric sex is actually a discipline which should be developed over weeks and months. We can't really do it justice tonight. But we can try out a couple of its techniques."

"Okay."

"It's about building sexual energy, abstaining from orgasms, and letting the energy circulate back into the body."

"Ah."

"Don't look so disappointed," she said, nose crinkling. "I said we'd adapt it for tonight. I've made up my own rules."

He laughed, and she felt a surge of affection for him. Poor Rusty. Deep as an ocean, seething and restless, confused and hurting. She wanted to hug him to her, draw out all his pain, but all she could do was show him how much she loved him.

"Are you comfortable?" she asked softly.

"Yeah."

"Good." She wriggled until she felt relaxed, and then put her arms around his neck, leaning on the back of the sofa. "Now, one key thing here is to keep eye contact. I think it's going to be weird at first, but it's important, because there's no hiding when you're looking into each other's eyes, and tonight's about baring our souls, sweetheart."

For the first time, he looked wary, but he said, "Okay."

She took off her watch and placed it on the back of the sofa, where she could see it without having to move. "Right. The first thing we're going to think of is how we felt about each other before we got together."

"Okay," he said again. She'd wondered whether he might find this amusing, and make some joke, but he didn't. He seemed relaxed and calm, his arms around her, his fingers linked behind her back.

She settled herself. And then she looked into his eyes.

She'd always thought they were green. And they were, generally, but for the first time, up close, she saw how many other colors were within them, like an Impressionist painting. Around the pupils, which were large and sucked in the light like black holes, were rings of sand-colored yellow, surrounded by dark green petal-shapes, as if his glassy orbs reflected two sunflowers. Beyond the dark green petals was a cloudy blend of yellows and greens, but also flecks of blue and brown, and, right at the edge, tiny sparkles of gold.

She thought back to the time she first met him. He hadn't changed that much, still long and lean, more muscular now, still as restless, still as hot and sexy. She remembered how she used to sit on the low wall fronting her parents' house while the boys played soccer and rugby and basketball out front, Dan, Rusty, Toby, and several others. Her eyes had always fallen on the lad with the red hair, who seemed a tad more serious than the others. He'd laughed and joked with them, but he'd sometimes turn up with a bruise or a scrape that she knew wasn't caused by falling off a skateboard, because his eyes would be dark and broody. She'd wanted to go up to him and kiss the frown between his eyes until it went away, but she'd never been brave enough, and besides, he'd usually had a girl hanging around. Sometimes she'd found her gaze straying to them when they kissed, and she'd watched with envy, ashamed to be prying. But she'd been unable to tear her gaze away from where he'd cupped the girl's head possessively, and the way he'd pressed himself against her, making the girl giggle and push him away playfully. She'd dreamed at night about how it would feel to be that girl, having Rusty kiss her, press himself against her, lying hot and frustrated in her bed. Was it possible she'd been in love with him her whole life?

She thought about her eighteenth birthday, how he'd dragged her under the lemon trees and kissed her, and automatically her gaze dropped to his lips. They started to curve, as if he'd guessed what she was thinking about. He smiled, and she smiled back, wondering if he was seeing the scene playing before him, as she was, the smell of lemons and mandarins in the air, the warmth of the night wrapping around her like his arms, his lips cool on hers.

She shifted, knowing her smile had turned into a frown. This wasn't going to be as easy as she'd thought. His eyes remained calm, however, soothing her, and she sighed and settled. Her eyes flicked to the watch.

She licked her lips. Her mouth was dry. "Now we're going to think about the last few weeks," she said, her voice husky. "I want you to think about each sin, and about what we've done, and how you've felt."

Chapter Fifty

Rusty nodded. He felt relaxed and calm at last, the most relaxed he'd felt all week. Like he'd come home, that this was where he belonged, sitting there on the couch with Faith on his lap, her body warm in his arms, her beautiful brown eyes locked on his. He knew brown irises were the most common type in the world, but there was nothing common about Faith's eyes. The color of polished mahogany, they had a strange pattern of light brown circles he'd never noticed before. They reminded him of tree rings, dissected by reddish-brown lines radiating out from the center, making him think of sunlit trees, dappled leaves, and forests in autumn. They were such a warm color, which didn't surprise him, as he was sure the warmth of her personality radiated out through them.

He began thinking about their journey over the past few weeks. Watching porn in the motel, Faith moving on top of him so erotically, the DVD of the two girls in the background. He remembered how worried he'd been, but she'd taken him in hand, literally, recognizing he needed to be talked into it, knowing even then what he needed and how to make him feel better.

He thought about the first time they'd gone down on each other, and how he'd watched her in the moonlight, filled with awe at her beauty. Was that the point he'd fallen in love with her? Or had it begun long ago, with the moment she stood in front of him in her bikini, only fifteen years old, but hot as a model, with her taunting, saucy eyes?

The song changed, and he began thinking about the time at the lake, when she'd gone to all that trouble with the food, spending hours tempting him with oysters and figs and Lord knew what else. He knew the exact moment she thought about the Mars Bar, because a flush appeared on her cheeks and she lowered her gaze for a second, and he laughed, loving the way he could make her blush in retrospect. They kept giggling for a while, but he kept his eyes locked on hers, determined that he wasn't going to be the one to break the spell.

He thought about how she'd stripped for him at the hotel, and how she'd driven him to the edge afterward. It had been the first time he'd realized how hot she was, how much she understood what he wanted in bed. It had been a revelation, his first eureka moment, and the thought now made him wish he were back there, with three sins still to go.

Her eyes glittered with amusement, and he knew she was thinking about the handcuffs. He gave her an exasperated look, and she laughed, leaning forward to kiss him on the nose, the first time she'd touched her lips to him since she'd climbed on him. He sighed, and then their gazes met and he knew she was thinking about the beach house, and all the fun they'd had. And how she'd taken him by the hand and led him toward the darkness, and kept him safe when he feared he was going to be overwhelmed.

And now the seventh sin had arrived, and his time with her was nearly over. His own regret was mirrored in her eyes, but she smiled, moving forward a little more so she was just brushing his boxers.

Chapter Fifty-One

"Okay," Faith said softly. "The next step is about exchange of breath. We need to keep our breathing in sync. You breathe out, I breathe in, and vice versa. That way our energies are intertwining." She waited again for him to make a joke, but he still appeared to be taking this seriously, because he didn't move, his arms and hands warm on her skin.

Between her legs, she could feel he was erect and ready for her, but he didn't try to press it against her. He was going to wait for her. How sweet.

Tipping her head so their lips were almost touching, she breathed out slowly through her mouth, and then breathed in, watching his ribs rise and fall in response.

The music changed to Jose Gonzalez's *Heartbeats*, and she sighed, which he drank in, returning it to her with an exhalation. Her hands rested on the back of his head, and she stroked his short hair with her thumbs.

Close up, she could see every detail on his skin. The small chickenpox scar on his cheek. He'd shaved that morning, and now had a slight hint of stubble on his chin. If she were to move her face against his, it would burn her skin, making a slight rasping sound. His lips were slightly apart, the bottom fuller than the top, his straight teeth just visible. His breath smelled sweet, of biscuit and tea, and mint—he'd brushed his teeth before he came to visit her. The thought made her soften like butter on a radiator.

She couldn't help it—she moved a millimeter closer. Their lips weren't touching, and yet she could feel the pressure of his mouth over hers, as if their shadows were reaching out to kiss. He still hadn't moved, his gaze moving slowly over her face, as if he were drinking in the sight of her, trying to commit her to memory.

Their breaths were deepening, but still coordinated, and she felt as if she were drawing his energy into her body, sucking him into her lungs, oxygenating her blood with him, feeling him speed through her veins. Gradually, she became acutely conscious of every inch of their bodies in proximity to each other. The fact that her nipples were just brushing the hairs on his chest. The slight dampness of his hair beneath her fingertips. The soft stroking of his fingers on her back—when had he started doing that? The fact that, once again, her moisture was dampening the silky material of his boxers, her sex beginning to ache, so aware of the hardness of his body just an inch away from it.

Part of her wanted to pull him toward her, press her lips frantically to his, push aside his boxers, and let him slide all the way up her, but the other part was desperate to make this last. This might be the final time he ever touched her. The thought made her want to weep, but she kept the tears in check, knowing she had to keep calm, keep the emotion at bay.

She moved the final few millimeters closer. Now her breasts touched his chest, and his erection pressed against the soft dampness of her, making her sigh. Their lips brushed gently, sending a shiver running down her spine like cool water. He moved his hands up a little, his palms against her ribs, brushing her skin with his thumbs.

She gave in and kissed him softly, leading the way. First of all, she used just her lips, and then eventually opened her mouth and ran her tongue lightly across his bottom lip, reminding herself of the first time he'd kissed her, in the car. He replied with a sigh and did the same, and they deepened the kiss, but kept it slow and languid, concentrating on the feel and taste of each other's mouths.

Eventually, however, she couldn't help but move forward a little closer, and pressed against his erection more firmly, conscious of the cool material between them. Her soft skin parted to welcome him and exposed her clit, gently arousing her as she moved her hips from side to side.

Rusty sighed and his hands slid farther up, coming around to cup her breasts. For a moment, he just held them, not moving his fingers, his skin warm on hers, and then as she arched her back, he brushed his thumbs across the swollen skin of her nipples, causing them to tighten into tiny buds that he rolled gently between his fingers.

Faith gasped and lifted her head. Desire lit her nerve ends, exploding within her like fireworks. He stopped and slid his hands back to her ribs, and she exhaled, not missing the slight curve of his lips. He liked knowing exactly how to arouse her, gradually, as if he were cultivating a garden, teasing the seed of her desire, watching it shoot through her, gaining great satisfaction as it flowered into a thing of beauty.

She kissed him again, and this time he pressed her closely against him, their passion beginning to grow. She moved her hips, and slid her hands through his hair, tightening her arms around his shoulders.

He held her around the waist, moved toward the edge of the sofa, and stood. Lifting her easily, he held her up as she wrapped her legs around his waist. He carried her through into the bedroom, climbed onto the bed, turned, and lay on his back. She stretched out along him, reveling in the feel of his hard, muscular body against hers.

She kissed him for a while, and he played with her breasts again. When she lifted herself on her hands, he covered her nipples with his mouth, going from one to the other, then back again, arousing her with teeth and tongue until she began to wriggle in earnest against his silk-covered erection. Eventually she lifted herself off him for a moment, and he slid his boxers off. She climbed back onto him and leaned over him. Widening her thighs, she moved down until she could feel the tip of him enter her, pushing aside her swollen lips.

She slid down him slowly, feeling him stretch her apart until he filled her up. He sighed loudly, and she knew she must be slippery and hot, a velvet sheath around him. She sat upright, and he watched her as she began to move. Every now and again, she bent and kissed him, and he stroked her body, worshipped it with his hands and mouth, until they reached a point where they could no longer hold back the rising tide.

He turned her carefully until she lay under him, and pushed himself up on his elbows, looking down with such an expression of love that emotion tumbled through her like a tidal wave, breaking down the carefully constructed defenses she'd tried to erect.

"Come on sweetheart," he murmured, kissing her. "Wrinkle your nose and screw up your eyes the way you do when I know you're going to come."

"Don't embarrass me." Her cheeks grew hot at his amused, affectionate gaze.

"I like embarrassing you. I like the fact that I can make you blush all over." He kissed her again. "Go on, love. Come for me one last time."

One last time. The phrase tipped her over the edge, and tears came in a rush that surprised her. He didn't stop, though. He kissed them away as they leaked from the corners of her eyes, and continued to move inside her. Even though she was upset, the sensations in her thighs and abdomen continued to build. Gradually, she felt the familiar approach of her orgasm. It crept through her, beginning with a slow ripple like a stone dropped into a pool, causing a wave that radiated out from deep in her belly, down through her sex. It became a rush, and then everything tightened, and she knew he was watching her with satisfaction as she squeezed her eyes shut, the pulsing in her muscles almost too intense to bear.

He hooked one hand under her thigh to bring up her knee, plunging deep inside her, and as she finally opened her eyes with a gasp, she looked up to see his gaze fixed on her as he reached his own climax. He held her tightly, his eyes unfocussed, pushing deeper and deeper into her, and she could only lie there and watch with longing as he poured his love into her, saying her name, until eventually he was spent, and the wave turned into small ripples, and back to calm.

And then it was done.

Faith lay looking up at the ceiling and tried desperately to stop crying, biting her lip as he breathed deeply close to her ear. He lifted his head and looked at her. Withdrawing, he rolled off her and sat up.

He got off the bed and went out into the living room, and she pushed herself upright, wiping her face free of tears. He always hugged her after making love, and a cold sliver of panic slid into her stomach.

A few seconds later, he was back. He'd tugged on his boxers and jeans, and he was holding his T-shirt in his hand. She sat back against the headboard, her arms around her knees, feeling vulnerable without any clothes.

He looked at her for a moment before concentrating on turning his T-shirt the right way out before putting it on. Faith looked away, reached for her bathrobe, and pulled it on quickly. She wasn't about to have this conversation naked. It reminded her suddenly of Ripley in *Alien*, climbing into a spacesuit at the end before she faced the creature. Why had that jumped into her head?

Rusty shoved his hands in his pockets. The sulky, angry look had returned to his face. She stood and tried not to think about the fact that her thighs were wet from his lovemaking and she could really do with visiting the bathroom.

"So," she said calmly.

The muscles of his jaw were knotted hard. "I don't want you to talk about that on your website."

She stared at him. "I beg your pardon?"

"It was personal, private. Nothing to do with anyone else. I don't want you going into detail for all the world to see."

She cleared her throat. "I understand how you feel, and of course I won't go into detail. But I do have to talk a little bit about the method. It's part of my job, Rusty. You did agree to that, when you signed the contract."

He glared at her. "I didn't agree to being exploited."

She stared at him for a moment and then burst out laughing. "What are you talking about, you big girl? I've hardly exploited you. You weren't exactly reluctant, from what I could see."

Instantly, she could see she'd done the wrong thing. He lowered his eyelids, clenched his jaw, and his eyes darkened. "You think this is funny?"

"No." She sobered hastily. "It's nerves. You're making me nervous." She took a step toward him, but stopped as he backed up. "What's going on here? We both agreed this was how it would end. That's what the contract was about."

"But you would want to carry on dating me. If I wasn't ending it now." His eyes challenged her.

"And so would you if you weren't so obsessed with your family genes."

He narrowed his eyes. "Did you plan this?"

"What?"

"The sins. Did you plan them in this order, to make sure they had the maximum possible impact on me?" He put his hands on his hips, angry now.

"No…" She looked at him warily. Uh-oh. He was losing it.

He ignored her answer. "Reeling me in gradually. Tempting me with more and more erotic stuff. And then finishing off with this?" He gestured angrily to the bed. She raised an eyebrow, and he continued, "Staring into each other's eyes. Drawing it out as long as possible. Was it all a big plan to make me fall in love with you?"

Her heart leapt, but she knew she was fighting now not to keep him as a lover, but as a friend. "Rusty, I swear, there was no plan behind all this."

"You told me it was going to be difficult. You knew ending like this was going to be hard."

"I originally thought it would be a lovely way to end the relationship. Affectionate and warm. I didn't expect…" She bit her lip.

"What?"

Her eyes filled with tears. "Nothing."

He glared at her. "And now the waterworks. Surprise, surprise."

She bit her lip harder and forced the tears away. She could see his despair, his pain, glimmering behind the anger, but that was no excuse for speaking to her like that. She wanted to slap him, but she knew he was trying to antagonize her, to make this easier. And she wasn't about to make it easier for him to walk away. "Rusty, don't be cruel. That's not fair. I don't deserve that. I'm your friend."

He was breathing heavily. "How can you be so calm? Didn't you care for me at all? Was I just a quick shag, a notch on your belt?"

"A notch on my belt?" Incredulity filled her voice. "It must be a fucking small belt."

"But it's something you can boast about, isn't it? It must earn you a bit of respect with the girls, having Rusty Thorne?"

"Me and half the girls in this town," she snapped. "Stop being so bloody ridiculous."

"Oh, I'm ridiculous now, am I?"

He was being so incredibly unreasonable, and the worse thing was, she knew why he was doing it. It was the only way he could end this—by making her hate him. He couldn't bring himself to walk out, so he needed her to tell him to go. It was cowardly and pathetic, and she hated him for it, and then hated him more for making her do exactly what he wanted.

She'd begun to shake, and she was close to tears again, although this time they were tears of fury. "If only you'd look beyond the ridiculous barriers you've put between yourself and happiness. You're not the devil, Rusty. You deserve to have a happy-ever-after the same as anyone else. And not everyone's determined to cause you misery."

"There's no happy-ever-after for me." He glared at her, his jaw set. "I'm leaving, Faith. Moving away. It's the only way we can put this behind us."

She stared at him. He meant it, she could see. Fury rose within her. He was chickening out. Running away. She might have guessed. Facing up to the truth—that he loved her—would be so much harder. Staying was too difficult. Running away was easy.

However, even though she was angry with him, she still couldn't deny how gorgeous he was, standing there, eyes blazing, his whole body showing his defensiveness. Was it worth a last appeal? She decided it was, took a deep breath and let it out slowly. She forced a smile on her lips. "We could be happy, love, I know we could. You just need to believe that things can be better—you need to have a little faith."

"Been there, got the T-shirt," he said. "What else you got?"

She felt her face drain of blood. She stepped back and stuffed her hands in the pockets of her robe. It couldn't have hurt more if he'd slapped her in the face. "Well, screw you, Rusty."

"Yeah, sure." His pose was casual, taunting. "Do I need a contract for that?"

Humiliated, hating him, she walked out of the room, feeling like she'd swallowed a dozen razor blades. She stood by the front door and held it open as he followed her into the hall. She looked at the floor, close to breaking down, begging him silently to go, not to stay and be cruel to her any longer.

He walked toward her and paused when he was level with her. She continued to look at the floor. When he didn't move, she closed her eyes. *Please go, please go, please go.*

He hesitated, moved past her, and walked outside.

She slammed the door behind him, so hard the whole house seemed to rattle.

Then she burst into tears.

Chapter Fifty-Two

Mr. Thorne was quite possibly the worst teacher in the school—if not the whole country—on Thursday and Friday.

Rusty was well aware he was behaving like an idiot, but he felt completely unable to do anything about it. Usually in class, he was pleasant and courteous, treating the students like human beings, funny and engaging. For the two days following his argument with Faith, however, he was grumpy and fierce, snapping every time any student did anything remotely wrong. He sent kids to the principal's office for the first time in his five years of teaching and made his classes work in silence—the sort of teacher he hated, but felt driven to be because he was so miserable.

The last class of the week was year thirteen. Normally this was his most relaxed lesson, and the class had Biscuit Friday, students taking it in turn to bring in packs of biscuits to nibble at while they had a discussion on a topic they'd covered during the week. That day, however, he set them hard essay questions under exam conditions, spending his time glaring at the computer as they worked studiously, occasionally casting each other glances across their separated desks.

Part of his bad temper was due to reading Faith's blog. Although she'd given a general discussion of her idea behind the seventh sin, and suggested ideas for her readers to try, she'd very carefully skirted around any mention of what he'd done. It was surprisingly kind—he didn't deserve it, and her magnanimity annoyed him, made him feel about two inches tall.

Her readers had pressured her for details, but she'd still managed to retain her generous spirit, even though he was sure she must have been fuming at him. He read the last few comments sadly, resentfully, wishing she'd given a diatribe on him and men in general, been spiteful and vindictive, anything to make him feel better about the things he'd said to her on Wednesday.

WendyS: So you're definitely not seeing him again, then Faith?

Faith: No. The relationship was finite—we both knew that. That's why we signed a contract. Everything's good. It's time to move on.

WendyS: Is Mr. S. coming on tonight? We'd all love to chat to him.

Faith: I think he's busy tonight, sorry. I'm sure he'll be along to say goodbye over the next few days.

HelenB: Oh Faith, did it end badly?

SueAnn: Oh no.

Faith: It's okay, I knew it was going to be difficult. It was, perhaps, more difficult than I anticipated. I suppose I was stupid to think it wouldn't be. I thought I could have sex and keep my emotions out of it, but it proved impossible. I don't know if it's the same for everyone, or if it's just because I already had feelings for him. Either way, it's done.

Patsy: You okay, sweetie? We are here for you—you know that?

Faith: I know. I love you all! You've been a great source of support for me through all this and I've enjoyed relating my experiences. I hope my journey has encouraged some of you to experiment yourselves. I'm sad it's over. But hey, I'm fine—don't worry about me. I had such fun! And all good things come to an end.

He shut his laptop as the bell for end of school rang. "Leave your papers on the desk," he instructed the students as they started shuffling around. They all got up quietly, and suddenly he felt a wave of guilt that he'd been so hard on them. "If I can have your attention," he said, standing up, waiting for them to stop tucking their chairs under. "I apologize if I've been a bit growly over the last few days. You're good kids and you've worked hard. Well done for putting up with me."

Laughing, the students left the room while he cleaned the board. His throat felt strangely tight. He'd been thinking about leaving, considering where he should apply for another job, but that the thought made him sad. He loved the school, and his students, and knew he'd miss the place terribly. What choice did he have? How could he stay in Kerikeri, knowing he could bump into Faith at any moment?

The door shut and he turned around, stopping with surprise as he saw Charlotte standing there, the girl who'd nearly rumbled him when she'd seen him kissing Faith in the supermarket. Her friend hovered outside, watching through the window.

"Hey," he said. "Problem?"

She wrapped her arms around her bag, shifting from one foot to another awkwardly. "Is it really all over, sir? You and Faith, I mean."

He gave her a wry, warning glance and started packing his books away. "I don't have a clue what you're talking about, Summers."

"Yeah." Still, she hovered. "It's just… you both looked so in love. I remember thinking: I hope someone feels about me like that one day."

He stopped and stared at her. She flushed and looked away. "Anyway. I've gotta go. Have a great weekend."

"Yeah, you too." He watched her hurry out, then sat heavily in his chair.

He was due to go around Dan and Eve's, but he didn't really feel like it. Dan had rung earlier, saying Toby was coming around and did he want to join them and watch the rugby? Rusty had asked if Faith was coming, making his voice as casual as possible. Dan had been short with him, saying no, she wanted a night in on her own, and had mumbled something about "the whole stupid idea", which led Rusty to believe she'd told him a little about how their seven sins had ended.

Since she was old enough to go to the bar, he'd seen her nearly every Friday night, either at the bar or occasionally at a party, especially in the summer. Sometimes in the winter, they'd met at Dan's house, huddled around the fire, and either watched rugby or some awful horror movie, which usually made Eve hide behind a cushion and Faith hoot with laughter. He was used to seeing her regularly, used to her casting her comforting, warm glow on them all like a candle in the dark.

And over the last month or two, their regular meetings with the others had included an added frisson of excitement, and it had been fun to try to get through the evening exchanging clandestine glances, or the occasional furtive brush of a hand against an arm. But now he'd lost that, and he didn't even have her friendship to fall back on. He felt forlorn. Bereft. Like half a person, as if he'd gone into hospital to have a mole removed and they'd mistakenly amputated his left arm and leg. While he was dating her, he should have written "Not this one" on his heart in black pen. He kicked his rubbish bin, knocked it over, and sent paper all over the floor, felt guilty, and spent several minutes picking it up. Time to go and mope somewhere else.

He went home, had a shower, and changed into jeans and a black T-shirt, but took it off because Faith had started to comment on the fact that black was the only color he ever wore. Then he put it back on, annoyed that in his head he was still listening to her. Took it off. Put it on.

Eventually, in a dark green T-shirt, he sat and watched some stupid game show on the TV, trying not to think about how Faith would have made up ridiculous answers and not given a fig for the fact that her general knowledge was, quite frankly, appalling.

He went into his room and tried to read for a while—he'd recently downloaded a new, highly rated book on World War I, and he'd been looking forward to reading it, but he couldn't concentrate. Eventually, he put down the device and lay looking out of the window, watching the praying mantis on the sill and trying not to smile at the thought of how Faith would have squealed and demanded he go and remove it for her, although she would have insisted he didn't hurt it, like a regular Francis of Assisi.

By the time Toby came around to pick him up, Rusty was desperate for someone to talk to and decided he was actually looking forward to watching some rugby—anything to take his mind off Faith. They walked around to Dan's house shortly after seven, Toby carrying a huge pack of beer, making it clear how he was going to spend his evening.

When they got to the house, Eve opened the door and let them in. As soon as he looked at her face, Rusty could see something was wrong—she was pale, and her eyes looked scared.

"What's up?" he asked in a low voice as Toby, oblivious as ever, went into the living room.

"I don't know. Dan's been weird since he spoke to Faith earlier, but he won't tell me why."

"Do you think he knows?"

"I don't know."

Rusty's heart began to hammer, and he was tempted to turn and walk straight back out the door, but he lifted his chin and took a deep breath, forcing himself to go forward into the living room. It didn't surprise him that Dan might have found out about him and Faith. It had only been a matter of time—he'd been certain it would come out eventually. He was just lucky to have lived as long as he had.

In the living room, Toby sat on the sofa. He started taking the top off a beer and chattered away, oblivious to the frosty atmosphere in the room. Dan stood in the middle, hands in his jeans pockets. He nodded as Rusty came in, and Rusty nodded back, standing on the opposite side of the room. So far, so good. Balls still intact.

"Hey," Rusty said.

"Hey." Dan's eyes were cool.

Toby picked up the remote and started to flick over to the rugby channel, talking about the starting line-up and what injuries the All Blacks had suffered over the past week.

"Toby," said Rusty eventually. Toby glanced at him and followed his gaze to Dan, who was studying him with a slight frown.

"What?" Toby said.

Dan hunched his shoulders. "You got something you want to tell me?"

Toby looked at Rusty, then at Eve, then back at Dan. "Uh…do I?"

Dan studied him. Wariness settled over Rusty as he saw a glitter of anger in Dan's brown eyes. What was this about?

Dan's pose was casual, falsely friendly. "I spoke to Faith earlier."

Toby stretched his arms out on the back of the sofa. Rusty knew him well enough to see he was starting to get irritated. "Oh. Jeez, that would be a shock if I didn't know she was your sister."

Dan studied him again. "I know it's you, Toby."

"You know what's me?"

Shocking them all, he said, "I know you're Mr. S."

Rusty's heart thudded, and he closed his eyes briefly. He heard Toby give a short laugh. "Er, no, I'm not."

"She told me she'd finished it with him. She said she missed him. I tried to get her to tell me who it was, but she wouldn't. But when I asked her if it was someone I knew, she hesitated. Only for a second, but enough to confirm it to me."

"And so you decided to pick on me?" Toby seemed amused rather than angry. "I'm flattered you think Faith would be the tiniest bit interested in me, but you couldn't be more wrong."

"You asked her, that day by the pool. You offered your services." Dan's voice was sarcastic.

"Er…yeah." Toby looked at Dan as if he'd grown horns. "I was joking. Jeez, Dan, I wouldn't date Faith. You know I wouldn't. I think too much of you and her for that."

Oh, fuck. Cheers, Toby.

Dan was breathing more quickly. "I saw you kiss her that day she was supposed to have got back from seeing him. You kissed her on the cheek, and she blushed."

Toby glanced up at Rusty, clearly starting to get alarmed. Toby held up his hands. "I swear, Dan. I haven't touched her."

Eve was looking at Rusty now, tears in her eyes. He could feel the inevitability of the moment approaching like a speeding train, with him standing on the edge of the platform.

"I know you're lying," Dan said, his voice rising.

Toby looked indignant. "I'm not!"

"You fucking are!" Dan yelled.

"He's not," said Rusty, stepping out in front of the train.

"How do you know?" Dan snapped, glancing over at him.

"Because it was me." Rusty met Dan's eyes. "I'm Mr. S." Crash. The train hit him with the full weight of the knowledge of what he'd done behind it, almost making him reel.

All three of them turned to look at him. He tried to remember to breathe in and out, and forced himself to stay still and not leg it out the door.

"What?" Dan couldn't have looked more confused if Rusty had said he was about to climb Mount Everest. "What the fuck are you talking about?"

"I'm Mr. S. I offered my services that night after the pool party."

Eve had gone white. Toby leaned his head on the back of the sofa. "Oh Christ."

Dan walked slowly up to Rusty until he stood a foot away. "You?" He studied him for a moment. "You're the one Faith's been seeing?"

"Yeah." Rusty forced himself to meet Dan's eyes, but inside he was slowly curling into a ball like a spider poked with a stick. *Yeah. And you're the spider, boyo. Deal with it.*

Dan gave a short, sharp laugh. "I thought it might be Toby. I never thought it would be you."

"Hey," said Toby, indignant at Dan's low opinion of him, but they both ignored him.

"All this time," said Dan. "When I've been sick with worry, you've sat there saying 'Don't worry Dan, don't overreact', and all along you've been screwing her behind my back."

"It wasn't like that." Rusty's protest was half-hearted, because it was like that, and he knew it.

"I thought you had more respect for me than that." Dan's voice was rough.

Rusty heaved an impatient sigh. "We're not in the mafia, Dan. Faith and I—it had nothing to do with you."

Dan gave a humorless laugh. "Right. So that's why you didn't tell me when you were dragging her off to some cheap hotel." His voice was sharp enough to cut glass. "Showing her porn. Making her strip for you." He went suddenly still. Anger lit his eyes. "A fucking Mars Bar?" His voice rose by about fifty decibels.

"Oh no." Eve closed her eyes.

Why did everyone focus on the bloody Mars Bar? Rusty gritted his teeth. He'd gone through this moment a hundred times in his head, had played out what Dan would say, and how he would respond. He'd thought he would feel panic and guilt at betraying his best friend. But although initially he'd felt ashamed, to his surprise, all of a sudden, he felt none of those things. Instead, he felt a sweep of anger. "It wasn't like that," he repeated, his voice stronger.

Dan stepped closer, his eyes glittering. "You fucking bastard."

Rusty held his ground. "Easy, tiger."

"You going to explain yourself to me, boy?"

Rusty laughed. "Boy?"

"I'm older than you."

"By about three weeks." He frowned as Dan moved forward and forced him to take a step back. "Back off, Dan."

"You gonna make me?"

"Oh jeez," said Toby.

"Guys." There were tears in Eve's eyes. "Don't do this."

Dan's eyes were taunting, challenging. "Did you laugh about big brother Dan getting all protective while you screwed her, Rusty?"

"Sorry to deflate you, Dan, but actually you weren't uppermost in my mind while I was getting off with your sister."

Dan pushed him hard. Rusty stumbled back but immediately took a step forward. "If you're going to hit me, then hit me," he snapped. "Don't push me like a fucking girl."

"I can't believe you did it," Dan said through his teeth, breathing hard. "Not to Faith. I can't believe you'd do that to her."

"Do it to her?" Rusty gave a harsh laugh, glaring at his best friend, fury and pain making him reckless. "She handcuffed me to the bed.

And she wasn't complaining too hard when she asked me to *fuck her up the arse.*"

"You fucking *cunt!*"

"Oh shit." Toby leaped to his feet, but it was too late.

Chapter Fifty-Three

Dan swung at Rusty, who moved back quickly and returned with a right hook of his own. It connected soundly with Dan's jaw, and Dan stumbled back and fell to the floor with a crash.

"That's for her eighteenth birthday," Rusty yelled.

If he'd thought that would finish Dan, however, he'd been sorely mistaken. Dan grabbed Rusty's feet and brought him to the floor like a felled tree, and then he was on top of him. Fists flew, and Rusty felt Dan's knuckles connect with his eye. Again? White-hot anger surged through him, the full measure of fury and frustration of the past week flooding in his veins, as well as Dan's assumption that he'd taken advantage of Faith. *It wasn't just me.* The thought burned in his stomach. *She loved me back. She wanted it as much as I did.*

The two of them rolled, and, in the distance, he could hear Eve screaming at them to stop. He couldn't have cared less at that moment, however. He finally managed to get on top of Dan and drew back his arm for another punch, but suddenly Toby hauled him up. Three inches taller, thirty pounds heavier, and a whole lot stronger from all his building work, Toby was easily able to pull him back.

"Rusty!" Toby bellowed.

Rusty shook him off. He could feel his eye swelling. Dan struggled to his feet. His lip had split, and blood trickled down his chin. He took a step toward Rusty, but Toby immediately stepped in the middle. "Stop it, for Christ's sake!"

Rusty felt the fury drain out of him. He wasn't angry at Dan, not really. He loved these guys more than anything in the world. They were his real family, and here he was, trying to destroy it. "Dan…"

"Was she worth it?" Dan was so angry he was near to tears. "You've destroyed her, Rusty. She's so upset she could barely speak to me."

"Don't…" His chest hurt.

"Was it worth destroying our friendship for a quick shag?"

"Stop saying that! It was more than that."

Dan tipped his head in exasperation. "You going to tell me you love her now?"

The room fell silent. Rusty's legs gave out, and he sank onto the sofa and put his head in his hands.

Eve came forward to stand beside Toby. "He does love her, Dan. He told me."

He turned on her, eyes blazing. "You knew about this?"

"Yes."

"And you didn't think to tell me?"

"No, and I wonder why!" She took a deep breath. "I know you think you've let Faith go, but you haven't yet, not really. Rusty's not completely to blame for this. He shouldn't have slept with her behind your back, but she wanted him to—Dan, she's loved him since she was twelve, didn't you ever guess?"

Rusty looked up at her, shocked. She glanced at him and then back at Dan. "Oh for fuck's sake, don't tell me neither of you realized."

"I knew," said Toby. They all looked at him, stunned. "What?" he said. "I've got eyes, haven't I? I saw her face after you kissed her in the garden that night on her eighteenth. She looked like Brad Pitt had ridden up and whisked her off for a snog."

Rusty put his head back in his hands. His eye was throbbing.

Dan looked down at him. "Is it true? Do you love her?"

Rusty didn't look up. "Yes."

Dan was silent for a moment. He sat into the nearby armchair and leaned back heavily. Toby heaved a sigh of relief and sat in the chair opposite. Eve perched on the arm of Dan's chair and stroked his hair.

Dan kissed her hand, but continued to look at Rusty. "So what are you going to do about it?"

"I'm going to find another job, as soon as I can."

To his surprise, Dan laughed. "What sort of answer's that?"

Rusty looked up at him warily. "What do you mean?"

"I meant, what are you going to do to fix it? Are you going to tell her you love her?"

"I already have."

Dan frowned. "So…what's the problem?"

Rusty stared at him. "You're kidding me? After all that…" He gestured at the floor.

"It was one thing to think you're trying to get into her knickers only to dump her afterward. It's another thing to know you love her."

Rusty was temporarily speechless. He stared at Toby, who shrugged, then at Eve, who was beginning to smile. He felt a brief surge of hope, which quickly faded when he remembered why he'd promised himself he was going to leave.

"I haven't got anything to offer her," he whispered. "This is me we're talking about, Dan."

Dan studied him. "You mean Rusty Thorne. One of my best mates. Secondary school teacher, steady job, reliable income. Honest, solid, trustworthy. Well, until tonight." His lips twitched.

Rusty glared at him. "Don't mock me. You know what stock I'm from."

"You're not a fucking bullock, Rusty."

"You know what I mean. You know what my family are like. Every man for the last fifty years has been an alcoholic."

"But you don't drink," said Eve, confused.

"Yes, but that doesn't mean it's not inside me." He tapped his chest. "I can't get rid of it—the family gene will always be there. Do you think I want to curse her with that? I couldn't bear to hurt her, Dan. I just couldn't." His voice broke and he put his head back in his hands, fighting to retain some semblance of control.

Dan tipped his head onto the back of the chair for a moment. Then he looked back up. "You know your problem?"

"No, but I'm sure you're going to tell me," said Rusty tiredly.

"You're an egomaniac. You think you're responsible for the whole world. You think there's this gigantic, enormous, gargantuan—"

"That's three words that all mean the same thing," Toby pointed out.

"This colossal…" Dan glared at Toby, "…monster inside of you. And mate, there's really not."

"You don't know that," Rusty whispered. "I can feel it sometimes."

"Dude, we all get angry." Dan gestured to himself and Toby. "We're all Neanderthals."

"Speak for yourself," mumbled Toby.

Dan ignored him. "We can all beat our chests and roar our frustration at times. That doesn't mean we're going to turn into monsters, and it doesn't mean we're going to beat the women we love."

Rusty met his eyes. "I couldn't do it," he said simply. "I couldn't risk it, Dan. I love her too much for that."

Dan studied him mutely. All of a sudden, he stood. "Toby." He pointed at a cupboard in the corner. "Get out three glasses." He walked off into the kitchen.

Toby looked at Rusty and smirked. He got up and did as Dan bid, retrieving three tumblers from the cupboard.

"Er…" Rusty watched him warily.

After a few crashing noises in the kitchen, Dan came back into the room carrying two bottles of whisky and a bowl full of ice. He sat back in the chair and showed the bottles to Rusty before putting them on the table. "Lagavulin and Laphroaig—two of the best Islay malts a man can buy. Completely wasted on you. This is how much I love you." He twisted the top off one, and poured a large measure into the three glasses.

"I don't think so." Rusty stared at the tumblers.

"You screw my sister, you do as you're told." Dan dropped a couple of cubes of ice into the glass and held it out to him.

Rusty shook his head. "I can't, Dan."

Dan didn't move. "We're going to get you pissed as a fart, mate, and then we'll see just what monster you've got inside you. And if there is one there, and it comes out, we'll meet it together, all three of us."

"Four of us," said Eve indignantly.

Dan shook his head. "I need you sober. You know what to do, later, when the time comes." He met her gaze. Her lips curved, and she nodded.

Rusty felt a huge wave of emotion sweep over him. He'd just flattened Dan, given him a fat lip, screwed his sister when he'd warned him not to, brought their friendship to the brink of destruction. And still Dan wanted to help him.

The problem was, Rusty didn't want to leave the school, and he didn't want to leave the town. He didn't want to leave his friends, and the thought of never seeing Faith again was just about killing him. And because of that, he was finally willing to do something he'd never done in all his adult life, something he was so afraid of, it made his hand shake as he reached out and took the glass.

Unable to speak, he held the tumbler up. Toby took one as well, and they clunked the glasses together.

Rusty took a suspicious sniff of the amber liquid. "Fucking hell. It smells like the kind of medicine a great aunt would give you."

"Hold your nose, then." Dan knocked back half the glass in one go and Toby did the same.

Rusty held his breath and took a large swallow.

Chapter Fifty-Four

Faith had dozed off in front of the TV. It was late, around eleven thirty, and the half-eaten tub of chocolate mint ice cream in her lap was melting slowly.

The sharp shrill of the phone made her jump and splosh some of the sticky dessert in her lap. Cursing, she put the tub on the table. Her heart thumped. Was it Rusty? Who else would be ringing at this hour?

She answered it with a cautious, "Hello?"

"It's Eve."

Faith felt a brief flutter of alarm. "Are you okay? What's up?"

"Everything's fine. Kind of. Look, you need to come around."

"At this time of night?"

"I really need you here. Are you okay to drive?"

"Yes, but…I don't understand…"

"You will when you get here. Can you come?"

"Of course. Give me ten minutes."

"See ya." Eve hung up.

More than a little concerned, Faith changed her clothes hurriedly, grabbed her purse, and left the house. She puzzled over Eve's words the whole way, wondering if they'd had another argument, but then why would they want her there? Taking the turnoff for Eve and Dan's house, she drove down the long drive and parked out the front.

She got out of the car to see Eve outside, waiting for her. She could also hear music—well, singing, to be more specific. "What the…" She stood there for a moment, staring at an amused Eve. She could make out Dan's baritone and Toby's deeper voice. And there was a third too. Rusty?

"What are they doing? Starting up a band again?" As teenagers, the three of them had once played in a group, along with a couple of other boys. They'd played terrible heavy metal music that had no rhythm and nobody ever wanted to listen to.

"Not quite," said Eve, beckoning her in.

Faith finally deciphered what they were singing. It wasn't heavy metal. It was Justin Bieber's *Company*. Her eyes widened. "What the f...?"

"If you're surprised by that..." Eve rolled her eyes. "I've had to put up with them singing that old song by whatsizname... Bryan Adams, *Everything I Do,* for about half an hour, making up the words. Eat a pie for you. Wear a tie for you. You name it." She opened the door and went in.

Faith walked slowly into the house and closed the door behind her.

The room was dark, lit only by a table lamp in the far corner. Toby sat in an armchair, turned in the seat so his head was on the arm and his legs hung over the edge. Dan sat opposite him, slumped so far down in the chair he was almost on the floor. The back of the sofa faced her, but she could see Rusty's bare feet on the arm, crossed at the ankles.

Two bottles of whisky stood on the table, both about a third full.

Eve walked over to Dan and perched on the arm of the chair. "Faith's here," she said quietly to him.

Dan looked over at her. He was quite clearly plastered, his eyes coming to rest on her slowly, like a pair of ball bearings swinging in a Newton's cradle. "Hey."

She stared at the whisky and the glasses in his and Toby's hands and then at Rusty's feet. Surely not.

Dan went to scratch his nose, poked himself in the eye, and swore. Eve rolled her eyes again. Dan rubbed a finger under his nose, blinking at Faith slowly with the intense concentration of someone trying to pretend they weren't as drunk as they seemed. When he spoke, he said the words very slowly and carefully. "I haven't done anything. I've just tried to help out a mate, that's all."

"By getting him drunk?" She stared at him. "Oh my God, you know. About Rusty and me."

"Yep. The whole sordid affair."

She studied his split lip in horror. "What happened?"

"I called him a cunt and knocked him flat. After he'd hit me, obviously. Then we kinda got drunk."

Almost too scared to find out what state Rusty was in, she walked up to the back of the sofa and leaned over.

He had a tumbler in his hand, filled with a half-inch of amber liquid. The bottom of the glass rested on his chest and moved up and down as he breathed. Clearly, he hadn't heard her come in, or registered what Dan was saying. His eyes were closed, but she could see the left already bruised and starting to swell. He was singing softly to Lionel Richie's *Hello*.

She glanced up at Eve, who met her gaze and started to smile.

Faith looked back down. Her heart thumped. "Hey."

Rusty opened his eyes and winced. The glassy green orbs were clear and bright, however, and he didn't seem to have trouble focusing like Dan. As he blinked, however, his lids moved in slow motion, and she could see he thought he was dreaming. He was quite clearly outrageously drunk.

"It's me," she said. "You're not imagining things. Are you okay?"

"Faith?" He studied her face. "Wow, your eyes are, like, so weird. They make me think of dendrochronology." It took him three goes to get the word out. Faith raised her eyebrows. "Tree rings," he explained. "They're beautiful."

"Wow. You're completely rat-arsed, aren't you?"

"No. No." He blinked. "A little bit."

"Hey!" Toby had finally realized she was in the room. He pointed at her shirt. "Woo-hoo! Lady in red!"

Together, the three of them started a rendition of Chris de Burgh's classic. Eve sighed and stood up. "I think that's my cue to put the kettle on."

"Coffee all around," agreed Faith, unable to hide a smile.

She walked to the end of the sofa and leaned on the arm, looking upside down at Rusty. "Why did you do it?"

"Dan wanted me to unleash the demon." He gave a slight hiccup. "I think he thought of himself as St. George. You know. Slay the dragon." He imitated a spear thrust and nearly spilled his drink in the process.

"And?"

He sighed. "Well, you know I thought there was this terrible monster inside me?"

"Yeah."

"It turns out that it's less a T-Rex, and more a…hamster. Dan's quite disappointed."

Faith started laughing. "So you don't feel bad?"

"Nope. Just kinda tired. And miserable. Until you showed up." He blinked at her. "I've been an arse, Faith. A terrible fucking idiot. I know I deserve to be hung, drawn, and quartered for the way I treated you. Can you ever forgive me?"

Faith studied him. His green shirt matched his eyes, and his hair was ruffled and unkempt. He was so gorgeous it made her ache. Unable to stop herself, she leaned over him and pressed her lips to his, upside down.

When she pulled back, he blinked at her and said, "Oh." He leaned across and put his glass on the table. Then he said, "I think I need to sit up."

Faith stood and watched as Rusty pushed himself up and swung his legs around. "Whoa." He leaned forward, elbows on knees, and stared hard at the table. "Who moved the house?"

Dan and Toby started laughing. Faith sighed and sat next to him. "Jeez, you're going to have a hell of a hangover in the morning."

"Only what I deserve." He gave her a rueful smile and ran his hand through his hair. They studied each other for a moment. Her heart felt light as a butterfly, full of hope. He took a deep breath. "I'm sorry, Faith."

"That's okay," she said softly.

"No, it's not." He looked away. "I was awful to you. And it was totally unprovoked." He stumbled over the word, but got it out eventually. "You're much too good for me. You're, like, an angel. An archangel. With a halo." He gestured around the top of his head. "And I'm…"

"Beelzebub?"

He shrugged.

She laughed. "Sweetie, you're so not. You're a good man. I wish you'd start believing me."

He studied her, his eyes wide. "I love you. You know that, don't you?"

Faith's cheeks grew warm, aware Dan and Toby were listening with interest, and she heard Eve's muttered "At last" as she came in with a tray of coffee cups. Faith ignored them all, however, concentrating on Rusty.

"Yes, I know."

He blinked. "Will you marry me?"

Faith stared at him. The other three cheered and then burst out laughing. Rusty glanced at them before looking back at Faith. "What's so funny?"

"I have no idea," she said firmly. She handed him a cup of black coffee. "Drink this up, and then I'm taking you home."

"Oh yeah." Toby gave her a wink.

"Yes, like he's in any fit state to be doing anything like that," she said tartly, passing him a cup as well. "I have to say, guys, I think you've been incredibly irresponsible. You've probably given him liver poisoning."

Dan waved a hand airily. "He's a man—he can take it."

"Hmm." She looked back at Rusty, who appeared slightly confused.

"I meant it," he said.

"Shh." She gestured to the cup. "We'll talk about it later."

He took a sip of the coffee and winced. "Fucking hell! This is strong."

"It needs to be," Eve said. "Now drink up, all of you. You want to go home, Toby? Or crash here on the sofa?"

"I'll stay here," he said, looking like a forklift would have struggled to move him.

As Rusty finished his coffee, Faith said goodbye to the others. "I'll have words with you tomorrow," she told Dan firmly, but he just pulled a face at her.

She gave Eve a kiss. "Thanks for ringing me."

"No worries." Eve's eyes sparkled. "Rusty Thorne proposing. Who'd have thought?"

"He's out of his tree."

"Even so. Will you say yes?"

"I need to see if he meant it, first. I'll talk to you tomorrow."

Faith helped him to her car. He walked carefully, his arm heavy around her shoulders. She opened the door, and he slid in while she protected his head. Then she leaned across and clipped his seatbelt in.

He caught her as she did so and put his arms around her. She leaned on the seat, suddenly breathless. Even hammered, smelling strongly of whisky, he was still the most gorgeous guy she'd ever seen.

He kissed her, and she lingered for a moment before pulling away. "Come on, let's get you home."

"Home where?"

She shut the door and walked around the car to get in the driver's side. "My place. I'm not leaving you alone in this state."

He sighed and closed his eyes.

Faith drove home, her heart hammering all the way. Had he meant it? Surely not. It had been a knee-jerk reaction, born out of guilt. But even so, the fact that he felt he wasn't like his father and brother, an animal when inebriated, must count for something, mustn't it? Did it mean he wasn't leaving?

When she reached her house, she helped him inside and took him straight through to the bedroom. She pulled back the duvet and began to unbutton his shirt for him. He leaned one hand on the wall behind her, studying her face, his eyes half-lidded, smiling. "I love you," he said again.

She laughed and pushed his shirt off his shoulders as he tried to kiss her. "Undo your pants, you idiot."

He tried to do as she said, but in the end, she had to help him. He fell backward onto the bed, and she pulled the jeans off, dumped them on a chair, made him lay the right way around, and covered him with the duvet.

"Don't go," he said as she stood up.

"I'm just getting a jug of water. You're going to need it." She went into the kitchen, filled up a jug, and brought it back to the bedroom with a glass.

He was already asleep.

She put the jug and glass next to his side of the bed, undressed quietly, pulled on a T-shirt nightie, and slipped in beside him. Talking would have to wait until morning.

Her bed was warm with him in it. She curled up beside him, studying his injured eye, glad she hadn't seen the fight with Dan. It would have made her cry. She leaned over and kissed the sore spot gently.

He'd hurt her, and the pain he'd caused her wasn't going to disappear overnight. But he'd also asked her to marry him. She knew the dream was as insubstantial as a rainbow. But it was beautiful, all the same.

Chapter Fifty-Five

When Rusty finally awoke, it was light, and he lay there for a while, looking out at the garden. Someone—presumably Faith—had opened the sliding door to the decking, and a light March breeze blew in across the duvet, cooling down his hot forehead. The sun's rays pooled on the edge of the bed. The other side was empty, although a dent remained in the pillow.

He rolled onto his back and covered his eyes with his arm. It had been a hell of a night. He'd vomited at least three times, possibly more—it was all a bit hazy—struggling to the bathroom in the wee small hours, completely disoriented because he wasn't in his own house.

But he'd been glad he wasn't at home, because Faith had been there beside him. She'd talked to him firmly, cleaned up behind him, bless her, returned him to bed, and forced him to drink water, stroking his forehead as he dozed off once again. He didn't deserve her, and he felt embarrassed about what an idiot he'd been. But it had been kind of nice as well, having her fuss over him like that.

He turned his head and saw she'd left two painkillers on the bedside table, along with a glass of fresh orange juice. The clock said nine thirty. Sighing, he pushed himself up and took the pills. His mouth tasted like it had had a team of rugby players partying in it, and the orange juice was refreshing. Then he turned over again and looked out once more at the garden.

He hugged the pillow to him. People often said they couldn't remember what they did when they were drunk, but he could remember the whole evening, even though it felt as if he was looking at it through a fogged-up window. He remembered watching the rugby with Dan, Toby, and Eve, wincing every time he took a sip of the whisky, but gradually growing used to the fiery, medicinal taste, until eventually he was knocking the glasses back as much as the other two. He thought of Dan, continually topping up his tumbler. Bastard. He'd known how Rusty would feel in the morning. He touched a finger to his sore eye gently. Dan had exacted his revenge in his own particular, Machiavellian way.

But he'd deserved it. Rusty had spoken the truth when he said that he and Faith were nobody else's business, but even so, he knew he shouldn't have slept with her without telling Dan. Dan wasn't her father, but he was the closest thing she had, and he clearly saw himself in that role. He was only looking out for her, and Rusty had violated that trust in the biggest way possible.

He thought about Faith and wondered where she was. In the living room, presumably. He could remember when she'd turned up at the house and leaned over the sofa, saying, "Hey." When he'd opened his eyes and seen her, his heart had nearly leaped out of his chest and boinged happily along the hall like a kid on a space hopper.

He lay on his back and looked up at the ceiling. He'd asked her to marry him. He remembered it clearly, and had meant it, at the time. What had she said? She hadn't said yes. She'd said she'd talk to him about it when they got home, but he'd fallen asleep. He couldn't remember her looking ecstatic, the way a woman was supposed to when a man asked her to marry him.

He lifted his arm and rested his hand on his forehead. What on earth had made him propose, drunk as a skunk, in front of the others? Maybe he'd wanted to prove to them, especially Dan, that he was serious about her, that it hadn't just been a fling. Or had he done it because he needed her to know how sorry he was? Like that was going to help. He'd been vile toward her, and the last thing she needed was a drunken idiot to declare he wanted her to put up with him forever.

But where did that leave him now? He was going to have to talk to her about it, and there was no way she would suddenly have had amnesia overnight. She was going to remember his proposal.

Did he want to marry her?

Rusty had never thought about what it would be like to live with a woman. Ever. He'd always been certain it would never happen. He'd carefully skated around the issue, not entertaining thoughts of having a wife or children. That life had never been for him. He'd never been a window shopper, figuring what was the point in looking when you didn't have the money to buy, and thinking about long-term relationships posed the same problem. Girls had stayed over occasionally. But he'd never cleared out a drawer for anyone—never put their coffee mug next to his.

But now? Had that changed?

He thought about how he'd felt when he'd drunk more alcohol than he'd been certain it was possible to drink in one night. He'd waited for the family demon to rear up inside him, but he'd only got more lethargic as the evening had gone on, and everything had got funnier and funnier. Eventually, he'd realized there was no demon, just tired, rather boring Rusty, not quite the fierce tiger he'd always dreamed he'd be, but rather a sad panda of a man, unhappy and forlorn without the girl he'd probably lost for good.

And now that he knew he didn't have anything to fear? That there wasn't something hidden inside him, waiting to rise up and destroy any relationship he had? He thought of Faith, and the way she'd been there for him during the night. What would it be like to come home to her every day after school? To sit at the table and eat dinner together. To go out as a couple, or cuddle in front of the TV and watch back-to-back DVDs. To go to bed with her, and make love to her all night, every night.

The thought didn't scare him. It made him incredibly happy.

He sat up, only seeing then that his clothes had disappeared and she'd put an old T-shirt and trackpants—presumably left there by Dan when he used to come and stay with Eve—on the chair, with a razor on top. He got up gingerly. He didn't want her to see him just yet. Picking up the clothes, he went into the en suite and had a shower, hoping to scrub the smell of the alcohol off. He washed his hair, had a shave, dried himself, and got dressed, all carried out slowly and cautiously, conscious that any sudden movement made his head spin. He didn't have a toothbrush, but he used her mouthwash and then the comb she'd left on the side to get his hair in some sort of order.

He looked at himself in the mirror. In spite of a rapidly darkening black eye, he seemed younger, brighter somehow, as if he'd finally managed to get rid of the tarnish that had stained him for so long. He wasn't a monster. He was just a guy. A guy very much in love.

Now all that remained was to see if Faith felt the same way.

He went into the kitchen. Faith was frying bacon and turned as he leaned against the doorjamb, hands shoved in his pockets. He smiled at her sheepishly, relieved when she smiled back. "Hey," he said.

"Hey." She motioned to the chair. "Sit down. Bacon sandwich coming up."

"Bacon?" His stomach growled uneasily.

"Believe me, a fried breakfast is the best way to deal with a hangover. Soaks up all the alcohol."

He shuddered at her description, but shrugged and sat, watching her as she put the bacon in between slices of bread and covered them with HP Sauce before slicing them in half. She put the plate down before him with a mug of tea, and sat opposite him, tucking into her own sandwich. He surveyed his cautiously, his stomach churning. But the bacon smelled good, and eventually he realized he was hungry and ate with gusto, making her smile.

They said nothing for a few minutes and ate quietly. The radio was on in the corner of the room, and the sunlight lit the bubbles that floated up from the dishes soaking in the sink. Was this what married life felt like? If so, he could deal with it happily.

He finished off the sandwich and licked his fingers, not missing the way her gaze followed the movement, then clasped his hands around his mug of tea and sipped it.

"How are you feeling?" she asked.

"Better. A bit…"

"Delicate?"

"You've obviously been here before."

"A few times." She pushed her plate away and picked up her own mug. They sipped their tea.

He cleared his throat. "About last night…"

"It's okay," she said hurriedly. "It's an unspoken rule that what you say when you're drunk is forgotten about in the morning."

"Faith…"

"I don't expect anything." She met his gaze imploringly. "Just tell me you're not leaving, Rusty."

"I'm not leaving."

Relief lit her face like fireworks in the sky. "Oh!" She sat back in her chair and gave him a wonderful smile. And that kind of did it, really.

Chapter Fifty-Six

Faith watched Rusty put down his mug. He scratched his head. "I know I was terribly drunk last night."

"Er, yuh-huh." She smiled, studying him. Apart from his swollen eye, he looked quite good, clean, shaven, and calm. And he wasn't leaving. She couldn't explain how happy that made her. She just wanted to be around him, even if they couldn't be together.

He smiled back. "Even so, I remember everything I did. And said." Meeting her gaze, and holding it, he took a deep breath, stood, and pushed back his chair. Her heart began to thump as he walked around the table and knelt before her. "Faith, I've been an idiot. I've treated you like shit, and if you tell me to get lost, I'll completely deserve it. But I promise you, if you let me, I'll spend the rest of my life making it up to you. I don't have a ring yet. But… Faith Alice Hillman—will you marry me?"

She stared at him. "Huh?"

He raised an eyebrow and waited.

"Rusty…" She stood and pulled him to his feet. "Sweetheart, it doesn't have to be all or nothing." She touched his cheek. "You were drunk last night, and we're all kinds of crazy when we're drunk. I told you, I don't expect anything."

"I know. Your answer is…?"

She studied him, shocked. His eyes were clear, his face open and honest. He meant it. "You really want to continue to see me?"

"I think that's what 'Will you marry me?' generally entails."

She shook her head. "We don't have to get married, Rusty, not yet. Not until we're sure. We can have years together exploring each other before we have to commit."

"I'm sure," he said. "Is that a no?"

She blinked, her mouth open.

He laughed, stepped closer, and cupped her face. "Don't you want to marry me, love?"

"M… marry you? Really?"

"Uh huh. Marry. Get hitched. Tie the knot. I can call you the 'old ball and chain'. 'My better half'. 'Little woman'. 'The missus'." He grinned.

"I…" Her mind had gone completely blank.

He kissed her. "Walk down the aisle with me, Faith." He kissed her again. "Wake up beside me every morning." And again. "Make love to me every night." And again. "Have my babies."

"Babies?" A tear ran down her cheek.

"If you want them." He wiped the tear away. "The family demon seems to have skipped a generation, but I can't promise it won't rear its head in the next. I'd understand if you said no because of that."

"I never say no because of something that might happen, Rusty. If it were to happen, we'd deal with it. But I don't think it will. How could a son of yours ever be anything but an absolute sweetheart?"

He bit his lip. "So you wouldn't mind having a husband who's a hamster, not a T-Rex?"

A husband! He really wanted her to marry him. "I love you, Rusty," she said, half-laughing, half-crying.

"Yeah, I know. Since you were twelve. Can't believe I never realized." He tucked a strand of hair behind her ear.

She rubbed her nose. "Eve, I'm guessing."

"And Toby. He said he saw your face that night I kissed you on your eighteenth. He's surprisingly observant for a Neanderthal." He kissed her again, longer this time. When he eventually pulled back, though, he sighed. "You still haven't answered me." He gave her a beseeching look. "Don't make me beg. It's so undignified."

A light came into her eyes, and her lips began to curve. "Oh, I fully intend to make you beg, but not in the way you mean."

"Oh my."

"You terrible man. Are you going to continue to corrupt me if I agree to marry you?"

He smiled wickedly. "Absolutely."

"Then the answer's definitely yes," she murmured, and, winking at him, she linked her arms around his neck and started pulling him toward the bedroom.

Chapter Fifty-Seven

Faith Hillman's Blog

So... We've come to the end of the Seven Sexy Sins. The contract has expired, and my Mr. Sinful has fulfilled his obligations. I said it was time to move on, and although it made me want to cry, I meant it.

Apparently, though, he wasn't quite ready to let me go :-) Mr. S. has asked me to marry him!

There's a lovely photo of us to the side of this article, which my brother took with his phone when we told him we were going to get married. Mr. S.'s real name is Rusty—well, Richard—but we all call him Rusty because of his red hair. And he's a teacher. Not quite a fireman :)

So, what's the moral of this story? That maybe it's not as easy to separate sex and love as I thought it was. Or maybe it's that if you already have feelings for a guy, it's best not to go to bed with him, because it's never going to end well.

Actually, that's a lie, because it's ended very, very well. Here endeth the lesson.

Faith x

*

Excerpt from the 2106 comments
Georgia: OMG squeeeeeee! I can't believe it!
WendyS: I'm crying right now. Bawling my eyes out like a loon.
Patsy: LOL. I could have told you that was going to happen from Sin One.
MrS69: Evening all.
HelenB: Rusty!
SashaT: Mr. S.! You old romantic, you.
MrS69: Yeah, well, what can I say? She won my heart.
Jules: Awwww!
Faith: Are you trying to get in my knickers, Rusty?
MrS69: Always.
SueAnn: Hahaha! You two! I can't believe you're getting married. It's the most romantic story ever.
Faith: It is, a bit.

Karen: I think it's wonderful.
MrS69: Me too.
Yolanda: Will there be photos of the wedding on your blog, Faith?
Faith: Absolutely! I hope you're all going to help me. I'll need guidance on dresses and stuff.
Patsy: We're here! You'll have to have an online bridal shower.
Faith: What a great idea!
MrS69: As long as you all join me for an online stag night.
SashaT: LOL of course!
Patsy: Seriously though, we're so pleased for you both. I'm sure WendyS isn't the only one who has tears in her eyes right now. I'm so glad you were able to work things out.
Faith: Yeah, me too. I can't imagine a life without my best friend.
MrS69: Aw. Are you trying to make me cry?
Faith: You are, though. My best friend. Promise you'll always be?
MrS69: I promise.
Karen: Are there likely to be little Rusties on the way soon?
Faith: Ah... I think it's too soon to be talking about that kind of thing
MrS69: Definitely.
Faith: Oh! LOL! Okay!
Karen: Yay!
SashaT: Hey, Faith, are you going to promise to obey him in your vows?
Faith: Ha! Absolutely not.
MrS69: We'll see. Now get your butt over here, Hillman—I haven't had a kiss for about ten minutes.
Faith: Ooh, yes sir...
SashaT: Are you two on computers in the same room?!
MrS69: We're on our laptops. In bed.
SashaT: Of course you are. Silly me.
Faith: I'd better go. Mr. Sinful is getting frisky. 'Night everyone!
Patsy: Goodnight, guys :) Have fun.
MrS69: Oh, I think that's a given, don't you?

The Heartfelt Series

Book 1: Mr. Sinful (Rusty)
Book 2: Mr. Seductive (Toby)
Book 3: Mr. Sensational (Felix)

Find out what happens next in Toby's story – Mr. Seductive. Available from most major retailers.

Excerpt – Chapter One

All day long, the ground had rumbled beneath his feet.

Toby thought he'd grown used to the sensation of living atop some monstrous beast that stirred restlessly in its sleep, but even so, as he placed his groceries on the supermarket conveyor belt, he couldn't help looking at the checkout assistant with alarm when the tiled floor trembled again.

She swiped an item across the scanner and smirked. "I'm guessing you're new to Christchurch."

He retrieved his wallet from his back pocket, not missing the amused glance from the young lad packing the carrier bags. "Actually, I've been here six weeks. I thought I'd got used to the shocks."

"Don't worry." She met his gaze with a flirtatious bat of her eyelashes. "If there's an earthquake, I'll protect you."

He grinned. She couldn't have been older than eighteen, and her tiny frame wouldn't have protected a mouse. "I might hold you to that. I scream like a girl when I'm scared, though, I have to warn you."

She giggled and gestured to the keypad. "When you're ready."

He swiped his debit card. About ten feet away, a toddler yelled, echoing loud through the afternoon quiet of the supermarket, and he glanced around. The boy sat in a shopping trolley and clearly wanted to be somewhere else. His mother had fastened his safety belt. The boy did *not* want it fastened.

Toby's lips twisted. His own mother had told him how he used to show her up in supermarkets. She'd said people staring made it worse, so he was about to turn away when something about the woman caught his eye.

Average height and slender, she had sleek brown hair pulled off her face in a clip. She wore long brown pants and an orange top so bright it made him want to don his sunglasses. But the bag resting on her hip was what caught his attention. The slogan on the chocolate-brown material read *Life is Short, Read Shakespeare* and bore an illustration of the English bard.

There was more than one bag like that in the world, surely. It wasn't her.

Having finally fastened the belt, she glanced over her shoulder.

Their eyes met. Toby inhaled sharply, his heart giving a gigantic thump as adrenalin surged through him. A vivid image of the woman lying naked, eyes closed in sublime pleasure as he thrust inside her, shot through his mind. Whoa. That was the quickest he'd achieved an erection since he was fourteen.

She stared at his face, and then her eyes widened as she obviously realized she wasn't dreaming.

He couldn't think what to do or say. The toddler squawked, but the woman remained staring at Toby, shock apparently freezing her feet to the floor. Even from across the aisle, he could see the flush fill her cheeks. So she remembered the holiday in Fiji too, then. She'd been so hot in bed, she'd almost set the covers alight.

He opened his mouth to say something—anything, conscious of the checkout assistant watching them both with amusement.

And then a huge bang shook the supermarket, and the world fell apart around him.

He ducked instinctively, swearing as the ground heaved. Crash after crash echoed through the building, shelves tipping and tins falling to the floor.

The checkout girl squealed and dropped to her knees, crawling under her till, and the packing lad ran around to join her. Toby froze, unable to believe his eyes as the tiled floor at the other end of the supermarket rose. *The monster's awake.* The thought shot through his head crazily, and he ducked again as a nearby display of boxes exploded into the air as if it weighed no more than polystyrene.

A wail brought his attention back to the woman and the trolley, and with alarm he saw she was having trouble getting the toddler's belt undone. Stepping over fallen bottles of bleach, he ran toward her and skidded to a halt by the trolley.

"I can't get it undone." She tugged with panic at the plastic clip, trying to keep the wailing boy's hands out of the way. "First I couldn't fasten it, and now it won't come apart."

Toby took the two sides of the belt in his hands and wrenched it open with brute force. He lifted the boy out of the trolley, tucked him under one arm, ignoring his squeals, and pushed her toward the exit. "Quick!"

They'd taken two steps when the ground split under the nearest shelving. The metal racks crashed down on top of the trolley, crumpling it as if it were made of tinfoil.

His heart in his mouth and the boy tight under his arm, Toby ran toward the exit. Even before they were halfway there, he realized they weren't going to make it. The ground buckled ahead of them, spilling tins and packets across their path, and she stumbled and fell.

She pushed herself to her feet and then fell again as the ground heaved, throwing her off balance. Under his arm, the child cried out, clamping his arms and legs around Toby, and Toby tightened his grip, determined nothing was going to wrench the boy out of his arms.

He bent and put an arm around the woman's waist and heaved her up, half-lifting and half-dragging her across to a table against the far wall. Pushing her underneath, he passed the child to her and then followed them under, covering them with his body as a horrendous bang echoed through the building.

Clouds of dust filled the aisles, and he put his hand over the boy's nose and mouth as it blew over them. For a moment, he couldn't catch his breath. Grit filled his mouth, and his lungs burned as he tried to inhale. A huge crack split the air, and something came crashing down onto the table. For a brief, scary moment, he thought the three of them were going to be squashed into a pancake. But the table held.

He'd tried to tuck his legs under and only realized he hadn't been completely successful when something fell on his feet. Swearing loudly, he curled around the woman, pushing the boy between them, and held them both tightly as the world continued to wrench itself apart.

In all, it could only have lasted about forty seconds, but it felt like a lifetime. Toby had never been so scared. The noise was deafening, crashes and screams and hideous screeching sounds that must have been the twisting of metal beams, but made him think once again that somewhere beneath the earth's surface medieval monsters were battling it out and ripping each other apart with giant teeth.

And then, all of a sudden, it stopped. In the distance, glass continued to shatter and displays crumbled. The ground trembled, but it stopped heaving and throwing them up in the air. For a moment, though, he stayed where he was, too frightened to move. He'd been in an earthquake. He couldn't believe it.

Then, finally, he turned onto his back and pushed up onto his elbows. He had a vision of looking at the bottom half of his body and seeing his legs missing, but to his relief they were intact. He wiggled both feet, relieved when the worst he felt was a stinging where falling debris had bounced and grazed him.

Next to him the boy shifted, and Toby looked down, thankful to see both the toddler and his mother still in the land of the living. She pulled back and lifted the boy with urgent hands, presumably checking for blood and making sure he was breathing. He coughed and rubbed his grit-filled eyes with his tiny fists, but he didn't cry.

"Thank God," she whispered, clutching him to her.

Her eyes, huge in her dust-streaked face, met Toby's over the boy's head. It couldn't have been a less romantic setting. Toby knew he must look a sight, covered in gray dust and probably blood too, judging from the throbbing behind his left ear. But at that moment, all he could think was *I found her*, and in spite of their predicament, his heart swelled.

"Hey, Esther," he said.

She blinked. "Hey, Toby."

"We're alive," he observed. "Result!"

She laughed with relief. "Yeah."

He couldn't help himself. Slipping a hand behind her head, he leaned forward and pressed his lips to hers. He'd only meant to snatch a quick peck, but to his surprise, she opened her mouth, her tongue searching for his. He moved his arm around her, drawing her to him, and they exchanged a deep, dusty, heartfelt kiss.

A sneeze brought them apart.

The boy coughed. "When the ground went bang, you said fuck," he accused Toby.

Her eyes widened. "Charlie!"

"I did," Toby said, still feeling the press of her lips on his. "Sorry about that, but the situation kind of called for it." Charlie had a round, plump face, curly blond hair—now covered with dust—and big brown eyes.

Eyes the mirror image of his own.

Toby's gaze slid to Esther's. He calculated rapidly. The boy looked about two and a half years old. He'd met her on holiday in December. Three years and two months ago.

No. Surely not.

She met his gaze calmly. Then, without saying anything, she rolled over and crawled out from under the table, bending to pull Charlie with her.

Toby pushed himself backward and got to his feet. Only then did he comprehend the extent of the devastation. The whole west wall of the supermarket had collapsed, and sunlight poured through the open roof, highlighting the rubble. All around, the cries of hurt or trapped people echoed through the building.

"Jesus." Horror filled him. How long would it be before the emergency services arrived?

Esther had picked up her son, who'd started to cry. She tried to soothe him, stroking his back, whispering in his ear.

"Is he okay?" Toby took a step toward them, but she moved backward, tightening her arms around the boy, and he stopped. She didn't want him near the kid. The exultant feeling that had swelled inside him died down.

She stroked Charlie's hair. "He lost Bear."

"Bear?"

"His Pooh Bear. It's okay—it could have been a lot worse." She looked around. "Damn it. I dropped my bag somewhere under all that rubble too."

Behind them, a hanging beam fell to the floor with a crash, and they all jumped.

"We've got to get out of here in case the place collapses," Toby said. There would be time later to talk to her about the boy. For now, he had to get them to safety. Debris had blocked the exit, but the window nearby had broken, giving access onto the street. "Come on, and mind the glass."

He led the way over to the window. Shards of broken glass still jutted from the frame, so he removed them carefully before climbing over. "Pass him to me," he instructed her, holding out his arms.

She hesitated for a moment, then handed the boy across. Toby held him in one arm and offered a hand to help her, but she ignored it and climbed over on her own. Letting his arm drop, he turned his attention instead to the child.

Charlie snuffled against his dust-streaked shirt. "Bear," he mumbled. "I want Bear."

"Shh, it's okay." Toby stroked his hair. His heart pounded. "I'll find him for you."

Esther took Charlie from his arms. "Don't make promises you can't keep," she said sharply. "I've never lied to him, and I'm not about to start now."

He put his hands in his jeans pockets, unsettled by her defensiveness. "I'm not lying. I'm going back in there. I'll keep an eye open for the toy."

Her eyes widened. "You can't! It's dangerous—it could collapse at any minute."

"There are people trapped in there."

"The emergency services will be here soon. It's their job. They always say never to go back into a building after an earthquake."

He shrugged. "I've got to do it. I can't stand here while people are in there, in trouble."

She crushed Charlie to her. Her large eyes met his, hard as emeralds. "You're not being brave—you're being an idiot."

The comment stung. He wasn't doing it to be a hero. The thought of going back made his stomach clench. But there had been other children in the shop and housewives buying the family shopping. The young checkout girl and the teenage boy who did the packing. How could he live with himself if he went home without knowing if they'd made it?

He glanced over at the building, then back at her. "How will I find you again?"

"I'll find you," she said. She must have seen the wariness in his face, because her expression softened. "I promise."

His gaze fell to Charlie. "Is...is he mine?"

She swallowed. Then she gave a small nod.

His eyes came back to her cool, emotionless ones. How could she be so calm? A hundred different emotions roiled inside him, and he clenched his fists in an attempt to keep them in.

What a day to find out he'd fathered a child. He was going home at the weekend. He'd booked the flights, and his best mate was getting married in a week's time—he had to be there. And after that, he had plans for his life. Things he wanted to do.

Bringing up a child wasn't one of them.

He couldn't think how to put his emotion into words. One day, he would have liked to have had a family. But not yet. His friends and family teased him constantly for being a Peter Pan. What would they say when they found out he had a son? Not that it appeared he had any choice in the matter. He was a father, whether he wanted to be one or not.

Nobody would blame him if he left the scene now to work things through with her. He hesitated. Then, behind him, someone screamed.

"Be careful." He ran back to the window and climbed over the ledge into the building.

*

Available at most major retailers.

About The Author

Serenity Woods is a USA Today bestselling author. She lives in the sub-tropical Northland of New Zealand with her wonderful husband and gorgeous teenage son. She writes hot and sultry contemporary romances with a happy ever after, and would much rather immerse herself in reading or writing romance than do the dusting and ironing, which is why it's not a great idea to pop round if you have any allergies.

She is the author of over fifty romance novels. You can check them all out on her website.

   Website: http://www.serenitywoodsromance.com
   Facebook: http://www.facebook.com/serenitywoodsromance
   Twitter: https://twitter.com/Serenity_Woods

Printed in Great Britain
by Amazon